Taming Fire

A novel by Aaron Pogue

Published by Consortium Books, 2011.

TAMING FIRE

First edition. June 21, 2011.

ISBN: 978-1-936559-02-2

A Consortium Books public work. Written by Aaron Pogue.
For copyright information concerning this book, please visit
http://www.ConsortiumOKC.com/writing/copyright/

10 9 8 7 6 5 4 3 2

My name is Daven Carrickson, son of shamed Carrick the Thief. I've been called Daven of Terrailles in mockery, called Daven of Teelevon in celebration, called Prince of Chaos by men and monsters.

In the spring of my seventeenth year, when I was a shepherd called only Daven, they came to take me to the Academy of Wizardry.

1. Swords

On a pretty spring day early in the month of Korhah, I stood with sword in hand on a grassy hillside and faced a tall and angry opponent. Sweat burned my eyes and I could taste it salty on my lips. I blinked, and the glistening beads on my eyelashes flashed momentarily in the bright sun. Then he advanced. I stepped quickly to the right, fell back a pace. My muscles burned despite the chill breeze that brought goose bumps to my arms. I started to turn, feinted slightly and whirled the other direction. Two quick steps. I counted time by the thud of quick feet on the grassy turf. Timing was everything—timing and terrain. My eyes darted to the edge of the little brook, slippery mud that he always forgot, but it was too far for me to press him now. Too far for my failing strength.

He attacked, quick and vicious. The sword he swung was heavier than mine—and newer—and I fell back half a step under its blows. Then I stopped him. His arms were stronger than mine, too, and his energy was new. My side ached, my head throbbed. I sighed, danced left as I sighed, and barely avoided a wild swing. Then a desperate smile stole across my lips. He couldn't see it with his shoulder turned away. I brought my sword up quickly. Falling forward, twisting, I lashed out and caught him just beneath the shoulder, felt the resistance against the tip of my weapon just as I crashed against the unforgiving ground.

For a long while I lay there, trying to catch my breath, trying to ignore the pain in my shoulder. Then I finally rose

1

to one knee and grounded my sword before me for support. I forced a smile, forced myself to breathe evenly, forced myself to stability as the cold wind danced across my aching body. My toes were in the brook, and I could feel the cold water seeping through old and worn leather.

Very, very slowly then the victory seeped into me. I had won, again, and the fight was done. Cooper stood above me now, frozen mid-stride and glaring at me hatefully. He should have won that round, and he knew it as well as I. A single point of brilliant blue light shone just below his shoulder, bright even in the afternoon sun. Wisps of yellow and white light trailed along his sleeves and chest, and mine as well, but the blue was the death shot, marking my victory. The same magic that made the air dance with color held him motionless, and the anger in his eyes made me glad of those few moments to catch my breath.

Slowly and unsteadily I pushed myself up. "It was a good fight, Coop." The anger in his eyes never changed. "You did well. I got lucky." He said nothing, so I counted the seconds beneath my breath and reached out to steady him when the spell expired. He fell against my arm, but instead of catching his balance he threw himself forward, hurling me down to the ground beside him. He grimaced when his shoulder struck the earth, but there was satisfaction in his eyes. It was a small victory in defeat, a bit of honor stolen.

I ground my teeth at the pain, but forced myself to calm because I was too tired to do anything else. Groaning, I pushed myself up again, and leaned against the ancient oak as I brushed some of the dirt and grass from my clothes. Mocking, Cooper said over his shoulder, "Sure. Good fight." After a moment I stepped away from the tree, knelt and washed my face in the cold brook. I rested there for a moment before turning to scoop up my battered sword and carefully sheathing it. There were already soft footsteps on the turf as two of the others stepped forward to take their turn, so I moved quickly out of the sparring area.

Cooper was sitting now among the other boys, gnawing a bit of dried venison and nodding at whatever they were talking about. Most of them were sitting on a rough-hewn wooden bench that Cooper's dad had made for us. Cooper was sitting on a large stone in front of it, which left me only a place on the grass. At Cooper's feet. I sighed and turned toward the road.

Bron yelled to me, "Daven, where are you going?"

I answered him without looking, "Back to Jemminor's. I still need to water the flock before supper." I stopped, a cruel smile stealing across my lips, "Good luck against Kyle."

They all laughed, then, and I almost decided to stay and watch that fight, but I had four wins for the day and those were points hard earned. That was some honor. I wasn't about to give that up by sitting on the grass before them. So I turned back down the graveled path, forgotten among the jibes at poor Bron, and headed for my master's house.

He was my master by choice—my employer—and I was a shepherd by choice, which still surprises some people. To me it was an opportunity to be free. I worked through the morning and afternoon out in the grassy hills of the luxurious Terrailles province. Every day I walked where the herds walked, watched over them and chased off any predators or poachers—though both were few in this land. I had a room in my master's house, a place at his servants' table and regular meals. More important by far, I had evenings off to practice the sword.

It had taken months to teach the other village boys what I knew, months more before any of us were good enough to practice with real weapons, but now we met almost daily. I taught them forms, and they taught me treachery. We dueled sometimes—the careful and polite sport of the capitol's nobility—but far more often we fought, a frightening blur of muscle and motion, of anger and desperation. All of it was governed by a little spell that I had brought with me—a child's enchantment, a referee and scorekeeper in the middle air. I had brought them together, and I dreamed that among that little group of boys I was king—or general, perhaps, of a ragged little army of miscreants. They didn't know—especially Cooper, whose family had a name—but I considered myself their liege, and they respected me as no one else had in my whole life.

At Jemminor's farm, I watered the sheep. It was heavy work, lugging bucket after bucket of water from well to trough, but it was work I did twice a day. The work of a shepherd is walking and carrying, and I had grown strong over years of it. The meal of a shepherd is a feast compared with that of a beggar boy in the capitol, and I had grown soft on too many of them, but I enjoyed that gentle luxury at the servants' table. I fell asleep on a soft bed under new quilts, and dreamed of being a soldier. It was a quiet life, and I loved it.

A shepherd's day begins before the dawn, and starts off with the smell of honey and oats—for the sheep, not the shepherd. I dumped several handfuls of sweet grain in a trough near the saltlick, then filled it the rest of the way with dry hay from the barn. The sheep came crowding in before I was done, pressing hard against my hips and legs, but I shoved between them to drop the last of the hay in the trough, then waded back out.

The day was bright and warm, and I spent long hours out in the hills with no one for company but the milling flocks. I stared up at the blue sky as soft white clouds drifted slowly by. I ran my hands through the waist-high meadow grasses as I strolled, a hundred sheep around me. I sat for an hour on a cool, mossy stone beside a quiet brook and listened to its bubbling. I enjoyed the silence, enjoyed the peace, but all day I felt the evening calling me forward. My hands strayed often to my belt, but the sword wasn't there. I had work to do yet, but the evening's fight called me on. I smiled and waited. Just like every day.

But when I climbed the low hill outside of town at the end of the day I was disappointed. I was half an hour late, and all the others were there already, but there was no sound of clattering blades, no shouts of encouragement or rage. I stepped up into our clearing and found them all sitting on the bench or spread in the grass around it, leaning forward with elbows on knees and listening intently to Cooper, who sat on the stone before them and spoke with solemn grandeur.

As I approached, Kyle tossed me a soft roll without ever looking away from Cooper. I caught it and took a bite, and I moved closer, curious. Cooper glanced up, saw me, and smiled. He looked delighted. It was the first time I had ever drawn that reaction from him. I stepped up next to Bron and nudged him and he scooted over, crowding Kyle but making enough room for me on the bench. Just as I sank down, Cooper said something that made my blood run cold.

"What?" I said, glaring at him suspiciously, "What about the Guard?"

Several of the boys scowled at me at the interruption but in a moment their eyes swiveled back to Cooper, waiting excitedly for his answer. He only laced his fingers behind his head and gave me a satisfied smile, lips pressed tight.

Kyle finally threw his hands up in frustration and said, "Coop's going to join the Guard!"

I shook my head. "That's impossible."

Kyle nodded. "It's truth. I heard it in the village green. His dad bought him a commission, and he leaves next Kingsday!" His eyes shone with excitement, they were all almost shaking with excitement.

I felt my heart sink. "Nothing so special about that," I grumbled.

Bron snorted. "You've spent too long in the sun. It's addled your brains."

I shook my head, trying to fight a panic building beneath my ribs. "No," I said, to myself as much as to them. "Don't let your daydreams fool you. It's not so fun being in the Guard." Every eye was on me again, most of them wide in disbelief. I swallowed a lump in my throat, "It's a lot of work. Think about it. And hardly any excitement at all."

Cooper grinned at me. His eyes sparkled. But Bron seemed offended. "Be serious, Daven. It's the biggest thing that's ever happened to any of us! He's leaving, he's going to see the world." For a moment he lost his intensity, gazing dreamily up at the clouds, but then he shoved me lightly and I slipped off the end of the bench, "You'd be ecstatic if it were you. You've always wanted to join the Guard."

I opened my mouth to answer but Cooper interrupted. "Guard wouldn't have him. He's got no family, no name, no skills. Leave the boy alone, Bron, he's just a little jealous."

I was already on my feet, and in an instant I whirled on him, my rage erupting. "My skills dropped you dead yesterday, Cooper, and you know it. After winning three other fights that day, too! I—"

"You cheated," he said, lacing his fingers behind his head. "If you'd fought fair I would have torn you apart."

Kyle laughed uneasily, "Come on, Cooper. Calm down. Daven's never cheated, he's just fast...." He pressed a hand against his side where I'd accidentally bruised him the day before, winced, and continued. "Calm down, both of you. It's all just a game."

I took a step back and placed my hand on the hilt of my sword, my chest swelling in my fury. "It is a game. Maybe. Here. But in the Guard it will be real."

Cooper shrugged. "I'm ready."

"No," I said, and the sick fury in me boiled in my stomach. "You're not. You're arrogant and pampered and a fool. And the first time you get a break from guarding pig farmers and building roads, Cooper—the first time you face an enemy with a sword—you're going to die." I took a deep breath, trying to see clearly, and let it out slowly. "Or maybe you'll remember your fights with me and turn and run."

"I think not." He rose gracefully, slowly like a cat uncurling, and I saw the shiny hilt of a new sword at his side. He hooked a thumb behind his belt. "Your *lessons* amount to one simple reminder: real foes cheat."

My voice dropped to a whisper, "I never cheat."

He snorted. "You *always* cheat!" He took a step closer to me, too close, and looked down his nose at me. "It takes honor to stand. It takes honor to face the charge. You run and sneak and hide and attack from behind and the sides like a coward—" he hesitated only a second, but his cruel eyes were locked on mine when he added, "like a criminal."

I bit back my anger, forced myself to stillness before I answered. When I did, it was in a normal voice. "There is one thing you always forget, Cooper." I turned to the others, slipping unconsciously into my lecturing voice as I repeated words I'd told them time and again. "When you face a stronger opponent or a larger opponent, remember this: you'll rarely win a game of subtlety with a brash charge."

I expected nods from them. I'd been teaching them for years. But now instead they just turned, all as one, to get

Cooper's assessment of my advice. In one day I'd lost everything, because his father bought him a commission.

Cooper spoke with patronizing indulgence. "This is not a game to be won whatever the cost. This is a nobleman's sport, and you *corrupt* it when you...you...."

Bron gave a tired sigh. "Coop, we don't even duel that much. Mostly we fight, and that's *not* a nobleman's sport."

"And that's what you'll be doing in the Guard," I said. "Fighting."

Behind me, Bron grunted his irritation at my interruption. But then he went on grudgingly, "It's true. And Daven does it right. Just let it go. Here, on this field, he's the best of us."

Cooper sneered. "You're far too kind. I'll say it like it is, like none of you has ever dared to say. He's a dirty little sneak. He's the least among us!"

Bron didn't answer right away, and that hurt. When he did, his words were measured. "If you mean in wealth, you've got it and I don't think he'd argue. But if you're talking skill with a sword...the shepherd will probably still be better than you even *after* the Guard teaches you how to do it right." For a long time Cooper only glared at him over my shoulder, and knowing Bron he met the stare levelly. After a minute Bron added, "He's just good."

Cooper opened his mouth to respond, then shut it. Still looking past my shoulders his eyes went wide. Then a stern, dark voice fell among us, "Better than Guard training, eh?" There was a slightly foreign lilt to the words, but more compelling was the authority and power behind that voice. Coop let go of me and took a long step back. I took a quick step away, then turned to see who had spoken so.

A man stood just at the head of the little gravel footpath, his shadow darkening the ground between us. His condescending gaze ran over the line of boys seated on the bench, then back to Cooper and me. Finally he gestured at me with the riding crop he was carrying, "You're more skilled than a Guardsman? Eh?"

The crimson sun behind him buried his features in darkness. His face was narrow and bony, his eyes deep and lost in shadow. His lips twisted in a mocking smile as he took one long, fearsome step forward. His clothes were much finer than any worn by the people of the village, but my gaze kept drifting to the heavy broadsword that hung on his belt.

When I did not answer, he seemed to grow impatient. "Well, you are the boy Daven, no?" I could only stare at him, and his brows came together in anger. "Answer me, boy! You are Daven, son of Carrick the Thief, correct?" I flinched at the name he used, but after a moment I stammered an answer, nodded, and he seemed to relax a little.

"I have been sent a long way to find you, Daven, with little explanation as to why a penniless peasant should command my attention. But now I understand. Everything is clear, yes? Here is a boy with no training who could school the soldiers of the Royal Guard." For the first time I noticed the greens and browns of his uniform, the crest on his shoulder, and recognized him for a Green Eagle, a member of the king's elite guard. He saw the recognition in my eyes, and his shone with malicious glee.

With a slow gesture he reached up to unclasp the cloak hanging from his shoulders. "This is something I must see," he said. He glanced at my eyes, but I couldn't find any answer. I gave a tiny shake of my head, but he pretended not to see it. He folded the cloak neatly, then dropped it on the end of the bench Coop's dad had made. He passed a gaze over the row of boys sitting in rapt attention. They all stared back in awed surprise, Cooper with a satisfied grin across his face.

The Green Eagle shook his head and strode out past the stump to our sparring ground. He turned in a slow circle, taking in the terrain, and I watched him note the mud-slick patch at the edge of the stream, the treacherous little pocket where a groundhog's burrow had sunk the earth, the knotted root of the oak that broke the ground more than four paces from its trunk.

Then he turned to me, his left hand resting casually on the hilt of his sword. "Well?" he asked.

I licked my lips. "I...I can't fight you."

The soldier grinned. He looked like death. "You must."

"No, I'm sorry. It was just...I'm not as good as a Guard." Beside me Bron nodded fervent agreement, and I felt the stab of it in my heart. Everything I'd fought for, lost. I sighed. "He spoke in haste."

"Regardless," the Eagle said, and his voice was hard. "I have come all this way, and I find you all dressed up for battle. I would see you fight."

Bron jumped to his feet. "I'll show you," he said. "Let him fight me. You can see why I thought—"

The soldier's terrible gaze swept to Bron, and the young man stammered to a stop. For a long moment the soldier said nothing, only stared, and then Bron took a long step back.

The soldier nodded. "I don't want to watch you," he said. "I want you to watch me." He ran his imperious gaze down the line a third time, this time commanding each boy's attention before moving on. "I want you to see how a king's guardsman handles himself."

Then his gaze snapped back to mine, and he drew his sword with a long, whispered rasp. He ducked his chin, and said, "Ready?"

Now I looked down the line of boys. Bron, who had spoken up for me. Kyle, who always had to find courage to face me, and always listened so carefully when I explained what he had done wrong. Dain who had been my first friend in town, though he had grown distant when the stories followed me in from the City. Gavin was strong and slow and shy, but he had found the worn-out old scabbard I wore on my belt and made it a gift to me. And even Cooper was impressed enough with my ability to feel threatened.

And now, in the dying light of a beautiful day, I would be made to look a fool. I took a deep breath, and let it out. I nodded once, to forestall the old soldier's impatience, and drew my sword. It was dented all along the blade, rusted so deeply in spots I couldn't possibly polish it away. The fine silver chain meant to wrap its hilt had been replaced with tight straps of leather, and even that was getting loose, now, and almost worn through. It usually felt easy and familiar in my fingers, but standing before the Green Eagle it felt like a frail and broken thing, and so did I.

For a long minute I stood there on the edge of the circle. I could feel the others watching me, waiting, and I nodded again and stepped forward. As I went to meet him I spoke the words out of long habit, "Watch over us, keep score for us, decide for us." The soldier tilted his head in curiosity as I invoked the spell, then he chuckled.

"You say prayers for yourself, too. I should expect as much. Well, God watch over you, boy, because it's time for us to begin." I had no response to that, but it mattered little. I fell into the stance I had learned, shoulder and elbow in line with the soldier, narrow blade held blocking everything from my waist to my eyes. He took a place in front of me, body turned differently and both hands gripping the short hilt of his broadsword. Gavin always liked to play at two-handed weapons, but I knew my victories over his clumsy thrashing were no preparation at all for the style of a true soldier.

11

He flexed his arms, stretching, then relaxed into a ready stance. "So, you have the skills to train a Guardsman?" He mocked me, low enough now that only I could hear. "You're so certain you will live through *your* first encounter?" My eyes went wide, and he nodded knowingly, "Ah, yes, I heard it all. You're a little arrogant for the beggar son of a thief. They think highly of you, though." Somehow, I didn't think he meant the boys watching us, but I couldn't guess who else he might mean. He gave me no time to consider it.

"We shall see," he said, and like a whisper he glided across the grass. He flowed as he moved first to one side and then the other. At the last moment his blade darted out and crashed against my own, flinging it from my hand. The soldier stopped in his tracks, his weapon hanging forgotten at his side.

For a long moment he stared at me, then shook his head in disappointment. He stepped up until I could feel his breath hot on my ear and spoke in a quiet voice filled with terrible menace, "Retrieve your weapon, child, that we may finish this. I mean to see these skills of yours."

I glanced over at him, and felt a blush beginning to burn in my cheeks. "I'm sorry—" I started, but he shook his head.

"I don't want your apologies. I want to see how you fight." A smile creased his cheeks. "I want them to see."

I closed my eyes and clenched my stomach against the sudden flurry of fear, then swallowed hard and turned aside to recover my weapon. When I turned back he had reclaimed his position near the center of the circle, and I moved opposite him. I lifted the sword again, but this time I could not hold it steady. Fear set my arm to trembling, and in my fear I squeezed the hilt too tightly. The muscles in my legs and stomach were tense. Everything was wrong, but I knew no way to make it right.

I took a deep breath and tried to concentrate on the terrain. He stood a pace closer to the brook than Cooper had yesterday, but there was no way I could force *him* back. I had at least ten paces to the edge of the clearing, but he could easily press me so far. The tree was to my right, so it would hamper my swing much more than his. I tried to clear my mind, to release myself to the habits of the fight, but terror kept intruding.

He raised an eyebrow at me, smile still on his lips. Then suddenly he lunged, the tip of his sword just barely striking the middle of my blade, and I responded perfectly. Half a step retreat, withdraw and replace the blade, setting it familiarly instead of responding to his beat. He nodded, ever so slightly, and came at me again, this time swinging a wide and powerful swipe that would have caught my sword near the hilt, but I dipped low and reached for his wrist. I recognized the practice forms he was using against me, and instinctively responded. He was teaching me a lesson from the fourth chapter of my book.

I relaxed a little, then. He *had* said he intended me to have a lesson, to see my skills, and that was just what he was doing. Perhaps, I thought as I parried a half-hearted thrust, perhaps I could impress him, too. As I fell back a step I noticed my left foot slid a little too easily over the grass and remembered the splash of the stream in spring slicked the ground over here. I adjusted for it, retreated another step, always parrying his blows. Maybe if I did well, I could get invited to join the Guard myself. Right in front of all of them, as I fought a Green Eagle.

I built the daydream in my head as he pressed me back, but as I retreated I slowly, subtly moved with the hope of placing the tree at his disadvantage. White light danced around the back of my right hand and fingers and I realized there was a very light trickle of blood running down to my wrist. I checked quickly, trying to see two things at once, and saw several tiny nicks on my wrist as well, and one on my shoulder. Of course, there were no marks on my opponent.

I focused too much on these little injuries and was caught by surprise when he suddenly fell back, then came on me *á flêche*, darting forward and lunging with a low cut that scored my hip. I felt blood flow, damping my leggings, and there was a flash of yellow at the hit. For a moment the soldier looked puzzled, but he pressed his attack. I fell back quickly. He made a move from chapter six, a clever strike, but I danced aside and came back with a variation on the normal riposte that nicked the edge of his hand. His brows came down, and he came forward.

He cut me again, on my right shoulder, and I ran to escape the next strike. I dove, rolled, and came up just in time to block another attack, but his blade moved like lightning and he nicked me twice more before I found a defensive posture. He pushed me back with textbook maneuvers and battered through my defenses without apparent effort. It seemed that every time he swung he cut me somewhere, small wounds, just enough to draw blood. Each time he cut me I felt the little pain, and each time he blinked in confusion at the sparkle of white or yellow, but pressed on with his attack. They had to be fierce, vicious thrusts to penetrate the ward of my spell, but I had expected such from him. He was a man trained to kill.

And suddenly I saw it coming. I was still clinging to my daydream, still hoping to somehow impress him, but as the blood flowed and sweat burned in the hundred little nicks and cuts, suddenly I realized that he was tiring of the game. Tired of testing my skills, tired of impressing these village

14

brats, and most of all tired of using up his great honor on a little nuisance like me. I could see the end of his patience in his eyes, and see his solution to that, too. One, two, three strokes away and he would finish me and be done with the bother.

I parried a shoulder cut that nearly knocked me down, then retreated from a stop-thrust. He came at me again, and I fell back, farther and farther, desperately hoping to somehow keep him at bay for a moment more. I wanted to find some way to impress him still, some crazy way to win, but he was overwhelming me now at every pass. I fell back, almost running backward, and he pursued me like a thunderstorm. Then I felt my foot start to slip on the wet grass. I had only a moment to realize I had come too close to the stream before both my legs went out from under me. I landed hard, and as my feet shot out in front of me I felt them connect with his ankles, and he began to fall. The soldier had no time to respond, no idea how. His arm was drawn back for a killing blow but as he came falling forward he tried to bring the sword down, his instincts curling him into a midair turn that aimed his shoulder for my stomach.

Desperately I threw my hands up to try to catch him, crossing my arms before my face, and as he hit me I felt the sword knocked from my clumsy grasp. His knee smashed hard into my right thigh, his other foot scraping the side of my left calf, but I was most afraid of the weight still hanging above me, of the shoulder to my midsection. I tensed against his fall, but it never came.

After a moment I opened my eyes and found his, hateful, inches away. He hung suspended above me, his sword stretched out over my left shoulder and his body almost parallel to the ground. His lips were curled back in an animal snarl and his eyes flashed madly. It took me a moment to comprehend, and then I noticed the bright blue line

15

where his neck and shoulder met, searing against his skin. In his fall he'd struck the blade of my sword and the spell considered it a fatal cut.

I scrambled carefully out from under him, grabbing my sword and hastily backing away. Even with him frozen in place I could not tear my attention from him. Suddenly I realized he would not consider my victory an end—when the spell released him he would be on me again, and I would not stand a chance. The thought drained the last of the excited energy that had driven me. Weak, empty, I fell to one knee and counted the slow seconds as the spell expired. I clutched my sword before me, now in both hands, and held it out in a defensive posture. Any moment now he would be free, and—

"Boy," his breath was cold death, and I realized he was speaking through the pressure of the spell, "I did not come to kill you, but you will rue this witchcraft!" He paused, straining to draw breath, and then went on. "You will regret this."

My breath caught as the spell expired, and somehow he caught himself short of falling. Instead he was instantly on his feet, and with a single stride he reached me and cast aside my little practice sword with a contemptuous swing. He pressed the sharp tip of his own weapon against my throat.

I heard a sound behind me, and it must have been Bron, but he didn't even make a word before the soldier's cruel glare swung that way and shut him up. "My business is with the boy Daven," he said, pronouncing the words like judgment. "This is no more of your concern. You will go to your homes."

They shifted uncomfortably, and Cooper took a step forward. I didn't dare turn my head, couldn't tear my eyes from the blade biting into my skin, but I knew Cooper by the sound of his footfall even before he spoke behind me. "You've shown him his place. You can let him go now."

The old soldier's eyes narrowed to slits, a cold fury focused on Cooper behind me. "A new recruit of the Guard doesn't give orders to an officer, let alone a Green Eagle." His nostrils flared, his breath escaping in a contemptuous *huff,* and he snapped. "Get out."

They went. None of them dared defy the man. I couldn't blame them. I heard their retreat, heard their steps crunching down the hill and back toward town, but kept my gaze fixed on his.

When he looked back at me, he seemed thoughtful." I knew your father was a thief, boy. It's an old crime, mostly forgotten, but I imagined it was for that that the magicians tore me from important duties. But now I understand. You dare to work witchcraft against an officer of the King's Guard, by the full light of day. I can only imagine what else you would dare to do."

I trembled as I knelt there, afraid to move for fear of that blade against my throat. I could only stare into his eyes as he spoke his terrible accusations. "The king respects the power of the Academy wizards. It serves him well. But it is a dangerous thing, and it cannot be risked in the hands of one without name, without honor, and without training. It was wise of them to send me, after all. Few men have the courage to do what must be done."

My heart thundered in my chest. My mouth was dry as summer dust, my stomach an aching knot. I shook my head and tried to find a voice. "No," I said softly. "No, you don't understand."

He ignored me. He looked around, over my head toward the bench where my friends had been a few minutes earlier. Then past it, out over the lovely fields of Terrailles that rolled out to the distant sea. His gaze swept over the rough path that led back down into town and he nodded once. The soldier looked around carefully, and then returned his attention to me.

The sun set.

He whispered, "Now you will die."

The sword rose high above his shoulder, still clasped in both hands, and he set his jaw in grim determination as he turned to swing it down with all his weight behind it. My eyes were locked on his, his eyes burned into mine for an eternity as that blade fell. Slowly...so slowly....

And then it stopped.

I stared up at his still form for a long time before I realized it was utterly motionless. I watched the shadows on his face merge, stared into his dark eyes as the last glimmer of day faded, and finally I took another breath, counted another heartbeat. I was alive, somehow, and he was frozen into a perfect stillness far beyond the magic of my little spell. I sat staring up at him, awestruck that I was alive, wondering who or what could have done this to him, until a sound intruded on my thoughts.

At first it was the whisper of clothes, the grinding crunch of footsteps on gravel. With that intrusion other sounds returned. I heard the water once more dancing softly to my left, heard the cicadas whistling in the night, and far off the cry of a hunting falcon. Then I heard a voice, grumbling in complaint and annoyance between panting breaths. It had nothing of the cruelty I'd heard in the voice of the soldier before me, but authority enough to shame him. Mind still reeling with terror, I rose slowly and turned toward the path to face this new surprise. Somewhere deep within my tired mind there was a spark of curiosity.

I saw first some gray hair, and then a round and cheerful face twisted into a grimace. As he came into view I saw he was wearing a plain gray robe, belted with a blue silk scarf but otherwise unadorned, and he carried a long, thin staff that he jabbed viciously into the ground at each step. He was walking quite hurriedly up the hill and puffing with the effort of it, all the while muttering to himself.

Then he caught sight of me and the soldier frozen behind me, and he stopped short. He was perhaps a hand shorter than me, but when he stepped forward to face me I felt an instant respect for the man. His annoyance disappeared in a flash, replaced by a kindly smile as he reached out a hand to clasp my shoulder, "You must be Daven, no?"

For a long while I stood there, blank and silent after that terrible question. This stranger only stood patiently, squinting at my features by the thin light of the stars. After a moment he demanded again, "Well, boy, you are Daven? Daven son of Carrick?" He caught himself, but I heard the name on his lips. Carrick the Thief. I shuddered, afraid of these strangers coming for me in the night.

"I have done no wrong, sir."

He breathed an exasperated sigh. "So you *are* Daven?" I nodded, afraid, and he continued. "Good. Good to hear, boy. I have come a long way to fetch you."

His words struck me like blows. Another stranger come to fetch me, this one clearly no soldier but somehow he frightened me more. I began to back away from him, stumbling on the ground my feet knew so well. "I—I have done no wrong," I stammered.

"Silly young man!" He said the words under his breath, but I caught them in the cold night, and they seemed a curse. Mad with terror I turned to sprint into the darkness, to lose myself in the night, but his hand fell upon my arm. At the same time he spoke, his breath bearing a strange word that meant nothing to me but somehow carried with it a world of meaning. In an instant my heart grew calm.

For several heartbeats he stood watching me warily, but all my fear was gone. When he was satisfied, he took a step back, releasing me, and continued in a normal voice. "I have come a long way to fetch you, Daven, and it would not do for you to slip out of my reach now. I need you to listen to me and to answer my questions. I hope you will forgive the things I do for need."

I nodded in agreement, but he wasn't paying attention. Instead he stared past my shoulder to the top of the hill. After a moment he stepped past me and tapped the end of his tall staff on the frozen form of the soldier. "Why..." he spoke thoughtfully to the night. "Why would Othin behave so?"

The answer sprang unbidden to my lips. "I offended him, sir. He was protecting his honor."

The stranger barked a laugh, but there was something cold in his eyes as he examined the weapon frozen in the soldier's hand. "There could be no honor in something like this. He acted rashly." He turned to me then, spoke words that sounded meaningful though they held no significance to me. "It is never wise for us to punish the weak for the injuries the strong have done us."

I nodded.

"This...." His attention was on the statue once more. "This was a mistake I should have foreseen. I regret how close it came to tragedy. I regret what it put you through. I'm glad I caught him before he did serious harm. You—" The wizard stopped, and a look of sheer surprise stole across his face. It seemed so inappropriate, so foreign on his dignified features, and it was quickly lost in a more fitting look of contemplation. "You are quite a remarkable fighter, Daven."

He stepped closer to the still form and tapped the extended sword with his staff. It fell free of the soldier's grasp, landing with a dull thud in the thick grass. "In Othin's homeland there is a tradition, Daven, that when a man loses a duel his only honor is in surrendering his blade. I believe you have rightfully won this."

He hesitated a moment, considering, and then reached out to tap the sword belt draped from Othin's shoulder to hip, and that too fell free. He scooped the sword up clumsily and forced it into its scabbard, then held the belt out to me as a gift.

I didn't dare touch it. Instead I met the wizard's eyes and asked, "What do you know of my fighting?"

His eyes shone as he returned my gaze, "When you bend reality, Daven, reality remembers. I can see much of you in this place, and it makes me think perhaps there is a hope after all. I've found you in the nick of time, and it seems you may exceed even my own lofty expectations." His voice trailed off, and still he stood there in the night, arms extended toward me.

Finally the awkwardness overcame my fear, and I reached out to take the belt. He nodded once, satisfied then whirled to face down the hill, nothing more than a shadowy motion in the darkness. "Come, it is quite late. Let us finish this discussion at your master's home."

He started confidently along the graveled footpath, down and into the village. I followed the old man into the night, never doubting he knew the way.

2. Sorcery

The gravel crunched with every step, holding back the silence of the settling night. Before us and below, Sachaerrich waited in the darkness, probably bustling as its citizens went to their meals though no sound reached us. Alone, we walked slowly alongside the gentle brook that bubbled down the hillside.

After a moment the old man spoke. "Have you enjoyed your stay in Sachaerrich?"

"It has been nice." My legs ached from the brief but frenzied fight, but I tried not to limp as we walked. By now the little wounds were nothing more than a distraction. "The village is a quiet place to live. The people are friendly."

He looked at me for a moment, considering. "You have made friends here, then?"

I shrugged. "Friends enough. Goodman Jemminor provides for me, and there are several of us that play at swords, sometimes."

He chuckled. "Play at swords? You are modest. Still, it is good to hear you have friends. Will you miss them when you leave?"

"No." I answered without thinking, but after a moment the question struck me as odd. "Why do you ask? I've nowhere to go."

"Everyone leaves eventually, Daven. I imagine you'll be leaving soon."

I nodded. Once more silence fell as we trudged on, then the stranger spoke again. "I am looking for a swordsman,

Daven. I need a young man about your age, who knows how to use a solid weapon but is willing to participate in...nonstandard training." He hesitated, his eyes on my face. "Would you be that man?"

For a moment excitement bubbled within me, like my daydream come true, but I fought it down. "I am just a shepherd. The most I've ever dreamed of is a place in the Guard." My voice sounded gloomy even to my ears.

"And you just proved yourself worthy of one." He chuckled, waving vaguely back up the hill behind us. "You showed yourself worth more than that, even. You fought a Green Eagle and—"

"I didn't fight him, though!" He blinked in surprise at my outburst, and I shrugged, "I mean...I didn't ever even hit him. He fell on me. He *fell* on me. It was just a trick of the spell."

"Ah!" He said, holding up a finger, "Even the spell commends you, Daven. That is a surprisingly complex adjudication for such a young man. The fact that you can work it—"

"I can't though." I was being rude, interrupting him, but he kept trying to call me more than I was. My father had been the last person to speak to me like that, and his words had all been lies. I said, "It's just a little spell. I bought it for a silver coin from a man in the City. He saw my book, and offered it to me. Anyone can do a spell like that. It's just words."

He looked at me for a moment more, his eyes sharp in the night, and then he said, "Ah. Well. True enough." I heard disdainful laughter hidden in his voice.

We walked in silence again, while the stars came out to shine, and I began to feel bad for arguing like that. Finally I sighed and said, "What do you want a swordsman for, anyway?"

His eyes cut to me, a moment's gaze, and then they were on the road again. "I wish to try a little project, with the king's approval. I mean to make a new kind of soldier, to train a swordsman with some of the skills of magic and see what he can do."

I shook my head. "Why would you do that? The king is disbanding whole regiments in exchange for the handful of wizards produced at the Academy. What value could there be in teaching someone both?"

He smiled. "I don't know. We've never tried it, so who could say?"

"I could," I said. "Anyone could. A wizard can call down fire and summon lightning. A wizard can simply lift his enemies into the air, or..." I waved back over my shoulder, toward the silhouette of the Green Eagle still frozen on the hilltop. "Or bind them in place from a hundred paces away. For someone who could do that, what use is a sword?"

"That's a complicated question," the old man said. "And one the other Masters refuse to consider."

"Oh." I nodded. It should have been obvious. I felt an emptiness gnawing in my stomach, but I kept it from my face. "You're a Master of the Academy."

"I am." His gaze was heavy on me, his words thick with understanding. "And I have been a Justice and a sometime adviser to the king. This is not the first time we've met, though I doubt you would remember me. You may call me Claighan."

I nodded. I couldn't speak. I remembered him, if only as one dark and threatening form among a long row of them. This was one of the men who had condemned my father far beyond the measure of his little sins. I squeezed my eyes shut, and the wizard gave a tired sigh. But he went on as though he had noticed nothing. "I've come from the capitol to ask you to be my test subject. It will be a great opportunity—"

"Thank you," I said, battering down daydreams and desire, "but no. The Academy is no place for me."

"Daven," he said in a paternal chide that set my teeth on edge. "I will make arrangements. You will be treated with the utmost—"

"No!" I raised my voice, breaking the stillness of the night. "I refuse! Do you understand? I have no place there. Besides... I'm happy enough here." He opened his mouth to say more, to argue with me, but I shook my head. "No. Thank you for your interest, but I can't do that."

He measured me with his eyes, then he shrugged and turned back down the path. A moment later I followed after, catching up quickly. We walked in silence most of the way into town before he said quietly, without turning, "There is more to you than your history."

I looked at him sharply, anger in my eyes, but he never looked up from the road. "Since the moment I met you you've been thinking of your past," he said. "Of the dark stain of your father's name."

I wanted to say, "A stain you supplied." I didn't. My father had never denied his crimes, but the punishment had been too harsh. Far too harsh.

Instead I scowled at the path beneath my feet and grunted. "My life has been nothing but that stain." I stomped along beside him for several moments, but he said nothing. "It's true. As far as my memory reaches, my whole life has been dictated by the consequences of his actions."

He still didn't look at me, but his voice was cutting now. "Do you really think things are so simple? Do you really think you can blame all your tomorrows on your yesterdays? It's your life. It will be whatever you make it."

"Then why am I here?" I was shouting, somehow, all my control broken by his calm. "You think I chose this life? I ran—ran as far as I could—and when I collapsed it was in this village."

He shrugged. "There's your beginning. You *can* make more of yourself. You already started, by coming here. Even before that! Perhaps your father's actions made you a beggar and an orphan, but it was by your own ingenuity and will that you survived. It was by your own passion and determination that you found someone to teach you swordplay."

He shook his head, and his words came out heavy. "Your whole life you have worked to forge your own path despite your beginnings. And now I am offering you one way to finish that path. You can choose your own road—*make* your own, if you have to—and end up where you want to be, not where your strength fails you."

Again silence. Finally I asked the question, "Old man, why have you come here tonight?"

"I came for you."

"The soldier said the same."

"I came to give you a new life, Daven. To offer you choices and hope and, if you so desire, all the honor this kingdom has to offer."

I stopped despite myself. Honor. Just the word made my hands clench into fists, but the offer was too much to believe. I regarded him with narrow eyes. "How?"

"From all directions, in the darkness, a great terror approaches this world." He looked at me for a moment, reflected starlight blazing in his eyes, then took a step back and continued along the path. I followed.

"That is not an answer."

He sighed. "I mean to fight the terror, and I would make a weapon of you."

"Why would you choose me, though?"

He shrugged. "You have the...very specific qualities that I need. And, to be frank, you have neither family nor any other obligation to stop you. And... the circumstances behind that were not entirely just. I would make what amends I can."

"No one owes me any amends."

"You are wrong," he said. "The king was wrong for what he did."

My breath caught in my throat and I found my head whipping left and right, looking for someone who might have overheard, but the wizard clucked with irritation.

"It would be dangerous," Claighan went on. "You would have to risk your life daily for the sake of your people—"

I waved aside that warning. "I have always wanted to be a soldier."

"I know." He nodded, his gaze locked to a spot just in front of his feet. "And they won't have you."

I felt a cold fist clench around my stomach and twist. I had to blink my eyes against the sudden pain. "They have taken on commoners before—"

"That was before," the wizard said. I could hear compassion in his voice, but he made the words hard. Definite. "The army is dwindling. Given the king's obsession with the Academy, I think soon the only military positions left will be decorative titles for pretty little lordlings."

I shook my head. "They need good workers to make the roads, to keep the peace."

The wizard shook his head. "The work can be done by hired hands," he said. "And order maintained by...." He sighed and nodded. "By the threat of swift justice."

I nodded, too, and turned my head away.

Sometime later I felt his hand on my shoulder. It was surprisingly light. Frail. "But you will be more than a soldier, boy. You will be an army. You will be a weapon."

I couldn't believe him. I had seen too much of the world to believe him. But I couldn't imagine why he was trying so hard to deceive me. "Why, though? Why would you give this opportunity to *me*?"

It took him a while to answer, and even when he did he seemed uncertain. "There are...costs to what I would put you through. Expenses too great to ask of a normal man. Of a *happy* man. I searched long and hard for someone like you, Daven, and when I finally heard of you it was like a blessing. Everything I have heard tells me you are the perfect child for my designs."

"Where did you hear of me? What did you hear?"

"In Chantire the rumors hang as heavy as the stench, you know. When I realized I had a need for an unhappy man, I went searching in those dark streets, and I heard of a lonely boy who somehow survived the slums. I asked questions about this child and learned he loved to practice with a toy sword, that some fire drove him to survive when others like him had given up, and most importantly that he rarely begged and never, *never* stole for his bread."

I chuckled darkly. "What's called stealing in the rest of the realm isn't always called stealing in Chantire."

"It matters not. The important thing was the determination, the self-reliance. I heard these beautiful rumors and then finally, at the very last, a drunken carriage driver casually mentioned that the boy had been gone for years. Gone without a trace. I searched the entire town for some sign of you, for a whisper of where you'd gone, but there was none. Then I made my first mistake: I asked the king to find you for me."

We walked on for several steps before the significance of that statement struck me. "The soldier? The Green Eagle?"

"He is one of Timmon's most able trackers, and the Justices have employed him before to bring in vagabonds. I do not know whether I failed to make clear the nature of my need for you or his own pride overwhelmed him, but he was never sent to threaten you."

"Why did you come, then? If you sent him for me, why didn't you just wait?"

"I did not send him, the king did. I would never have chosen a Tiran for Academy business. No, while Othin began searching for you across the Isle, I searched in my own way. Time and need drove me farther than I would have wished to go, but with my magics I finally found you just days ago, and I hastened here as soon as I knew."

"You came just in time." I thought of the soldier frozen on the hilltop, thought how close he'd come to killing me. "You saved me. If you had taken a day longer in your search, if your horse had stumbled along the way and delayed you an hour...."

He laid a calming hand on my shoulder. "My need was great enough to save, even if fate had not been."

"And now I am found, what will you do with me?" I swallowed, and chanced a look in his direction. "What are these costs I must pay?"

"You must leave, again, and perhaps forever. You must take on a new life and become something completely new." He hesitated, then said reluctantly, "Even with the support I can provide, you may have to survive in a place that does not welcome you, perhaps a place where you have no friends."

"I can do all those things. They are no cost to me."

He smiled, a secret and knowing smile visible now in the light from the village. "That is why I have come so far, my boy. Now lead me to your home that we may be on our way."

Our path led directly to the green at the center of town, six torches blazing in the night to light the common yard and the merchants' shops all around it. Ignoring the cobbled walk that surrounded the green, I cut across the thick grass toward the north, leading the old man quickly through and out of the village. An old road turned to the east, the King's Way, but we followed a newer one north. We came upon a low stone wall that ran beside the road in perfect regularity, and then upon a gate where a steward waited in the evening chill.

"Hey there, Daven. You bring a guest tonight?"

I nodded to old Wen. "He's from the City."

The old man stepped in front of me, suddenly tall and proud, and looked down his nose at the stooped steward. "Please inform your master that the Master Wizard Claighan has come from the Academy at Pollix to speak with him." Wen stood in awe for a moment before ducking in a clumsy bow and clutching at his hat.

"I will inform him right away, sir. Please, come in." He opened the gate and then stepped aside, bowing the wizard through. "Will you have dinner, sir? I believe there is still time to set another place."

Claighan nodded, "Yes, please arrange a plate for me. Run ahead." He spoke the words with a casual air of command and Wen obeyed, darting up the path to the manor. The wizard followed at a more stately pace.

I bit my tongue. He had been kind to me, inexplicably so, but a wizard could demand respect from any lord in the king's lands. He certainly had the authority to talk down to a country steward. Still, he seemed to sense my disapproval, and he shot me a brief look. "I believe things will go better for us if we take things very seriously from here on out."

"What do you mean? Jemminor is a kind man. We won't have any problems with him."

"People behave differently when wizards are around." He caught my shoulder and I stopped, still some small distance from the house. An orange square of light fell across the marbled steps as Wen threw open the door. Claighan watched until the door was shut again. "I need to be certain you will follow me, Daven, before I speak to this man, but I fear I do not have time to explain everything to you. This I can say: I would take you to the Academy to learn wizardry with some of the nation's brightest young men, and with the full support of the king behind you. Would you give up your life here for that?"

"I already told you I would."

"So you did. So you did. Now tell me again."

I frowned and said, "I will."

Before I could say any more he cut me off, nodding. "Very well, word of my arrival should have reached your master by now." I started to step off the path, but he caught my arm. "No Daven, tonight you enter by the front door. Come."

We walked to the end of the path and up three short steps, where Wen stood once more waiting for us. He threw the door open then slammed it shut when we were through. I grimaced at the stain my muddy boots left on the thick carpet in the entrance. The air in the manor was warm after the night chill, and the smell of roasting lamb roused my empty stomach. We stood alone in the hall.

After a moment's wait the sound of heavy, hurried footsteps preceded Jemminor into the little foyer. The look on his face was terrible, foreign. His eyes shone with suspicion, his lips pursed in anger. He stood at the end of the hall, looming over us both and glaring from under his brows. He jabbed a finger at the wizard. "You are Claighan?"

Claighan nodded.

"You've no business here in Sachaerrich! All of us are good folk. All of us." His eyes darted to me, then back to the wizard's face. Still Claighan said nothing.

"I've done no wrong. No one in this house has. The boy," he faltered for a moment, bit his lip and then resumed with a bit less steam, "the boy has committed no offense since he left the City. If he's done anything else...." Again he glanced at me, again it stopped him for a moment. "Surely you can't hold him accountable for something done so long ago!"

Claighan stepped forward, his staff ringing as it struck the wooden floor. Jemminor fell back before him and retreated two steps before he knew what he was doing. Then he stopped, tried to draw himself up again, but somehow the wizard's authority dwarfed him. "Jemminor," Claighan called, and his voice echoed off the walls of the little foyer. "I have come on the business of the Crown. Would you defy that authority?"

At first his mouth worked soundlessly, but finally he said, "No. No, I'm loyal to the king—"

"That is good to know. I am here for the king, for the country, and I would hate to think you would oppose me."

Jemminor grunted. "We have done no wrong, wizard." I was amazed at the change in his attitude, mumbling now the same words he had shouted moments ago. "We have none of us done any wrong."

Claighan seemed to grow impatient. "And I have brought no accusations, Goodman. I have requested a dinner. Have you a place?"

Jemminor nodded.

"Excellent. Go see to the table and send your wife that I may speak with her."

"She has done no—"

"I understand." His eyes flashed with impatience that belied the calm in his voice. "I only wish to introduce myself." Jemminor nodded then turned and scurried off. I stood astonished.

"Claighan…why was Jemm so afraid?"

"Wizards are seldom popular where the common man gains power, Daven. I do not wholly understand why, but I wholly regret it. There are those that see us as tyrants and terrorists, and men like your Jemminor are the first of this sort."

"Is he wrong?"

He looked at me, then returned to his casual observation of the room. "That is a shrewd question, Daven. And a dangerous one. I invite you to speak with me as freely as you would—my own life hangs on your education—but be careful in your treatment of the other Masters. As much as possible you should strive to be respectful and go unseen."

I looked around at the empty little room, trying to see what caught his interest, but finally decided he was focusing on other things. His answer tickled my mind—for one, it was not an answer at all. It was also ominous. I was still mulling his words when Lady Sherrim swept into the room, her silk slippers noiseless on the hard floors.

"Greetings, Master Claighan!" She curtsied politely, her finest dress whispering as she dipped. "I am honored to have you in my home. Please, please, come into the sitting room while dinner is prepared. Rest, and tell me of news at Court." The wizard smiled to himself before bowing slightly. He murmured some answering pleasantry and slipped past her into the sitting room.

I stepped quickly forward and caught Sherrim's arm. She threw a surprised glance at me, and I ducked my head, suddenly sheepish. "Sorry, ma'am." My voice was a whisper, and she answered in kind.

"It's fine, Daven. Just speak quickly. What do you need?"

"You…you were so proper! I've never seen you—" I blushed, and squeezed my eyes shut. "I'm sorry. I'm just surprised at your reaction. And Jemm's."

She smiled, but her eyes were sad. "I have more experience with such men than he does. And I heard how things went for Jemminor. I could not afford to imitate him." Claighan took a seat in the next room, settling his staff against the wall next to him, and the sound of it drew Sherrim's attention. She went on hurriedly. "We behave as we must in these situations, Daven. I fear we will lose you no matter what I do."

I started to answer, to reassure her, but she motioned me to silence and hurried into the room where Claighan waited. I hesitated in the doorway, wondering whether the state of my clothes or my presence in the sitting room were the more pressing demand and finally let my fear decide for me. I had no desire to see the proud Lady Sherrim bowing and scraping for some wizard, no matter what he had offered me.

I darted downstairs to my room to change into some cleaner clothes. My room was cold and damp, as always, and I took several long, slow breaths of the cool air to clear my head. Then I opened my eyes and caught an impression of how I must look. I was shivering, excitement and fear wrestling each other inside me. I still had the sword belt clutched against my chest, and when I realized that I dropped it like a poisonous snake. It landed on the straw pallet I used for a bed, and I took a long step back. No matter what the wizard said, that was far too fine a blade for a boy like me to own, and the soldier—Othin—was not one to forgive a theft like that.

I could hardly give it back to him, though. I turned my back on it, trying to forget it while I changed quickly into cleaner clothes. Then, without glancing back, I left my little room and rushed upstairs. I stepped into the sitting room just as Jemminor entered from the other door.

"Dinner is ready. Please join us in the dining room."

Sherrim offered a nervous smile as she rose and brushed some nothing from her skirt. Claighan leaned heavily on his staff as he rose to his feet, then turned a gracious smile to Jemminor and Sherrim. "It smells wonderful. Let's see what your cook can do." He swept out of the room, all grandeur, and the master and mistress were only left to follow, a bit dazed.

In the dining room, Claighan waved me to a seat on his right. I sank down into the cushioned chair before the elaborately inlaid table where I'd only eaten one or two meals in all the years I'd worked here. Two servants entered, the arms of both full of fine plates and silverware, which they placed carefully around the table while darting curious glances at me. I smiled back and shrugged, but they averted their eyes as though I were Jemm or one of his guests.

Claighan tasted the food placed before him, sampling each piece delicately, then took a slow sip of the red wine. Then he sat back and fixed his gaze on Jemm. "Master Jemminor, this is an elaborate dinner and a quite impressive manor." His tone was friendly, but his eyes were dark. "I have seen few as extravagant outside the City."

The muscles on Jemm's jaw clenched, but he made a polite, "Thank you." He hid his nervousness in his wine glass, taking a deep draught and waving to the servant to refill it.

Claighan watched Jemm take another long drink, then the wizard turned his head away to study a tapestry hanging on the wall. Almost offhand he said, "By the looks of it you own some rather extensive fields as well. I've heard rumors that in certain seasons you employ nearly every son of this town."

Jemminor stared at the wizard's turned head. He wore undisguised suspicion and anger on his face, and it didn't lesson when his eyes cut briefly to me. "I don't take your meaning," Jemminor said at last.

The wizard turned back and quirked an eyebrow at him. "My meaning? I only offer you my compliments. Your property is flourishing."

"Just so," Jemminor said, his eyes narrow now. He looked over to Sherrim at his right hand, but she did not look up. She kept her sharp eyes fixed on her plate, though I could tell by the tilt of her head that she was listening intently. Her knuckles were white around her grip on a delicate silver fork.

The men didn't seem to notice. Jemminor took a deep drink of his wine then licked his lips. He turned his attention back to the wizard. "Your compliments are well and good, but you must forgive my curiosity. Why have you come here?"

"Oh, Jemm!" Sherrim said, chastising, but it was a tiny sound. She raised a hand to his shoulder and went on without raising her voice. "He is our guest."

Claighan smiled across to her and shook his head. "It is no matter. Goodman Jemminor's hospitality and grace are spoken of throughout Terrailles. He has done nothing but live up to that reputation."

Sherrim went pale and her shoulders fell, but Jemminor heard the wizard's words as a compliment. He nodded to Sherrim as though vindicated then turned all his attention back to the wizard. "Thank you. I know there must be more to your visit. I'm sure you didn't come here just to discuss my field hands."

The corners of Claighan's mouth quirked up as his only answer, but Jemminor caught on quickly. He sucked in a deep breath, let it out, and then his gaze moved to hang on me. "Just so," he said. "Just so."

"I do have some interest in Daven's fortune," Claighan said. "I found him out upon the hill, where he teaches the other village boys to fight."

"Oh, yes. Yes. He's handy with a sword, this one. Sharp as they come, and...and a good teacher, too," Jemminor said. "So I hear, anyway. I figure there's no harm in it." He cast a sidelong glance at Claighan, testing, and the wizard only nodded.

"Of course not," he said. "Boys will be boys."

"Just so," Jemminor said, and I saw a smile threatening now. His eyes shone with more than just the wine. "He, uh...he never misses a day's work, either. Don't misunderstand about the swordplay. It's good exercise, good training, but the boy knows how to put in a full day's work first."

"And how did he come to be in your employ?" Claighan said. He gave the question no real weight, all his attention apparently on his knife and fork as he cut a slice of the newly-served beef, but Sherrim's head lifted enough for her to throw a furrowed gaze at the wizard.

Jemminor was paying no more attention than the wizard now. He helped himself to a thick cut of roast. "The boy's been with us four years now. Five?" He frowned and looked over to Sherrim. She nodded, and Jemminor repeated the gesture. "Five years. He came into town one morning, tired and dirty and smelling like the dungheap, but Sherrim told me, 'You give this boy work to do,' and how could I say no to her?"

He spared a smile for her. She raised her head then, and Claighan took the opportunity to catch her eye. She took a little breath and nodded. "He did. And Daven has worked for us since."

"So generous of you," Claighan said. "Has he been loyal?"

Jemminor spoke over his wife's answer, "Oh, yes! He's always done a full day's work for us, and always worked harder than any of the others, too!"

"Excellent! Good to hear." Claighan leaned forward, watching Jemminor's face closely. Baiting him. "I'm going to need a hard worker."

Jemm scowled at that. "Oh, well, as to that...I can hardly just let you take him away."

Sherrim rested a hand on the back of his, trying to catch his attention. "Jemminor," she whispered, "he is a wizard."

Jemm shook her hand away and shrugged one shoulder. He met Claighan's eyes levelly. "Even wizards must respect property, Sherrim. He can't just come around taking good hands—"

"He can," Claighan said calmly, his gaze still locked on Jemminor's face. "At his sole discretion." He paused, as if considering a different tack, and then reached for a purse on his belt. "But for the sake of argument, let's pretend the wizard were willing to pay. How much is Daven worth to you?"

Sherrim shook her head, mute with fear, but Jemminor frowned thoughtfully. I could see him adding columns in his head.

"Master Claighan," I said quietly. "You don't have to do this—"

"I do." He said the words without glancing at me, and there was a cruel finality in them that set my blood cold.

"I've already said I'll go," I tried again, talking to Sherrim and Jemminor now. "I'm sorry. I'm not staying."

"Hush," the wizard said. "We are discussing important matters."

Sherrim glanced up to meet my eyes across the table. She licked her lips, and then let her gaze fall to her lap again. Jemminor stretched his arms behind him, reaching up high and flexing muscles large from hard work in the fields. Then he tucked his hands behind his head and fixed the wizard with a shining gaze.

"I figure he's worth four silver vints a week."

Sherrim made a noise. A tiny little squeak. It was the sound of her breath escaping her. Her shoulders fell, her lips pressed tight together, and she laid a desperate hand on her husband's. He didn't notice. His eyes were all on the wizard's purse.

Claighan's eyebrows went up in surprise that couldn't have been feigned. "Four vints?" he asked incredulously. "A reliable field hand might be worth one vint, anywhere in the kingdom."

"And it's as I said," Jemminor said, spreading his hands. "The boy is more than reliable. He's talented and smart and dedicated. He's strong and young and focused. He's worth four vints a week."

"Surely two would be more reasonable," Claighan tried, but Jemminor cut him off.

"Four vints if he's worth a penny."

Claighan held Jemminor's gaze for some time. "Just so?" he asked.

"Just so."

The wizard nodded slowly, untying the strings of his purse with a studied care and then reaching one of his long, bony fingers into the satin bag to stir the coins within. "That does force me to ask one more question, of course." He said it almost offhand, but Sherrim nodded with a terrible certainty. Claighan's mouth twitched in a sad smile in her direction. "How much do you pay him?"

I blinked at the question. I hadn't really thought of it when the goodman named his price. As Claighan said, any good field hand might hope to earn one silver vint a week. But I was different. I had nothing. They didn't pay me in king's silver; they gave me a room and meals. They gave me clothes and food.

Neither of them spoke. Sherrim looked defeated and Jemminor flustered, but neither of them provided an answer. I looked back and forth between them, waiting for someone to speak up, and then I opened my mouth to speak for them.

Claighan hit me with a look of such dark fury that the words died in my throat. Then he spoke them for me.

"Room and board," he said. He looked me over. "And rags. And a cast-off, ruined old sword when you could have bought him a perfectly good one for one week's wages. In this political climate." His lips twisted in distaste at that last.

I looked down at my hands. The sword had been my own. But they had not been cruel masters and I had to speak in their defense.

"Claighan, don't. They gave me a home—"

"They took far more than they ever gave you."

I shook my head. "They have been kind. I like walking in the fields."

"And Jemminor likes the profit your efforts have made him."

Jemminor winced at that, despite the frustration suddenly hot in his eyes, and I realized with a shock it must be true. I shook my head.

"It doesn't matter," I said.

"It matters," Claighan said. "Watch his eyes. Watch how his lady tries to hide from the truth she knows. Think, boy! Think how a landowner like this, overextended, might value the help of a sturdy young man. One who never asks for his wages. One who'll work without rest. One worth more than a dozen merchants' sons all by himself."

Sherrim flinched at every accusation, as though he were striking her. Jemm's fury boiled, and I saw behind it shame. Misery. I shook my head again.

40

"It doesn't matter!" I shouted now, cutting him off to protect them. My breath came hot and fast. "I don't care what I might be worth. They aren't monsters. This life has been better to me than any I have ever known."

"That doesn't satisfy me!" Claighan roared, unleashing on me the anger he had so carefully concealed from Jemminor.

I flinched away from him, and he winced. He pressed his eyes tight closed, then drew himself to his feet. He looked down on me for a moment, hovering on the edge of a deep regret, and then turned to Jemminor and Sherrim with all the deep, quiet authority I had felt in my first moment with him.

"I am taking the boy away," he said. His pronouncement brooked no argument, and none was given. Sherrim nodded and Jemm just scowled across the table. Claighan scrubbed both his hands across his face, looking deeply tired, then shook his head. He met Sherrim's eyes. "Thank you for your hospitality. It was a fine dinner. I regret that I cannot stay for dessert."

She nodded, dumb, and he turned to me. "We should leave now, Daven. It is a long walk to the capitol. How long will it take you to pack your belongings?"

"Only a moment, Claighan. I have very few things." Sherrim sighed at that, and I felt a blush burn in my cheeks, but the wizard only nodded.

"Fetch them. I will wait for you in the sitting room."

I darted downstairs and tossed my shirts—all dirty now—into a weathered leather bag that I had brought with me from Chantire. Other than that there was only my work knife and my ragged copy of an outdated dueling text. I looked around for something else I had gained in my years in Sachaerrich, but those were all my belongings. I couldn't avoid looking at the Green Eagle's broadsword, sheathed on the foot of my bed. I thought about leaving it there. I thought about trying to explain to Sherrim, but I couldn't even imagine what I would say.

I was going to the capitol. I could leave it with the guards there. I nodded once to myself, scooped up the belt, and crammed it into the long leather bag. Then I pulled its drawstrings tight, slung the pack over one shoulder, and headed upstairs.

Sherrim met me just outside the sitting room. She whispered so Claighan would not hear her as she pressed a small leather purse into my hands, "This is for the work you've done for us, Daven."

I shook my head. "No, ma'am, there's no need. Thank you, but—"

She shook her head fiercely, cutting me off. "They are wages well earned. He was not wrong about that. But please do not think poorly of us. Do not let him convince you we misused you."

"You were always kind to me, ma'am, and the master provided a home for me when no one else would have. I won't forget that." I stood for a moment, considered hugging her, but finally decided against it. "Thank you, Sherrim. Goodbye."

"Goodbye, Daven." She slipped off down the hall as I stepped through the door into the sitting room. Claighan looked at me with one eyebrow raised.

"I am glad that relationship, at least, could end well. Cherish the memories more than the silver, boy. I fear you will be alone for a while."

I wanted to snap at him. I wanted to point out that during one dinner he had tarnished every memory I'd had. I wanted to send him away without me.

But more than that, I wanted to see the world. I wanted to find my place—not just one where I was accepted, but one where I belonged. For a long time I'd hoped that would be the Royal Guard, but perhaps the old wizard was right. Perhaps it could be the Academy instead. It couldn't be any worse than I'd survived before anyway. I forced myself to shrug, not a care in the world. "I can handle alone," I said. "Let's go."

"Very well. We take the King's Way to Sariano. We should be no more than three days on the road, if we move quickly." In the quiet darkness we slipped out of the front door. A light rain began as we walked the neat path across the manor lawn, and by the time we turned onto the road we were drenched. Claighan's voice came to me through the cold, wet night. "Smile, Daven. You're beginning a new life."

3. To See the King

The rain poured down throughout the night until my sodden cloak dragged at my shoulders and an icy stream of water flowed down my back to fill my leather boots. Claighan ignored the rain, walking with a brisk step and the hint of a frown tugging at his lips. His eyes were on something far off, and he mumbled to himself as he walked.

Trying to ignore the bitter downpour, I watched him as he walked and saw his distraction growing with every mile, saw his concern and frustration building. At one point he stopped and whirled with fear in his eyes, but when they fell on me, he smiled.

"Ah. Daven. You are there. Good."

Without another word, he turned back east. I followed.

Long before morning the heavy downpour dwindled, though rain still fell in a heavy, chilly mist. I shrugged out of my cloak and wrung it out as well as I could, then flung it back around my shoulders and jogged a few steps to catch up with the wizard.

"Claighan." He didn't respond, so I tugged at his sleeve. "Master Claighan! Stop."

He turned to me, but it was a moment before he seemed to see me, and then he shook his head. "What? Oh, Daven. Oh, dear me. I'm sorry, boy. I've been...distracted."

I frowned at him. "You have. We've been walking all night. We must've made twelve miles. Do you mean to walk straight to the capitol?"

"If we can, boy. If we can."

I shook my head. "Don't you think we should stop? For a rest?" I looked away, a blush burning softly in my cheeks, but out of concern for him I pressed on. "Surely you must be tired."

He shook his head. "I have no time to be tired. The world is moving against us." He eyed me up and down, concerned. "But perhaps I ask too much of you. Are *you* tired?"

I shook my head. "No," I said, and it was almost the truth. "Just a bit cold. But...." I didn't dare say it.

A smile touched his eyes, and he turned and started down the road again. "But I'm just an old man." He laughed, and it was a sound of satisfaction. "Since yesterday's sunrise you've worked a full day in the fields, fought a Green Eagle to the ground, walked away from the only home you've ever known, and trudged—what was it? Twelve miles through a downpour. And you're worried about *me* being tired."

I nodded. He snorted. "You're a very physical one. Strong. That'll be a problem. Not unanticipated, but a problem."

"What do you mean?" I asked.

He shrugged. "It's complicated. I'll explain more when we get to Souport."

"What's at Souport?"

"Boats," he said. "More importantly, I've arranged a demonstration that will help you understand. In the meantime, you must just trust me. Come on." He turned back to the east. "Let's get there."

"No." I stopped, and he walked several paces before he noticed and turned back to me. I glared at him. "I need you to tell me something."

"What's that?" He sounded impatient, and stamped his foot unconsciously.

"Why were you so cruel to Jemminor?"

"What looks like cruelty can often be a kindness," he said with a carefully cryptic air. He turned his back on me and started down the road again, but I did not budge.

"That's not good enough," I said, and my voice sounded loud through the patter of cold rain. "Tell me why."

Claighan turned back to me again. He held my eyes for a moment, and then said with gravity, "He is a small man who has gotten very good at pretending to be something better."

I shook my head. "That's not it either." Claighan opened his mouth to argue, to hurry me on down the road, but I stepped closer. "It was something to do with me."

He narrowed his eyes. And then he came a step back to me, searching in my eyes. Instead of answering, he said, "What would it have to do with you?"

"I don't know," I said, giving him half a shrug. "There was something you wanted me to see. Perhaps you just wanted to make sure I didn't go back, that I would see them for the monsters they were, but you didn't...." He shook his head in a slow no, and I trailed off. He held my eyes for a moment, then jerked his head on down the road. After a moment I nodded and we started walking again.

"It wasn't that," he said.

I nodded. "Then why?"

"You were right. Surprisingly right. There was something I wanted you to see."

I thought for a moment, replaying last night's events in my head. "Sherrim? Something about—"

He shook his head. "No. I have no interest in Sherrim. Or Jemminor."

"Me? You didn't show me anything about me! It was all Jemm's misdeeds. Jemm's mistreatment. Jemm's greed."

He frowned, just the corner of his mouth turned down, but I felt his disappointment. I fell silent, mind racing. After a while I sighed. "I'm sorry. I don't know. I can't see the subtlety to it because it was all so strange. I had never considered them like that. Never even considered how I fit into it."

Just like that his frown disappeared, and his eyes glittered. He shook a finger at me. "Precisely," he said.

I closed my eyes, moving automatically at his side. "I don't understand."

"It is what we spoke of before. You have lived too much of your life in the context of your past. You accepted your lot on Jemminor's farm because it was better than what you had experienced before. Not because it was as good as you *deserved*—"

"No," I said. "I mean no disrespect, Master, but that is not a luxury of my class." I growled deep in my throat. "I cannot live by what should be. I live or die by what is."

He didn't answer immediately. He watched me. Then he sighed. "As I said before, you are a physical one. Practical. And that is a problem."

I shook my head. "No, wizard. That is the only reason I'm still alive."

"I won't argue that," he said. "But that will be a problem for your Academy training." He fixed me with his piercing eyes, and I felt suddenly naked. Deeply exposed. "The wizard lives in the world of what should be. What might be. What *could* be. For a wizard, 'what is' is just a starting point."

I nodded, but my head began to spin. I opened my mouth to answer but felt a sudden dizziness, a wave of nausea that gripped me, and I clenched my jaw against it. I focused on the road for a half dozen paces before the feeling passed, and I nodded again. "Let's walk for a while."

He didn't look my way, didn't see the moment of weakness. And he seemed glad of my suggestion. "Yes," he said. "We should press as hard as we can. There are terrible things happening in the world, and I seem to have challenged them to a footrace."

I fought through another wave of dizziness, and focused on keeping up with him.

Later the shower trailed off. The unrisen sun splashed spots of pink on the thick gray clouds, but the light held no warmth yet. My legs grew tired, and over time that ache faded to a chill that sapped my strength, but I didn't dare admit my weakness to the wizard. He was lost in his own world again, now, and I stumbled along the cobbled road behind him, falling farther and farther behind the old wizard as time passed. We walked the sun into the sky and the heavy clouds out of it, and still Claighan showed no sign of slowing. He walked on without me, mumbling to himself and staring east as though he could already see the city ahead of us.

At some point short of noon he suddenly stopped. He turned to me then with the most clarity in his eyes that I had seen since leaving Sachaerrich, and examined me with a careful scrutiny. "My goodness, boy," he said. "Are you used up?"

I nodded, too tired to speak. He shook his head. "You should've said something, Daven. You're exhausted. Come." He waved me to follow, then stepped off the road into the waist-high grass. I followed him, stumbling wearily. After a moment he had lost me, but I heard him call out from ahead, "Come on. There's a nice comfortable rest up here. Come on!"

The world spun around me as I walked, but I followed the sound of his voice and emerged from the tall grass to find him standing in a clearing. A red brick fireplace stood in the middle of the field, without wall or roof, but it had a tall chimney that reached high into the sky. A warm fire blazed on its hearth, and I dropped my cloak as I stepped over to it to warm my hands. Claighan smiled, delight sparkling in his eyes. "You need some sleep. Go ahead." He waved toward a four-poster bed with heavy cotton sheets and thick blankets. I looked at him for a moment, uncomprehending, and he laughed.

"Think of it as a dream, Daven, but you need your rest. I pressed you too hard." Still I watched him, and he shrugged. "Get into bed. Sleep. I will stand guard."

I did as he said, taking time only to pull off my heavy boots before slipping under the warm covers. The mattress was thick and full, and the pillow soft under my head. In minutes I was asleep—perhaps I was asleep before I ever saw the bed—and it was some time later before Claighan woke me.

I was stretched out in the grass, a pace from the King's Way. The wizard knelt over me, shaking me lightly awake. "Daven," he said, "Daven, wake up. You've had a long rest, but we should press on."

I stretched, and sat up. My clothes were dry, though they still felt stiff. "I had the weirdest dream, Claighan—"

"I know," he said, rising and brushing the dirt off his knees. "Now put on your boots. We've got miles to go."

He tossed me my boots, and as I pulled them on he was already starting down the road. I jumped up and stamped my feet down into them, then set off after him.

It's three days' walk from Sachaerrich to the capitol. We made it in less than two, though it took all our strength. Twice more we stopped, and both times the wizard made an inn of the grasslands, though we only slept a few hours each time. Every time I awoke the bed and fire were gone, the comforts of civilization just a dim hallucination, but I felt well and rested. I *felt* like I had slept in luxury.

Our last stop before the City came just shy of sunrise on the second day, when the wizard urged me to get some rest before making the final push. Twice before I'd slept in the conjured bed, both times so exhausted I could remember almost nothing of it after, but now the thin light of approaching dawn dragged at me, and this time I had trouble finding a comfortable spot on the bed.

When at last I drifted off it was to a fitful sleep, plagued with dreams of cruel, mocking men and terrifying beasts. I dreamed of wars and conflagrations, and then at last I dreamed of drowning in deep black waters. The sensation was so real it finally ripped me from my slumber, and for several minutes I wrestled with the heavy blankets bearing down on me before I remembered where I was.

I was alive. I was healthy and well in a comfortable room, buried under blankets made of magic. I sat up, looking across at the chimney without a wall, and the absurdity of my situation struck me.

The bed beneath me wavered, vanished, and I fell to the hard ground with a thud. I winced.

"Claighan," I called out, rising and brushing the dirt from my pants. "Claighan, are you there?" I looked around, and my eyes fell on the impossible fireplace again. I had only a moment to consider it in confusion before it disappeared—and then I thought perhaps it had never been. I was standing waist-deep in grass, and there had never been a clearing.

There were still two paths through the grass, where grown men had walked through and bent stalks on the way. One led back to the road. I followed the other.

Claighan knelt some distance off in the grass, a long way from the road. I watched him, but he neither moved nor spoke for a long time. Finally I moved next to him and fell down on my knees, imitating his posture.

Nothing happened, so I closed my eyes.

There was nothing, only darkness, except...I thought perhaps I saw an image, nightmare sky above a mountain all in flames. It felt like a memory of the dreams I'd suffered before, but more real. The image became clearer, and I looked out at monsters spreading wings within the flames and soaring up into the sky. Dragons flew high, the world aflame below them. It was the sensation of a heartbeat, an instant, and then it was gone, but the memory hung in my head all full of pain and sadness and fear.

I felt Claighan's hand on my shoulder, and then he spoke, his voice heavy with strain, "That was a brave thing to do, boy. You could have seen—"

"I saw," I said, and his eyes only widened for a second but I spotted his surprise.

"You are a brave boy. Or foolish." He put a hand on my shoulder and pushed down, rising, then held out a hand and helped me up. "But it is good that you can see at all, even if you spy on things you'd be better not to know. I'm sorry you woke before I moved you. Such enchantments rarely survive surprise."

He laughed again at the look on my face, then began wading through the grass toward the road. "Come, Daven. We are nearly there."

I followed him to the road, then followed him to the capitol. We arrived at noon, the old man speaking to empty air all the way.

The guards on the city gate nodded to Claighan and waved us through, and for the first time I entered Sariano on the King's Way. I'd spent most of my life in the dirty streets of Chantire, a slum district no more than a mile or two northwest, within the same walls. But now, walking the proud streets of High Hill, it seemed I was entering the nation's capitol city for the first time. Grand shops lined both sides of the street, three-story inns and noblemen's mansions vying for places along the lower end of the boulevard. I walked with Claighan, and men and women in the crowded street parted to make way for us, sometimes even sweeping low bows as we passed. I wandered up the street half dazed, memory challenging my senses in a dizzying confusion.

Last time I had walked these streets I'd been an urchin, a boy of eleven or twelve years, dirty and poor, weaving in and out among the tight crowds with curses following me all the way. I'd been a beggar, sad and hopeless on a muddy corner in the pouring rain. I'd never walked High Hill to bows and hellos, every eye following me in interest and admiration. I suddenly felt the weight of the purse Sherrim had given me, and I felt my eyes drawn to the shops along the way.

Claighan was three long paces ahead of me when he glanced back over a shoulder and saw me tarrying. His eyes snapped impatiently up the hill, to the distant golden shine of the palace gates, and then back to me. "Come, boy! Quickly. We are close."

I tore my eyes from a weaponsmith's displays and forced myself to catch up with him. I kept pace for most of a block, but I couldn't help notice the shops lining the way. I remembered what Claighan had said about the price of new swords, too. I mustered some courage and plucked at his sleeve. "We've been two days on the road," I said. "We've made fantastic time. Surely we could spare a moment."

He glanced down at me, irritated, then his brows came down and he gave me a longer look. "What would you do with a moment? We are here to see the king."

"For you to see the king," I corrected him. "You have no need of me."

He cocked his head to the side, curious. "Of course I have need of you, Daven. Haven't you been listening?"

I shrugged, impatient. "Yes. Yes, you need me. Your promising young swordsman," I said. "And yet I have no sword. And I look more a shepherd than any kind of promise." He snorted a laugh at that, and I grinned back. I pressed the advantage. "You go and speak to the king. I have money enough in my purse to find a blade and a change of clothes. Tell me where, and I will meet with you later."

He shook his head, still laughing, and fell back into his hurried pace up the hill. I could only follow after. "You needn't spend time shopping, boy. I have new clothes waiting for you at the palace. And you *do* have a sword, or have you forgotten?" I frowned at him, and he waved vaguely to the long leather sack slung across my back.

I remembered Othin's blade. I shivered at the thought of it. And then, as I followed close on Claighan's heels, we came in sight of the palace gates and another thought stopped me dead.

The Green Eagles. They were the king's personal guard, and they were thick in the city. Two of them stood at attention outside the palace gates we were approaching. Neither of them had the same long, scarred face of the man who had tried to kill me in Sachaerrich, but the palace would be crawling with Green Eagles. If he'd had a horse he could have beaten us back here. He could be waiting for me anywhere inside there.

Claighan stopped, surprise and concern glowing in his eyes. "My word, boy, what's come over you?"

I shook my head, mute with sudden fear, and he laughed. "It *is* an intimidating experience to go before the king—"

"No, I have no fear of the king," I said. In finery or a shepherd's travel-stained tunic, it mattered not. The king would pay no more attention to me than to a bit of dirt on the rug. No, my fear was all for the petty fury of one of the king's bodyguards. But before I could say more Claighan cut loose a great roaring laugh and clapped me on the shoulder.

"Of course you don't," he said. He applied a touch of pressure between my shoulder blades, gentle but insistent, and I fell automatically back into motion. As we walked he nodded to himself. "Of course you must be nervous, so I will tell you something of what to expect. But first, we must gain admittance."

The palace sat at the top of the city, its famed golden gate making the northern edge of the world's wealthiest plaza. There to my left was the great marble mass of the Hall of Lords. To my right, the public exchequer's building. The shops here bore no signs and displayed no wares. They were offices for scribes and land registers, for the moneylenders who financed trade expeditions and wars. We stepped into a plaza filled with lords and ladies, and I felt like the same grubby little urchin who had begged for bread just downhill from here.

The guards at the gate looked at me the same way, but Claighan never even slowed. He propelled me along a half-step ahead of him, and with barely a glance at the guards he said officiously, "Academy business, boys. Got to see the king."

They glowered at me, but they made no move to bar our passage. Inside the gates stood another courtyard—this one almost completely empty—and in spite of the busy press of people beyond the wall the courtyard here held an eerie quiet. Our footsteps rang against the marble paving stones as we crossed to the high-peaked doors of the palace.

More guards stood at attention there, a clerk between them, but instead of challenging us he fell easily into step with the wizard as we approached. "Master Claighan," he said. "We expected you sooner." The wizard only gave a grunt in reply, and the steward ducked his head. "Master Edwin is waiting for you in the summer suites. There is a sitting room nearby where the boy can make his preparations. The clothes you requested are waiting." He cast a glance my direction, and without a hint of distaste added, "I shall send for a washbasin as well."

I would have laughed at that if not for the fear in my heart. Every crossing corridor seemed to boast a guard, every deep-set doorway, and the guards all wore the same beautiful, terrible uniform as the man I had so offended. Claighan and the steward bowed their heads together in conversation, making arrangements, but I could not spare a thought for them. I paid no attention to the fine, wide halls we walked down—to the expensive hangings on the walls or the exquisite portraits. I lost track of the path we took down huge arching hallways, up wide marble staircases, and past narrow windows looking out on manicured gardens.

Claighan stopped abruptly and I barely caught myself short of stumbling into him. He frowned at me and then shook his head. To the steward, he said, "Thank you for your assistance. You've been a great help. I will not forget it."

The steward ducked his head and disappeared down the hall. Claighan's attention was instantly all on me again. "I'm sorry, Daven. I know things have moved quite quickly, but within the hour that should all change. I have...opponents who would thwart us for no more reason than their own pride. But none would dare speak against you once you have the backing of the king."

I felt my eyes go wide. My stomach turned over. I realized my mouth was hanging open. I swallowed. "You want the *king* to sponsor me?"

He nodded hurriedly. "It is no small thing, but the need is great."

I shook my head. "That's why you thought I was afraid." My knees buckled, and I had to grab the wall to keep from falling. "I'm going to *speak* to the king?"

Now Claighan's eyes went wide. "Wind and rain, no! No," he chuckled, but it sounded forced. "But you must be presented before him. Hold your tongue, bow as low as your joints will let you, and keep behind me. That is all I need of you."

I nodded slowly. I took a breath, and met his eyes. "And if he refuses?"

"He won't refuse," Claighan said, but his voice didn't carry the same certainty as the words. "He must not. But if it comes to that—if he cannot be convinced here and now—then we will have to find some patience." He swallowed nervously, and dropped his eyes. "I can find us rooms here in the palace, or at one of the manors on High Street. It will take some time. Weeks, likely." He grimaced. "And I'm sorry to say it won't be terribly exciting, but I can begin your teachings in some small way while I move the necessary pieces into place."

I fought not to smile. He offered me weeks of luxury and apologized for the inconvenience. I could tell the delay troubled him greatly, though, so I kept my expression stern and asked, "Why wait here? Why not move on to the Academy while you 'move pieces'?"

He didn't meet my eyes. "Without the king's backing it...it wouldn't be prudent to take you to the Academy."

I stared at him for a moment, and for a heartbeat he looked small and perhaps even nervous. Then I understood, and I felt the same. "Of course," I said. My voice sounded surprisingly cool. Insultingly so. But I could not force any warmth into it. "Because, as I said before, I do not *belong* at the Academy."

Fire flared in Claighan's eyes. "There are some who see it that way," he said. "Are you so weak-willed as to agree with them?"

I turned to the wall, closed my eyes and let my forehead fall against the cool stone. "Life has taught me to respect my limitations, wizard. That is not weakness."

He sighed, and when he spoke I heard his disappointment. "So desperate for honor," he said. "So desperate for pride. And so determined to leave matters in the hands of those who would deprive you of it."

Anger flared hot in my chest. What could this wizard know of such things? I turned on him, but before I could speak I saw the determination in his eyes. And I understood. "You really mean it. Don't you?"

He frowned, just a slight crease between his brows. "Mean what?"

"You're doing all of this for my pride. Why? Why would a Master of the Academy and a confidant of the king care about the feelings of an orphaned shepherd?"

His eyes held mine. A fatherly smile tugged at his lips, but it didn't reach his eyes. He spoke soft and low. "I barely care about you at all, boy."

"But that first night you said it was to make amends—"

He shook his head. "No. You deserve amends, but I cannot make them. You deserved some touch of dignity, but the Green Eagle wouldn't give it. You deserved fair reward for your efforts, but Jemm never offered it."

"But why? Why do you care?"

"Because I need a decent swordsman still young enough to learn magic," he said, with a simple sincerity. "Because you have no ties to hold you back. And because until you learn to believe in your own authority, you will make a truly miserable student of magic." He took a long step back, and looked me up and down. "Wizards do not receive the respect they deserve, Daven. They *take* it, from man or from nature. That is what I have been showing you all along."

He nodded past me to a servant scurrying down the hall gripping the edge of a fine ceramic basin in one hand and the handle of a heavy pitcher in the other. "Get cleaned up, get dressed, and join me across the hall." He waved to another door. "And be quick about it. Time is of the essence."

With that he turned on his heel and swept across and through the door, leaving me alone. The servant hurried past me, shouldering through the door to my sitting room, and I followed him in. He set the basin on a tall, narrow table and poured steaming water that smelled very lightly of flowers. Then he laid out two small towels he'd carried tucked in his belt, and turned to me.

"Will you need anything else?"

The question was almost absurd. I needed...insight. Understanding. Patronage. Instead of answering, I stepped past him and sank down into one of the wide, deep chairs against the wall. I let my head fall back and closed my eyes.

What was I doing? What was I really hoping for here? That the king—the king of the Northlands, the Isle, and all of Southern Ardain—would smile upon me and sponsor me to the Academy of Wizardry? It was laughable. I was worse than nameless. A quick bath and a change of clothes would hardly change that.

I thought back on my last conversation with the wizard. I left a pleasant enough home without a thought, for just the promise of honor, but until just now I had never bothered to understand why. And he still hadn't said it outright, but there was much significance in something he'd said. "I barely care about you at all."

That...that I understood. That I could believe. And with that piece, I could understand more of what he'd said before. "A great threat approaches," he had said. "I would make a weapon of you." It wasn't *about* me. I was just a piece on the board, a pawn to be moved into place for another one of his schemes.

Perhaps that should have offended me. Perhaps it should have frightened me. It didn't. All my life I had wanted to be a soldier, and this was no worse a fate than that. And in exchange he had offered me a place of honor. He would teach me how to make my own honor.

I nodded, eyes still closed. I smiled. All I had to do was impress a king. I laughed, low and dark, but I had my instructions for that, too. Stay close and stay silent. I could do that well enough.

I heaved myself to my feet, suddenly feeling strong and sure. I was surprised to find the servant still standing just inside the door, watching me patiently. I glanced around the room and spotted the neatly-folded pile of clothes, checked that there was enough water in the basin, and turned back to him. "That will do nicely," I said. "Thank you."

He nodded once, mute, and left me there alone.

I stripped out of my filthy clothes. I washed my face first, then soaked one of the towels to scrub quickly at my body, and used the other to dry. I did it swiftly, but by the time I was done I felt clean and fresh and ready to face anything. And then I turned to the pile of new clothes.

A moment later a finely woven red cotton shirt hung almost to my knees over a pair of doeskin pants that fit almost as though tailored to me. I also found a pair of plain leather boots much like mine, but these were new and fresh as mine had never been. I considered the already bulging pack I'd slung carelessly into a chair and rejected any thought of adding my filthy clothes to it. Instead I left them there, piled neatly on the floor beside the empty pitcher and my mud-stained boots.

Then I turned to the last of my new finery, a dark blue cloak, thick and luxurious. I slung the cloak around my shoulders and stepped to the door. It was heavier on my shoulders than any of the tattered cloaks I'd worn before, and that weight seemed to strengthen me. I grabbed the strap of my pack in one hand, straightened my back, and left the room.

Across the hall I found the door Claighan had pointed out standing closed. I tried the handle, but it was locked. I heard voices within, low and furious, but I could not make out any words. I raised a hand to knock, and then a soft voice stopped me.

"Probably not your wisest course of action." It came from behind me. A woman's voice.

I jumped. I spun around. I fell back against the door with a *thump* and heard a curious exclamation from within the room.

She grinned, one corner of her mouth doing all the work, and I felt a flush rise into my cheeks. She raised an eyebrow. "It's not any better when you knock with your shoulder blades."

I stepped away from the door, cast a glance back at it, then moved out into the middle of the corridor. It was a young woman who'd startled me, maybe a year older than me. She sat up very straight on a low bench set against the wall opposite Claighan's door.

She had chestnut hair long and loose, charcoal eyes with just a hint of blue to them, and sun-dark skin that was out of place—but still quite alluring—on a nobleman's daughter. She had to be that. She wore a white silk blouse that was deliciously tight-fitting, and loose gray riding skirts that showed toned calves and pretty little feet accustomed to fine carpets.

Without thought, without embarrassment, I studied her from head to toe. I saw her smile quirk, saw her eyes sparkle, but she didn't object. Perhaps she even twisted a bit here and there as my eyes roamed, showing herself to full advantage.

Then she uncurled from her place on the bench and moved toward me like a breath of wind. She smelled like a summer sunset. She came too close and raised a hand to toy idly with the collar of my too-fine shirt.

"You've got the costume," she said, distant and thoughtful. "But you certainly don't play the part too well."

I found a breath, and then I stammered, "What part?"

"Of a prince," she said. She looked up through her lashes at me.

I chuckled and she frowned. I shook my head. "I am not a prince."

She took a slow step back, and shrugged. "Of course not," she said. She waved a hand toward me. "Not even a little. But you've got me curious. Wizards and kings rarely have time for visits from a..."

I held her gaze. "A shepherd."

"A shepherd?" Her voice rose a little at that. Then she breathed a little laugh and shook her head. "Of course. You almost look like a beggar from Chantire."

I smiled. "I have been a beggar from Chantire."

She nodded. "I thought so. That's the part you looked when you came in." I felt the surprise show on my face a heartbeat before she answered it with laughter. "Yes," she said. She nodded toward the room where I had changed. "I've been waiting here the whole time."

I felt my blush burn brighter and ducked my head. I took a breath. I met her eyes again, and they were waiting. They were delighted. They were lovely.

I licked my lips and tried a bow. "I am Daven," I said.

She returned my bow instead of offering a hand. "And I am Isabelle," she said.

"Just Isabelle?" I asked.

She arched an eyebrow at me. "Just Daven?" I spread my hands, flustered, and she laughed again. It sounded like moonlight. She came half a step closer and tilted her head to look up at me.

"I am Isabelle of Teelevon, first-born daughter of the Baron Eliade. Come all the way from the farthest corners of the Ardain to find myself a prince to take home with me."

I sighed and spread my hands. "Alas. And I am not a prince."

"Indeed not," she said. She looked up and down the hall, and then stepped closer still and lowered her voice. One conspirator to another. "But you keep working on that act. Hang onto the clothes. Maybe before long you'll be able to pull it off."

For a long moment we stood like that, our noses inches apart, her charcoal eyes wide and serious. Then my mouth broke in a grin, and hers answered it. I laughed, sharp and loud and utterly astonished, and she gave a little shrug—still smiling—and stepped away again.

I laughed myself out, then met her eyes. She waited. I shook my head. "Are you always so kind to beggars from Chantire?"

"Oh no," she said, suddenly serious. "No, not to most of them. But there's a special place in my heart for princes."

I looked at her for a long moment, and my breath escaped me again. "I'm only a shepherd," I said. My eyes lingered on hers, and I had to lick my lips again. "But I'll certainly let you know if I'm ever anything more."

She blinked, surprised, and then opened her mouth to answer. Even as she did, I heard the door behind me open. A servant was going through with a tray loaded with silver goblets and a glistening silver wine jug. Beyond him I saw Claighan, red in the face and arguing with another old man, and I felt a little shiver shake me. I remembered how important all of this was, how much depended on my appearance before the king, and here I stood in the hall flirting with a girl three times my better.

I turned back to her. I took half a step, half reached for her hand with a thought to kiss it farewell. My heart pounded and my anxiety rose and I gave a little shake of my head and met her eyes one more time. "I'm sorry," I said. "I must go."

Her lips parted, her eyes widened, but behind me I heard Claighan speak my name and I settled for a weak little wave. The cloak flared dramatically around my heels as I turned. Perhaps I looked the prince, but I felt the fool. I left the girl behind and went to see my wizard.

Though he'd spoken my name, he hadn't been calling me. I slipped into the room without a sound and found a sprawling salon, richly-appointed, with a fire roaring in a fireplace on the outside wall. Claighan and the other old man were arguing, waving their arms and speaking with fierce faces, but mostly in low voices that didn't carry across the large room. The servant I'd followed stepped past the couches in the middle of the room and placed a pitcher of wine and several glasses on the small serving table there.

Then he turned and caught sight of me. He moved quickly back to me, whispering. "The Masters, they are not happy. Perhaps you should speak with them another time?"

I smiled in spite of the nervousness that suddenly danced in my stomach. "I have little choice. I'm here with Master Claighan."

He shrugged. "Princes fear to tread where wizards argue, but young men will always do what they will." He slipped the silver tray under his arm and stepped past me, but just before he reached the door he turned and whispered back to me, "But don't forget that I warned you." And then he left in the same quiet way the servant had left my sitting room. I sank into one of the plush couches and waited for the old wizard to notice me. He did not.

Instead, their voices rose higher and higher until finally I could make out what they were saying. The argument still did not make much sense, except that I could tell Claighan was defending himself. The other said, "I don't care how far you've come, you must leave!"

"It is *not* that simple! This is more important than one man's pride, Edwin."

Edwin's voice was cold when he answered. "Do you have any idea how dangerous your words are? You risk your life just—"

"This is more important than my life. This is the world, and I cannot afford to tremble before the governor of three small bits of land."

Edwin shook his head. "If I had ever suspected you might be this big a fool, Claighan, I wouldn't have taught you so much as a seeming!"

"You taught me more than magic, Edwin," Claighan said, pleading without backing down. "You taught me to see truth, and to do what must be done—"

"I taught you to survive. I don't care how great the peril, you can help no one if you are dead, least of all this boy."

Some of the fire went out of Claighan's voice. Most of the hope was already gone. "This boy is more important than anyone else on this island. This project is, anyway. If I just give him up to die over some stupid soldier's grudge—"

"He will not die! I have said that already! We can arrange for his safety, but it is a serious accusation, and the king harbors more affection for that guard than he has ever held for you."

Claighan snorted, and Edwin fixed him with an irritated glare. "A new student can be found, if it comes to it," Edwin said. "A new Master is harder to come by. You must be wise, and above all else, you must be patient. "

"There is no time for patience!"

"There is no time for foolishness! Stop. Calm down. Think about the situation, Claighan. Nothing good could possibly come from this encounter. Not now. An hour ago, perhaps—"

"You don't understand. Too much rests on this. The timing will only get worse if Seriphenes figures out what I intend."

"You have explained it all to me. I'm even helping you, remember? I *understand* the situation with the boy, but you don't seem to understand that the world goes on outside your little schemes." Claighan started to protest, but Edwin spoke over him, "I know how important this is to you, but thanks to the troubles in the Ardain we *cannot* proceed as you had planned. Not now."

"It is not my fault."

"You said that already."

"Lareth should not have gone over to the duke. I don't know what happened."

"No matter how we train them, they are still only people. He was tempted by the power, that is all. It is not your fault."

"I know!"

"And the king will see that, but you must give him time. For now—"

Claighan's shoulders fell. "For now we must wait."

"Exactly. I am glad you understand."

"I understand. I do not like it, but I understand." He sighed and fell against the wall, all his strength gone. "What will we do?"

"Take him to the Academy and keep him hidden. I will let you know when things are ready."

Claighan shook his head. "The Academy is too dangerous. I will find us rooms in one of the nobles' houses. Perhaps Souward—"

Edwin cut him off with a raised hand. "That is too close. Get him out of town, Claighan." He held the other wizard's gaze until Claighan nodded meekly. Then he smiled, satisfied.

But Claighan frowned. "What of other business? What of our demonstration?"

Edwin shrugged. "I arranged it as you asked, before, and I have not had time to contact them. You will have to deal with things."

He nodded, tired. "I will. Perhaps it will still serve its purpose." For a minute he stared at the floor, lost in thought, then finally shrugged. "You are right, there is nothing I can do. We will wait, and...hide." Again he paused. "You will tell me as soon as things are calmer here?"

Edwin nodded. "These things will blow over. You have always been dear to him."

"I hope you're right. For the sake of the world. You must let me know as soon as—"

"Claighan, I *know*!" The elder wizard was getting exasperated, but Claighan pressed.

"You don't understand. I need a thousand more like him. A hundred thousand. One man cannot face the dragonswarm, but I must prove myself in him before they will let me train any others—"

"And if you face the king's wrath *now*, you'll never train even the one. Run. I'll take care of things."

"Fine." He said, "Daven, are your things ready?"

I jumped when he addressed me, then started to my feet and turned to face him, fighting the blush in my cheeks. I took a deep breath to calm myself.

"I have no things, Claighan. I am ready."

He studied me for a minute, then turned to Edwin. "You see how the boy is? He's always ready. He never falters. I have it on good authority he's worth four vints a week for his work ethic alone. It could have been perfect."

Edwin smiled with a sad look in his eyes, patting Claighan on the shoulder. "It will be perfect, Claighan. Your vision will save us all. For now, though...for now you must go."

Claighan opened his mouth to answer, but he was interrupted by the sudden, clear ringing of a bell. It had the sound of a small bell, one a nobleman might use to summon an attendant, and it came from beyond the doors at the other end of the sitting room. I frowned across at Claighan, confused, but he exchanged a look of terror with his master a heartbeat before the doors behind me flew open, smashing against the walls.

I dove away from them, to the center of the room, and found my feet as eight guards with loaded crossbows stormed into the room and aimed their weapons at Claighan and me. Edwin did not seem to interest them. I considered ducking behind the couch for cover, but fear froze me in place. Claighan slid slowly away from the other wizard and came to stand behind me. The guards did not object. I noticed sweat on the foreheads of several of the soldiers. I noticed fear in some of their eyes.

For several tense seconds we stood captured in that frozen tableau before the sound of soft leather boots scuffing on the marble floor interrupted the crushing silence. Then off to our left the sitting room's other doors opened. The room beyond was a sprawling library or office, and I could see a country gentleman seated in a plush chair beneath one of the tall bookcases. It must have been the Baron Eliade, Isabelle's father, come from farthest corners of the Ardain with news for the king.

The king himself now stood in the doorway. He was a man in his late forties, a crown on his head and fire in his eyes. He wore fine but sturdy clothes, and several large gold rings shone from his right hand. In his left he held the royal mace as though prepared to use it in combat, and the strength of his stare belied the gray in his hair. I almost fell to my knees before the king, but no one else in the room moved. I stumbled forward, caught myself, then stood looking awkward. Everyone ignored me.

Edwin stepped forward, fear in his voice. "Something troubles you, my lord?"

"Oh, yes," the king said. His smile was small and forced. "I have just received grave news from my good cousin Eliade. These are tidings that require our attention, Edwin."

"I have just heard as well, Your Highness," Edwin said. He stopped to swallow, then gestured behind him. "I have been speaking with Claighan—"

King Timmon screamed, cutting off the wizard, "*I do not want you to speak with him!*" He stopped, struggling to regain control of himself, then pressed on in a cold voice. "I hold this man personally responsible for the emissary's treachery. He is a traitor and a conspirator to rebellion. He does not need a firm lecture from his old master; he needs to be *punished!*"

Claighan started to speak but Edwin stepped over and caught his arm, whispering something to him. Timmon's anger built. "You have not even lectured him, have you? Do you conspire, too, my good Edwin? Have all my wizards betrayed me?"

Edwin's eyes grew wide in shock. "Not in the least, my liege! You are correct in all things." He released Claighan's arm and walked quickly around the couch to stand by the king. "You are right, my lord, I was overindulgent with him. I forgave him much because he was a former student, but you have shown me my error." He turned to us, an apologetic look in his eyes, then looked back to the king. "I will make an example of them, Your Majesty. None will dare stand against you again!"

Before the king could respond, before I even knew what was happening, the old man whirled to face us and threw his arms out, shouting some terrible word of power that made the whole room shudder. Bright light flashed in blue and red and blue again, blinding me, and in the same instant a fierce heat flashed through the room. It wrapped around me in bands hair-thin and strong as steel, and before I could find breath to scream the bands began to tighten, digging into my skin. Then I felt a wash of sudden cold all around me, the crushing bands were gone. I sensed darkness outside my tight-shut eyelids.

For a moment I thought I was dead, destroyed by the wizard's magic, but then I felt a touch light on my arm and Claighan's voice drifted softly to my ears. "We haven't much time, Daven. We must move quickly. Come." When I opened my eyes I was staring at a wall of crude wooden slats. Suddenly the smells and sounds of a stable flooded me, and I realized somehow the wizard had cast us out of the castle. I peeked out the front door and saw we were still in the palace courtyard.

Claighan turned away from speaking with a groomsman and said in a whisper, "We must move quickly, but everything is prepared. Hopefully we can escape without the king's notice. As soon as the carriage is brought around get in quickly. We have a long ride ahead."

He started to turn away but I caught his sleeve. "Claighan, will Edwin suffer for this?"

He looked down at me, the hint of tears in his steely gaze. "Not if we are careful, Daven. Not if we are swift. Come, the carriage is here." We hurried across the courtyard and into the carriage, and as night deepened the king's own horses took us surely and swiftly from the palace where the king raged against us. That is how I met the king, and how I left his audience.

4. Fugitives

The seats were cushioned and covered in satin, with plush matching pillows strewn in the floorboard. But the luxury of the carriage was lost on me. I knelt on my knees by the door, curtain cracked just enough to peek out and watched the courtyard flash past. I strained to see behind us, to listen for any sound of alarm in the streets as we approached the city gates. The road rattled by beneath us, sharp clop of horses' hooves punctuating the grinding rhythm of wooden wheels against cobblestones.

We passed out of the city without incident, and a mile south of town my nervous strength finally drained from me. I collapsed back onto my heels. Above me the curtains swayed with the constant roll of the carriage and did little to stop the chill draft that flowed in from the night. Every bump in the road jostled me, throwing my shoulder hard against the wooden box of the seat, but I didn't bother moving.

Claighan sat with arms crossed in the corner opposite me, staring at nothing. His eyes were sad, his body bent in dejection. The confrontation with the king had hurt him. And again, as he had on the road from Sachaerrich, he mumbled to himself as he laid plans. I tried at first to talk with him, but he ignored me. I spent a while watching the night flow past outside, but the darkness and the cold wind robbed the sights of their interest.

Two long, squat chests rested in the luggage area atop the cabin, apparently arranged beforehand and carrying

Claighan's possessions. I had my sturdy leather bag inside with us, stuffed full and taking up most of the floorspace. Every now and then I looked at Claighan to see if he was still awake. He always was. He never answered when I spoke to him.

I tried to think, to understand what had happened. Apparently Claighan had not won his race. The king had called him a traitor and conspirator to rebellion. I had heard Claighan speak of the king in less than glowing terms, but it had never seemed beyond the scope of an Academy Master's pride. This was something else.

Rebellion. I closed my eyes and thought of Cooper's commission to join the Guard. I thought of regiments disbanded to be replaced with Academy wizards. The king's army had only one serious engagement at the moment: the constant, quiet threat of rebellion in the Ardain. But if they were taking on new Guards....

I raised my voice across the small cabin. "There's a rebellion, isn't there?" Claighan didn't even seem to hear me. I looked down at my hands. "There's a war."

He gave me no answer, but I didn't need one. I had heard more of the conversation with Edwin. They'd spoken of a wizard tempted by power, going over to the duke. That would be Duke Brant. If he were involved, if he had access to a battle wizard of his own....

I let my head fall back against the wall of the carriage, and felt the same distant, disconnected shock that seemed to have wrapped itself around Claighan. A traitor, Academy-trained. I would have killed him by my own hand. One man, probably some soft nobleman's son swollen on the pride of his own power and lusting for more, and he had cost me whatever future Claighan had been willing to offer me.

I opened my eyes and looked across the cabin. "What was his name?" I asked.

Claighan raised his head. He met my eyes. "Lareth," he said. "And he has cost us everything."

Before I could get another answer from him, he let his head sink down onto his chest again and descended back into his toneless muttering. I tried to draw him out, tried to learn more, but that was as much as he would give me. A name. Lareth. I felt my lips peeling back in a snarl, intended as much for the king's quick temper, for Othin's petty rage, even for Cooper's sneering disdain.

And now...now we would go into hiding. Not in the princely luxury of the capitol, but in some quiet little village across the channel, or perhaps in the hostile halls of the Academy. Claighan would pull strings, and Edwin would do what he could. He seemed to have considerable influence. And while they strove to return to the king's good graces, I would play my part, too. I would study under Claighan. He could teach me, if I could just draw him out of his dark reverie. I would practice the sword. I would be ready next time, to show the king I was worth sponsoring.

It wouldn't be easy, and I knew enough of the treacherous games noblemen played to know it wouldn't be quick. But I could wait. This still offered me greater opportunities than I could have hoped for herding sheep in some quiet Terrailles township. It might be slower, but that could even help me. Things had been moving awfully fast.

The more I thought about it, the calmer I became. My heartbeat slowed, my brow smoothed, and gradually the knots in my shoulders began to relax. At some point during the night I drifted asleep. I slumped back into the corner and let my head fall against the polished wood because the bench was too narrow to stretch out on. The shaking of the carriage wall bruised my head, but I eventually ignored even that, and sank into a shallow sleep. For hours more we rolled on, my dreams constantly tinged with the little sense impressions of the night journey. Finally a coarse, low shout interrupted one of my dreams. The carriage jolted to a stop and I sat up, looking around. A thin gray light suffused the cabin, starlight and some stray beams from the moon cutting in through the curtains. I yawned and stretched, grimacing at the stiffness and pain of half a night's journey.

I heard the same voice growling through the night and realized it was not the voice of a friendly stableman come to help unhitch the carriage. Of course not. We wouldn't make Souport until well after dawn. So why had we stopped? I heard another shouted order and grew cold. *Who* had stopped us? My tension returned. It had to be the King's Guard. I sank quietly down off the bench and darted back to my place at the window, peeking past the curtain.

I expected to see soldiers in uniform, though it would have been difficult to get word here so quickly without the help of another wizard. I did see several shadowy forms in the night outside, gathered at a careful distance and brandishing arms that flashed in the moonlight. They did not wear the uniform of the Guard, though. They wore clothes as ragged as mine had been, and I saw faces smeared with mud. One man stepped forward into the light cast by the carriage's lamps, and as he approached his words became clear.

"Get down from there, old man, or I'll stick you clean through! Lewin, Kent, get the luggage!" I heard a thud as the old driver jumped down from his high perch and landed by the roadside. The sound was followed by the clatter of two men climbing the steps to the top of the carriage. These were not soldiers, but thieves. Brigands had stopped us on the King's Way, on the Isle.

My heart began to pound, my mind racing. Forgetting my caution, I threw myself away from the window to grab for my leather bag in the far corner.

"Claighan," I hissed. I fumbled at the drawstrings for four desperate heartbeats then growled under my breath and tore at them until they broke. Then I reached within and drew the Green Eagle's sword from its sheath. "Claighan, wake up!"

The blade was magnificent, the balance perfect. I barely had room to hold the weapon upright, but I did my best to position myself within the cramped space, facing toward the voice of the bandit leader. He was still croaking orders in that low bark of his. I bumped the wizard with my hip, trying to wake him without making a noise, and he gave a little snort and blinked his eyes in a confused flutter.

But before I could catch his attention I heard a rattle as the leader of the brigands took the handle of the door. His growl turned to a shout as he flung the door open, a battle cry intended to startle us awake and terrify us, but I was waiting.

I fell forward onto my right knee, let my right arm straighten, and in those movements I drove the sword forward and down in a textbook-perfect thrust. Behind me, Claighan cried, "No!" but I could not have stopped myself. I had spent years perfecting that maneuver, practicing under the protection of our silver-penny spell, until my body drove the blade straight and true without any thought from me. But there was no magical pressure and dancing lights to stay the sword's sharp tip this time. I caught the thief just below the eye, felt the thin bone crunch on both sides of the skull, and in that instant his cry was silenced. He fell off the blade and landed in the roadside grass with a wet thud. I knelt there, arm still extended and blade glistening, and stared down at the dead man on the sod. I forgot the other bandits in the night, forgot the danger and the fear. I leaned forward and vomited, trembling through my soul at the thing I had just done.

In an instant the wizard was beside me. I lay trembling on the floor of the carriage, but I heard him curse softly above me as he looked out into the clearing. The other bandits stood in a loose circle, looking bewildered. Claighan spoke mystical words that felt strangely familiar. I felt a flash of blinding light and an instant's searing warmth, and that quickly his spell was done. Everyone was gone, bandits and driver alike transported far away. I lay still on the floor of the carriage, panting and sick, and a terrible silence fell around us.

Claighan knelt and put a hand on my shoulder, turning me over to look at him. "Daven, this...." He struggled for something to say. I could only stare at him. "This should not have happened."

I shivered, head to toes, and squeezed my eyes tight shut. I realized even now I was filled with panic. I fought for control of myself, I fought to slow my thundering heart. "There were brigands, Claighan. On the king's road. They attacked us. I—"

He smiled at me, his eyes filled with sadness. "You did what you knew, Daven." He looked with regret at the torn cords of my leather pack, at the blood-stained broadsword still in my hand. "You used the only weapon you know." He straightened, then he reached down and caught my hand, pulling me to my feet. I sank limply onto the uncomfortable bench, my mind still reeling.

"I killed him."

"No, Daven, I killed him. This was a terrible mistake." He pressed a hand to his forehead, scrubbed it over his eyes, and nodded. "I have been far too distracted. But you...you need to sleep."

"I couldn't possibly sleep!"

"You will sleep. I will help you. Close your eyes." I sank back into the corner again, pulled my knees up before me and wrapped my arms around them. I was still trembling. When I closed my eyes I saw a man's bloody, lifeless face. The tears felt cold against my skin. I fought to keep my eyes closed as the old wizard chanted, fought to ignore that hideous image, but it leered at me and I felt sick again.

Claighan's hand on my shoulder was no comfort as he chanted in a low, soft voice. I heard him falter once, and I heard great sorrow in his voice, but even as his words washed through my head the gruesome images remained, and finally I jumped to my feet, crying out. Claighan stepped back and let the spell die away, concern in his eyes.

"I am sorry, Claighan. I'm sorry, but the visions...."

"I understand. It is probably for the best. We have far to go." I waited for his direction, but for a long time he stood staring at the wall of the cabin, thinking. Finally he sighed and sank down onto the bench. "There is no easy way out of this. There may be no way at all." He looked up at me, as if suddenly remembering I was there, and then changed his voice. "Daven, we must continue on our way. The king is *not* pleased with us, and when he hears of this he will be less so."

"He would blame us for the bandits?"

"He would blame me for them. It was my fault. We must move on, but we have no driver now—"

"I can drive." He threw a questioning look at me, but I persisted. "I drove for the nobles when I was a boy. It's how I paid for father's...for father's food. And mine. I drove carriages in the city for almost a year."

He nodded. "You did. Yes, I think I knew that. Well, there is one answer at least. You will drive us to Souport and I will make arrangements from there. Climb up front and sort out the reins." I did as he instructed, trying to ignore the sounds of effort that came from behind me. He was putting the corpse inside the cabin. The corpse was going to Souport with us. I grimaced and turned my attention to the horses. They were a fine team, and the road was an easy one. I counted seconds under my breath. Finally Claighan climbed up onto the seat beside me, panting from the effort. He met my eyes for a moment then quickly looked away. "We are ready, Daven. Just follow this road."

I clucked to the horses and snapped the reins. They started off at a quick but even pace. They knew the way. I sank back against the wall of the car and watched the land-scape slide past. The air on my face was fresh and cold. I drove for hours, until the red-gold glow of morning touched the sky over my left shoulder. I watched the sun climb into the sky and let the cold night fade into the dark-ness of memory.

I thought about the things the wizard had told me on the road to the City. I thought about my father who had died in a dank cell for stealing a loaf of bread. I thought about the man I'd killed, and Claighan's earlier mention of a demon-stration on the road to Souport. I thought of his answer ear-lier, "No, Daven, I killed him." I was lost in these dark thoughts when a soft, dangerous voice spoke from the air between us.

"Claighan, can you hear me? It is *exceeding* important that I speak with you." I nearly jumped from my seat, but the old wizard merely shook his head and pulled a small, ornate mirror from within his robes.

When he held it up to his face it showed the king's ad-viser instead of Claighan's reflection. "I am here, Edwin. I expected to hear from you."

There was silence, then, "Claighan, this is grave business. What—"

"Another mistake, that is all. Another in a string of trag-edies. I hate what has happened, but—"

"What *has* happened? I do not understand. I have only the reports from the men you sent me, and they are quite confused."

"I was distracted. I lost myself in concern for what happened at the palace and I forgot about what awaited us. Daven...the boy proved himself a most remarkable warrior. Once more he surprised me with his ability, and this time—"

"This time was one too many! If what they tell me is true, I don't know that I can save you."

"You don't have to save me, Edwin. Do what you must to keep yourself in favor. I am certain we can reach the Academy before his soldiers, and then I can return to set things straight. Until then, distance yourself from my name."

"You have no idea." His voice sounded sad. "Timmon believed I had killed you. He was outraged. For a moment he forgot his anger and...and he nearly cried. That simple trick almost won you free, but I cannot hide this. Too many of the soldiers knew you were involved."

"I know," Claighan said. "I understand the importance of this, but I cannot change the past. I cannot undo what has been made, I can only shape the uncertain. You taught me that."

"I did. I did." He sounded as though he wanted to say more, but the silence stretched on, and finally the old man's face faded from the glass.

Claighan put the glass away. "I hope he does not pay for my mistakes, Daven. Too often we pay for others' mistakes."

I didn't know what to say to that. After a time I shrugged. "You said something like that before."

He nodded. "It is something I think on often." Silence stretched, and then he added, "I have made many mistakes this season."

We rode on, and the sun rose high.

Then I drove the carriage over the crest of a hill, and in an instant Souport stretched out below us. It rolled lazily down into the sea, its houses and markets scattered across a long slope that ended at the grand harbor. The gray stone houses all had roofs of white slate that made a mosaic of the town, splattered here and there with the colorful markets. At the bottom of it all the great sea crashed against ancient stone docks, the noonday sun splintered into a sparkling mist that hung over the harbor and dazzled my eyes. I stopped the horses and sat for some time staring down over the view.

Claighan noticed when we stopped and sat forward, looking down and squinting against the bright light. Finally he nodded. "Very good, Daven. Very good. You've brought us to Souport. Go on down into the town." He stretched an arm out toward the spindly piers that jutted into the sea. "Straight to the docks. We haven't much time."

I went down the King's Way, passing broad boulevards paved with granite blocks. Near the bottom of the hill the sound of the sea danced rhythmically through the air and I could taste the salt tang on the breeze. Claighan caught my attention just as we approached the docks and waved me over to a dirt-floored alley near the sprawling stables there. I turned down the alley and before I'd even stopped Claighan hopped down from his place and started walking back to sunshine.

I ran to catch up with him. "You're just going to leave the king's coach?"

"Edwin will deal with it."

"But shouldn't we wait?" I asked. "There are...things in that carriage that must be explained!"

"I will explain later. Right now our main concern must be getting off this island before the king's guards find us.

They will know I have come here." He was carrying the strap of my pack in one hand, and as we stepped out onto the main road he passed the pack over to me. I noticed that the sword had been replaced in its sheath, and the broken strings knotted inelegantly to hold it closed. It felt unbearably heavy, but I slung it over my back and kept pace with him.

He stopped at the intersection to look back up King's Way, though he could not have discerned anything within the jumble of crowds. After a moment he turned toward the sea.

A low stone wall separated the harbor from the rest of the town, and we passed beneath a decorative stone archway to get to the docks. A skinny man with ink-stained fingers met us just inside the wall. He bowed briefly before fixing us with a sharp, appraising look.

"I am the harbormaster here. How may I help you gentlemen?"

Claighan pulled a small signet ring from his finger and pressed it into the man's palm. "I am Master Claighan from the Academy and I have instant need of a Swift."

The man examined the ring closely then passed it back, nodding. "You are in luck, Master Claighan. Three Swifts arrived this morning and are only just now ready to depart."

Claighan bit his lip, a thoughtful frown creasing his brow. "Three, you say? When did they arrive? Do you know whom they carried?"

"Only Masters, of course. I believe Seriphenes was among them, as his Young Swift is one of those at dock. There were others, as well, but I spoke only with Seriphenes." He paused for a moment, examining Claighan's expression, then added, "I am certain they intended to speak with the king, Master Claighan. They hired four coaches and set out immediately for the City."

Claighan cursed under his breath. "We might even have passed them on the way here. And Seriphenes among them...." He shook himself, apparently returning to the here and now, and looked at the harbormaster. "Thank you for the information. I am sure it will be quite helpful. I...I will have need of all the Swifts. Please find men to man them, and lead the boy and me to one of the Old Swifts, if you would."

"Are you certain, sir? As I said, the Young Swift Master Seriphenes is in dock—"

"We will not ride the Seriphenes. That would be an ill omen in a voyage already too full of them. Please arrange passage on one of the Old Swifts for us, and prepare all three to sail." The harbormaster started to turn away, but Claighan caught his arm. "One thing more! If any other Swifts arrive and any of the king's men ask permission to ride one, you are to deny that permission."

"My lord, I am certain I could not—"

"The Swifts are and have always been the property of the Academy, harbormaster, and have nothing to do with the king! We only allow them passage as a courtesy."

The thin man looked around and lowered his voice. "My lord, refusing the king's request would be something close to treason."

"I have done worse than that today. My order stands, and you are bound to obey it."

Looking sick, the harbormaster turned and disappeared into one of the small buildings along the wharf.

Claighan forgot him. He turned to me. "Come, the Swifts always dock at the east end." He led me to a pier where three magnificent boats rested lightly on the water. The afternoon sunlight glowed dully off the silver-gray sides of the ships, but the white mainsail reflected it in a blaze like a torch. The boats looked tiny against all the great fishing and merchant galleys farther down, but their decks held only one mast, and the rigging stood high above the ship, leaving most of the deck space free. I saw two men on each of the Swifts, scurrying about and preparing to sail.

As we made our way out onto the pier, a dockman sprinted up behind us and pointed to the second ship on our left. It took him a moment to catch his breath, but finally he panted, "You're...to board...the Old Swift...Master Edwin."

Claighan nodded, smiling despite himself. "Master Edwin. Excellent." He strode quickly up the gangplank and I followed close at his heels. The two sailors I had noticed earlier turned away from the main mast as we stepped up onto the deck and both saluted Claighan. He shook his head. "That is enough of that. We sail to Deichelle. Can you get us there by morning?"

One of the sailors stepped forward. "You will be eating your breakfast there, Master Claighan. Now—" he cut off, staring past us in surprise. We turned together and found a dozen of the king's soldiers trotting along the harbor toward the Swifts' pier. They saw us, but in the same instant Claighan cried some word of command, and the Swift leaped forward into the small waves of the strait. I looked back and saw both of the other Swifts darting away as well, pulled as if on strings out into the water and already speeding south with sails full. Sailors on the other ships looked about in confusion, but as I watched they shrugged it off and returned to their duties.

Claighan clapped me on the shoulder, then tightened his grip. "Wind and rain, you're shaking, boy. That was a close call, but things shall get better from here on out." I looked over and up at him, hoping to show him my gratitude, but his eyes were on something far off and they bore none of the confidence his words had expressed.

He looked back to the harbor quickly dwindling behind us. "Although, with Seriphenes in the capitol...." He trailed off, his eyes grim.

I ducked my head. "That danger, at least, is behind us."

He squeezed my shoulder again, and nodded. "Indeed. Indeed. Now we must prepare for the dangers ahead."

I sank down on the deck, leaning against the railing, "There has been nothing but danger since you turned your eyes on me, wizard."

He sighed. "It is a fair accusation." For a while I thought he was going to say more, but he fell silent. I watched him.

After a time I said, "Who was it that I killed?"

He flinched away as though I'd stricken him. His grip on my shoulder tightened in something like a spasm, and then he let his hand fall away. "I do not know his name," he said, "but he was a captain of the King's Guard."

I nodded. Pain blossomed high in my stomach, and I felt it reaching up into my chest. I blinked, and my eyelashes glistened a bit. I swallowed and found my voice to ask, "Why?"

Claighan lowered his eyes. "Do you remember what I said on the road to the City? About your being too physical a spirit and that causing problems in your training?"

I nodded slowly, and he nodded back. "I had a solution planned. I meant to demonstrate for you how creativity and will can do something easily that physical force can only do with effort."

"You...." I sighed and shook my head. I caught my breath. "You were supposed to thwart the robbery."

"Indeed."

I felt my fingernails digging into the palms of my hands. My fists were clenched so tight my knuckles hurt. I closed my eyes. "You set it up. You were going to teach me a lesson."

"Indeed."

"And you fell asleep."

For a long time he said nothing. He caught his breath with something that sounded like a sob. He let it out with something like a sigh. I waited another heartbeat for him to say again, "Indeed."

I opened my eyes to meet his gaze. My chest ached. My shoulders ached. I said, "You have made me into a murderer."

"And a fugitive of the king's justice," he said. "And once more someone else must pay for my mistakes. It is deeply unfair. But I attempted too much. I strove too hard. Eventually even a wizard's body fails him."

"You fell asleep," I growled. "And now an innocent man is dead."

I expected him to flinch again at that. He didn't. He didn't sob, either. He held my gaze for four heavy heartbeats, then he raised his chin half an inch, and every trace of uncertainty melted from his expression. "I do what must be done," he said. "It is a tragedy. But one innocent death will pale to nothing against the threat that is coming."

I felt my jaw fall open. My fists at last relaxed, fury fading in the face of the wizard's madness. "Nothing?" I said.

He nodded slowly. His eyes were serious. I would get no apology from him. He would have sacrificed everything in this mission. I thought back to his conversation with Edwin, to the things he'd been saying about the greater threat. I remembered what he had told me on the road to the City and shook my head. "What is it?" I asked.

He tilted his head, waiting for me to clarify, and I asked, "What is the dragonswarm?"

The wizard held my gaze. "There are old legends, myths, that tell of a time when the dragons began waking." He said it almost offhand, but there was a terrible intensity in his eyes.

My mouth was suddenly dry. I had to swallow. "Which dragons?"

"All of them," he said. "Enough to fill the sky to black at noon. Enough to burn the world to ash."

I chewed my lip. I remembered the strange vision I had intruded on during our trip to the City. The whole experience felt like a dream, but the image of the dragons in flight stood out stark within my memory. Enough to burn the world to ash. I believed it. "That would be a fearsome thing," I said.

He nodded and said nothing.

It did nothing to change what I had done. It did nothing to lessen the dangers I now faced from the king's justice. It only added new nightmares to be feared. I fought against them and fought to catch my breath.

The ship flew south, dancing along the waves. Warm sunlight bathed us, and a cool spray occasionally touched my cheek, my hair, the skin of my neck. For a while I tried to think about that instead of the dangers. It didn't work. At last I said, "Why did you recruit me?"

Claighan's mouth turned down in a sour frown. "This is the fourth time you've asked me that."

"And the answer never satisfies." Before he could respond, I pushed myself to my feet and faced him. "Am I to be another battle wizard in the Royal Guard?"

He shook his head and I nodded. "I thought not. Am I to be an answer to a rebel army?"

His head sank, but I saw another little shake no. I nodded again. "You mean for me to fight dragons."

His eyes found mine. They burned with a vicious fire. "All of them."

He was a madman. He was my only hope for refuge now, for redemption, but he was clearly a madman. But I remembered again a vision of the dragons waking and my breath caught in my throat. "It's just a story," I said. It sounded unconvincing even to me.

Claighan stepped away from the rail. "That is what everyone insists," he said. "It is a comforting thought." He turned and walked away.

Hours later I was still sitting at the deck rail when Claighan came and joined me. I stared out over the waters slipping past, afternoon sun flashing gold and silver off the dancing waves. I didn't look up as the old wizard joined me, just spoke to the wind. "Three days ago, at this moment, I was putting sheep in Jemminor's pen."

He sank down to rest on his heels for a moment, then sat stretched out on the deck beside me. He leaned his back against the rail and drew out an old, ornate pipe. While he filled it, he nodded at my comment.

"An hour later you fought and conquered one of the king's elite guards."

"I had a job, a home, a family...."

"You had a closet *dug* from the basement wall, Daven. You had one pair of pants and two shirts. You had a task-master."

I nodded. The waters danced by while a light blue smoke drifted up and away. "It was home to me. I had friends."

"Do you wish to go back?"

"No." After a moment, "Could I if I wanted to?"

"At this point...no. You *could*, but they would find you eventually."

"Of course." A school of fish skipped past, one great shadow just beneath the surface. "What now?"

"Now we go to the Academy. You will be safe there, and in time I will go back to the capitol to set things straight."

"Won't he kill you?"

Claighan smiled. "Wizards are not easy to kill. I imagine I'll survive."

I nodded. In my head the sheep were bleating, the sun beating down on a cold pasture, the flock milling idly beside a quiet stream. Terrailles had plenty of quiet streams. I sat in the shade of an old tree and watched the day melt.

"Tell me about magic."

The wizard snorted at me, and I took it for a question. I turned to face him and waited until he met my gaze. "You set that up," I said. "You did all of that so you could teach me a lesson about magic." I took a deep breath and let it out. "So go ahead. Tell me about magic."

Claighan looked up at me, then took the pipe from his mouth and stood to face me. "There is...reality. We all know reality, and we are all part of it, but..." he looked around, tapped the deck of the boat with his foot, "nothing that we sense is real. The world we work with, live in, is a flexible framework we build on top of the underlying reality."

I nodded. He chuckled. "Fine, pretend to understand me." He drew a deep breath, and turned to look at the sea over his shoulder. "The inner structure is Chaos. It is the *power* on which we build reality as we know it. Like the deep currents, fast and strong, far beneath the water's surface."

He pulled a scrap of parchment from a pocket of his robe, frowned at it for a moment, then flicked it over his shoulder. I watched it slice down through the air to settle lightly on the water's surface. It stained to dark, but even when it was soaked it didn't sink far. Claighan faced the other way, so he watched my eyes instead of the paper, but he nodded.

88

"We are not creatures of Chaos, humans. We are creatures of Order. We do not fare well among the rushing and tearing forces of the deep currents, so we prefer to live our lives somewhere far removed. We're driven by the power of Chaos, but we live above it, away from it. We take a million little filaments of nothing and drape them over the Chaos like a dress, until our reality is shaped by true reality, *changed* by true reality, but it is far, far separated from true reality. Then, and only then, does the world make any kind of sense to us."

While he spoke I stared out over the waters. Now before my eyes they danced across a deep, terrible web of pulsing filaments. Claighan went on, "Every time we speak, every time we accept some sensory impulse as real, we help maintain that façade that keeps the human sane. Once you understand the façade, though, you understand it's not *real*. It's not *necessary*. So whether you see a harmless wave over there, or," I felt him wave a hand behind me, and in the distance the sea waters rose into a terrible wall that came hurtling toward us, matched with a roar that shook the boat, "or a great tidal wave, either way it's the same thing, and your mind makes use of it."

Terror gripped me as the waters rushed toward us. I grabbed the rail and tensed every muscle in my body preparing for the impact, but through all the fear Claighan's words fell like little drops of rain, and at the last the crushing wave splashed harmlessly into the sea below and was gone.

My fear did not disappear so quickly, though. My heart still raced and my stomach burned sour. I threw a frantic, furious look at the wizard, but he seemed entirely at ease. The sailors beyond him were as well, casually going about their chores.

I caught my breath and frowned at Claighan. "So it is all illusion?"

"It is *all* illusion, but the 'it' is bigger than you think. It's not magic that's the illusion. Not at all. No, *reality* is illusion—a complex, communal hallucination that keeps us all sane—and we as wizards bend that hallucination to meet our needs. The underlying fabric is the real power, the real substance, but it is not something I would toy with."

I turned back to the sea, trying again to imagine the complex web of energies I'd envisioned before. I thought of great and terrible powers far beneath the feeble illusion of reality and imagined taking hold of those powers, bending them to my will. "Is that... is that what you would teach me?"

He sank back down to his place on the deck, relit his pipe with a word. "No. Even Masters of the Academy rarely study such forces. It is not in our power to shape them, but when you understand how they work you gain insight into everything *else*. When you can see what is real, it becomes a somewhat trivial matter to change what is illusory."

"And that is everything," I said.

"And that is everything." He tapped a finger to his temple and nodded to me. "No, you do not need to learn sorcery to become a special power. You need only learn the practice of will in support of the practice of body. I believe that alone could make all the difference." He took a deep breath, and let it out in a sigh. "Though I don't know that I will be able to teach you at all."

Two days ago he'd ripped me from Jemminor's resistant arms, and now he was almost ready to give it up. So much had gone wrong, so quickly. I frowned, thinking it over, and then I said into the silence, "Who is Lareth?"

His eyes narrowed. "You're perceptive." He wrinkled his nose. "You have heard of the duke Brant?"

I nodded. "A lord of Southern Ardain, right? He has been trouble for years."

"He's the lord of Tirah, one of the most important cities in all Ardain. Second only to the capitol in all the kingdom, probably." Claighan shook his head. "And he is more than trouble. He has been working his way up to treason for years now."

"I've heard rumors."

"Well, the rumors finally came true late last year. The king's taxmen didn't return, which probably means the dozen king's soldiers sent with them were killed. That means war."

"Rebellion," I said.

"In the middle of our nation. It will tear us apart, and it is not something we can afford, not now. Our army is too small as it is. So I advised the king to seek other methods. We sent one of our recent graduates to the Court, and I advised the king to use him as an emissary, to negotiate a peace that would not send thousands of soldiers to die on Sarian soil."

"What happened?"

"He turned. The wizard, Lareth, ceased contact with the crown on the same day he reached Tirah, and ever since there have been reports of a powerful magician fighting for the rebels."

We both sat for a while, those terrible words hanging in the air between us. "And the king blames it all on you?"

"Of course."

"And since I was with you...."

"The king has a very short temper, especially of late. He was prepared to hold you as a traitor just for being in my presence."

"Of course." I forced a smile I could not feel. "Then it hardly matters that I have added another high crime to my record."

91

He shook his head. "I have made many mistakes, Daven, and I fear now you shall have to help pay for them. I...regret that."

I looked at him for a long time. He was small and frail again. I gave him an easy little shrug. "I've been paying for my father's mistakes all my life," I said. "I can pay for yours, too."

He did not look sad when he turned to me. He looked proud. "If only I can make it work, it will still be worth it. Give me time, and I will make you a legend."

I shook my head. "Give me another hole in the wall, another job to fill my days, and I will be as happy as I was before. Give me anything else and you've done me a favor."

He rose and tucked his pipe away somewhere in his robes. "You are a good boy. Better than most." Out over the waves the sun was setting, casting deep crimson rays into the ocean's depths. "I am going to sleep, we have a long ride tomorrow. There is another bed in the cabin, if you like, or you can take one of the rooms below. Good night."

He left, his boots thumping on the weathered wooden planks. I sank down to lie on the deck and stared up at the sky. I watched until the stars came out, a billion brilliant points penetrating the night's darkness, and I thought of yesterday and tomorrow. And then I thought of dragons.

5. At Gath-upon-Brennes

I woke to the sound of voices, danced softly from un-consciousness by the rolling of the boat. The early morning sunlight cut in sharp rays above and painted a picture on the deck, but I was in the shadow of the low rail. I sat up with a yawn, stretched sore arms, and looked for the source of the voices.

Near the helm Claighan stood talking with one of the two sailors. The sailor looked confused, and the wizard's strained patience showed clear on his face. I moved a little closer to listen.

"No, no!" Claighan said. "The *others* tie to the Swifts' docks. *You* sail into the harbor and tie to a normal dock."

The sailor shrugged, "All right, but they will know the ship on sight, anyway."

"I will take care of that. It is a simple thing. Just be care-ful docking." The sailor scowled at him, but Claighan had already turned away. The old wizard smiled when he saw me. "Daven! You're awake. Excellent. Come into the cabin, and I will arrange your disguise."

"Disguise?" I asked.

He caught me by the elbow and led me toward his cabin. "Yes." His smile slipped. "Yes, according to these sailors the king has a strong garrison in Deichelle. And we know he now has access to at least one wizard hostile to my cause. Edwin will have done everything he can, but still I suspect there will be guards waiting for us at the harbor."

Sudden fear gripped my heart, but the wizard seemed unafraid. I did my best to feign the same casual air and simply nodded. Even when I'd lived in Chantire, I'd never run afoul of the king's justice. I had seen what that kind of life did to my father.

I shuddered. "Will we be able to escape them?"

"Oh, easily." Claighan said. "The king has not had time to prepare a proper search for us and I doubt even Seriphenes would have made a traveling to come this far." He hesitated, but his hand rose up and felt the empty air, and he smiled. "Anyway, it seems unlikely. They *will* have communicated with the garrison here. That is a simpler matter. But these soldiers should have only a few words of explanation. I will weave some simple illusions—make us merchants or farmers, I think—and we will slip quietly through the town, pick up a couple of horses, and be on our way to the Academy before anyone notices our passage."

He pushed open the door to the cabin. The room was small and cramped, with two beds against the walls and a tiny area between them. Claighan sat on the edge of one bed and waved me to the other. He began digging in several small leather pouches strewn across the bed, searching for something.

I tried to sound casual as I interrupted his search. "So we ride to Pollix?" My heart sank when he nodded. I was not a skilled rider. "That will not be a quick way to travel. Can't you...." I didn't know how to finish the question. "After all your talk of problem-solving, surely a wizard could do *something* better than riding."

He stopped fiddling with the pouches' contents and sat staring blankly at the bed for some time. After a while he turned to me and said, "Magic is not a...simple thing." He paused again, searching for the right words. "I told you last night about the illusion of reality. People *need* that illusion, most of the time. That's why it exists. When wizards change that, people see flashy magic and mysticism because they need some kind of explanation for their sturdy, reasonable reality suddenly shifting."

I nodded. "That makes sense. But—"

He discarded my interruption with a wave of his hand. "Most magics are that easy for people to cast aside. They think in terms of 'spells' and rites and even a pillar of fire that just destroyed some poor farmer's house, when really a wizard only changed the seeming of reality so the house *was* destroyed. The how of it is a mere matter of perception. That's how it *usually* works, and people adapt just fine. But to do what you suggest...." He fought for the words once more. "To bridge vast distances—to make a traveling as we call it—that would require me to shift *all* the fabric of reality between here and there. I must make it so, for us at least, there isn't really *any* reality between where we are and where we are going. That makes the intervening space...soft. It doesn't feel real for weeks afterward. It makes people uncomfortable, and it makes magic there...a bit too easy."

"You do it, though." He looked at me sharply, but I shrugged. "I've heard about it. Everyone's heard about it. Magicians travel like that all the time. Edwin cast us out of the palace and you sent the... the bandits back there."

He sighed. "Of course. It's *possible*, and I know how, and there are those even among the Masters who use travelings far too lightly." His brows came down angrily. "But I will not. Besides, the distance is of great importance. Edwin's projection threw us perhaps a hundred paces. If I were to send us from here to the Academy it would weaken reality across half a thousand miles of farmland." He shook his head, sure and serious. "The things we do with magic only hasten the day of the dragonswarm, and I mean to delay it as much as I can."

I leaned forward. "You really believe in the dragon-swarm? Here and now?"

He frowned. "Yes," he said. "I do." He shook himself and met my eyes. "But not as here and now as the king's soldiers." He returned to his search and began to draw out some herbs. Finally he withdrew a small bit of folded parchment from the bottom of one of the pouches. It looked old, and he moved with deliberate care as he pulled it free of the other items in the bag.

"Now, here is our map." He unfolded the parchment, and my breath caught. It was an ancient map of the Ardain, divided into kingdoms. It must have predated the FirstKing. Claighan chuckled at my response.

"This is the only map I have handy. I'd intended to present it to the king as a gift for his Royal Collection." He very carefully spread it out and traced a finger from the north coast to a place just above the center of the map. It was a long journey—half a thousand miles. "We will avoid towns for the most part, but we cannot miss them completely. We will stop here, at Dann, and here at Gath-upon-Brennes, and I believe that will be all. We can slip through both towns quickly, change horses if ours have problems, and be at the Academy by the middle of next week."

He folded the map with care and returned it to his pouch, then turned to look at me once more with a frown of concentration. "Farmers, I should say. Returning from market." He spoke strange words, unintelligible but alive, and as they hung in the air, writhing, they took on a more powerful aspect. Something in the world around me began to...flow. Everything—the boat, the bed, even the air in the room—everything suddenly became soft. Pliable. I felt dizzy at first, but nothing seemed solid enough to support me. Then in an instant I felt a tightening, and a sudden constriction as Claighan's voice dwindled, and then all was real once more. The ship rolled heavily to one side, then settled back, and when I had my balance again Claighan was sitting with a satisfied smile, staring at me.

"They won't know you from any other country boy, gone to town to sell your father's goods." A cry came from without and Claighan's smile returned. "And now we are there. Come, Daven, and see the Continent."

Just as we emerged from the cabin, the ship rolled lightly, bumped softly against the padded docks, and settled to a stop. The two sailors darted forward and dropped a gangplank in place, moving swiftly. The small port was nearly deserted, with here and there a sailor hurrying past on some errand, and nowhere a sign of curious townsfolk or anxious merchants. Two other ships rested quietly against a pier further down, no sign of movement or business on their decks.

As in Souport, a low wall bordered the dock area, with a gateway through into the city. Just inside the wall stood a knot of fifteen soldiers, armored and armed and looking surly in the early morning sun. As I stepped to the gangplank, I watched half a dozen soldiers swarm onto each of the other Swifts. A captain remained by the barrier wall with a handful of guards around him, and as we made our way across the empty docks he stared at us. Claighan grabbed my elbow as if he needed steadying, but his breath reached my ear. "Be calm. They'll never know you." My heart pounded despite his words.

The wizard stepped up to the guard on the gate and nodded toward the Swifts. "Some bit of commotion, eh captain? What've them wizards got up to now?"

The captain glanced down at him with a look of disgust. He took half a step away from the disguised wizard. "It's all king's business, old man. Move along." Claighan opened his mouth to ask something else, but the soldier jerked a thumb toward the gate. "Now!"

Claighan shrugged then shuffled through the gate and down the lane beyond. I followed him, entirely unnoticed by the captain. Before I slipped through the gate I glanced back toward the Swifts still swarming with soldiers, and I looked toward ours, too. It wasn't there. In its place, instead of the glamorous magical vessel that had flown across the sea, sat a battered old ferryboat, the boards of its hull nailed on three layers thick, and so coated in tar that not a bit of wood showed through. Its rigging was a mess, its sails tattered, and even from twenty paces away it reeked of old fish. I frowned at it, trying to see the truth within the illusion, but Claighan grabbed roughly at the back of my collar and dragged me on my way.

We turned down the first major street and once we were a good distance from the docks, he stood straight and began to walk with his usual strong gait. "As I said, boy, they had no idea what to expect. No trouble at all."

"They'll find out soon those ships were empty."

"Aye, that they will. They'll catch on pretty quick that our ship was a Swift, too. The seeming on her doesn't run very deep. That's why we need to be out of town. Come this way." He led me directly through the town, walking as though he knew the way well, and near the south end of town he stopped at a large inn. "I know the keeper here. Go around to the stables and wait for me there. I'll only be a moment."

Minutes later we were mounted on two fine Southern horses, slipping quietly out of the town with a loaded packhorse following on a lead. Deichelle had no walls, and consequently no suspicious guards to scowl at us as we rode out onto the royal highway that stretched all the way to Tirah. Claighan glanced back over his shoulder once, just as the town slipped from sight behind us, and sighed. "Don't grip so tightly, Daven. You're scaring the horse. We have a long ride ahead, and it wouldn't do to wear him out early."

Despite his warnings I clung to that horse in terror, as the world jolted and shuddered and the hard road rushed past far too quickly.

We pressed hard across the open country, walking the horses almost as much as we rode them. Despite their fine breeding, their endurance would only carry them so far. Unaccustomed as I was to the saddle, I needed the breaks as much as the horses did. We drove the horses past sunset, until the darkness fell so deep even Claighan could not justify the risk. Then we continued on foot until I was ready to drop.

At last the wizard decided it was time to stop. He found a bit of scrub large enough to tie the horses' leads, and we spread out thin palettes to sleep a short night on hard earth. There was no more imaginary feather bed, nor even a normal fire in the chilly spring night. He told me again as he had before, "When you bend reality, reality remembers." And he refused to leave a glowing trail for Seriphenes to track us by. I had learned to feel a cold chill at every mention of Seriphenes's name.

Master Seriphenes and the rebel wizard Lareth and Othin the Eagle. I had enemies in high places. It seemed absurd. These men had turned me into an outlaw. Three more hard days followed like the first, and I spent dark thoughts on my enemies as I ate dried beef and hard rolls and drank from icy streams and slept short nights on the cold earth. Before dawn each morning we packed up and pressed on.

By afternoon of the fourth day Claighan was sure the king's men were on our trail. He looked back often, cursed under his breath, then pressed his horse for a bit more speed. We flew due south, sometimes on the road and sometimes through farmers' fields. I thought of us hiding, of us passing more softly through the terrain and leaving no tracks, but Claighan had no interest in such subterfuge. "We have a lead on them, Daven. We must press that! We are still far ahead of them, and in four days at most, perhaps only three, we will be safe in our sanctuary."

"Will we?" I asked him, wheezing with the exertion of the hard pace. "Will we be safe?"

Claighan frowned and did not answer.

"I won't be," I said. "You said as much at the palace. And Seriphenes is a Master there. The same Seriphenes we're running from."

Claighan nodded and threw an anxious look back over his shoulder. But then he met my eyes. "The king's authority does not reach the Academy. Within its walls, the will of the Masters is sovereign. And Seriphenes is just one of many. We will be safe there."

I ground my teeth against the horse's jarring gait, even at a trot, but forced out the words. "Even me?"

He hesitated for a heartbeat before nodding. "Of course. I will extend you my protection. That will be enough." His eyes held worry, though, and I waited for more. After some time he opened his mouth again, his piercing gaze fixed on the horizon, then said almost under his breath, "As long as we can pass quietly through Gath."

"What if they catch us? What do we do then?"

He looked at me, some sad humor tinting his eyes. "You stay still, and stay alive. I will do what I can with magic. But I will not fight them if I can avoid it. We have already killed one of the King's Guard." His eyes turned sad at the memory, for just a moment. "And that will look less like an accident if we do anything to harm others. For now, though, we have no concern for such things. We ride."

So we rode, hard and fast across beautiful country that never gave pause to our horses. All around us stretched beautiful fields of grass, cut here and there by shallow streams. There were no fences, no walls, and throughout the sunny days there were no villages. This land was littered with little towns, but Claighan had planned his path well, and our unswerving route would take us to only two towns—one late at night, and another where the Masters of the Academy held high favor.

Sometime near sunset on the fifth day I glanced back— just for an instant, I tore my eyes from the land blurring before me—and I saw what had made Claighan curse each time he turned. A small cloud of dust burned gold and red in the setting sun; distant, barely visible on the far horizon, but it followed us where no road went. I turned back, sank low against the neck of my horse, and clung to that racing animal as if it were hope itself. Claighan saw it all, he nodded, then turned his face into the wind as our horses raced on.

Once again we pressed well into the night before Claighan finally called to me to stop. I jerked on the reins and half-fell, half-slid out of the saddle, crashing to the dusty ground before the horse had stopped dancing. Claighan stepped down beside me, his boots slapping softly against the earth, then helped me to my feet.

He looked into my eyes with concern. "Are you yet alive?"

I chuckled darkly. "I am. Yet." I shook off his hand and gave him a smile. "I am fine, Claighan. It has been a hard ride, and I have little practice at such paces."

"You have done well. You have done marvelously. And you must do it again."

"I know. I realize that." I stretched sore muscles, trying to relax, but the memory of a dust cloud haunted me. "How long of a rest?"

He chuckled. "More than a rest, Daven. The horses are near dead. We will sleep until dawn." He pulled a wineskin from the packhorse's bags and pressed it into my hands. "Have something to drink, then find a place to sleep. I'll try to find some food for breakfast."

I sank down where I was, cradling the wineskin like a child. "Are you sure we have time for this, Claighan? They were so close behind us!"

He interrupted the business of unsaddling my horse to pat me on the shoulder. "We have time. They will not risk their horses in the night, not even as much as I did. And you need rest almost as much as the horses do. Worry not, I will take care of you."

I grumbled something acid as I sank down in the dirt. I think he heard me, but he never replied.

Breakfast was berries and some hard rolls that Claighan found in his saddlebags. I washed my face in the cold water of a stream, and then we were on the horses again. I had gained some amount of mastery but I still felt small and un-comfortable perched atop the powerful beast. The air was bright and clear, the sun crisp against the blue sky, but my mood was dark and jittery. I rode tense, still unsure, and tried to ignore the bruised and strained muscles that com-plained with every step.

Claighan, too, sank into a bleak mood before the sun had even reached the sky. He glanced back often over his shoul-der, and finally said. "If I stare too hard I'll bring them on us myself. But then...." He trailed off, then reined up and backtracked for some distance. I stayed on the farmers' footpath, trotting steadily on until he returned. "They must be close, Daven. It's daylight, and they will not have given up. We must be wary."

"I'm too weary for wary, wizard." I gave a dark chuckle at my own words, and it became a long, low, coughing fit of laughter. Claighan shot a worried look at me.

"Daven!" He stopped, glancing over his shoulder as if the soft bark might have caught the attention of a great army. "You must pay attention. We are close enough to refuge that it would be a great shame to be captured now, but we are not close enough to feel safe. Watch every step. I'll be right back." I nodded, making my face serious, and after a moment he seemed satisfied. Again he fell back to search for signs of pursuit. Again I kept on, and after a moment he hurried up beside me and led me to a gallop for most of a mile. And then again we fell to a canter.

We continued in that way throughout the morning of the sixth day, Claighan constantly on edge, and I plodding dutifully down the path. We were walking the horses when we topped a long, low hill and saw far before us a sprawling town bustling in the late morning. Claighan glanced over when my jaw dropped open, and his eyes flicked back ahead. "Gath, at last! Get on your horse, boy! Up! We must appear absolutely unremarkable when we pass through the gates. The people here should not have heard of us yet, but if we draw attention to ourselves we are lost."

I shivered. This was not a farming town, lost in the rolling hills of the Ardain. This was a city. Even from here, miles away, I could see the bustle of it. So many people, and if word of us had gotten out, any one of them might recognize us. I couldn't make myself move. "We're going down there?"

"We are," Claighan said, and his voice had a vicious snap to it. "Now. Get on your horse!"

There was such a tone of command that I couldn't help scrambling up into my saddle, and Claighan nodded in satisfaction. I settled into a trot beside him then shook my head. "What is this place?"

"Gath-upon-Brennes," he said, almost reverent. "Home of kings and warriors. The town itself is a monument." A great river came thudding into the city from our right, poured beneath half a dozen bridges and then into a great half-moon lake that filled the very center of the town. Beyond that the river rushed out the other side, beneath another dozen bridges. Even from afar I could see thickly clustered homes and markets, but the packed warren of streets and shops seemed to wrap around some unseen wall, and a great green garden blossomed in the midst of the bustling city. From nearly a mile away I could see the wash of colors from all the flowers.

I couldn't feel the beauty of it. My stomach turned. "This is foolishness, wizard. What if they recognize us?"

"Recognize us?" He looked over at me with a lazy laughter in his eyes. "The Academy is less than a day's journey from here, so wizards are a common enough sight. And how would anyone know you from any other common boy in the world?"

I shook my head. "It's not me, or you," I said. "It's us. Together."

He glanced at me again, but this time the laughter faded to a scowl, and I nodded.

"I know all too well how rumors spread," I said. "They've chased me my whole life. And news of a wizard turned traitor to the crown, hunted by the King's Guard and traveling with a young man who killed one of them...."

He nodded, brow furrowed. "I see what you mean."

I reached up to tug at his sleeve, trying to urge him around the city to the east, but he shook my hand off.

"No," he said, and dragged me back. "You make a good point, but we cannot avoid Gath. We must cross the river Brennes either way, and passing by the town would cost us nearly a full day. That would be foolishness this close to our destination."

"Worse to walk into a trap," I said. "By the same reasoning, they must know we'll be headed here."

He threw a sharp look at me, and I snapped my mouth shut. Then he shook his head. "You are not wrong, Daven, but I find myself too anxious to reach the safety of the Academy's walls. We seem to have outrun our pursuers, and I cannot imagine a gossipy farmer making better time than we have."

"But what if Seriphenes sent word for the king?"

"Then we shall have to deal with that," Claighan said. "It would be worse if the whole populace were on the lookout for us, but I suspect the king's orders will have been kept close. If we can escape the attention of the guards, we should be fine."

I rode at his side in silence for a while. Then I said, "And how will we do that?"

"We will split up," he said, and I could feel the heavy regret in his voice. "You are right. Either of us alone is inconspicuous enough, but together we may be lost." He sighed and pointed down the path ahead of us. "You will go in by the north gate, and follow the King's Way through the heart of town. It cuts west across the Great North Bridge."

From our vantage I could clearly see the path he pointed out. It was an easy route, and it led directly into the sprawling garden along the west bank of the lake.

He nodded. "I'll enter through the Farmers Gate in the east wall and take the Great South Bridge on the southern end of the lake. Wait for me in the park."

Alone, in the city. I shivered at the thought of it. "Will you dress me in illusion again?"

He shook his head. "No. As I said before, no one here will know you by sight, but if there happens to be another wizard in town, he would recognize the seeming, and it would draw far too much attention." He took a deep breath and puffed it out slowly. "I'll need to travel undisguised for the same reason. That may be trickier."

"Then let us pass the town altogether. I'd rather spend another night on the road—"

"No," he said with some finality. "No. The risk is slim, and we have wasted too much time already. We must begin fixing things, not allow them to continue getting worse."

I bit my tongue against a dark retort. Things could get quite a bit worse if we were caught in town. He would not be moved, though. I leaned forward in my saddle, checking my route through the city once more, and then I turned to him. "I will wait for you in the gardens."

He nodded. "Until sunset. If I do not come by then, slip out through the Empire Gate and follow the King's Way south toward Pollix. You'll know the road to the Academy when you see it."

I nodded. My stomach roiled with a sudden fear, but I took slow, steady breaths to calm myself as I always did before a fight. I reached over my shoulder to the sword hilt, just barely jutting out of the top of my travel pack, and prayed it wouldn't come to that.

Claighan saw it all, and then he nodded grimly. "It must not come to that," he said. "Run if you must. It will not go well for you if you are caught, but it will be worse if you kill any Guardsmen."

Any more, I corrected, but I did not say it. Instead I nodded back. He glanced over his shoulder to the north, but still there was no sign of pursuit—neither on the road nor in the sky above. I took his meaning, though, and spurred my horse forward. I heard him do the same behind me, veering off to the east to enter through a different gate.

I covered the last half-mile to the city walls at a gallop, then slowed to a canter as I approached a pair of bored guards beneath the shadow of the gate. One of them waved me through without even looking. The other gave me a glance, then turned his attention back to the road. I felt an itch between my shoulder blades as I passed, and it persisted for more than a mile down the road, but when I finally allowed myself to look back, they were still waiting in the same position, same bored faces. I turned my attention back to the road ahead and made my way through the city.

As I moved, comparing the city around me to the view I'd had of it from afar and above, I came to realize just how vast the gardens at its heart really were. The whole city seemed to point toward them, and here and there throughout the busy mercantile district I was passing through were hints, reminders of the gardens that made up the city's glory. I saw flowerpots in nearly every window, and little flower gardens tucked into every alley. The city was a rainbow of color and scent from thousands of flowers, exotic and plain. They mingled with the sights and smells of a busy city, the combined scents of sunflower and sweat, of daffodil and dung. As the afternoon breezes eddied and whirled I was assaulted and inspired by turns.

The people of the city paid it no mind at all. They paid far more attention to me, riding high above the cobblestone streets and gawking like a country boy come to town. I tried to rein it in, to hold myself with a bored, busy air. I doubt I did a very good job of it, though. I felt the weight of every gaze that passed over me, and far too often it belonged to a uniformed soldier. They wore the livery of the city watch, but they would be no slower to answer a warrant from the king than the most dedicated Green Eagle.

That left me tense and jumpy, and I passed the nervousness on to my horse. He became skittish and a little wild in the press of the city, and once while I was busy looking back over my shoulder at a pair of guards I'd seen talking close, the beast spooked beneath me and startled forward, knocking a shoulder into a goodman and sending him sprawling.

I scrambled down and helped him to his feet. He was more polite than I could have hoped for, but I couldn't count on the same treatment again, and I could end up in the hands of the watch as much for a skittish horse as for my actions on the Souport road.

So I stayed on my feet. Claighan had a longer way to go anyway, and I felt much less exposed leading the horse. I'm sure he appreciated the rest. And there, on my feet, I felt entirely lost within the crowd. In an instant I felt most of the tension escape me. Mounted I'd been terribly visible, but walking with the flow I found the crowds of the city more a blessing than a curse. Suddenly no one paid me any attention at all, and I drifted with the current of the city, flowing inexorably toward the gardens.

It might have taken me an hour to reach the bridge, and by the time I came in sight of it, most of my earlier fear was gone. I felt a touch of nervousness again when I saw the two guardtowers set into the foot of the bridge, but I moved closer and found them empty, roped off, and from the look of it they hadn't been put to use in a very long time.

The bridge itself was a marvel, an imposing military structure unlike anything I'd ever seen before. Made entirely of heavy worked stone, it arched up high over the surface of the river. And though it only stood fifty paces from one bank to another, the sides were dotted every three paces with either a small, closed guardhouse or a stone crenellation which could provide cover for an archer facing out. There were even several places where slits in the stonework allowed a glimpse of the river rushing below. As I spotted each clever new strategic structure along its length, I'd picture it in use. I walked from one end to the other with the thought of fighting in my mind, my imagination rich with thoughts of defenders trying to hold me back, of attackers trying to force me from some bulwark. It was a marvel, and I could easily imagine the full length of it dripping with blood.

At the far end my boots slapped against packed earth rather than worked stone, and in an instant I returned to the real world. Here, too, stood two long-abandoned guard towers, but no foes barred my way. Instead I looked out over a beautiful, flowered field—sculpted to seem like wild nature. A cool breeze blew steady off the great crystal lake, dancing among the many flowers and carrying on it only a sweet perfume—the odors of the city now gone. I resisted the pull of the lake and turned instead to my right, following a winding path until I came to an ancient stone wall. I remembered the view from outside the city, and here found before me the actual structure that held the bustling city away from this place of serenity. Through the stone I felt the dull throb of noise from the city without, but the flowers and trees that grew close here kept these worlds apart.

For a long while I followed the path along this outer wall, marking the location of the Empire Gate that Claighan had mentioned. By my guess I'd have to wait at least half an hour for him to meet up with me, and likely more. So I walked my horse beneath the shade of the trees, keeping out of sight as much as possible, and reveled in the quiet calm of this refuge.

I walked in and out of shadow, felt the warm sunlight wash like waves across my skin, and from time to time heard ripples of a child's laughter break the silence. The path wound around, slowly bending away from the wall, and led me back toward the garden's heart. Suddenly the trees on either side of me gave way and I stepped out into the full afternoon sun, and there directly before me was the shore of the lake. I stopped, astonished, hushed by the lapping of dozens of tiny waves against a stony shore. Here and there along the shore families were stretched out on sheets, eating a picnic lunch beneath the trees or simply enjoying the afternoon.

I turned, fascinated. There to my left, in the far distance, I could see the bridge I'd come across. And to my right, the Great South Bridge that would bring me Claighan. Even as I thought of him, I spotted him riding high on his fine Southern steed. I shook my head, smiling in sudden superiority as I thought how conspicuous he seemed. And then, with that thought, I felt the creeping tension I'd shed come washing back in.

It started as a little worry, but I couldn't shake it. I watched Claighan climb the arch of the bridge, nearly a hundred paces distant, and the hair on the back of my neck tried to stand up. I took a step in his direction and felt a sudden knot of fear in my stomach. Something was very, very wrong.

And then I spotted the guards waiting for him at the foot of the bridge. They wore no uniforms, but I could see it in the way they held themselves. In the way they waited. In the way they watched their enemy approaching. Ambush.

Once I recognized it, I saw the rest. There were two or three more moving along behind him, pretending to be part of the crowd, but they moved in perfect formation, barring any chance of retreat for him. There was another ahead of him, never looking back, but he kept pace with the wizard, and then I spotted another on the other side. They'd be ready to respond if Claighan did something before he reached the ambush, and ready to lend aid if he fell into the trap.

The tension that had been building in my chest exploded into panic. I reached instinctively for a sword I did not have strapped to my belt and darted rapidly toward the bridge. It was too far. Before I could be halfway there, the wizard would be in the midst of their trap. As I watched, two more men stepped out from among the trees to join the two waiting at the foot of the bridge, and I saw hints of movement deeper in back. Fear made my heart a hammer, crushing my ribs and lungs in its sudden pounding. I dropped my horse's reins, dropped my pack, and ran for all I was worth toward the bridge.

And as I ran, I shouted across the great distance. "Look to, Master Wizard! Claighan! Ambush in the gardens!"

I heard an answering snarl, an angry shout. It didn't come from the bridge ahead of me, but from nearby to my right. Too late I tried to turn, and saw a form already blurring toward me. It was another of the guards dressed in plain clothes, and he hit me at a full sprint. He buried his shoulder in my ribs and threw me up and back. I flew through the air and splashed down in the shallow waves of the lakeshore. The river-smoothed stones bruised me where I landed, but they did nothing to slow me. I slid into knee-deep water. The cold was a shock, and I had to throw myself frantically out of the water.

Coughing and sputtering, I whirled, trying to orient myself. The splashing of footsteps nearby helped. I turned that direction, blinked water from my eyes, and just had time to see the wide swing slamming toward my head. I ducked it, faster and more nimble than he had expected me to be, and

I danced left of him and swung my right elbow hard into the back of his shoulder. It threw him off-balance, and his momentum carried him down into the water.

I wasn't in the clear, though. Three more soldiers stood four paces back, penning me in. They came slowly closer, waiting to see if their companion could catch me before they stepped into the water. The thought didn't give me much courage. I wasn't nearly a good enough swimmer to try it for an escape. I did consider trying a sprint south. If I could get past the one on my left, I knew I might be able to join the fight near Claighan. Surely he could help me. Before I took my first step, though, I spotted two more guards standing farther back, watching me carefully while they readied heavy crossbows. If I made a run for it, if I broke free, they'd be able to shoot me down without any effort at all.

Distance was against me. Desperate with a sudden panic, I pounded two quick steps through the surf and then threw myself at the guard on my left. My right shoulder crashed hard against his shins and I grappled with him as he fell. I got a fist knotted in the front of his shirt and hauled myself up as he went down. I slammed my free fist hard against his jaw, then dropped the other hand to his belt and closed it around the hilt of his sword.

Then I twisted and got my feet under me. I kicked off hard, throwing myself clear of the stunned guard and taking his sword with me. I flew to my feet, stumbled three quick steps with no kind of balance at all, and crashed into one of the other two guards who had tried to ring me in. I aimed a clumsy blow at his jaw, too, as he started to fall, but he wasn't quite so stunned as the first had been. He brought both arms up, and though he couldn't bring his blade to bear he got in a good shove that flung me on my back.

I swept again into the froth of the chilly waters, and the third swordsman was upon me in an instant. I brought up my stolen sword, trying desperately to defend myself. He grinned down at me, fury in his eyes, and lashed out at me hard with a heavy longsword. I twisted away and snapped my blade up in time to deflect the blow. I aimed a swipe at his midsection to buy a moment's time, then tried to rise. He pressed me hard. I tried to dance aside as I rose and brought my sword to bear, but I still caught the tip of his blade in a long score against my left arm. The cut burned, the blood flowed, and the cold water on my skin stung still more, but I kept moving. I dodged another swing, then met the next with a perfect parry and reversed, slammed the hilt of my sword against the base of his neck. He fell with a splash and lay still as the water washed through the links in his armor.

All of that happened quickly, but the guards still facing me had overcome their surprise and as soon as the one was down, two more were upon me. They seemed cautious, confident in their numbers, and I felt the fear building in me. I retreated steadily before their attack, still ankle deep in the lapping waves, still uncertain on the sandy footing, but I dared not break for the firmer shore because of the crossbowmen waiting there. So I retreated, carefully and slowly, and did everything I could to keep these two men between me and a pair of crossbows built to penetrate plate armor.

The swordsmen quickly grew impatient of my maneuvering, and began attacking with more force. Sweat half-blinded me, wet clothes stuck heavily to my arms and legs, and the two attacked in almost perfect unity. I was good— better than I'd ever really believed—and they were playing careful. Still, they battered me even with the force of the blows I deflected, and I felt my strength giving. Every block or parry came a little slower than the one before; I knew any moment now another cut would get through. I fell back, calf-deep in the waters now, and they followed. A cold wind came dancing off the waters and chilled me despite the heat of combat, and I had to fight sudden shivers.

And then a larger wave smashed against the backs of my knees and I began to topple forward. One of the guards grinned at my falter, but I let the water wash me forward, and just as the wave hit him, I lashed out. My stumble turned the attack so I hit him with the flat of my blade instead of the edge, but it slipped off the armor on his shoulder and crashed hard against the side of his head, sending him sprawling.

But even as I fell forward, the other guard turned to finish me. I kicked out under the water and felt my boot connect with his ankle, and he stumbled back. Grimly I kicked against the sand underfoot and scuttled away in the water. I reached down and shoved myself aright as I moved. It was a clumsy maneuver, but I was able to gain my feet while the other swordsman was still cursing his damaged ankle. I almost grinned then, as the fire of battle rushed through me. I took two great, noisy leaps forward, swinging my sword high to finish him, when suddenly a new fire shot through my leg.

In an instant I lost all strength. I fell forward into the chill waters. I looked down as I fell, astonished, and saw water stained black and red around my left calf. A heavy crossbow bolt stood clear against the stony bed of the lake for just a moment before another wash of blood obscured the waters. I slammed down after it.

I fought to rebuild my mental image of the scene, to figure out where I should be. There was still another crossbowman ready to fire, and another swordsman close at hand. I struggled to regain my feet, but panic had me, and I merely splashed about in the water. Pain washed in wave after blinding wave over my torn leg, and mingled with fear and weariness it nearly drove me mad. I fought for control, fought to simply hold still and await death with some dignity, but I kept floundering uselessly.

I felt as much as heard a heavy step splash down beside me. I sucked in a deep breath, though it was half water, and gripped the threaded steel of the sword hilt as if it could preserve me. The tip was buried in the earth beneath me, and I hadn't the strength to wrench it out and into any kind of a block. Not in time. Not with him so close. Not with the threat of a crossbow bolt through my chest if I ducked the wrong direction. At last I fell still, paralyzed by my fear.

Every muscle in my body tensed until my bones creaked, but no blow came. I coughed, sputtering, and waited for the felling stroke. Instead, I felt a bony hand grip my left shoulder, just above the cut, and with surprising strength pull me straight to my feet. I nearly fell again when my leg began to give, but the hand steadied me, kept me upright.

For an instant I simply stood there, breath burning in my lungs, amazed I was still alive. But the wizard's words burned bright in my memory. *It will not go well for you if you are caught.* This man behind me had shown me some mercy, but I could not afford it. Still tense, I unleashed all my strength like a spring wound to the breaking point. I ripped the sword free of the earth and spun with all my might. The blade flashed up in the air, flinging out a fine spray of water that sparkled in the evening sun. The sword, too, glittered as it soared through a graceful arc and then down. I twisted at the waist and drove the blade home with all my strength.

Something happened, then. Rapidly. I felt invisible cords, bonds, almost casually snake around me. They whispered out around the blade, flowing like the ripple of a little springtime breeze but a heartbeat later they grew firm. They bound me in place like steel. The blade stopped as though I had thrown it against solid stone. I hung in the air, motionless, imprisoned by the air itself. I found myself trapped, helpless, and staring into the surprised eyes of Claighan. It was he who had pulled me from the waters. His robes clung heavy and wet to his legs and a shallow wound spilled blood down his cheek to stain his gray beard. The edge of my stolen sword dripped lakewater onto his collarbone from less than a hand's breadth away.

As I watched the astonished fear in his eyes drained away. I felt the same dizzying blur of emotions: recognition and horror and finally relief that he had stayed my hand. But relief lasted less than a heartbeat. My mental image of the field of battle fell back into place, and I growled at Claighan through the bonds holding me. "Let me go! Now!"

His brows pinched in a frown, but he did not argue. He twitched a finger, and the bonds that held me were gone. I almost fell again into the waters, but I held my feet and forced myself to ignore the pain. There was another crossbowman with an easy aim at Claighan.

I shoved past the wizard to lurch painfully up out of the water and onto the shore. Three long paces brought me face to face with the crossbowman. I had the sword stretched out before me, ready to strike, but there was no need. The crossbowman stood frozen, an arrow half-drawn, trapped in the same bonds that had held me a moment before.

I turned back to Claighan and nearly fell again. The immediate danger past, my strength went out of me, and it was all I could do to stand upright against the pain in my injured leg. The wizard took several hurried steps up out of the waters and came up to take my weight on his frail shoulder. Again I was surprised by the old man's strength.

"You saved me," I said. "How did you escape the ambush?"

Claighan didn't answer me. Instead he turned me from under my shoulder and pointed back toward my horse. He started me walking, and I had to grind my teeth at every step to keep from screaming. I felt the wizard tense beneath my arm, too, responding to my pain. We made it three paces, then he said with sadness in his voice, "They beat us to Gath."

In spite of myself I chuckled at the comment. "Yes, Claighan, but we beat them *at* Gath. We won!" Claighan shook his head, his expression grave. He started to answer, but the heavy sound of steel on stone drew our attention to the south bridge behind us. I craned my neck and saw more soldiers hurrying into the gardens. These wore the full uniform of the King's Guard, and they immediately began forcing their way through the trees toward us. A crossbow bolt buried itself in the wet earth several paces away, then another a pace closer.

I looked at Claighan. I pulled away from him to free my arm and raised my sword against the distant attackers.

Behind me, Claighan clucked in irritation. "No more killing, Daven. You've done enough evil for the sake of my plans. There are other ways." I heard him sigh, but in an instant he cried out in a thunderous voice three quick words that melted from my mind. And then he began a more complicated chant, arms waving in slow circles.

I had some guess what he was about, and with a desperate motion I flung myself forward and grabbed the strap of my traveling pack. I reached for the reins of my horse, too, but before I got there I felt the air around me grow tense, as though lax strings had once again been drawn tight around me. The sensation was more violent this time—the threads seemed to slice into me, heat and darkness exploding in my head. A piercing tension flooded my skull, and then a soft white light washed across my vision and I saw a tall, rectangular doorway standing in the open air before me.

"One step will take you to refuge, Daven. Find your safety! Go!" Despite his insistence, despite the pressure on my soul, I hesitated. The soldiers were too close, and I could see at least one of them lifting a heavy crossbow to his shoulder. I tried to cry out the danger, tried to argue with the old wizard, but he planted a hand between my shoulder blades and shoved, and I fell forward through the light.

Somewhere far, far away I heard the twang of a bowstring, heard an old man's cry of pain, but time and terrain washed up around me like the gentle waves of the lake. They eddied slowly around my dazzled mind then pulled away, faded, and left me in darkness.

In the blink of an eye I left Gath-upon-Brennes far behind.

6. The Academy

Light and darkness faded back together again, melted into each other and settled on normal patterns. Slowly color returned and with it my senses. I lay sprawled in a dusty courtyard, sick patches of dry grass here and there about me, but the ground beneath me packed so hard the dirt seemed one great paving stone. Rather than trying to stand, I rolled over onto my back and saw a massive pair of doors towering high above me, set in a stone wall some forty feet tall that stretched off to the right and left. The doors reached nearly to the top, set in a great pointed arch and every inch of them covered with runes and mystic symbols. For a moment I thought I saw an image in the etchings, a great white dome arching high against a green field, but in an instant the image faded and left behind only carvings in wood.

As I lay resting, staring up at the afternoon sky, I could still feel a strange tension in the air, an uneasiness that pointed like an arrow to the north and west. The sensation lay heavy on me, and in my mind I saw clearly the gardens I had just left, the guards standing stupefied just feet away, but my eyes told me I was elsewhere, and a shake of my head dispelled the garden and the soldiers with it.

I heard the rapid slap of shoes against the hardened earth and craned my neck to see half a dozen old men sprinting awkwardly toward me, fingers grasping at the air while they ran as though they could feel the invisible cords. One of them darted in the lead, tall and thin and clothed all in black. His eyes were dark beneath a frowning brow, and his hair hung in black waves nearly to his shoulders. He approached me directly, pointed a long finger in my face and barked, "Stranger, how dare you intrude here!"

From my side, down by the ground, a weak voice coughed then said, "Let be, Seriphenes." Claighan had made it through. I felt a wash of hope, but a stab of breathless pain immediately drove it away. Claighan groaned and said, "This boy is with me. You would not challenge me yet, would you?" The dark gaze of Seriphenes stabbed just as sharp as the pain in my leg, his scowl only deepening as he turned it toward Claighan.

"This bloody lump is Claighan?" Seriphenes said. His voice was nearly a whisper, dark with ominous portent. He took a slow, careful breath, then turned and said in a more neutral tone, "It is Claighan who has come so precipitously into our midst. He is injured apparently, so any trial must wait—"

Another of the old men interrupted Seriphenes. "A trial?" He nearly laughed, but the look he shot Seriphenes was stern and chastising. "He clearly acted out of need, and that we may forgive. Archus!" A young man who had been lurking at Seriphenes's side suddenly looked up, scowling. "Archus, help Claighan inside and take him to the priest. He will need attention, and quickly."

The words gripped at my heart, and I rolled onto my side to get a look at Claighan. He sprawled on the ground next to me, one arm pinned beneath him and a leg bent awkwardly to the side, and with a small pool of blood collecting beneath his ribs. His robes were torn on the left side, below his chest.

He reached for me, placed his right hand on my shoulder, and surprised me by hauling me close enough to whisper, "You are safe here, Daven. Be silent and go unseen as much as you may." His voice grew quieter as the young man called Archus stepped near, and Claighan said in a failing whisper, "Not everyone here is a friend, but none should be an enemy."

His grip relaxed, then, and we fell apart. I watched, panting through my own pain, while Archus helped Claighan struggle to his feet. The young man sneered whenever the wizard showed his pain, and I felt an animal fury burn inside me at that. Claighan's words held my tongue, though. With groans and grimaces Claighan finally attained his feet, and leaning on Archus's shoulder he made his way toward a large, low building that stood some twenty paces away across the courtyard.

After all Claighan's warnings I expected unkind words from the cruel-eyed Seriphenes, but he only sniffed down at me and strode off in the same direction Claighan had gone.

Instead, it was the man who had called Seriphenes down earlier who spoke to me, while the others trailed off toward the buildings. The one who stayed had bushy white eyebrows and a beard to match, eyes as gray as a summer storm and a pair of impossibly delicate spectacles balanced on his nose. He looked me up and down, considering. "So," he said, "at last we meet Claighan's little experiment."

"Daven," I said, trying to keep my tone polite. "Of Terrailles."

"Carrickson," he corrected. "We know precisely who you are. And word of your actions on the Isle has reached us as well." My heart sank. I would be a prisoner here instead of in the City. He shook his head, disappointed, and I felt it echoed in my heart. "We will keep you here in safety until Claighan is recovered and your case can be fairly made. Until then, you are to behave as our guest. You may attend classes—"

I brightened, astonished. "Really?"

He frowned at the interruption, but nodded. "Claighan made it well known that he intended you to be his apprentice. By our laws, that choice is wholly his. No matter the rumors we have heard, you shall have the education his authority grants you... until the council can convince him otherwise."

I bowed my head, doing my very best impression of meek. "Yes, my lord."

The other nodded once and picked back up where he'd left off. "You may attend classes, but only as a mute observer. You will not make any disturbance, you will not make any trouble on our grounds, or you will be handed over to the Royal Guard *immediately*. As easily as you were brought here you could be deposited in the dungeons of the royal palace. Bear that in mind, boy." He started to turn away, then stopped and added, "This Academy will be no haven for criminals. Unless Claighan can make a good case, you should not expect much kindness here."

I shivered at that, and nodded, but he was not done with me. He dropped a heavy hand on my shoulder—heavy enough to make me wince at the shock of pain in my injured leg—and caught my eyes. "Did Claighan warn you about Seriphenes, boy? Or perhaps Leotus? You know he has enemies here?"

I nodded, mute, and he nodded back. "I'm not one of them. They have their little schemes, their power plays, but I am the Chancellor. I have no loyalties to their games. It is my sole duty to protect this school. And right now, you are a threat to it. Do you understand?"

I nodded, but he wasn't satisfied with that. I fought to catch a breath, shook my head against new waves of pain, then groaned through clenched teeth. "I have no desire but to learn, Chancellor."

He frowned at me, as though I might be mocking him, then spun me around to face the towering doors. I gasped in pain, but he ignored it.

"It is said those doors only open one way," he said. "You will not be welcome here—I can guarantee you that—and those doors are designed to keep intruders out, not to keep freeloaders in. Leave when you want, and you will not be missed."

He stood for a moment waiting, expectant, as though I might push through the doors that very instant, but I did not budge. It took all my pride to keep myself upright, but I did not budge.

When he saw I wouldn't go, he shrugged behind me and dropped his hand from my shoulder. "Well enough, boy. It's your choice. Just don't wait too long. Once judgment is passed, running won't be an option." Again he paused, again I stood firm. Again he shrugged, then turned briskly and began walking across the courtyard, not looking back. "Very well. Follow me, then, and I'll find you a room."

A single building bordered the great courtyard, made of two immense halls stretching north and south, with a third connecting them near the middle. Two tall, wide doors in the middle of this crossing hall made the building's main entrance, but the dark wizard strode quickly toward a small oak door set in the end of the east wing. He pulled the door open harshly, muttering something to himself as he did, then stooped to fit through the small doorway. Hopping awkwardly on one leg, clenching my teeth at the pain in the other, I followed him into a dark, narrow hall lined on both sides with plain wooden doors. The Chancellor stopped at the very first one on the right and pushed it open, stuck his head in to look around, then stepped back.

"Fine. This shall be your room as long as you stay with us. Number one east wing, in case you get lost. Enjoy your visit." With that he turned and stalked off down the hall like an angry cat on the prowl. Far down the hall I saw a cluster of boys standing near a doorway, but they rapidly dispersed as the old wizard approached them. I watched, a little afraid, until he was lost in the far shadows before I entered my room. I closed the door firmly behind me.

A thin mattress hung halfway off a simple wooden bed, its legs scored by the teeth of mice or rats over the years. A desk stood in one corner, and a plain armoire beside the door. Other than that the room was empty. I collapsed onto the edge of the bed and rested my head in my hands. The blood on my arm was dried and dusty, but the scratch throbbed a little. The wound on my leg was worse, but somehow didn't hurt nearly as much. I brushed my hair out of my face, wiped the sweat from my eyes, and looked around the room again. I started rolling up the leg of my pants to examine that injury, but the motion brought a new lance of pain and a wash of fresh blood down my ankle.

I ached; the sweat and dust caking me made me feel nasty, but something much larger was pressing at my mind, and I was avoiding it as much as I could. Claighan was gone. I was alone. I sat with elbows on knees, staring at the cold stone floor. I was alone and hated already. I thought of the old wizard's cruel voice, of the cold eyes of the other Masters. I thought of the boy Archus, on Seriphenes's heels, who had stared at even Claighan with such contempt. This place was no haven; it was no home. I began to run my eyes along the stone blocks of the walls, the tiles of the floor, tracing the little paths between that always led back to each other.

I was alone.

I cried. Tears mixed with blood and sweat, and hopelessness burned in my soul. My hands fell together in my lap, my eyes fixed on them, and I wept without a sound and wondered what I was to do.

My door creaked, and the sound threw me to my feet, heart pounding. I screamed at the flash of pain that drove up from my calf and stabbed hard into my hip. I fell back down to my bed and had to blink away tears and blackness before I could see.

When I did, I found a boy standing in my doorway. He peeked around the edge of my travel pack, holding it with both arms and not quite tall enough to look over the top of it. He had a thick mop of brown hair, big blue eyes now opened wide in astonishment, and a round nose. He dropped my pack to the floor with a *whumph*, and I saw his mouth twisted into a great O in his surprise. I nearly smiled at the sight, in spite of everything.

He was a scrawny little boy, and he looked terrified by my howl. I forced myself to take several short, sharp breaths while I pushed the pain away and then focused in on him.

Then I nodded toward my bag on the floor. "Are you the butler?"

His eyes went even wider. Then he took a step back, and his eyebrows pinched together in anger. And then he laughed. It was almost a giggle, high and sharp, and it took his breath away. Then he fixed his eyes on me. "The butler? I'm the Chancellor's apprentice!"

I sighed and hung my head. "I'm deeply sorry," I said. "I had no idea."

"Keep your sorries," he said.

He came to stand over me, though I was nearly eye-level with him even sitting on my bed. He looked me over and said, "How much of it is true?"

I closed my eyes and shook my head. "None of it, or close enough."

"They say you killed a king's Guardsman on the Souport road just to win an argument with Claighan. They say you bested one of the king's elite guards and won his sword in fair combat." His eyes shone with boyish enthusiasm, and he took a step closer. "They say you fought half an army in Gath-upon-Brennes and laid nine men low."

I shook my head. "Barely half that," I said. "Although I suppose the rest of it is true."

He barked a laugh, a grin splitting his face. "Oh, they are *not* going to like you here."

I frowned. "Everyone keeps telling me that."

He shrugged. "They're right. You'll just have to show them all you're true gold. Excellence covers a multitude of sins."

"You're asking a bit much. I'll be lucky if I ever walk again."

I said it in jest, but his eyes shot wide again in horror, and his head whipped left and right in a terrified panic. I had to stifle a laugh, but he sank down on his knees next to the bed and looked at my bloodied leg in horror.

"I'm so sorry, Daven! I let my curiosity get the better of me. I'm supposed to bring you to the Kind Father. Can you stand?"

I wanted to laugh at the terror in his eyes, but the pain washed over me in waves with his words, and I clenched my jaw to keep from screaming at him again. Fighting tears, I slid to the edge of my bed and pushed myself upright. I'd hoped to catch my balance on my good leg as I had done coming in here, but the sudden rise made me dizzy, and I nearly fell to the stone floor.

The boy caught me. When my weight fell on him he grunted sharply, but he held me upright and wrapped an arm around my waist to steady me. "It's kind of a long walk, but I'll help you. Let me know when you need to rest."

In good health I could have made the walk in four or five minutes, but hobbling as I was it took me nearly fifteen, and every agonizing hop of the way sent fire searing through my body. While we were still in sight of my room the boy began to breathe heavily. When we finally stopped in front of a carved oak door in a larger hall, I was glad to be able to take my weight off him. I leaned against the doorframe, and he huffed a great sigh of relief. He sagged against the wall, too, but leaned forward to knock on the door while I caught my breath.

The door opened to reveal an elderly man draped in yards of thick, embroidered robes until he seemed a mound of red and violet cloth. A violet ribbon around his temples and a gold sun medallion hanging around his neck named him a Beneficent Priest, but he looked with no kindness on the boy before him.

"Themmichus! Haven's name, I always expect to see you before my door, but I am never pleased to find you there! What have you done this time?" Only the hint of a smile belied the harsh words. The boy must not have seen it, because he seemed cowed to fear. He didn't speak a word but pointed mutely down to my leg. The old priest turned, surprised to find me standing so close, and as his gaze reached my bloodied calf his mouth fell open. Concern washed away jest and mock anger, and with a soft-breathed prayer he caught me up in surprisingly strong arms and bore me back into his office.

I heard Themmichus call something from the doorway, felt the priest respond above, around me, but the words were fast fading into nonsense. If the journey from my room to this office had strained me, the priest's lifting me broke my last tenuous hold on consciousness. I realized this man would care for me, by oath and by law, if anyone in the world might. I sighed behind closed eyes at the thought, and then I let the pain drown me and fell back to a blistered peace.

I woke in absolute darkness to the sound of a feeble cry. I blinked, hoping my eyes would adjust to the dim light, but there was none. I searched my memory and eventually remembered my trip to the Kind Father's offices. I remembered a bed like a high table and gentle hands on my injured leg, murmured prayers and the smell of blood and fire. I shivered at the shard of memory.

Then I heard a noise, not ten paces away, but muffled by a door or wall. It was a furtive sound, a careful one, but it held the sharp brutality of violence. I frowned in the darkness and, without thinking, rolled off the bed to land at a crouch on the floor. There was no pain, no weariness even, and for the first time I realized this must be a dream.

And then I heard the sound again, and once again a pathetic little moan. Curiosity dragged me across the room, and caution made me quiet. I moved by touch and distant memory and found my way to the door. I turned the knob with all the care in the world, and it didn't make a sound. I eased the door open a crack, and then I saw a light.

It was faint but unflickering. A dull green glow, entirely unnatural, and it came from an open doorway on the other side of the Kind Father's main office—another room like mine. I saw the shadow of a man stretched grotesque against the wall and ceiling, the sharp line of a beard stabbing down from his chin, the great draping sleeve of a robe hanging off powerful arms. I saw one of those arms rise up in shadow, then slash down in what looked like a backhand, and I heard another desperate groan. And I heard what sounded like a chuckle.

And then I thought of Claighan. I remembered him, broken and bleeding on the ground beside me. I thought of him helpless in the bed, of the cruel-eyed Seriphenes or the sneering student Archus lashing out at him, and I felt a great fury build in me. I was strong now. I was whole. I could defend him against this cruelty. I balled my fists, tensed my legs, ready to hurl myself across the gap and into the room.

An outer door opened and I barely stopped myself short of gasping in surprise. I fell back on my heels and sank low to the ground, heart pounding, desperate to remain hidden. I recognized the form silhouetted out in the hall. It was Seriphenes, tall and terrible, and he lingered on the threshold for the barest heartbeat before his eyes narrowed on the eerie green glow from the other room and he stomped in. He pulled the outer door closed behind him with more restraint than I suspect he wished, but he did not make a sound.

He crossed the office in three long strides, and darted into the other room. I heard a growl like an angry dog's begin low in his throat, and I could see him clearly in the eldritch glow. His eyes narrowed to slits.

"Lareth," he snapped. My blood ran cold.

Lareth, the rebel wizard. The traitor who had turned the king against us. He was the same who had been striking a helpless Claighan. I felt my teeth grinding together so hard it hurt, and I forced myself to relax lest the sound of it gave me away.

The other wizard answered with a voice like summer honey, smooth and sweet and languorous. "My dear Master Seriphenes," he said. "What brings you here?"

"I thought I sensed the shape of a traveling," Seriphenes answered, his voice cold. "Of a pathway stabbing off hundreds of miles to the south of here. I *thought* perhaps I recognized the workmanship—"

129

"Nonsense," Lareth said, and I could imagine him waving a hand dismissively. "I have learned new tricks. My workings are undetectable."

Seriphenes growled again. "You always were stupid. There is no such thing."

"There is," Lareth said. "I'm sure it was simple intuition that brought you here. Or, perhaps, a desire to see justice done."

Seriphenes frowned. "Justice is doing well enough on its own. There is no reason for us to stain our hands with it. And there is certainly no reason for you to be *here*—"

"What, am I unwelcome at my teacher's table?"

"As long as you are in open rebellion against the king," Seriphenes hissed, "it would be *wise* for you to keep away."

Lareth took a step closer. "I have been too long without news," Lareth said. "I began to feel abandoned."

"You stupid child," Seriphenes said. "This king is not a forgiving one. If he suspected anyone in these walls so much as spoke to you, he would bring the whole of his army against the Academy."

"Let him try," Lareth said lazily. "I have seen just what his army is worth. I've slain a thousand men by my own hand, with just the least portion of the things you taught me."

Seriphenes looked around. His eyes passed right over me, but he could not have seen me. "You would be wise to keep such words to yourself, even when speaking to me. I do not condone your actions."

"And yet my actions are set to prosper you greatly." Lareth chuckled, dark and low. "Astonishing that the king's wrath turned against the one who suggested he send *someone* to speak with the rebels, and the old fool never gave a thought to the failings of the man who trained the traitor up."

"King Timmon doesn't trouble himself to know the details of our apprenticeship process." Seriphenes's lip curled in distaste. "Admittedly, he does not trouble himself to know that much at all."

Lareth laughed, delighted, and clapped Seriphenes on the shoulder. "There's the mentor I know and love." His shadow turned away, washing across the ceiling. "Come, try your hand at the doddering old fool. If we don't abuse him a little, the Kind Father just might bring him back after all."

Seriphenes's lips curled in amusement, but he shook his head. "I've always admired your zeal, Lareth, but I suspect you might nearly be a dangerous maniac."

"I am practical," Lareth answered, and some of the honey left his voice. "I don't *truly* enjoy this sport, any more than I do killing king's Guardsmen. But it is so much easier to do under the persona of a madman."

Seriphenes cocked his head, curious. "Fascinating," he said. Then he shook his head. "That conversation must wait for another time. I have told you, Lareth, you must stay away from the school until you are ready to end this foolishness with the rebel army. So long as you are openly in defiance of the crown, you must wait for me to contact you as I may."

Lareth turned back to him, and for a long time he said nothing. Then he stepped closer and lowered his voice. "Find more opportunities, Master. It is a dangerous world out there, and I would hate to face it without your aid."

Seriphenes frowned. "I will do as I can, as I always have, but if we are caught—if anyone so much as suspected—I could help you not at all. I might even be driven to living the same squalid life you've chosen for yourself, and I would not like that at all."

Lareth laughed. "It's not so bad. Living off the land. Sleeping under the stars."

Seriphenes sneered. "I prefer my creature comforts. Now go. And do not come back."

Lareth started to answer, but Seriphenes raised one hand and silenced him. A moment later the green light flashed, so bright it seared dark spots behind my eyes, and then it was gone completely. I sat in the darkness, stunned, thinking over everything I had just heard and trying desperately to comprehend it.

And then a new light flared in the office as Seriphenes summoned a white flame of his own to light his way out of the office. It happened before I could even move, and he passed within a pace of me. The light washed over me, and his gaze followed it.

For a terrible moment his cold black eyes met mine.

And then, for reasons I cannot imagine, it passed on over me. He made no comment, gave no indication he'd seen me at all. He slipped through the outer door and closed it so quietly behind him I didn't even hear a sound.

Fear and fury bubbled up within me. Seriphenes was a traitor to the crown! It seemed he must have seen me but that didn't matter now. He had to be stopped. I threw open the door above me, and it didn't make a sound. I flew across the Kind Father's little office, and my movements felt eerie. Dreamlike. I drifted like a mist across the room and threw open another door that made no sound.

I washed out into the wide corridor lined with benches and stone-brick walls, supported with carved-wood pillars, and lit with fixed points of magical light. I remembered it bustling with students during the day.

But none of that was there now. Not the students, not the pillars, not the corridor, not even the lights. Outside the door of the Kind Father's office was only blackness, thick and deep and stretching out forever.

I could hear footsteps on stone, though. I turned toward them and saw the shape of Seriphenes, strangely-lit in all the darkness. He had his back to me, and as I watched he whisked away. I tried to run after him, but I drifted too slowly, and soon he faded and was gone.

That left me in perfect darkness. I tried to hurry after him. I tried to turn back to my room, but there was no light anywhere. My heart raced, and fear bubbled up in me, but there was nowhere to go. The darkness washed around me like a nightmare, and I screamed and screamed without making a sound.

Sometime later, sunlight kissed my skin and glowed red through my closed eyelids. It summoned me gently back to consciousness with light touches on my arms and face. I drank in a deep breath, opened my eyes and blinked against the brightness. The air was heavy with the sweet smell of apple blossoms, even at this time of year, and thick, lush grass made a more comfortable bed than the mattress in my room. Slowly I sat up and realized with a start that I was whole again. I pushed back the tattered leg of my pants and examined my leg, healed clean without even a scar.

"Nice, isn't it?" The small voice made me jump, and I realized for the first time I wasn't alone. Behind me Themmichus was sitting on a large stone thick with moss. He held a crisp apple in one hand and rested his chin in the other. "Kind Father said you would be well, but I've never seen such concern from him. You must have been hurt worse than I realized. What happened?"

I shrugged, suddenly uncomfortable. "I haven't had a good week."

Themmichus waited for more, and when I didn't offer it he laughed. And then harder, and he gave a shrug. "How could I forget? You killed a dozen Guardsmen in Gath-upon-Brennes."

My stomach turned sour at the joke, but I kept it from my expression. "Yesterday it was nine," I said, and he only laughed harder. I scowled and shook my head. Then I climbed to my feet and looked around. "Am I dreaming?"

He popped to his feet beside me. "If so, you're not very good at it," he said. "And I don't know why you roped me in."

"It's just...." I ducked my head, thinking. I could remember the incident in the Kind Father's office, but it held an eerie unreality to it. An impossibility. Seriphenes a villain, conspiring with a traitor. Lareth, the man at whose feet I could lay all my troubles, come in the night to wreak petty vengeance against my only ally in this place. It was all too much.

Themmichus stood beside me, looking up into my face, and after a moment he frowned. "How are you feeling? Should we go back to the Father? He told me to watch over you."

"No," I said and forced a smile. I tilted my head back to feel the sun on my face, the cool breeze in my hair, and my smile grew a shade more genuine. "No need," I said and began strolling idly among the apple trees. He fell in step beside me. I reached out to trail my fingers through the flower blossoms on a low shrub and shook my head. "What is this place?"

"Kind Father thought you could use some sun," he said. "Said it wouldn't do for you to be waking up in darkness. So he brought you to the Garden. I asked after your health one too many times, so...." He trailed off, looking uncomfortable, but after a moment he finished with a weak smile. "He told me to watch over you. Protect our famous new warrior child from all the dangerous monsters prowling these grounds."

I was supposed to laugh at that, but I thought of Lareth, of Seriphenes, even of the quiet, dreadful threats the Chancellor had offered me. I couldn't quite manage it. I gave him a sickly grin, though, and he settled for it.

"Anyway, main reason I'm here is to make sure you wake up in time for classes. Lhorus caught me this morning—said he'd heard from the Kind Father that you and I were friends now." He chewed his lip at that, and his eyes didn't quite meet mine. I suspected he would come to regret expressing any concern for my well-being. "Anyway," he said. "The Chancellor has decided you should begin with private lessons to get you up to speed."

"Lessons now? Right away?" I felt a panic bubbling in my chest. Then I turned to look the direction he'd been waving and found myself staring at the wall of the dormitory's west wing. My jaw dropped open. "This is Academy grounds? But...but I was in the courtyard yesterday and it was nothing but dust and dirt!"

He chuckled at that, then started off toward the building. "Follow me. There's something I should show you."

I stumbled along after him. We took a twisting path among the lush fruit trees, surrounded always by a cool breeze, but as we reached the north end of the dormitory building the trees began to thin, and the breeze died down. I followed Themmichus around the corner of the dorm and saw another building, just as large, sitting to the north. The boy waved at it. "That's the Learning Halls. You'll learn about them soon enough." Ignoring the sprawling buildings on either side, he led me down the wide lane between them toward another courtyard that seemed more like the one I remembered.

As we reached the end of the lane and stepped out into the barren yard, I realized just how stark the contrast was. The ground was entirely bare, broken here and there by large rocks that jutted out of the earth like some monster's huge gray teeth. The sun seemed somehow warmer here, barely a hundred paces from the Garden, harsh and unforgiving. Dust hung in the air, though no breeze lightened the stifling warmth.

For a long time I just stood staring at the cruel courtyard. It was a miserable bit of land, and someone had gone to great lengths to make it so. "Why?" I asked. "Someone *wanted* it like this?"

The boy grinned, a spark gleaming in his eyes, and put on a creaky, condescending voice. "Ah, child, understanding can be found in the most remarkable places." He chuckled. "The Masters say it helps us to understand the balance of everything. There are times and places where the world is soft and beautiful, but times and places when the world is hard as stone. So they gave us the Garden and the Arena."

"One for recreation, one for punishment?" I guessed.

He shook his head. "Not really. They don't ever really tell us where to go. But when they find us loitering in one yard or the other, they like to ask us why we're there. You should probably be prepared for that."

I frowned. "What's the right answer?"

He shrugged. "Oh, I don't know. Just make something up."

I laughed. "Really?"

"It's always more about being able to say something clever than something right."

I looked out at the desolation for a while, then I looked over at Themmichus. "You ever come up with anything clever?" He shrugged, but I saw a blush rise in his cheeks. "You did!" I said. He didn't answer, and I bumped his shoulder. "You're supposed to be looking out for me, remember? I could use a hint."

He shrugged again and ducked his head. "One time the Chancellor caught me in the Arena and asked me why. I said I figured they were trying to train the nobility out of us, and the sooner I got that done the sooner I could get on with my education."

"Training the nobility out of you?" I frowned, thinking about it. "And what did the Chancellor say?"

Themmichus grinned. "He took me on as his apprentice then and there."

I laughed. Themmichus led me over to a boulder jutting out of the ground and took a seat on it. I stood over him, taking in the rest of the courtyard. After a while I asked, "How'd you come up with that?"

"Well...you spend enough time out here, moving between the two of them, it's easy to start getting philosophical. Besides, my father talks like that all the time. Eventually you just pick it up."

I looked down at him and fought a grin. "Who's your father?"

He glanced up at me and away, fast enough I almost missed it. His answer came exquisitely casual. "Just a minor baron. No one you'd know."

Something in his voice made me doubt that. For whatever reason, he wanted to keep it to himself. I felt an instant, deep sympathy for him. It might have clouded my eyes for a moment, but I did my best not to let it show.

He wasn't looking anyway. He stared out at the Arena grounds and shook his head. "I'd sometimes stand in the corridor between the two, considering them both, and think that our lives are like that. No matter who we are." He gestured back over his shoulder, toward the distant Garden. "Sometimes it will be cushy, sometimes you'll get your way

137

and have servants to get it for you." Then he patted the stone beneath him with a wry grin. "But sometimes you're all alone and afraid and helpless. We spend time at both ends of the corridor, and our training encompasses it all."

I tried to understand that. Living with the power to shape the world to their whim, these men still chose to face the hardship. I wasn't sure if it was clever or foolish, but as I stared out over the starkness of the barren, broken earth, I felt at home.

Themmichus waited. He watched me as the thoughts sank in, then nodded. "Most of the students are scared of the Arena for a long time, but after a while we almost all end up taking our lunches here. There's something refreshing about the plainness of it, the harsh reality."

I leaned against the stone next to him and he clapped me on the back, but then I sank into my own thoughts, and he into his. For a while neither of us spoke. Then a bell rang, high in a tower at the north end of the campus, and he jumped to his feet with fear in his eyes.

"Haven's name, I forgot to show you to your class. Lhorus is going to kill me."

I rose more slowly to my feet and smiled down at him. "Blame it on me," I said. "But first, show me the way."

He bobbed a nod and hurried off, back up the Arena to the corridor between the two buildings, and then dragged me through the great double doors into the Halls of Learning. As we went he chattered by my side. "Most new applicants get a week of interviews and instruction before the actual lessons begin, but Lhorus said you're a special case—naturally—and the Masters want you to begin immediately. I'll show you to your class, but it's a private lesson and I'm not allowed to watch."

He walked half a pace ahead of me, constantly looking back over his shoulder and begging me on with his eyes. I tried to keep track of our path, but he hurried me through broad corridors and around numerous corners, past hundreds of identical doors. Then he stopped at one among the many, knocked politely, and pushed it open. The room beyond was dark and empty, and he heaved a great sigh of relief.

"You'll have to wait for him here. I need to get to my own classes, but meet me for lunch. That same big rock in the Arena." He glanced down into the dark room, then looked both ways down the hall. He shrugged. "Lunch if you can make it, dinner if you can't. Private lessons sometimes go long. But find me. Please?"

I nodded to him and reached out to clasp his shoulder. "Thank you, Themmichus. I'll find you."

He gave me a grin that split his face, ducked his head, and then darted off down the hall.

I stood for a moment, alone, and gradually became aware of the sound of voices. They were not new, but with Themmichus gone the silence in the hall deepened until I could hear a distant, muted murmur all around me. I took two steps and realized it was coming from the doors.

I listened at one for a moment and heard the muffled sound of a lecture. At another I heard a low, eerie chant, and at yet another the brittle roar of a blazing fire. I smelled no smoke, though, and heard quiet, casual discussion coming from the same room. I shivered.

Magic. Behind these doors, magic happened. And I was about to have my first lesson. A sudden fear frolicked in my stomach, while nervous excitement settled in just above my lungs, pressing down. I moved back to my room, the one Themmichus had shown me, and sank down to wait by the door. I had barely settled into a crouch before the steady thump of boots on stone broke the uneasy silence. Fighting my own excitement, I looked toward the sound of the footsteps.

7. A Challenge

A young man came around the corner at a quick pace, his face set in a scowl. Tall and thin, he wore a beard that looked more mature than he did. When his eyes fell on me, though, they were sharp and compelling. "Daven," he said crisply, "you are to be my student. Rise."

We entered the room, a great auditorium intended for twenty to thirty students, with benches and tables standing in long rows, five tiers above the floor. On the floor of the room stood a podium, four crude wooden chairs, and a large slate only half erased. My teacher led me down to the floor and sank into one of the chairs, waving me toward another. When I was seated he dragged his chair a little closer to me and simply stared at me for several minutes.

From the moment he arrived he'd been wearing a look of anger and frustration, but as he examined me now I watched his expression slowly change, melting into curiosity and perhaps even pity. After a long while he sat back, crossed his arms, and said, "Daven of Terrailles, why have you come here?"

The question had no ring of formality to it. I recognized his own curiosity and tried to answer honestly. "I had no pressing business elsewhere, and I was invited here. It sounded exciting."

"You were invited. By Claighan, no?" I nodded. He nodded. "That is a sad business. Do you know why Claighan chose you?"

The answer was complicated and I wasn't entirely sure of it, so I just shook my head.

He nodded. "Neither do the Masters, apparently, but some are quite suspicious." He paused for a moment, thinking, then leaned forward again. "You already have great powers turned against you, Daven, and your only real defender is on his deathbed. Are you certain you wish to stay here?"

I shrugged, "Claighan said the king could not reach me here, that I would be safe. I wouldn't know where else to hide."

"It's not the king you need fear, Daven. He is only a minor power in this world. If you make enemies within these walls, they can undo you in ways the king could only dream of."

My mouth went dry at the thought of Lareth's cruelty, of Seriphenes's dark eyes passing over me, but I told myself it had only been a dream. Still, some of the fear must have shown in my eyes, because my teacher gave a curt nod. "Yes, you understand. I do not think excitement is reason enough for you to stay here. I'm not at all certain you should."

I thought about it for a moment. Then I frowned and met his eyes. "Do you want me gone?"

He shook his head. "I have almost no interest in you at all." The words rang with an eerie echo of Claighan. My only ally. My teacher went on. "I have been appointed to teach you your preliminary lessons, but beyond that I've no emotional tie to you. I have heard some of your story, heard most of the rumors, most of the lies, but I see you before me as just a boy, caught up in something he cannot comprehend."

He rose and began to pace as he spoke. "Everyone says you came here for the power, that you want to escape your peasant roots. I don't see it." He looked at me briefly, looked away. "There's a rumor that the Masters mistreated your father, and some say you're here to learn the magic necessary to avenge him. That, I think, is ludicrous. To me it seems...just as you said. You answered an invitation, and find a place more hostile than you could have imagined."

"And so I should run from the threat?"

"It wouldn't be a bad idea."

I considered it. "I thought....." I started, and then had to swallow against a sudden pang of regret. I tried to laugh it off. "I will tell you the truth. I thought I would find this place all comfort and luxury. I thought I would find wise old teachers anxious to grant me untold power and authority." I chuckled darkly. He only nodded.

I licked my lips. "This place is not what I expected. But I did not come for the comforts or for the easy power. I came here because I have nowhere else to be, and because someone thought it would be worthwhile to teach me something new. If that opportunity is still available, as long as it is available, I would like to find out if he was right."

He stopped pacing. He weighed me in his eyes again until my shoulders began to itch. Then he shrugged. "You are an interesting young man, Daven. This should be...interesting." He stepped close to me and extended his hand. "My name is Antinus. I shall be your instructor."

I stood to shake his hand, mumbled some pleasantry, and sank back into my chair. "And that was all to satisfy your curiosity?" I asked. He nodded, and I nodded. "I expected as much. Is there any more, or may we begin?"

He chuckled, but returned to his seat. "We may begin, though much of the early part of your training will be little more than discussion. I suppose for most of it I will be answering, you asking, but there is still much we must learn of each other before we can investigate the power. For instance, have you ever knowingly worked magic before?"

"I learned a spell which my friends and I used for sword practice. I probably worked that several dozen times at least."

"Interesting. A spell in the Elder tongue, that you read off a card, or a bit of paper?"

I shook my head. "Not the Elder tongue. More of a ritual chant. But otherwise yes."

He nodded. "That won't count for much at all. Anything else? Have you ever reshaped anything? Ever studied under a real wizard? What about a priest? Ever trained for the cloth?" At each question I shook my head but briefly before he moved on. "Very well, what sort of training do you have in craft or trade? What is your professional intention?"

"I tend sheep," I said. I shrugged, both hands palm up. "I drive coaches. I have done some tanning and helped a village baker. And I can handle any sword. My main interest has always been to become a soldier."

He grimaced at each part of my answer. "So those bits are true? You will be a challenge. They say the more adept you are with the physical world, the harder magic becomes. I suppose you'll be my masterpiece."

Before I could respond, a booming voice interrupted our conversation. "Not a masterpiece, Antinus. A failed experiment." I looked up toward the door, and recognized the arrogant young man who had helped Claighan out of the courtyard. His lips were dark and red as a courtesan's and twisted in a vicious sneer.

Archus. Seriphenes's apprentice. All his features stood stark black against his pale skin. Dark eyes, bored, told me his contempt. Dark brows, drawn down, told me his distaste. Dark hair, neatly combed and hanging loose like his master's, told me he knew the luxury I would not find here.

He took a heavy, dramatic step down into the room, his eyes fixed on mine even as he finished speaking to Antinus. "Unfortunately," he said, "it's going to be my time wasted, not yours. You are dismissed."

Antinus flew to his feet, face red with anger. "I am not interested in your dismissal, Archus. Daven is to be my student. I have specific instructions from the Chancellor—"

"Your instructions have changed." Archus cut him off coldly. As he passed Antinus, Archus casually handed him a folded bit of paper without ever taking his eyes off me. The note bore a wax seal which made Antinus go from flushed to pale, and as he read the message within his face sank in defeat. He turned to me with pity in his eyes, perhaps even compassion, but only shrugged before turning and darting up the steps and out into the hall. All the while Archus kept his hateful gaze locked on me. When Antinus was gone and my eyes snapped to meet his, Archus grinned evilly.

"Now your instruction begins. Sit."

Fighting to hide my frustration, I moved to obey. I took a step toward my chair, but he clucked sharply. "Around here, Daven, we are concerned with propriety. It wouldn't do for you and me to be on the same level, would it? You may take a seat at one of the benches, and I shall instruct you from here."

A caustic reply sprang to my tongue, but I bit it down and moved swiftly to take a seat at one of the long benches. Archus smiled smugly. "Now, have you pen and paper?"

For a moment I stared at him, astonished. "Not at all. Should I?"

"Most students think to bring such supplies to their lectures. I'm certain you'll remember it in the future. For now, let us focus on more immediate matters. What do you know of magic?"

"Nothing at all, I'm sure."

144

His grin flashed teeth. "So modest of you! Or perhaps the simple truth. I understand your pathetic old mentor had little time to instruct you on the journey here, as you were pursued by the King's Guard. Correct?" I nodded. "And you've had no magical or religious education growing up, correct?" I nodded. "In fact, you've had no education of any sort, is that correct?"

"I know more than you could possibly imagine." I fought to keep the words cold, almost frozen, and the fact that I responded at all clearly surprised him. He took two long steps toward me and glared directly into my eyes.

I expected a haughty challenge, perhaps some dreadful lecture, but his voice was light with sarcasm. "I'm sorry I didn't specify. Sheep herding doesn't qualify as education here." He chuckled to himself, stepped back to the middle of the floor. "No, I meant more academic study. Can you write?" I had to shake my head, not trusting my voice. "I expected not. Can you read?" I gave a curt nod, and he chortled. "Oh ho! That is something, at least. One surprise in you, but so far you're not shattering my expectations."

I pushed myself up, shoving the bench back with a harsh growl. "Who do you think you are?"

"I am the first apprentice to Master Seriphenes," he said, staring into my eyes. "I am the first heir to the Pollix duchy. And I will be the first wizard to wear the FirstKing's crown." His black eyes blazed. "And who are you?"

"I am but a humble shepherd," I said, and my voice came out a growl. "But I have come here to do good."

He snorted. "Good. You bring the king's wrath down upon our walls, you stain our reputation with your filthy common blood, and you waste our time with a mind unfit for the simplest workings. You are a nuisance."

My patience snapped. I couldn't even manage fury, just frustration. I waved back toward the door at the top of the stairs. "Then why not leave me to Antinus? Why insist on taking over my training yourself?"

"Because my master asked it of me," he said, and his eyes glittered cruelly. "Because my master considers you a threat to this Academy. Because my master trusts me to keep your contagion contained."

"How?" I meant it to be a challenge, a sneering demand, but it came out stammered and weak. I cleared my throat and tried again. "How do you intend to contain me?"

He grabbed the chair Antinus had used and sank down into it. He tilted back, balancing on two legs, and laced his fingers behind his head. He spoke to the ceiling instead of meeting my eyes. "I have full oversight of your training," he said. "I will be your personal tutor throughout your stay at the Academy. I decide when you are ready to attend lectures, when you are ready to study basic workings, when you should be allowed to commune with more advanced students."

My heart sank with every word, but he went right on. "And I decide when you are out of line. When you need correction. When you need punishment." That turned his smile into a wolf's grin. He tipped his chair forward and the legs came down with a *bang*. He caught my eyes. "Leave tonight, and save us both some trouble."

"I will not leave." The words came out a growl, and somewhere in them was a truth that hadn't existed before. Even while speaking with Antinus I had been uncertain about my future here, about my right to even stay within these walls, but I would not bow to this prat. "I will not leave the Academy. If you are the only teacher I'm to get," I invested that with all the contempt I could muster, "then at the very least you should attempt to teach."

He studied me for a moment through narrowed eyes. Then he shrugged, and climbed to his feet. "Fine," he said with a dismissive wave. "Fine, you have passed the first test. You have the necessary will, the necessary determination. If you're willing to face me," he smiled, "you're strong enough to face at least a few weeks of classes. I just had to know."

I offered him a smile, but it was not a friendly one. "I'm glad I pleased you."

He didn't respond. Instead, he turned his back on me, staring up at the slate on the wall, and took on a lecturing tone. "Magic, as you know, is the reshaping of reality. We do not make or break reality; we don't even bend it. We take the fleshy bits, the extra, the skin on the skeleton, and we move it about, but the underlying model never changes. Does that make sense?"

"Claighan said something of the sort, yes."

He whirled and I saw a deranged fury in his eyes. "Do not speak that name!" He trembled, and despite myself I shrank back from him. He stalked toward me. "Whatever I hold against you," he growled, "whatever threat you are to the Academy, you at least have not yet damaged the honor of the Masters. But that man...that *imbecile*...is a stain on everything this Academy has ever accomplished. I won't have you speaking of him here. Understood?"

I glared at him, unbelieving, but he seemed to take my silence for assent. "Very well," he said, and I watched him take control of himself. "Then I shall continue." He turned his back again, and all the emotion fell from his voice. "Your magical power, your ability, derives almost entirely from your faith and your force of will. Both of these things can be trained, can be developed, but both demand some starting point within your own personality. If you have no strength, the training will do you no good."

He turned back to me again and met my eyes. "So we must ask the question, Daven: What strength do *you* have?"

I thought of Claighan challenging my master at his dinner table. I thought of him offering me the Green Eagle's sword. We had spoken of this on the road to the City, and he had lamented how much I lacked. My mouth suddenly felt dry, my chest gaping empty. Claighan should have been my teacher, telling me these things. Instead, I had only Archus, and he smiled down at me, waiting for an answer.

"I don't know," I said.

He smirked. "Of course you don't. That's why we're here. One of the first tests of any new student is a weighing of his magical power, to determine his potential. A reality exists—a small one, an insignificant one, but one that is part of your right-now life. In a moment, you are going to do what you can to reshape it, to rearrange it, and I shall focus on doing the same."

He leaned down, bringing his eyes to a level with mine, and put on a mask of helpfulness. "The heart of the test is this: You try with all your might to make the change I suggest, and keep at it. As you do, I will very slowly, very slightly at first, begin to apply my own will to managing the same feat you are attempting. At some point, the force of us both will overwhelm the reality we know, and things will change. I will determine your power by how much of the magic is mine, and how much your own. Does that make sense?"

"I understand the basics, I suppose, though I have no idea what you mean in specific."

He raised an eyebrow at me and his mouth twisted in a sarcastic smile. "How could you know the specifics? I haven't taught you any yet." He straightened and took a step away from me, then turned back again and began.

"The very first thing I need you to do is relax. Relax completely. Your muscles must be calm but much more importantly your mind must be fresh and alert, free from distractions. Do you understand?"

I fought to contain a growl. A storm of anger and injury against this man boiled within me, battling a flood of self-doubt and fear. For a moment I felt my throat tighten, and the thought of relaxing seemed impossible. But old habits held my panic at bay. I caught a deep breath and held it for a moment, and then began a brief exercise that I had learned with my sword work. It was the second chapter of my book. Relax the mind and body, so the muscles can respond according to their training.

I closed my eyes and imagined waves like water lapping at my toes and then at my ankles and rising slowly up my body. Each wave washed in with a sense of cool relief, and then ebbed carrying away my tension with it. The exercise was old habit, familiar like nothing else in this place, and in the space of three deep breaths I was completely relaxed. I exhaled softly, feeling the tension go, and then opened my eyes and met Archus's surprised stare with a small smile.

"I'm ready."

He frowned. "We shall see. When the spirit is calm, the mind's eye may see. The second part of any magic is a perfect awareness of your surroundings. You must now take a moment to get to know this room. Learn as much of it as you can, and be prepared to imagine it with your eyes closed, to *see* this room—not one like it, but this actual room—from your imagination alone." He sank down into his chair once more, relaxed, then gestured impatiently. "This shall take a while, so begin."

I almost laughed at that. I wanted to laugh at the old Claighan, so sure my background in sword fighting would pose a challenge here, and all these other wizards married to the same belief. Relaxation. Environmental awareness. I closed my eyes and drew up a perfect recollection of the circle where I had fought my friends outside Sachaerrich. And then a perfect memory of the lakeshore in Gath-upon-

Brennes, where I had fought a contingent of the king's Guard. And then, without even trying, a perfect model of this room.

A bench on the second tier stood slightly out of place. There was a scrap of parchment on the floor off to Archus's left. Four pieces of chalk sat in a tray beneath the slate. I could see Archus even with my eyes closed, track his every movement by tiny sounds and sense impressions, by fitting him into the picture I held so clear.

This was magic? I felt a grin twist at my lips. Control. How often had I preached that to the boys from my village? Everything I'd learned, everything I'd taught them, had been about understanding and control. Of course I could work magic. I looked out into the classroom in my head and imagined I could feel the world around me as a soft illusion. Everything in the room showed in that image, and thinking back on things Claighan had taught me, I imagined it was nothing more than an illusion stretched taut over something deeper. If I pressed a finger against the slate, it might bend like doeskin leather. If I willed it, that bench on the second row might settle into place.

The sensation buzzed in my head. My skin felt flushed, and for the first time I felt a great desire to learn this magic. Not to prove myself against Archus or defend the embattled Claighan's grand experiment, but for my own understanding. I longed to reach out and pull back the veil, to find the core of truth that rested behind the stale world I'd always known.

I waited long enough that he might be satisfied with my pause, then I opened my eyes to meet his. "I am ready."

He laughed, "Already? Perhaps you don't understand—"

"I am ready, Archus. Please continue. Teach me magic."

Finally he shrugged. "Very well, we shall continue. When the spirit is calm and the mind's eye sees, all that is left is the work of the will. Close your eyes." I did, and felt him come to stand over me.

"Now," he said, "do your best to imagine the room we are in, do your best to recreate it in as perfect detail as you may." He invested his words with heavy sarcasm, certain I would fail, but I easily regained an image of the room. I shifted my awareness, until I saw it as though I were looking down from a spot just above the door. This I could handle.

"I am ready," I said.

"We shall see," he said, with a tone that left no doubt what he expected to see. "The door. Is it open or closed?"

He snapped the question as though to catch me off guard, but I casually replied, "Closed."

"Correct. The body of your test now will be the simple process of opening the door. Understood?"

"No."

He waited for me to ask more, but I was caught in my imagination, moving my awareness down and to the left to stare directly at the closed door. Finally I asked, "How?"

"It is simple. Whether the door is open or closed...that doesn't matter. The fact that it is a doorway is important— in fact, doorways and walls are surprisingly important—but open and closed shift constantly, and they don't hold too well. So, you know that with your eyes open the door would be closed, right?"

I nodded.

"Now, in your imagination, you must create an image of this room, of *this* door, but with the door open. Then you must believe that the image in your mind is the true reality, that your memory is only tricking you but your imagination shows you truth."

"How?"

He growled softly in frustration before he answered. "By your will," he snapped. "By your faith. That is all it takes. Believe, desire, and create. Now, begin."

I tried. In my mind I spoke the words, "The door is now open! Poof!" But the image stayed the same. I wasn't fooled by words. I knew the truth.

I tried to change the image so that the door was open, or discard this image and create a new one with an open door. But that was not real. The image in my mind was the truth. It was the room I might have to fight in. Whether the door was open or closed mattered very much if I needed to beat a hasty retreat or back an opponent into a corner.

When I closed my eyes and saw the room, I saw the world as I could count on it. I would not hesitate to stand up and walk among the rows of tables and benches, to dance up and down the steps without even glancing, because I knew the accuracy of my memory. This change, though, demanded something different—almost something opposite of what I knew. The tools seemed the same, but the harder I tried to work the magic, the more real my belief in a closed door became.

I began to feel a tension building in the air about me, a heavy, oppressive air that weighed on my body and taxed my lungs. I screwed up my face, frowning in concentration, but the more effort I poured into my imagination the more it seemed I should just stand and walk to the door. It would be so much easier to open it by hand!

And with that thought the whole image fell apart. Instead I saw myself rising within the room, walking calmly and easily to a plain door, and pulling it open by hand. No magic, no power, no buried truth. Only the stale world I'd always known. And as I watched that little pantomime unfold before me, I felt all hope for power, all magical ability at all fade from my feeble grasp like a tide sinking back to sea. I could never have anticipated the great sense of loss, of emptiness that I felt in that moment.

I sighed a great sigh and let my shoulders slump, falling back against my seat. I allowed my eyes to open and stared at the cursed door for one long heartbeat, and then it whispered effortlessly open, swinging easily and rapping lightly against the inner wall before settling to silence. Ashamed, I turned to face the grinning Archus.

"That," he said darkly, "was the most pathetic thing I've ever witnessed. You actually showed *no power at all*. I've never even *heard* of that happening! The door didn't *budge* until I opened it on my own!"

Shame and rage met in a great clashing front that hurled me to my feet. Before I even knew I was on my feet I flew over the long table and landed directly in front of him, grabbing the front of his shirt in my fists. "You arrogant bastard!"

He didn't twitch, but snapped a word of command, and a wall of air threw me back to crash against the wooden table I'd just hurdled. He took a moment to arrange his shirt again, brushed at his sleeve, and then stepped up to loom over me. Half of his mouth curled up in a sneer.

"You should watch your mouth, little Daven. Students are not permitted such harsh language around their masters."

I tried to stand, to lunge at him, but found myself still bound by his magic. I recognized bands of air, like those Claighan had used to trap me at the lakeshore, snaking over my chest and shoulders, my waist and knees. I stopped struggling and instead spat at his face, which took him by surprise. "Let me go, coward! Face me like a man, with sword in hand."

"Oh, Daven." He shook his head slowly. "You should know threatening your master is considered poor form, too!

And, as I said, I am responsible for setting your punishments. However I see fit." His eyes danced. "But I'll forgive both your offenses this time. After all, you're just a shepherd, and it will take time to tame you." He turned his back on me and started up the stairs toward the door. He made it halfway, strolling with an easy arrogance, then turned back to me as though in afterthought. "But...perhaps I would do well to continue your education by other means. Meet me in the Arena at even bell, with your sword, and we shall settle this."

With that he left. I struggled to stand, but his bonds were still in place. I screamed after him, crying curses, but his footsteps trailed off down the hall and I heard no other reply. It was a long time before his magic faded and I could push myself up off the floor to make my way wearily to my room.

I had missed lunch with Themmichus and wasted much of the afternoon pinned on my back on that floor. I didn't know where I was supposed to find dinner, or when, but as I stepped out into the courtyard between the Halls of Learning and the dormitory, I saw evening fast approaching. Bloody sunset bathed the corridor in red shadows. I set my jaw. I'd missed dinner, too, then.

I whipped the door to the dormitory open with more force than I needed. The halls beyond were empty and my footsteps echoed, high and thin, as I stomped my way back to my room. I saw no one. As I went, my shoulders twitched. I licked my lips and fought to suppress a snarl. My hands balled in fists, and I made a conscious effort to relax them, but moments later they were clenched again. I began walking faster and then finally broke into a run for my room just as the great bells of the tower began tolling the evening hour. Archus would be waiting. Hate and fear clawed at my heart, crushed on my lungs, but neither overwhelmed my desire for vengeance. He would pay.

When I came to my room the door was standing open. I exploded through it and saw my travel pack still fallen where Themmichus had dropped it. I spared it less than a thought, stepped over it, and drew the Green Eagle's sword with one furious motion, then turned on my heel and darted from the room. I sprinted down the hall, feet pounding against the stone in time with the thunderous beat of my heart, and burst through the little wooden door that opened onto the Arena.

And I stopped. The courtyard was packed with students, and every one of them faced toward a little clearing at its heart with a palpable expectation. I understood in a flash. I understood why Archus had left me trapped in the room, and why the halls had all been empty. He had gathered them here for this, to witness my humiliation.

Of course. He was the first heir of some southern nobleman. Of course he would have some facility with a sword. I had watched noblemen duel, though. A dark grin twisted at my lips, and I began shouldering my way forward. He couldn't know how hard I had studied. He couldn't know how viciously I would fight. He had bought his own suffering with that one act of cruel arrogance. I finally broke through the crowd and into a ring of richly dressed young men. Archus stood opposite me in an open area almost exactly the same size as the one I'd fought Cooper in years ago.

No, days. I shook my head, and my grin faded. Days ago, I'd been just a shepherd. But I had killed since then. My path had changed. I set my jaw, raised my sword, and met Archus's eye.

He smiled. He laughed and raised his voice. "So you've come after all. Let's dance."

I dropped the sword to my side and sneered at him. "I hate to dance. Let's fight." He scowled as a chuckle went up from some of the closest students. He came a step closer and answered me.

"You would brawl like a dirty beggar." He shook his head in disappointment. "You're a disgrace, Daven, and you don't belong here. You bring shame on the school, and to-day you have dared to challenge your master." He dropped his voice, dropped his eyes to lock on mine. "Prepare for your second lesson."

He reached up to unclasp his cloak, and it fell in a soft rustle to pile on the dusty ground. One of the nearest spectators darted forward to take it up. Beneath the cloak he wore new clothes, all of black silk and resting lightly on his pale skin. He pulled a long, light rapier from a sheath on his belt and settled into a northern stance, left hand held arcing up to head height behind him. He hopped from one foot to the other like an excited race horse. "Come fight me, then."

I looked around for a sympathetic face in the crowd, but the closest all seemed to be Archus's friends. They wore the same elegant finery on their soft frames, the same arrogant sneer on their hateful faces. I had no cloak to drop and my clothes were simple cotton, but they were much like what I'd always worn, and I was comfortable in them. I rolled my shoulders once, then raised my sword in a simple capitol stance, and settled to wait for him.

But when his eyes finally fell on the blade, his mouth dropped open. "Where did *you* get a sword like that, shep-herd?"

I kept my voice low for him. "From a duel, lordling. I took it from a Green Eagle."

He snorted, but when my face didn't change his expression did. "Impressive. I'll examine it more closely once I've won it from you." As the words left his mouth he moved. With a smile like a striking hawk's, he came gliding forward.

He used the rapid, careful steps of a trained swordsman. Within three paces I had a measure on how he moved, and I rushed to meet him.

We crossed swords once, almost formally. But instead of falling into a flurry of flashing blades I disengaged and then lunged, forward and to the side. I struck out once, more against his blade than at him. It threw his weapon wide even as he turned to follow my motion. I quickly reversed my lunge and closed with him, face-to-face from less than four feet away.

I slashed my sword up to cut his cheek, to score a point off my clever motion, but he moved with astonishing speed. He managed to bring his blade back around and deftly parried my attack. His riposte came just as swiftly, and I was lucky to send it wide of my right shoulder.

At that distance our fight was a desperate, dizzying whirlwind. His sword and mine danced around each other, seeking frantically for some purchase. A deep, cold silence filled the courtyard around us. The boys closest must have been straining to see what was going on, and those farther back straining to hear some indication from them. But for a long moment, we merely tested each other in speed.

The observers couldn't have followed us. I couldn't even keep up consciously with the motion of our swords. Instead I fought to maintain my relaxation, to know our positions, and allowed my muscles to respond more on instinct than thought. Training turned my wrist, jabbed my arm forward or pulled it back, rolled the hilt of my sword lightly over my fingertips. I moved the blade on nothing more than a sense of the pressure and angle of his weapon against mine, but it was enough to keep me safe.

He was terribly skilled, and faster than I, but everything he did was with textbook precision. For two passes I allowed my guard to lapse on the *terce*, and on the third pass his perfect strike came *in terce*, straight out of the book. But I was not there to receive the blow. As his lunge carried him forward I dove free of him, coming up behind and to the right.

He caught himself short of falling and whirled to face me. Surprise and irritation flashed across his face, beneath a light sheen of sweat. I grinned as I moved to meet him, but I hung just an inch outside of the appropriate range. For two or three passes we fought like that, and I could tell that the distance was irritating him. So I pressed an attack and took a long step forward, bringing us face to face. I thought to lock swords with him and then just shove him over—I was clearly stronger than he—but as I slid in close to him I saw his mouth move.

At the same time his left hand suddenly swung out, as if he were throwing a haymaker at me from three paces away, and a great gust of wind reached across the distance to deliver the blow for him. Pain flared across my ribs and I had to take three quick stumbling steps just to keep my feet. Before I could set myself, before I could turn to face him again, he attacked me from behind.

I felt the tip of his sword cut into my left shoulder, sharp and hot. Blood washed down my back and anger flooded me. I threw myself into a tight turn and dove toward him. I swung my sword in a high arc to draw his attention up, and while his blade was still rising to block it I leaped forward and crushed his forward foot beneath my heel.

He cried out in surprise and pain and then lashed out again with another gust of wind that pushed me away and beat me down to the ground. I tried to fight it, tried to attack him through the spell, but he moved forward with the gusts of air and attacked as he did it, the tip of his blade darting past mine to cut me along the arm and shoulder. I fell into desperate defense, but beneath the torrent of air I couldn't even maintain enough control for that.

Finally I gave up, crawling miserably in the dirt, trying to escape his attack, but a too-familiar force wrapped me in tight bonds and lifted me into the air. I was helpless against his magic, and he put me on display. He lifted me up high enough for everyone to see, and then with another gust of wind set me slowly spinning. Humiliation burned hotter than the searing wounds he had inflicted. Then Archus stepped forward, sneering up into my eyes. "You are pathetic, Daven. Go away."

I could not answer, whether from the spell or my own shame I do not know, but after a moment more my spinning broke our eye contact. For a moment I could breathe again. For a moment, I hoped it was over. I squeezed my eyes shut and prayed for an end.

It didn't come. Instead, I suddenly felt the cold tip of his blade cut into my right shoulder. He did it with that same textbook precision, pressing just deep enough to tear the flesh. He allowed my motion to do most of the work for him, slicing my skin open in a long, shallow gash as I kept turning. He waved the blade up and down as I turned, giving shape to the scar, sinewy like a serpent's tail. I felt blood wash down my back, felt sweat burn in the long wound, felt the presence of Archus like a cancer behind me. I heard sounds from the assembled students—some cries of outrage, maybe, but mostly catcalls and jeers and laughter at my humiliation. Archus was laughing, too, and the ring of boys closest to me roared.

A flood of emotion came—rage and fear and terrible shame—but behind it came a great thudding wave of pain and exhaustion that blended with the darkness of coming night and washed me into unconsciousness. I dread to think what indignities they might have done while I hung unconscious in their midst, but when I woke the ordeal was over.

When I awoke, I was in my room. I was in my bed, propped up against the wall, with my legs stretched out before me. It was dark, deep in the night, and there were no candles burning. There was enough light through the cracked door that I could vaguely see the figure leaning against my writing desk. Tall and thin, and idly toying with the sword I had taken from Othin. Its naked blade glittered in the thin light.

For a moment I thought it was Archus, and my heart quailed. I must have made a sound, because he looked up. I saw dark eyes narrow, and then he pressed himself up and stepped over to face me, the sword resting almost forgotten in his hands.

Seriphenes. He looked down at me for a long moment then nodded toward my shoulders. "Are you feeling much pain?"

I glared up at him. It dawned on me, though, that I didn't feel the agony Archus's torture should have caused. I felt a flush of relief, even gratitude, as I recalled the Kind Father's healing magic. I shook my head in a little no, rolled my shoulders to confirm it—

And cried out at a flash of searing cold fire across my back. I could feel the sinuous trail of Archus's cut. It didn't bleed, but it burned with a vicious chill. Seriphenes grimaced.

"I'm afraid our magic lacks the...finesse of the Kind Father's treatments," he said. "But you will live."

I ground my teeth against the pain. He smirked.

"It will scar. I thought perhaps...that would be for the best." His eyes glittered whenever he paused, and his nostrils flared. I took short, sharp breaths and regained my composure. As long as I stayed still, the pain gradually faded.

He watched me for some time and then nodded. "You know why I am here?" I shook my head. His eyes widened in surprise. "Truly? You have no idea?"

I took a slow breath, and then met his eyes. "Because your apprentice tried to maim me?"

"He did maim you," Seriphenes said coolly. "That I undid it does not detract from the effectiveness of his actions. Credit where it is due, yes?" I glared at him, but I did not speak. He nodded.

"I am here to speak with you about your role in the Academy."

"You and everyone else," I growled. "I'm not leaving."

He considered me for a moment. Then he nodded, one curt jerk of his chin. "So I have heard," he said. "And so you have shown. And as I'm sure you have been told, we cannot tolerate your causing trouble at our school."

"I am not the one maiming students," I said coldly.

He smiled, his lips tight. "Just so," he said. "And that is why Archus is currently on...suspension. And that is why he was not allowed to keep the weapon he clearly won." He looked down at the Green Eagle's sword, and his lip curled in distaste. He turned and placed it on the writing desk then wiped his hands clean and turned back to me. "And by the Chancellor's order, it is not even to be taken from you."

"I appreciate the Masters' generosity," I said. "Why are you here?"

"I am here," Seriphenes said, his words a little clipped, "because *someone* must tell you how a student behaves at the

Academy of Wizardry, and Archus's little *stunt* has caused that burden to fall on me."

I met his eyes for a moment and shrugged. I had to fight down another yelp of pain at the motion, but I kept it hidden. "How about you let me get some sleep, and I'll ask Themmichus for some pointers tomorrow morning?"

His lips curled in a smile that never reached his eyes. He held my gaze for a long moment, and then began as though I hadn't spoken. "You are expected to comport yourself with civility, nobility, and dignity. You are to speak to the Masters, and to any teacher, with nothing but respect. You are to refrain from inciting *fights* or otherwise causing disturbances with your fellow students, and you are—in every possible way—to keep from drawing my attention."

Those last words fell from his tongue like shards of ice, and I nearly flinched away from them. I made myself hold his gaze, though, and after a moment he nodded.

"Of every ten days, you will set aside six for training with your personal tutor, two for lectures with the other first-year students, and one for personal training and evaluation by the Academy masters. Your remaining day will be left to your leisure, although I suspect you will need it for studying. Your first day off will be tomorrow, and you can spend it healing."

He half-turned toward the door as he rattled on. "Meals can be had at the kitchens north end of the Halls of Learning, and new clothes from the commissary," he nodded pointedly to my shoulders again, and I realized the fine shirt I'd worn from the king's palace was now in tatters. "If you have more expensive tastes you can also place orders there for goods from Gath, although...."

He didn't bother finishing the sentence, and I couldn't muster the outrage to glare at him. I only stared back at him. I did my best to look bored, while I groaned inwardly

162

at the thought of six days a week trapped in a room with the horrible Archus.

He nodded and headed for the door, but when he reached it he stopped and turned back to me. He hesitated for a moment, weighing his words. "I regret Archus's actions," he said. "But you should know he was on direction from me to convince you to leave. I have spread the word to everyone who will listen. *You should not be here.* I don't care about your pride or about Claighan's grand ideas. I want you gone, boy, and in time you will go. Until that happens...keep out of my way. Keep out of my way, and you may leave here alive."

With that he left my room. It was a long, long time before I fell asleep.

8. An Education

I spent the whole of the following day alone in my room, healing and sulking. Around lunchtime Themmichus came to knock on my door and even called my name before he gave up, but I did not invite him in. Eventually he went away.

The next morning marked the beginning of my first regular week of study at the Academy. I woke with the morning bell, washed myself at my basin, and shrugged into one of the worn shirts I'd brought from my days as a shepherd. The smell of sheep's wool and honest sweat had become part of the fabric. It should have been a touchstone, real and familiar, but it felt sharply out of place in this house of nobles' sons. I grimaced, but there was no time to replace it now. After my morning's lecture I could visit the commissary.

Lecture. I set my jaw. I sucked an angry breath in through my nose, and pushed it out again. Archus. I closed my eyes. There were soldiers looking for me outside these walls. I knew that much. The king wanted me in chains or worse. This place was my only refuge, but it was a kind of prison anyway, wasn't it?

I took another slow breath. There were opportunities here. They wouldn't come easily, but when had anything come easily? If I could survive this place, I would have magic to show for it. The king's cold dungeons offered no such benefits.

So I rose and reached for my door. But I stopped, a grim smile tugging at my lips. Then I went back for Othin's sword, sheathed it, and hung it from my belt. It was a long walk from my room to my appointed class in the Halls of Learning, and I drew looks from everyone I passed. I heard them talking, but I did not slow, did not look to left or right. I went to meet Archus with a weapon at my side.

In the end, I was late. I missed my turn, took a wrong staircase, and had to try three classrooms already full of students before I found my way to the right corridor. That meant Archus would be waiting already. It meant he would sneer and call me down for my tardiness. Fear and anger and irritation boiled in my stomach, but I forced them down. I took strength from the weight of the belt on my hip. I wanted to hesitate when I got to the door, to turn away, to draw it out. I didn't. I grabbed the handle and ripped the door open and stormed into the room.

And looked down on the startled face of Antinus. The young man who had once been appointed my tutor was sprawled across a chair on the floor below, flipping impatiently through the stiff leather pages of an ancient book. He met my eyes. Then I watched his gaze fall to my tattered shirt. Then to the immeasurably expensive sword on my hip. Then back to my eyes again. He raised one eyebrow. "In my studied opinion," he said, words slow and even, "you have come prepared for entirely the wrong kind of training."

I felt a flush burn in my cheeks, but it could not compete with the sudden rush of relief and excitement. I started down the steps. "Where is Archus?"

"Ah," he said. He nodded once. "Of course. Archus is not here. And I will not excuse an absence to be spent on so frivolous a thing as tracking him down and murdering him."

I ducked my head, offering meek acceptance. "Very well. I'll save that for my free time."

He laughed, and it was a sound warm and rich. He gestured me on down to a chair opposite him, and when I was seated he considered me for a moment. "In all earnestness, Daven, you must not go about dressed like that. I'm to be your tutor. Archus is suffering administrative reprimand for his part in your altercation. Leave it at that."

I looked away. "I cannot leave it at that."

"You can," Antinus said. "Or you will be cast out. And that would stain my honor." He put a bite into the words, and I ground my teeth.

"I understand," I said.

"Be sure you do," Antinus said. "I did not want you for my student, but you were assigned to me. And when it comes down to the truth, I believe you deserve your opportunity here. Many do not. I will do my best to see that you get your opportunity, and a part of that is restraining you against your wilder notions."

I nodded my head, trying again for meek. It did not come so easily this time, because there was less joking in it. I took a deep breath. "I'll do my best."

"I expect it of you," Antinus said. Then he leaned back, releasing me from his gaze, and laced his fingers together behind his head. "Now, let us speak of magic."

We sat for four hours, on the floor of the empty lecture hall, and we talked. He spent more time asking questions of me, as he had at our first meeting, but then he moved into explanations of his own. There was little new—much of what he said that first day overlapped things Claighan or Archus had said—but he was building a foundation. He took time to teach me the language, the terms we would use to discuss the complex and strange practices of a working wizard.

We broke for lunch. He led me through the maze of halls, and I was more careful to learn the path this time. We talked more as we walked, and he showed me the way to the kitchens. He took a plate and then cast a glance at me. "I'll see you back in class in an hour. Don't dawdle. If you hurry, you can drop the belt in your room, grab a bite, and even visit the commissary in that time. *If* you hurry."

I nodded and took my own plate to my room instead of following Antinus to the Gardens or seeking out Themmichus in the Arena. An hour later I found my way back to the room, dressed in a plain gray shirt that was nonetheless finer than anything I'd ever worn as a shepherd. Once again Antinus was waiting. He nodded at my shirt, at the missing sword, and then waved me on down.

I expected more discussion, or perhaps lecture, but instead he led me through an exercise meant to help me visualize my surroundings. I quickly recognized it for what it was.

"Oh," I said with a little laugh. "This is unnecessary. Archus told me of the need, but I am already able—"

"You're not," Antinus said. "If you were able, Archus would not have won."

I shook my head. "I don't mean I'm a wizard, but these tricks to help the mind's eye see—"

"Hush," Antinus said. It was not cruel, but it was final. He nodded. "You see the world as it appears to be. That you can do so strongly is not an asset. You must see the world as it is. Now begin again. Close your eyes."

And that is how we spent the afternoon. He led me through a dozen exercises meant to help me relax, to prepare the mind and body for the practice of magic. They felt familiar, half-seen reflections of the exercises I knew so well from my sword work, but there was a subtle difference in tone and texture. I grumbled at first, irritated at his insistence, but I did as he said.

For another four hours I did little more than breathe and relax and imagine, but by the end I felt as tired as though I'd spent a full day in the fields. And by the end I was ready to admit I knew nothing. My head throbbed, and I felt a failure.

When a bell tolled suppertime, he nodded once and climbed to his feet. Then he surprised me. He stepped up and extended a hand to me. "Well done, Daven."

I tilted my head, confused. "Really?"

"Really," he said. "Quite remarkable. You have much to learn. But, too, you have learned much. I shall make a wizard of you yet. Be here tomorrow. On time."

I ducked my head in a nod, and he left the room.

The next two days of my education passed much as my first had. I spent them alone in a lecture hall with Antinus, and he tried to lay a foundation. Antinus was clever, careful, and almost kind. He did not reach out to me, he did not invite me to eat with him or commiserate over my mistreatment. But he did not speak down to me, either. He did not go slow unless I needed it. He expected me to excel, and I seemed to meet his expectations.

The fourth day saw me seated in the back of a lecture hall taught by a doddering old Master named Leotus. Leotus laughed, sharp and sneering, when he first saw me step into the room, but otherwise he paid me no attention. For my part I sat in a back corner and tried to understand what he had to say. When we broke for lunch I slipped out quickly. I shared a quiet meal with Themmichus against the wall of the Halls of Learning, and he told me not to worry about it. Leotus never made any sense to anyone.

I entered the class for my afternoon lecture and found Seriphenes staring up at me. I expected another derisive laugh like I'd gotten from Leotus, or perhaps some outburst, but the Master merely raised an eyebrow, then beckoned me down to the front of the class.

I felt the eyes of a dozen students turn to me and fought a shiver of fear. I swallowed a lump in my throat and wondered what the professor would say or do. He just waited, tall and dark and terrible. I stepped up to him, and it seemed inevitable that he would put me on display—humiliate me in front of the class.

Instead he moved his head close to my ear and spoke softly. "I have spoken with your tutor, Daven, and you are not prepared for the topics of this class. I will evaluate your progress in three weeks' time. Until then, you are dismissed."

He straightened, and his eyes turned back toward the class. Dismissed. He had done it as politely as he could, but still I felt the sharp sting of injured pride. I turned and started back up the stairs toward the door, and I felt all those eyes on me again. Seriphenes raised his voice behind me, launching into a lecture, and it was as though I were not there at all. I closed my eyes and pressed on up and out of the room. When I reached the hall, I had to struggle to catch a breath.

It was foolish. I closed my eyes and worked through one of the exercises Antinus had taught me, but I fumbled it three times before I switched to one from my fencing book. That served me better. I regained my control and slipped away down the hall. I went to my room and spent four hours working forms with my sword.

That was good honest work. By the time the bell rang dinner I was dripping with sweat, arms and legs and chest all weary, and my heart felt good. Themmichus and I shared stories over smoked turkey and crusty rolls and I went to bed feeling satisfied.

On my fifth day I met a spare and absent-minded Master named Bennethis in his study for private lessons. He asked me four questions, patted me on the head, and sent me away. I spent the afternoon running laps around the Arena.

And then the cycle started again. Three days in training with Antinus, a day of lecture with Masters Alteres and Bennethis, and then a day of rest that I dedicated to hard work. But this time I answered my door when Themm came knocking at lunch time. His sister had sent a bottle of fine wine to celebrate his apprenticeship and he wanted me to share it. I offered to grab a couple plates of food for us, and he told me where to meet him in the Arena.

I was just coming back from the kitchens and into the painfully-bright courtyard when I heard the sounds of an argument. I rounded the corner to find Themmichus backed against a wall. Four older boys were gathered around him, and they wore sneers and jeers that I recognized all too well. Themm's eyes were wide and his chest moved in and out with short, sharp breaths.

I didn't know the boys taunting him. I didn't really know anyone but Antinus and Themm. But I recognized some of them by reputation. The tallest was a Souward, dark and handsome and unimaginably wealthy. Beside him was the heavyset son of a powerful northern lord, and another who I recognized as a close friend of Archus's. The last had blond hair, bright eyes, and a distant claim to the FirstKing's throne.

They all had powerful names, and as I watched them looming over my only friend I felt a rage begin to burn in my heart. I'd heard whispers, I'd seen Themmichus hide his eyes when he walked with me in the halls, but I'd never seen anyone challenge him directly. I tried to keep my cool as I moved closer, but I heard Themm's voice break.

"Daven's not the problem here," he said. He drew himself up to his full height, still head and shoulders smaller than anyone he was facing. "You guys are the problem."

They laughed in sneering contempt and the northerner jostled Themmichus's shoulder roughly. "You must be kidding, Themmy! A shepherd, really? Is that how far your father's name has fallen?"

Themm's eyes flashed fury and I saw his fists ball. The brute noticed, too, and shifted his stance, but before either of them could make a move I stepped up next to Themm's shoulder. I met each of the others in the eyes. "What's going on, Themmichus?"

I felt him shift beside me, suddenly showing his nervousness. "Just talking with my friends," he said. "You could...you could come back in a few minutes."

I shook my head slowly and held the northerner's eyes. "No need for that," I said. I still had two plates piled with food, and I set them carefully on the smooth top of the stone Themm and I usually used for a table. I rubbed my hands together and turned back to the bullies.

"Master Seriphenes says I'm not supposed to be starting fights," I said. I gave the words more menace than I really felt. These weren't the simpering fops I'd taken Archus for. Even without magic two of these guys together probably could have taken me. I wasn't about to let them push Themmichus around without at least standing by his side, though. I met their eyes again and showed my teeth in a little snarl.

Themm tugged at my sleeve. "Daven, don't."

I shook my head. "Get out of here," I said to the northerner. "He's a good kid. Leave him alone."

Themmichus sighed beside me, frustrated, and he nodded to them. "Yes. Just...just leave me alone. Daven's my friend, and that's not changing."

I felt a little touch of warmth at that, but I held the icy glare. One by one the lordlings dropped their gazes. They shrugged and made condescending noises, but they backed away and left. When the last of them was out of earshot, I turned back to Themmichus.

"Are you..." I started, but I saw his chin come up, and I figured his pride had suffered enough. "You held yourself well," I said instead. "Thank you."

He looked up into my eyes for a moment, then he shook his head. "You're trouble. You know that?"

My mouth quirked toward a smile and I rolled one shoulder. "I do the best I can." I nodded toward our plates. "Venison and greens today. Should go well with your red."

He held my eyes for a moment, and he looked as though he meant to say more. He looked almost chastising. But then he shook it away, and forced a little laugh. "Anything would go well with this red," he said. "Have a seat."

The next several weeks passed like that. I spent most of my days locked in a classroom. The best of those days were the ones I spent with Antinus, learning the basic methods of self-control, of concentration, and of imagination. After a week I began to understand how I could make something change, and after two I thought I could at least try to open the door, but Antinus said it was against the rules. First-year students only did that sort of training with the Masters' supervision. Instead he told me to relax and imagine the door and see what I could see.

Themmichus told me that one day I would go through these exercises with a thought, and instead of simply relaxing I would find myself staring at a whole new world. Everyone spoke of "the world as it was," the world of energies and powers and realities that Claighan had mentioned to me a long time ago. The true world.

172

It seemed impossible, but every day in the Academy I saw the proof of it. I walked among men who could reshape reality with wish and word. I could barely imagine it, but the more time I spent among them the more I longed to prove that I could do the things they did. I had little need for magic, but I hated being bested by these spoiled children, and so I kept on trying day after day. Within my gray and pale world, where time slipped like wind between my fingers, the thought of achieving that true world compelled me.

And somehow Antinus saw that in me and always knew what to say to keep me going. Themmichus, too, teased me with displays of power and quiet, confident assurances that it would come for me. So day and night melted into a single desire, coaxed and fanned to life beneath the quiet gaze and gentle words of my teacher.

Every week I had one day to myself, and I always spent some of it studying, some of it chatting with Themmichus. I practiced my sword, too, if only in the privacy of my room. And every week I went to check on Claighan. It became a ritual, because every week the Kind Father turned me away. The old wizard was alive, but he was not well. He took no visitors, and the Kind Father said he could not even speak. I always checked, though, and daydreamed of the time he would recover and take me on as his own apprentice. Then, at last, I would learn the secrets he had meant me to know.

The rest of my days were not so pleasant. Every student of any rank spent two days per week in classroom study with the Masters, and though I was left out of Seriphenes's class, I had some hope for the others. I watched my classmates' first fumbling attempts, but as days and weeks rolled by I watched them slowly find successes. Sparks instead of summoned flame, coughs and rattles instead of violent motion, but at least they moved things. It was Leotus who used the closed door as an example—walking through the lecture

173

with precisely the same words Archus had used—and it took most of an afternoon in my third week, but by the end of the day every one of my classmates could open and close the door with a spoken word.

Everyone but me. I couldn't budge it. I couldn't summon sparks. I certainly couldn't light a candle, or project a thought, or catch a moth, or hang an image in the empty air. I watched my peers bend the world to their will, and no matter how hard I studied, how many questions I asked of Antinus or Themmichus, I couldn't do a thing.

At first I held some hope that my private lessons with the Masters might correct that. But after Bennethis dismissed me, I had to wait a week before meeting with Leotus who only took me into his classroom and repeated his lecture word for word, asking me to open the door. He started over, *explaining* everything, but there was no part I didn't understand. I knew the theory behind it. I knew the exercises. I knew what I was supposed to do, but I had no more luck opening the door for him than I had beneath Archus's taunting.

At noon the bell rang for lunch, and he gave a sigh of relief. "You tried hard, Daven. Well done. You're dismissed."

I didn't budge. "It's not enough," I said. "Why can't I work magic?"

He was already halfway to the door. He turned back to me, and I caught him rolling his eyes. "Sometimes it takes time," he said.

I shook my head. "I've watched a dozen spoiled nobles learn in a matter of weeks," I said. "I know how long it takes. *Everyone* but me can open that door."

Leotus threw his hands up. "Then perhaps you're not cut out for magic. Is that what you want to hear? It's the truth. We've all known it since you arrived." He took a calming breath and then gave a shrug. "But we have our roles to play in this charade. You have done well enough for today. You are dismissed."

I frowned. "But after lunch—"

"Play with your sword, boy. Or bang your head against a wall. I don't care."

Master Alteres was not so cruel, but he was no more successful. And then another week later Chancellor Lhorus spent a full day quizzing me on the things Antinus had taught me. We covered more than a month's worth of theory, and by the time we were done he was shaking his head, baffled. "I cannot say," he said.

I shrugged. "Leotus says I might not be cut out for magic."

The Chancellor shook his head sharply. "No. Magic does not work like that. Everyone can be taught. I have taught near enough a thousand students, and I have seen as many different strengths and weaknesses. But magic can be taught. It is self-control, concentration—"

"And imagination," I finished for him. I sighed.

He placed a hand on my shoulder. "And patience," he said. "And determination. And focus." He stopped. He tilted his head, and after a moment he nodded. "Focus. I suspect that is the issue."

I met his eyes. "What do you mean? I already do the exercises."

"As well as anyone I have ever seen."

"Then what—"

"That is self-control," he said. "By focus, I mean something...wider. Your life does not belong to the Academy. Your life does not belong to your study of magic."

I held his eyes for a moment and then hung my head. "I don't know how—"

"Of course you don't," he said. He squeezed my shoulder then climbed to his feet. "And perhaps Leotus is right at that. Perhaps you shouldn't be one of us, Daven. I cannot answer for you. It is a question for your heart. But you have a strong grasp on theory and a remarkable discipline. I cannot gauge your native strength until you can perform a working, but I believe you could have a true future among our ranks. If you *want* one."

I could not answer that. After a moment he nodded and left me there. The dinner bell rang, but I didn't move. Even bell rang, too, before I finally shook myself from my thoughts and dragged the long walk back to my rooms. I didn't sleep well.

It should have been an easy question. It should have been an easy answer. A Wizard of the Academy stood higher in rank than anyone else in the kingdom. In theory, even than the king, though I knew of no wizard who would test that claim. But it was not a political position. It was a place outside. Above. What law could govern a man who bent reality to his wishes? What strength could bind him, but the strength of the Academy itself?

But I had known wizards, and they were not gods. They were scheming connivers, as often as not. Claighan had been kind and clever—kind enough, anyway—and in the end he had proven weak and foolish. Here among the Masters I had found indifference, cruelty, arrogance, and among some of their prized pupils more of the same. And, too, there were the vicious monsters. Archus. The traitor Lareth.

What law could bind a man like Lareth, if not the law of the Academy? But Seriphenes, his old Master, barely called him down. He certainly did not bring him to heel. I frowned, reviewing that conversation for the first time in weeks. Its edges were soft, unreal, and I couldn't say for sure if it had been a memory or a dream.

But it didn't matter. Not here and now. If I were to have a place at the Academy, I had to give my heart to it. I had to make a home among these stained and broken creatures. And, dream or memory, that conversation told me what my heart felt of this place. Themmichus was a friend. But he was alone among all the school, and he had suffered for the kindness he showed me. That made this place no home for me.

Still, I had nowhere else to go. I pressed the Chancellor's words to the back of my mind. I went back to my studies with Antinus and continued to impress him with my memory and understanding. I attended classes and watched my classmates work through the budding first steps of their magic, and I strove to memorize every piece of it. Someday, maybe, the experience would be mine, and I would be ready for it.

In my fifth week at the Academy I woke at dawn to a single sharp rap upon my door. I dressed hurriedly and threw the door open, bleary and confused, and found Seriphenes waiting in the still-dark hall. He nodded once then turned on his heel. He snapped, "Come!" and marched off down the hall.

We passed through the building and on to the Learning Halls, where Seriphenes led me down a corridor I had never noticed before. Soon these halls would be bustling with other students, but for now the whole building rested beneath a calm silence. He stopped before a plain, narrow door, and turned to face me.

"Today you are to be my student," he said. "I am supposed to teach you magic."

I felt a tension in my shoulders and tried to relax. His lips pressed together, grim. He nodded. "I have spoken to the other Masters about your progress."

I licked dry lips and ducked my head in a nod. "Yes, Master Seriphenes?"

"Yes. Progress." He reached past me to open the door and gestured for me to enter. The room inside was dark, but I tried to show some measure of confidence as I stepped past the Master and into the darkness beyond. My second step brought me up against a wall. Before I realized where I was, Seriphenes closed the door behind me. The darkness was complete.

For several moments I stood there stunned, the silence punctuated only by my ragged breath. Finally, I said, "A closet?"

"Be still," Seriphenes said from without. "Watch."

I recognized the order, and closed my eyes. I needn't have bothered in the total darkness, but it was part of the process. I worked through the exercises Antinus had taught me, and realized with a start how easily they came. It was as Themmichus had predicted. With a thought, I settled into a disciplined frame of mind, then opened my eyes. The darkness was still there, though it did not press so close.

I said, "I am ready." My voice sounded strangely distant to my ears.

Seriphenes didn't answer. Instead, a brilliant white light suddenly flared in the room. I flinched away from it, but there was no heat, and my eyes quickly adjusted again. I found myself in a simple closet with low shelves along the walls stacked with parchment and ink, blank books and ledgers and chalk for the slates in the lecture halls. There was no chair, no stool. And there was no handle on the inside of the door.

The light remained just long enough for me to make those observations, and then Seriphenes said, "You are to duplicate this light." My breath caught, and the light winked out. The darkness came crashing back, and my training was not enough to protect me from it now. I grunted in surprise. I blinked my eyes. I felt my breath speeding up and forced myself through my teacher's exercises again. And then through my fencing exercises. And then, at last, I could breathe again.

But I could not see. I shook my head. "Master Seriphenes, I do not know this spell."

"There is no spell," Seriphenes said. "It is simply light. It is what you want. It is what you need. You have the knowledge. Now put it to use. Create the light."

I closed my eyes, began to build the visualization as Antinus had taught me, but frustration shattered my concentration. I slammed a fist against the inside of the door. "I can't, Master. I have not learned this level of working yet."

"You have learned enough. That you cannot work a seeming with all that knowledge in your head is a joke. It is a *problem*, Daven, that reflects poorly on every teacher you have ever had. I will not let it reflect on me."

"Then teach me," I said.

"I am."

I objected to that. I shouted at him, but he spoke over me. "You have your instruction. Create light within the darkness, and I will let you out. For my honor. And for yours. Make it happen."

That last cut at me. The words were on my lips, "I can't," but I couldn't make myself give them voice. So I closed my eyes, worked through my exercises, and built the visualization.

I saw the room in perfect clarity in my mind, remembering it suffused with a brilliant white light. I willed it to be so. I spoke my will. "Light!" One word, sharp and clear, and opened my eyes.

Darkness.

It crushed me. It suffused me. I felt my breath growing short again and forced it even. I closed my eyes and stepped through the process again. Slow. Deliberate. Careful. "Light!" And darkness. I tried again. And again. And again.

It must have been hours, though I had no measure of time. I tried, and I failed. And with each failure I felt something building in my chest. Terror like a rage. I felt my whole future in that moment. I felt a desperate need. I felt every failure, every misfortune, every injustice of my life in that darkness. Silent, empty, and heavier than sin, it bore down on me.

And finally I broke. I screamed, an almost animal sound. "Let me out! I cannot do it."

I heard Seriphenes's voice, cold and calm through the door. "A wizard must, Daven. A wizard must be able to perform a working, and you are here to become a wizard. If that is not your goal, you have no purpose here."

"I cannot do it yet. I cannot do it here. Not like this."

"You *must* do it here. Like this. This is the place of weakness. This is the time of need. Magic does not happen in a classroom or a study, but in darkness and fear. *Answer it.*"

I let my head fall against the door. "I can't."

"There is no room for can't in the place of need," he said. "You do, or you are dead."

"Please, just let me out. Dismiss me as you did at your lecture. Next time—"

"No," he said, and his voice brooked no argument. "No. It is my responsibility to teach you today. I will not shirk that responsibility."

"But I can't," I said.

"And yet you must. Begin again."

I did. I fought for calm. I tried in desperation. I tried in despair. I tried in building panic. I could not find the light. I pleaded with Seriphenes, but he only said, "You must." I pounded on the door. I screamed, again and again, but the door would not open for me.

Eventually I collapsed. I fell to the ground, knees bent before me, arms wrapped around them. I remember the almost physical force of the light when the door finally opened. The light washed over me, the dim glow of the mystical fire that lit these halls at night, and I heard the distant tolling of the even bell.

I was soaked in sweat. I felt beaten. My muscles were sore, my head ached, but none of that compared to the emptiness in my chest. I could feel the darkness, soaked through my skin and settled into my heart. I looked up and saw Seriphenes considering me.

He held my eyes for a long moment, no expression on his face. Then he turned with a swish of his long black robes and slipped away down the hall.

9. Word of War

I knew, then. I knew there was no magic in me. I knew I had no place here. But I had nowhere else to go, and I faced the threat of prison or death if I left the Academy's walls. So I went on with my classes, I went on pretending, but I did it all in a mechanical way. Time slipped by, unconnected from me. I lost track of Themmichus. And soon I lost Antinus, too. He would bring me a reading list, then leave to pursue his own studies. We all knew. I was only killing time.

Still I met with the Masters, and it went again as it had before. Bennethis dismissed me. Leotus repeated instructions I knew by heart. Alteres tried to guide me, demonstrated working after working, but I saw nothing. The Chancellor looked for some critical piece that I was missing. And then Seriphenes came for me again. I spent six months at the Academy, and three nightmare days locked in a sweltering dark closet while Seriphenes waited, silent and terrible without.

Time dragged on and on, and day after day I waited and hoped that I would make some breakthrough or receive some message from Claighan or notice *some* measure of real progress, but nothing happened. For seventeen weeks I put up with all the rude remarks, all the quiet, lonely hours, and all the frustrations of trying to move a world that refused to budge. Finally, as summer came to an end and fall began, a breath of change came to the Academy.

I first noticed it in the excited whispers passing along the halls, the half-formed rumors spreading like fire among the students and just beyond my hearing as I made my way from class to my room. I walked with head tilted, straining to make out the news that had everyone so excited, but I reached my room with nothing more than a nervous energy and a burning curiosity.

For a long time I sat on my bed, trying to focus on the reading Antinus had assigned me. But the words faded to gray before my eyes. I couldn't focus. Instead, my mind kept turning back to the puzzle. What in all this world could so powerfully capture the excitement of so many arrogant, spoiled children? A visit from the king?

My heart turned cold at the thought. Perhaps he was already here, wandering the halls with sharp eyes and a burning temper. He was a well-liked king, fond of festivals and indulgent with the people's wealth, but I had seen him face-to-face. In my mind, he was a monster prowling, a beast hunting me by scent.

Suddenly there came a banging on my door, and I jumped, my heart stopping in fear. Before I could move the door slipped open enough to admit Themmichus and then fell shut behind him. He looked as excited as all the rest of them, eyes wide, mouth open, more than a little breathless.

And then his gaze fell on me and he frowned. "Did I scare you?"

"No," I lied. "I was studying a volume that Antinus—"

"Of course you were. Well never mind that. Have you heard?"

I wanted to play it cool, to shrug it off. I didn't want to be one of *them*, bubbling with excitement at the newest gossip from court. But my curiosity would not let me.

And besides, it was Themmichus. I could not resist his eager grin. So I shook my head. "I haven't heard anything. What's going on?"

"War." There was a gleam in his eye, shadowed by a hint of fear but intense nonetheless. For a moment I simply stared at him, unhearing.

"War? In the kingdom?"

"War twenty miles from here! The king's army marches in the Ardain!"

I could see it in his eyes, then, and I understood. I understood the energy bubbling through every corridor of the Academy. I remembered it, from a quiet, spring afternoon on the hill outside Sachaerrich. I'd seen the same excitement in the eyes of my friends when they heard Cooper was going off to join the Guard.

My stomach clenched at the thought. War. Cooper was not made for war. He was made for long days in his father's shop. He was made for fire brigade, maybe, and he would have done well enough in a city watch. He would have done well enough in the Guard, too, when that had meant digging roads and settling tavern brawls—although he'd have done even better starting them—but he was not made for war. He would be on his way, though, and a thousand other promising young sons of happy, quiet villages.

Themmichus stepped closer, and a line formed between his brows as he frowned up at me. "Well? Aren't you excited? Think of the stories they'll tell."

"I'm thinking of one right now," I said.

He tilted his head, waiting for more, and after a moment I took a deep breath.

"I'm thinking of someone I knew," I said. "Someone who received a commission to the Guard just before I came to study here."

"Cooper?" I felt my eyes widen, and he laughed at me. "You've told that story a dozen times, Daven. Why are you worried about him now?"

"Because he'll be marching to war," I said. "He could be killed."

Themmichus shrugged. "I thought you didn't *like* Cooper."

"I don't," I said. I felt another pang in my stomach and sank back down on the edge of my bed. "I haven't thought of him in months. But here and now, I feel a deep sadness for him." I took a breath and closed my eyes. "And not just for him. For all the boys in these halls."

"Oh," he said, and he deflated. He took a step away and nodded. "All these little boys?"

I met his eyes. "Yes," I said, tired. "Honestly, yes. You're the best of them, Themmichus. But you're all...." I flexed my hands, helpless, trying to find the words.

He supplied them for me. "The rich children of an easy life." He spat the words at me and I hung my head.

"You think it sounds like fun," I said. "So did they. My friends in Sachaerrich. They thought it sounded like an adventure. But it's not. It's fighting. It's good people dying."

He stared at me for a long time, and I could not meet his eyes. Finally he said, "I thought you would be excited. I thought you would be more excited than all of us together."

I shook my head. "No. I have known the pain of loss."

"I don't understand!" He took a hard step toward me, stomping his foot. "Since the day I met you all you've ever wanted was to be a soldier! How can you look down on us—"

"It's not an adventure," I said, but my voice sounded weak in my own ears. He listened anyway, so I went on. "It was never about the adventure. I want to be a soldier because it is good work, laying down my life for a good cause."

"Why can't Cooper be doing that?" he asked. "Why can't that be the thing that has us so excited?"

I looked at him for a long time. I had an answer, but I didn't dare say it. Because they couldn't know. An easy life is too easily offered up for glory by a fool who cannot know the cost. "Because you have a life worth living," I said at last. "You have a name, even if you won't tell me what it is. You have the promise of power. If you want to change the world, do it that way." I took a deep breath and nodded. "I should be a soldier, because the only chance I have of ever changing the world is by the strength of my body. But you have so much more to offer."

His foot twitched, toes tapping rapidly against the cool stone floor. His lips pursed, and for a moment his eyes remained hard on mine. But then he blushed, and he dropped his head, and he nodded.

"I can understand," he said. "I can see why you would think like that. I'm just sorry you couldn't be happy." He sniffed and shrugged one shoulder. "I thought I might get to see you happy."

I looked away. "I'm sorry, Themm."

"They...they're offering an amnesty," he said. "I came to tell you that. The king has offered a general pardon to any able-bodied fighter from the Ardain who reports to the post in Pollix."

I stared at him, stunned. And then I felt a smile tug at my lips. "A rumor?"

He shook his head, short and sharp. "No. I received news from my father today, good and true. There's a call to arms across the Northlands, too, and every shipbuilder on the Isle has been pressed to service to build the ferry fleet. The king is looking to obliterate the rebel's forces."

I sat back. I rubbed my eyes then shook my head. I started to my feet. "You may get to see me happy after all, Themm."

He nodded, but there was sadness in his eyes. "I know. But I...I didn't want to tell you that part."

I shook my head, mouth split in a grin, eyebrows raised in confusion. "What? But why?" He bit his lip instead of answering, and I understood. I felt the joy fade from my eyes, my grin, but it still burned in my chest. I felt the touch of compassion cool beside it, though.

I put a hand on his shoulder and he looked up. I gave him a smile. "I'll miss you, too."

He shrugged, doing his best to look unconcerned, but he had to look away again.

I sighed. "I know you lost friends for spending time with me."

His eyes snapped up to mine, and there was something fierce in them. Offended. "You think so, huh? No, Daven. That's not it."

I let my hand fall from his shoulder. I frowned down at him, confused, and he frowned right back. "I lost friends because I saw the kind of people they were. For what they did to you. I lost friends because I walked away from them when I saw what a hero looked like."

"A hero?" I almost laughed, but he cut me off with a vicious glare.

"Yes. Because I saw you on your first day here. I saw you when you were torn and tattered and afraid. I saw you when everyone hated you and all you wanted in the world was to go away somewhere you'd be safe from all of it. And you didn't. You stayed. And you fought. You fought Archus when you didn't know half a seeming. And even after he made a mockery of you in front of everyone...." He trailed off, sputtering, then started again. "Even when Seriphenes locked you in a cell till even bell...."

He shook his head, and I saw tears in his eyes. "My father told me a long time ago that there are heroes, Daven.

And that they're usually not noble-born, and they're usually not much to look at, but that if I ever found one I should bind myself close to him and study at his sunburned feet." He sniffled, and wiped a sleeve at his nose. "And you were everything he ever described."

I fell back onto the edge of my bed. "Themmichus...I had no idea. I thought you were just...."

"Nice," Themmichus said. "You thought I was just nice. Because I'm little. You probably thought I could use a big strong friend, for that matter." His lip curled in disgust. "I fought for you, Daven. My name holds power, even here. I fought the Chancellor for you. I wrote home to tell my family what a remarkable warrior you are, and my sister has nearly fallen in love with you just from secondhand stories. My father sent a letter of complaint to Seriphenes that nearly got Archus expelled. I thought you were a good man. We all did." His shoulders rose and fell, and his face was flushed. His eyes flashed fire.

I hung my head. "But what am I supposed to do?"

"You're supposed to fight," he said. "Not in storybook wars. Not in stupid, bloody battles. You're supposed to fight the bullies and the powers and your own self-pity and become a real-life hero."

I looked at my hands. I couldn't raise my voice above a mumble. "I haven't seen you much, these last few weeks."

I felt his nod. "You haven't made the time," he said. "I thought it would pass. I thought you would find your spark, call your power, and then things would change."

I took a deep breath, but it did nothing to ease the tension in my chest. I let it out in a weary sigh. "I'm sorry, Themm. There is no magic in me."

"You haven't even been here a year," he said. "You cannot know that. Most of us have schooling all our lives before we ever come to study here."

"It's not about schooling," I said. "The Chancellor said so. It's about my heart. I don't *belong* here."

"Then change your heart," Themmichus said. He was begging. "You said it yourself. You have so much more to offer."

I should have met his eyes. I wanted to. I couldn't. "I'm sorry, Themm. I can't. I have tried and tried and tried." I thought of long black days trapped in a closet, desperate for any trace of light. "I can't."

He didn't answer. For a long time he stood there, towering over me despite his size. And then he turned, without a word, and left.

I sat there for a while feeling empty. He had been my only friend at the Academy. In some ways, he had been my only friend ever. He had believed in me. I wanted to go after him, to tell him I was sorry, to make it right.

But I couldn't. It had nothing to do with pride. It had to do with...well, with the world as it was. I would not stay here. Not now. I was going off to war, to take the king's amnesty. Anything else I said to Themmichus would ring hollow.

So I rose, said my good-bye to the open door, and took my travel pack from the armoire. I stuffed it with three sets of sturdy clothes from the commissary. I almost put the sword belt back in the bag, as it had been on our disastrous flight from the capitol, but a flash of memory was enough to stop me. I sighed, long and low, and buckled the belt around my waist for the first time in months. The weight of it felt good.

And then I heard a knock on my open door. Antinus stepped through then raised an eyebrow as he cast a glance at the sword on my hip. "I thought I told you to leave that in your room," he said.

I met his eyes for a long moment, and he nodded. "Not your room anymore?"

"Not for long," I said.

He nodded again. "I expected something like that when I heard the news. You're going off to be a soldier?" He didn't really wait for my nod. He leaned against the doorframe and breathed a little sigh. "You have been a good student, Daven. A remarkable one, even if you never changed a thread of reality. It was my honor to teach you our principles, if not our secret workings."

I felt tears sting my eyes. They weren't really for Antinus, but he was the one who got them. "You have been one of three kindnesses in this place. I thank you for taking the time and risk of teaching me. If we ever cross paths again, please consider me your friend."

He smiled, then solemnly we shook hands and said serious good-byes. Then he turned and retreated down the hall. Finally alone, I felt a fever of excitement and fear stirring in my blood, but as I turned to survey the little room I realized it was time to go. Now. With my heart set on a course of action, I couldn't stay here a moment longer.

I waited only long enough for Antinus to leave the hall. Then I took the washed-leather purse Sherrim had given me in Sachaerrich, still heavy with the weight of unspent pennies, and tied it on my belt. I slung the heavy leather pack over my shoulder and cast one look over my little room. In the blink of an eye I was ready to go, with everything I needed hanging on my back, and some weary flicker of hope in my heart for the first time in weeks. In an instant I exchanged one future for another in my mind, in the space of an hour I rebuilt my whole world. I don't know how I was able to do it so quickly, but I saw only suffering and frustration here, and I saw glory and freedom in the King's Guard. At last I had an easy choice.

I slipped from my room, turned left, and opened the little wooden door at the end of the dormitory hall. It opened onto the front courtyard, one none of the students ever really visited. As I stepped out into the late afternoon sun, I remembered why.

The Academy's front gates loomed, massive and scrolled with deep, curling runes that whispered with a dark, foreboding power. I felt the immensity of them from a hundred paces away, the finality of them, and a shiver chased down my spine. I took a step in their direction, and for a moment I thought I saw an image among the twisted curls that covered the gates. A face, lost in the intricate sigils. For a heartbeat it was Themmichus. Then Claighan. And then it was gone, and I knew it all for my imagination.

But it was enough to stop me. I stood beneath the gates, staring at them across a great dusty distance. Then I took a deep breath, and it settled in my chest like a heavy weight. I closed my eyes, turned in place, and returned to the Dormitory.

This time I didn't enter through the side door nearest my room. I went around to the main entrance on the south wall, and down the building's central hall as wide as a boulevard. Halfway down, on the right, I approached the familiar door to the office of the Kind Father.

I knocked as I entered, and the old priest looked up from his place behind a desk scattered with papers and open books. His eyes widened as I entered. "You're three days early."

"I'm here to say goodbye," I told him. "I don't care if he can't really hear me. I just need to say it."

He held my eyes for a long time, then shook his head. "You may have better luck than you expected," he said. "But you will have to wait."

I frowned. "Why?"

"Because he is awake." At those words I was in his office in an instant, and halfway across it before he continued solemnly. "And he is not here."

I stopped, but I had come far enough to see the truth of it. I could see into the room, and the bed was empty. I looked to the Kind Father and the question was clear in my eyes.

"This afternoon," he said, rising and coming to meet me. "He awoke shortly after lunch bell. And an hour later they received official word from the king about the war. When I sent notice to the Chancellor that Master Claighan was responsive, they came immediately and took him to a war council."

"Among the Masters?"

The Kind Father nodded. "The king has given them an ultimatum. They have three days to decide where the school will stand."

I chewed my lip, my mind racing, but then a thought struck me. I frowned and met the priest's eyes. "Why are you telling me this?"

He nodded to the pack on my back, to the sword on my hip. "Because you look like you're about to do something stupid," he said. "And because all the other students will have heard as much from their fathers. I thought you should be advised. Wait until the Masters make their decision before you make yours."

I held his eyes for a long moment, wondering why Themmichus hadn't told me. And then I knew. I nodded. "It would make no difference," I said. "The Academy is no part of my decision."

I saw the confusion in his eyes, but he didn't press me any further. Instead he spread his hands. "If you will wait in your room, I'll send a message to you when the Master is back. He will be back here."

I hung my head at the certainty in the priest's words. Then I shook my head. "No, thank you, Father." I left his office, took one step back toward the gates, and hesitated. I turned and headed the other way.

North of the Dormitory stood the sprawling Halls of Learning. Beyond that, in a courtyard that made a garden maze of long, low reflecting pools, stood a tower that rose seven floors above the earth. It cast a shadow across all the Academy, and at its top hung the ancient, eldritch bell that chimed the time for all the FirstKing's lands.

This was the Tower of the Masters. In six months at the Academy I had never set foot in it. I went there now. The doors of the tower were heavy oak, stained to black with age, and they swung open without a sound, without a touch, as soon as I approached. The tower had no windows, but firelight sculpted of magic traced in elegant scroll along the stone walls, a hand's breadth beneath the ceiling.

A small sitting room stood just inside the outer door, and beyond it a corridor three paces wide that seemed to run in a great circle around the outer edge of the tower. I followed it around to my right, unsure where to go. After a dozen paces I saw a stone staircase on my right climbing up to the higher levels, but the sound of voices dragged me on.

Another ten paces brought me to a pair of great doors on the inner wall. I heard voices beyond. The door was open only a crack, and beyond it I could see another ante-chamber, another pair of doors ajar, and beyond those must have been the council hall of the Master of the Academy, because I recognized their voices.

All of them, raised in outrage. My time in the Academy had been enough to teach me Leotus's sneering cackle and Alteres's airy wheeze. I heard Bennethis shouting himself hoarse, and the Chancellor calling for order. But it was the cold, heartless voice of Seriphenes that cut through the noise and settled them all to silence.

"Enough," he said. "Claighan, we have heard enough of your objections! Hold your tongue or we'll be forced to convene a council without you."

The Chancellor mumbled an objection to that, but the Master pressed on. "No, Chancellor. There is a time and place for his foolishness, but there are grave questions at stake here. We cannot be diverted by dragon stories when there is war on our doorstep."

"There is something worse than war," Claighan said. Though it was cracked with strain, I still heard dark foreboding in the old wizard's words. I took a slow step closer, quiet as I could, and prayed no one wandered down these halls to catch me spying.

Claighan stopped to catch a breath, and then he pushed on. "The dragons are waking. A gathering of forces is foolishness. I do not care about the politics. If the king puts ten thousand strong men in one place an elder red will burn them all to ash before the day is done. Consider the cost to our nation."

"So you vote against the king?" Seriphenes asked, and there was surprise in his voice.

"I vote for reasoning with the king," Claighan said. "He must be diverted from this action."

Seriphenes snorted in laughter, and I heard other chuckles within the council room. I pressed right up against the antechamber's outer door, though I didn't dare enter for fear of making some noise.

"That has served you well in your prior efforts," Leotus sneered. "Will *you* go tell the king to overlook a rebellion in his lands?"

"In our lands," Seriphenes said. "Pollix is a day's ride from here. Claighan's bedtime stories aside, we *should* be better served if the king did not bring his chaos to our door."

"But it is already decided," the Chancellor said. "Read the missive. The only question before us is whether we answer his summons or stand in defiance."

"We cannot war with the crown," Alteres wailed.

"Nor should we war with our countrymen," Seriphenes said firmly. "I do not believe the king will send his armies against us, no matter what we choose."

There was silence for a moment, then the Chancellor sighed. "We can claim neutrality in this. The king will not like it, but I suspect you are right, Seriphenes. He is unlikely to attack us directly."

Claighan grunted. "That is not *enough*. We cannot afford to let him draw this army."

"Be still!" Seriphenes shouted, and I flinched in spite of myself. I knew the outburst far too well. "Who could stop this king from calling this army? And what reason could we give him? That a Master he has despised anticipates some dark apocalypse? Have you even seen a dragon?"

"I have seen a dragon," Claighan said, and a stunned silence fell in the room. There was a rustle of movement, and Claighan said, "On our doorstep, as you say."

"I am not interested in the drakes that play in the forested hills around far Cara," Seriphenes said. He tried to make it cutting, but he faltered.

There was grim confidence in Claighan's answer. "I do not ask you to be. I ask you to consider the threat of an adult black no more than a day's ride from here."

"Impossible," Leotus cried, but Seriphenes did not answer.

Alteres spoke up. "I had heard rumors," he said. "From out of Pollix. In the Sorcerer's Stand?"

"Indeed," Claighan said. "I have seen it with my own eyes. It has a summer lair among the cliffs at the heart of the woods. And there are more. I've found signs of them among the hill breaks to the west, and in the highlands to our east. There are new stories of serpent strikes among the sailors of the channel, and I have stood in a shadow dark as night while an elder blue flew above me beneath the Drakespines to the north."

"Impossible," Leotus said again, but his voice quavered now. My own pulse raced, and I felt a weakness in my arms and shoulders. There had always been dragons in the histories and stories. The king's own father had killed a drake with his own hands before rising to the throne. But never so many as Claighan described. Never all at once.

"I lay no stock in the stories of fishermen," Seriphenes said, dismissive. "Nor in the tales highlanders tell. None of our histories describe any manner of dragon habitat there. The Drakespines, perhaps. It is a remote range, far from any significant populations. An ideal place for an elder to take refuge through the long years."

"And the Sorcerer's Stand?" Alteres asked. "You have an answer for that?"

"I have an answer," Seriphenes said, and Daven heard dark victory in his voice.

"No," Claighan said, his voice barely more than whisper.

"We shall settle it ourselves," Seriphenes said. "Three answers in a single action."

"No," Claighan said. "Don't be a fool. This is no hatchling drake—"

"I don't care if it's an elder legend!" Seriphenes said. "We are the Academy of Wizardry. We are the greatest power in this land. I'm tired of you slandering our power over guesswork and lies."

"The histories are clear," Claighan said. "Dragons do not obey our workings. We may not be able to harm them at all. That's why we must—" Seriphenes cut him off.

"I have seen the power in the Chancellor's hand," Seriphenes said. "I have seen my own terrible strength. Even yours, Claighan, is sufficient to make armies tremble. Tell me not of the histories. Did the wizards of yore have an Academy such as this to train them? We have unlocked mysteries and powers man has never known before. We can face a single scaled monster."

"You are a fool," Claighan said. "And soon to be a dead one."

"Claighan!" the Chancellor said, softly chiding, but Seriphenes cut over him.

"Leave him be," he said. "He is broken and sick with delirium. He speaks out of a melancholy. Does anyone else here truly believe we, combined, cannot answer the threat of a dragon?"

No one spoke. Claighan grunted, but he couldn't seem to find the strength to argue anymore. When Seriphenes spoke again, his words dripped with satisfaction. "Then, as I said, three answers in one. We shall settle Claighan's nonsense with incontrovertible evidence. We shall exterminate the threat of a dragon on our doorstep. And we shall demonstrate the power of the Academy to the king, before we stand in defiance of him. We shall hang the black beast's head above our gates, and let the king find soldiers willing to face a force capable of that action."

Silence fell on the room. After a time, Alteres spoke up. "Are you all agreed, then? Would you really stand in defiance of the king?"

"We will," Seriphenes said, before anyone else could answer. "We are the Masters of the Academy. Who is a king to call us like hounds to heel?"

No one answered that. I heard Claighan give a weary sigh, but he'd lost the strength to fight them. I stood there, stunned, leaning against the wall beside the open door.

And then a hand like tanned leather closed around the edge of the door inches from my ear. I startled back a step as the door swung silently open and a figure slipped through it. He was furtive, and I knew in an instant that he, too, had been eavesdropping on the war council, from within the antechamber. Likely he'd been the one who left the door cracked so I could listen in.

And I knew immediately why. He turned to me, and though I knew nothing of him but the shape of his wretched shadow against a wall, I knew him. He stank of sour sweat and cheap beer. His fine clothes were threadbare and grass-stained, and his long cloak showed the tatter of heavy use. His skin, too, was rough and sun-scorched, his features thin, and his deep-set eyes were dark with weariness and worry.

They fixed on me, and I expected him to shout. I expected him to run. I fumbled clumsily for my sword, stumbled one step back, but he flew to me in an instant. The traitor Lareth clapped one strong, stinking hand over my mouth. He slammed the other on my right wrist, trapping my sword in its scabbard, and hissed a word of power.

Empty air rained on me like the blows of a Guardsman's club. They cracked down on my shoulders and crashed against the backs of my knees, driving me down to the ground. And as I went the wizard went with me, stinking hand still clamped over my mouth. When I was flat on my back, he whispered another word and the crushing blows subsided.

He stooped there beside me, resting lightly on his heels. Then he threw one glance back toward the council hall. The Masters still muttered among themselves beyond the cracked door. Even as the thought crossed my mind the rebel wizard pulled a sturdy little work knife from his belt and pressed its tip into the soft skin beneath my chin. He pressed until the point bit against my flesh, then raised both eyebrows and removed his hand.

The Masters still lingered in their council hall. I knew I could cry out and bring them here—and he could slit my throat and disappear in an instant. So I held my tongue, trembling with fear and fury, and he watched my eyes with his head half-turned, as though he were also listening to the murmur in the other room.

After a moment he leaned closer. "Who are you?"

"Just a student at the Academy," I said.

His head twitched, and he frowned at me for a moment. Then I felt the knife tremble lightly against my throat and a cruel smile curved his lips. "Who knows you are here?"

I thought fast, closed my eyes for a heartbeat, and then looked up at him. "The Kind Father sent me," I said. "And I told the Chancellor's apprentice I would be here. And Master Claighan expected me."

"Ah," he said, disappointed, and then a moment later. "Ah. You are Claighan's boy."

I said nothing, but he saw confirmation somewhere in my expression. He grinned. "The things I'll be allowed to do to you...."

"You have done enough," I said. I tasted the bitterness in the words, and Lareth seemed to take great joy in it.

He hissed, "Tell me about it."

I wanted to spit at him. I wanted to hit him. I wanted to cry out, but I didn't dare. He rocked on his heels above me and pulled the knife away to rest his elbows on his knees. He was still close enough to kill me with one motion, but I saw my chance now. Delight at my predicament shone in his eyes. I remembered him beating Claighan for fun. He was doing the same thing now. He wanted to hear my pain, and I could use that. If I could keep him distracted long enough the Masters would find him on their own. And even Seriphenes could not protect this one if he were caught by the other Masters.

So I let my shoulders fall, let my very real frustration and anger show in my eyes. "You have personally cost me everything." I said. His eyes danced with pleasure. I shook my head. "Your treachery robbed me of the protection of the king."

Lareth gave me an unapologetic shrug. "A matter of unfortunate timing," he said. "I didn't even know you."

"That has made me a wanted murderer," I said, letting fear tremble in my voice. "And made my only patron a traitor still on his deathbed."

Lareth waved it away. "The old man had to go sometime."

I sat up, heaving my shoulders off the floor, and only stopped from striking him when he pressed the knife close again and I felt it break the soft flesh on my throat. He raised both eyebrows in threat and I sank back. I raised a hand to stop the trickle of blood, and he allowed it.

I looked away. "You've harmed far more than me," I said. "You've brought the whole nation to the brink of war."

"No," Lareth said. "The duke brought the nation to the brink of war. The king, in his arrogant pride, has pushed it over. And I, by the strength of my hand, shall settle the matter more swiftly than could otherwise be done."

"By your hand?" I sneered. "How will you settle the matter?"

His eyes shone. A smile of pure delight lit his face. He leaned close to whisper to me, pressing the knife's edge against the soft skin of my throat as he did. "I am going to kill the king. He sends his soldiers now, but they will not defeat us. They will not even find us. And when in time he comes in person, he will reclaim the city of Tirah. The brave victor again."

His breath flashed hot against my ear. I peered past his stringy hair, staring hard at the door to the council chambers, praying for them to come find us here.

Then Lareth drove those thoughts from my mind. "And then I will kill him. On the road to Tirah, surrounded by ten thousand of his men, I will strike him down and end this war." He pulled back, searching my eyes for the awe he knew would be there.

But there was no awe. There was only fear, desperation. This man would kill the king. That would not end the war, that would start an age of conflict like this nation had never known. I closed my eyes. I took a breath. And then I hit him.

From my place on the ground I threw a punch hard at his jaw, moving my other arm to push away at the knife against my throat. His shock saved my life, and gained me enough time to shout, "Claighan! Lhorus! Seriphenes!"

He snarled and fell forward against me again, and this time I knew he would kill me. I couldn't let him get away with that. I struggled, digging fingers hard into the wrist of his knife hand and clawing at his face with the other, but he didn't try to press the attack. Instead he caught a breath, and spoke a word. My world became pain.

I felt the traveling spin around me, violent and fast, threads sharp as knives and strong as steel snapping down against my flesh in all directions, then twisting tight. Squeezing. My vision faded to darkness. Then bursts of colored light flashed behind my eyes. And then it was over.

I ended up lying on my back, gasping for air. He stood over me, apparently unaffected, and pressed a boot down hard on my right wrist, pinning it to the polished wooden boards of a well-made floor. I felt my vision swim once more, watched unnatural colors wash in and out, and then at last the world settled back to normal. I found myself staring up at the side of a heavy office desk, two high-backed, narrow chairs off to one side, and a framed map of the Old Kingdoms hanging on the wall beside the door. I was in a study.

It wasn't Lareth's place. Not given his ragged clothes and dirty hair. This room belonged to someone else. From the looks of it, to someone of wealth and power. Someone of advanced education. And then a sudden understanding burned new anger into my heart. He hadn't bothered to take me away at all.

I felt the snarl twist my lips, and he laughed when he saw it. I ignored him, though. My right wrist was trapped, but I was no child. I spun at the waist, throwing my shoulders up off the ground and driving my left fist hard toward the side of his right knee. It might have been a crippling blow for all the ferocious strength I threw behind it.

But he spoke a word and danced back, and a web of magic air fell across me like a cast-iron blanket. It slammed me back against the floor and drove the breath from my lungs. Then he stepped forward and, pinned though I was, he brought his booted heel down hard on my right wrist once again. I screamed at the pain, but his weave of air stole even the expression of my agony from me. The wizard laughed.

And then the door flew open behind him. Seriphenes stalked in, eyes blazing. He threw the door shut and fixed a hard gaze on the wizard Lareth. "Give me three good reasons not to burn you to the ground."

Lareth grinned, lazy and delighted, and twisted his heel against my wrist. "First," he said, "for love of a prized and

202

cherished pupil. Second, for your own reticence to do what must be done. That stays your hand even as it makes me a terribly valuable asset to you."

Seriphenes's eyes stayed on Lareth, dark and demanding, and the traitor shrugged. "And third," Lareth said, "for apprehending your enemy's agent, spying on his betters."

The Master's eyes widened. Then they narrowed. They swung down to fix on me. Still, he spoke to Lareth. "You are a fool. A reckless, dangerous, terrible fool. You made yourself known to this one—"

"Easily enough remedied," Lareth said.

"No. Not without raising questions. He draws too much attention, wherever he goes."

"But look at him!" Lareth said. "He's packed for traveling. Let me take him back to my camp. Everyone here can think he has run away to join the war, and I can provide my unschooled soldiers an impromptu lecture on human anatomy."

Seriphenes made an irritated sound and shook his head. "No. No, that would not do. I must handle this myself." He considered me, eyes still narrow, then shook his head again. "Why have you come here, Lareth?"

"I had to know the decision of the war council."

"You did not trust me?" Seriphenes demanded.

"I honestly did not believe. Four good men of the king's. Five, with that old bastard suddenly awake. And somehow you carried a unanimous vote to defy him."

"They are easily swayed," Seriphenes said. His eyes lingered on me, and he frowned. "You have not stopped his hearing?"

Lareth shrugged. "I was still teasing him when you arrived."

Seriphenes considered me for a moment, and then the breath escaped him in a sound of regret. "It matters little, I suppose. He knows too much now."

Lareth gave a little bow. "Precisely why you should let me dispose of him, Master."

"No. I have other hands than yours, Lareth. And an opportunity has just presented itself."

Lareth frowned. Understanding showed on his face just as it came to me, too. "The dragon?"

"Four problems, now," Seriphenes said. "But it must be now. Keep him for an hour, locked up tight, and then let him go. And get out of here."

"What? We won't be sharing dinner?"

Seriphenes growled low in his throat. "You're a reckless fool," he said. "And someday it will get you very dead. Now more than ever, you must stay away from the Academy. I could not protect you if you had been caught."

He gestured down at me, turning it into a flourish. "But my master, *I* can protect me. See how well I've done?"

"Against a shepherd who cannot make a seeming of moonlight to save his soul?" Seriphenes snorted. "By all means, take pride in that. I've also heard your soldiers very nearly won an altercation with a loose formation of wild hogs. You're quite the tactical genius."

"Domesticated hogs, as it happens," Lareth said. His smile never slipped. "We lost three good men that day."

Seriphenes headed to the door, but he stopped before he opened it. He looked back at me, and I saw regret in his eyes. "Hold him," he said. "Do not scar him. He must be seen in public before the ruse is truly done."

And then he left, and Lareth turned his attention back to me. It is remarkable how much pain a wizard can cause without leaving the slightest scar.

10. The First Dragon

Worse than the physical pain was the memory of the wizard's threat. He meant to kill the king. The rebel duke had started this war, but the king had more than enough resources to quash a minor rebellion. The threat was not the duke, but the battle wizard who had joined him.

Yet even with Lareth assisting the rebel soldiers in battle, he was only one man. The threat had been of more lives lost before stability returned. More stupid soldiers like Cooper stretched dead on the battlefield. But this was something different. If Lareth could strike at the king personally, if he could actually succeed in this plan, he could break the kingdom. That was something Duke Brant never could have hoped to accomplish, but Lareth just might.

I winced beneath invisible blows, but I trembled in fear of the world torn apart. We wouldn't even need Claighan's dragonswarm. If Lareth killed the king, we could destroy ourselves.

But something struck me in the heart of my fear. There was an opportunity here. If I could just survive, if I could carry warning to the king, if I could thwart Lareth's plan, I'd be a hero. Forget the amnesty, if I could help the king break Lareth's power, I could end this war.

I found myself laughing at the thought, a low, dark chuckle that seemed to drive the wizard mad. He struck harder and harder, but I clung to my hope. Let him hurt me now. If I could just survive, I would destroy him.

He finally relented when the bell began to ring. I'd missed the supper bell while I was packing, but it certainly wasn't yet even bell. It rang differently, too, high and sharp and insistent instead of the slow, steady toll of the hour. It was a summons. Seriphenes had used his hour well.

A moment after the first tolling of the bell, the door to Seriphenes's office opened and Archus stepped through it. I'd gone five months without catching more than a glimpse of the apprentice. It hadn't been long enough. I would have been happier if it had been a lifetime.

The disgust in his eyes as they passed over me, curled up and crying on the floor, said he felt the same way. His gaze passed on to take in Lareth, too, and the two stood considering each other for some time.

They made a sharp contrast. Lareth wore his blond hair long and loose, and his blue eyes looked astonishingly pale against his sun-dark skin. His white tunic and black breeches had both been fine once, but they were both worn and well on their way to gray. He was probably still a year or two shy of thirty, but the years had not been kind.

Archus, though, could not have been more than nineteen. He held himself tall and straight, dressed in perfect black silk and satin to match his short, dark hair and his flashing eyes. It all stood in stark contrast to his pale, smooth skin. The only trait he shared with Lareth was his cruelty.

And contempt. The two regarded each other with undisguised disdain. Then Archus nodded, a peremptory gesture. "You've done your job. Now you should go."

The wizard sneered. "I do not take orders from children."

"You don't take orders from anyone but your own reckless folly," Archus said. "Regardless, there is quite a bustle of Masters about, and it would be worth your head if you were even glimpsed. So go back to hiding in your hole. I'll take care of the shepherd."

My stomach clenched at that, but there was nothing I could do. Chains of air bound me hand and foot, and a cruel muzzle pinched my mouth shut and left me barely enough room to breathe. I could only lay on my side and pant and pray.

The two of them stared in mutual hatred a moment more, until another peal of the bell pulled Archus's attention. He waved a hand in dismissal and turned away. He frowned, considering me like a puzzle, and then I felt the bonds of air stretch and shift, still clamped tight around me, but they rolled up my forearms like splints.

There was a break at my elbow, but more rigid force around my biceps, and around my thighs, and calves. I felt the air lock around me like perfectly-fitted pieces of plate armor. Then Archus considered his invisible handiwork for a moment and nodded in satisfaction.

He quirked a smile, bent a hand, and said, "Come." To my horror I obeyed.

Or, rather, the worked-air obeyed. The bonds around my right calf shifted, forward and up, and I had to bend my knee or let the bone break. The cuff drifted forward, then set itself, and the bonds on my left leg repeated the gesture. On the second step he moved my arms, too, jerkily at first, but before I reached the corridor he was controlling me like an able puppeteer.

I heard Lareth bark a laugh of approval behind me, and then the door slammed shut, and Archus guided me down and down to the floor of the tower and out into the red-tinged evening light.

The courtyard around the Tower of the Masters was mostly empty, though I saw the Chancellor hurrying across it at a distance. I fought Archus's bonds then. I struggled with all my might against them, but they might as well have been cast iron. I tried to scream against the muzzle on my mouth, but I couldn't manage much more than a moan, and he did not even look my way. Archus stepped up beside me, so I could see the satisfied smile on his face, and then he pushed me on ahead.

He led me around the northeast corner of the Halls of Learning, and onto the north edge of the Arena. The stark, dusty courtyard stretched half a mile before me, and as soon as we entered it I was overwhelmed by the bustle of motion. It had probably been this full when I had come to challenge Archus, but I hadn't had the attention to spare then. Now I had no control over my body, I could not even turn my head, so I stared out over the milling crowd as I trod inexorably ahead.

The whole of the student body seemed to be gathered in the Arena. All in a throng the students of the Academy were rushing out from among the buildings and into the courtyard. They didn't mill about, either. They organized into tight square formations and then moved smoothly to the south.

Among the rushing bodies I caught sight of someone familiar. Themmichus stood at the edge of the courtyard, standing on one of the rough stone outcrops to see over the crowd, eyes scanning desperately left and right. He was looking for me. I tried again to resist, to catch his attention. If Themmichus saw me with Archus he would know something was wrong. Muzzled or not, I'd find assistance from him. I threw my gaze hard against him, hoping to draw his attention with the weight of it, but he was mostly watching students flowing out from between the buildings. Archus and I were the only ones coming from the Masters' yard.

I had a thought, a spark of desperate hope, and I closed my eyes. I flashed through the exercises I'd learned from

Antinus, and then for good measure worked through them again, settling into a distant, removed kind of calm. I could still feel my heart battering, feel the pinching pain every time one of Archus's cuffs bent me to his will, but it was a flutter on the edge of my mind. I focused my attention and imagined the world as I needed it to be.

I didn't try to touch Archus's working. One wizard can undo another's magic, but it is a challenge of skill and strength, and I could not yet challenge Archus at either. I only hoped to catch Themm's attention. I marched on forward, without spending a thought on the motion, and instead poured all my attention into a gust of wind, a puff of force to bump Themmichus around so he would see me and my captor.

I poured every ounce of will into it. I built the belief in my head as they had taught me. I felt it settling slowly together, jagged edges falling into place. It congealed until it was almost real, almost believable. I expected him to stumble, to turn. Any moment now—

And then I felt a horrible pain on the back of my head and light flashed behind my eyes. My head didn't move, pinned in place by Archus's bonds, so I took the full force of the invisible blow. It shattered my concentration, my focus, even my careful calm. I scrambled to put it back together, but beside me Archus growled, "Don't. I can see what you are doing."

I felt a cold fear claw at my stomach, but I fought to force it away. I tried to regain the necessary self-control, but panic pushed it off. We were ten paces away from one of the fast-forming knots of students, and I saw Archus was guiding me behind them. In a matter of moments we'd be lost among the crowd. And then I heard someone bark Themmichus's name, loud and impatient, and as I watched helpless he frowned, jumped down from his vantage, and scurried to join another of the formations.

Archus didn't. Instead he marched me along beside the rearmost of them, and we moved slowly, steadily south toward a high platform that had been raised over the floor of the Arena. Two Masters stood upon it, dramatic in their long black robes. My eyes fixed on Seriphenes and I trembled within my shackles.

He turned his gaze on me, and I saw a single satisfied nod from him. There was no smile in his eyes, no cruel delight, nor was there any hint of mercy. He seemed grim and entirely committed.

The Master beside him was Leotus. I tried again to scream as we stepped up to the foot of the platform. I opened my eyes wide. I struggled against my bonds, but Archus stretched them with a thought and stole any slack I might have used.

The Master's eyes fell on me, and he gave a little chuckle. "Well, well," he said, amused. "Our little shepherd boy has come to join in our hunt. I'm sorry, Daven, but the call was for wizards. I've seen first-hand how little you can do. You'd be better served to pursue a career in the King's Guard. Or return to your fields—"

"No," Seriphenes said, cutting him off. "I sent for him, Leotus. I have hopes that when he sees the power at work in a real-world environment, he might find the breakthrough he needs."

Leotus swept his gaze to Seriphenes, and he frowned. "That seems a risky scheme."

Seriphenes shook his head. "I've tasked Archus with keeping him safe. My apprentice shouldn't have any trouble."

"A cruel task, that," Leotus said. He turned to Archus and gave him a wink. "I suspect your boy would prefer to be the one that bags the beast."

Seriphenes ducked his head in a slow nod. "I've no doubt he would. But he yet serves his punishment for reckless indiscretion."

"Oh ho!" Leotus laughed. He shrugged. "That was months ago! You are a cruel master." But he turned, gesturing with his whole body toward the foot of the platform. A portal stood there, like the one Claighan had opened to send me from Gath-upon-Brennes, but this one was twelve paces wide from end to end, a long rent in reality that showed a window on a forest glade that must have been dozens of miles away. As I watched, the last of the students' block formations filed through it. I could see the rest gathered there, waiting, and scanned desperately for Themmichus among them.

"Well, go on then," Leotus said. "Join up with your classes. Archus, take the boy with you, I guess."

"No," Seriphenes said. He placed a hand on Leotus's shoulder and shook his head, then he made a gesture with his other hand and a smaller portal opened directly before me. This one was just wide enough for Archus and me to pass through together, and it showed a darker bit of land, trees pressed thick, and rocky ground sloping steeply up away.

"I'd prefer them to keep their distance," Seriphenes said. "They are merely to observe, after all."

Leotus opened his mouth to argue, but after a moment he shrugged. He threw a compassionate glance to Archus then hopped down from the platform. "Watch close," he called back over his shoulder and headed toward the wider gateway. "And keep safe."

My eyes snapped back to Seriphenes, and I saw the same grim nod once more. He fixed his eyes on Archus and said, "You understand what you must do?"

I felt Archus nod beside me, and Seriphenes gave a little sigh. "Very well. Pay attention, be sharp, and do not make a single foolish mistake. You understand?" Archus nodded again, and Seriphenes weighed me, his eyes fixed on mine for the space of three heartbeats. Then he turned away, and stepped gracefully down to the earth. He headed for the other portal, too.

"When this is done," he said, "come find me in my study. I must know the precise details."

"Yes, Master," Archus said. "You will not be disappointed." Then I felt the same sharp pressure against my arms, my legs, against the base of my spine, and the dark-eyed apprentice pushed me through the Master's portal and into the woods of the Sorcerer's Stand.

I tensed trapped muscles against the twisting sensations of the portal, but felt...nothing. My last experience with a portal had tossed my mind about like a toy, but this time it was as though I had stepped through an ordinary door. I opened tight-squeezed eyes and found myself upon the forested foothills of a lone, ancient mountain. I looked around as much as my bonds would allow me, eyes straining, but there was no sign of the clearing that held the other students. I was alone with Archus.

And then I saw the dragon, and for a moment I forgot the fear and hatred I held for my captor. Instead I felt only a bone-deep, primal terror at the serpent shape dancing on the wind.

It must have been over a mile away, sweeping high through the air and then diving, a streamer of flame flickering on the breeze before it. It darted from view, diving in a deadly sweep toward the woods below, but in my mind's eye I saw it falling toward fifty half-trained students entirely unprepared. It swooped beneath my sight, but moments later it was wheeling back up, pursued across the horizon by little flashes of fire and light and a beam of searing energy that I could see clearly despite the distance.

I heard distant shouts, barely more than a whisper from here, and I longed to know how much damage was done. I thought of Themmichus, so full of principle and promise, and I hoped desperately that he was safe.

And then Archus reminded me that I was not. He grunted once, then stepped up the hill past me and turned his head slowly, scanning the hillside. He settled on a spot above us and to the left, dropped a hand on my shoulder, and spoke a word.

This time there was violence and pain, invisible strands biting sharply into my flesh as they had done when Lareth moved me to Seriphenes's study, and a heartbeat later I stood on rocky ground clear of any trees. The armor bonds that had clad me were gone, too, forgotten or destroyed by the violent traveling, but my legs gave out and spilled me to the earth.

"What are you doing?" I cried. I panted short, sharp breaths until the world steadied around me, and then I scrambled to my feet and faced him. He paid me no mind, brows knit in concentration while he scanned the hillside above us again. My hand fell to the hilt of my sword and for a heartbeat I considered attacking him. With his attention so focused on the dragon, I thought perhaps I could cut him down before he responded.

But I was not here to kill Archus. I was not here to kill a dragon. I had a far more important purpose to serve. I had to save the king. I was free of Lareth and away from the Academy. I could join the garrison at Pollix, take up the amnesty, and send warning to the king. All I had to do was survive. I watched the back of Archus's head for a heart-beat, but he paid me no mind. Then I turned in place and sprinted down the hill.

I made it three paces before I hit a solid wall of air. My forehead cracked hard against it and I rebounded off, and before I could recover he stepped calmly up behind me, his boots crunching on the gravel. He said, "No, that is the wrong way."

His hand fell on my shoulder and he worked another traveling. Higher up the mountain now, and I heard him make a satisfied sound. He didn't release my shoulder this time, and his grip was all that kept me on my feet. I spun at the waist and threw a jab at his jaw, but he stepped back and summoned air again to bind me.

It was not the elegant plates he'd used before, or the smothering blanket Lareth had called. It was more a belt that snapped around my arms near the elbows and gradually contracted until my upper arms pressed tight to my ribs. He didn't watch, didn't even look at me.

His behavior was odd. He didn't sneer at me. Didn't mock or punish. I seemed an afterthought, and he spent as little effort on me as necessary. Instead, his attention was sharp and focused, bent entirely toward a purpose I did not know as he scanned the mountainside above us one more time.

A shadow passed over me, and Archus's head turned slowly to watch its source pass above. He traced its trajectory, and a slow grin crept across his face. He turned to me.

"Once more," he said, "and then this will be done."

He reached for my shoulder and I tried to flinch away. The belt of air restrained me, though, and he made a second grab, pinched his eyes shut, and sent us up the mountain again.

The spell released the bonds around me, but before my vision had returned he had it in place again. I felt its tug against my stomach as it began pulling back and up, driving my elbows even harder against my ribs before it lifted me off my feet and up into the air.

I remembered him doing that in the courtyard at the Academy, putting me on display for all the students to see my shame. This time there were no laughing, mocking eyes. This time there was only Archus. And me.

And the dragon.

We were just above the treeline now, high up the mountainside and several miles from the site where the dragon had attacked before. I could just see the black scar of its fire marring a bit of woods, the tiny flicker of distant flames among the ancient trees.

There were few trees here. Instead it was all rock and dirt. Archus stood below me on a little ledge, a rare flat bit of land among the steep slope of the mountain's peak. Several paces beyond him the earth stabbed sharply up in a sheer cliff. The weathered stone face showed sharp gouges, the sort buck deer sometimes left in the trunks of trees with their antlers, and here and there it showed spots of coal-black soot.

And on the ledge around Archus there were corpses—of deer and bears and timber wolves, of sheep and cows and farmers' hogs. Some were rotten, some were charred, but none of them were picked clean. Carrion animals had not touched them, but something had feasted here, again and again.

The shadow swept over me again, and Archus lifted me higher into the air with a force of will. I strained against my bonds, trying to look up to see the dragon above me, but I could barely move. I collapsed against the belt and screamed at Archus.

"What are you doing?"

His eyes were not on me. They looked past me, high into the sky, attention wholly focused on the circling dragon. His voice was distant, too, as he answered me. "I am showing you what a real wizard is capable of," Archus said. "I am to convince you that you do not belong among us. And that you do not dare betray my master." He watched the dragon for a moment, eyes growing wide, and then he smiled to himself. "I believe you will find my case convincing."

The darkness that passed over me then was complete, black as night, and it did not flash by. Instead I heard the distant sound of beating wings, rapidly approaching. The dragon was coming for me. I felt my shoulders and neck tense, felt my whole body go rigid, but there was nothing I could do. It was coming for me.

Then Archus raised a hand, and a moment later he produced a wrist-thick beam of energy like the one I'd seen stabbing up from the forest floor before. It lanced past my right shoulder and I heard a sound above me, a snort, a *huff* like that of an angry bull. I saw surprise and frustration on Archus's face, and then felt a great buffeting wind slam against me, and the dragon rolled right past me. If my arms had been free, I could have reached out and touched it.

The thing was unimaginably huge. Its head alone was three paces long, from the tip of its snout to the base of its curving horns. The neck was even longer, sinuous and scaled, and behind it came broad shoulders supporting massive membranous wings. The thing's rib cage was probably larger than my room at the Academy, its hind legs taller at the joint than I would've been standing. Its long tail swayed behind it, drifting left and right with an immense, lazy power.

Rocking in the wind of its passing, I watched it swing out wide to my right, and then it curled back and flew like an arrow straight at Archus. I saw its jaw fall open, heard a cry from Archus beneath me, and then the beast unleashed a gout of flame that washed like a wave off the sea, three paces wide where it hit the ground beneath me. The fire rolled forward, consuming the discarded corpses and flowing over Archus as the great beast thrummed past directly beneath me.

The monster's momentum carried it by, sweeping out over the trees, and it left behind a fitful dance of dying flames on the hard, bare stone.

And Archus, barely visible through a thin layer of ash and soot that hung several feet distant from his body.

He gestured as though brushing a bit of lint from his shoulder, and whatever magical shield he had woven dissipated, leaving the black cake to drift like snow to the charred rocks below. The dragon curled lazily around, and when it spotted Archus it roared in defiance and frustration and came rushing back. Terror made my muscles weak and watery, but Archus faced the dragon's charge with a deep, perfect calm and began to chant the words of a spell. My eyes flew from him to the dragon and back, and hanging helpless as I was, I hoped with all my heart that he would win.

The dragon did not waste its flame again. It swooped in low, legs flashing to a gallop as it reached the ground, and moved straight from flight into a full sprint across the rocky clearing and straight at Archus. The wizard's apprentice didn't flinch, didn't budge. He continued his low chant. And when the dragon was ten paces distant, Archus cried out in a voice of certain power and light flashed all around him.

It was a single flare of light, bright as a sun, and the flash of it blinded my eyes. It must have done the same for the dragon because the beast roared and faltered in its rush. It stumbled, tail lashing violently as it tried to hold its balance, but it tripped and skidded past Archus on its right side. If I had been free I would have dashed in to open the thing's belly with the Green Eagle's sword, then and there, but Archus merely turned in place, tracking its motion, and I saw a confident smile on his lips.

Then he spoke again, and a dozen little silver flames began to dance over his palms. The dragon climbed to its feet some short distance away. It seemed hesitant now—not afraid, but patient. It turned its head and looked down on Archus, almost mesmerized by the young man's spell. I recognized the glowing globes of force that danced in the air before Archus—the spell had been one of Themm's favorite tricks—but the number and size and intricacy of the power Archus juggled astounded me. The dragon tilted its head like a bird and watched, waiting.

Suddenly Archus shouted a command crisp and clear, and the silver flames flashed through the air. Still the bolts of power danced, weaving together and flowing apart as they flew toward the beast. It never moved, and the silver lights struck the beast full in the face. Themmichus had once knocked me down with a bolt a tenth as strong as Archus's, but now a dozen globes of focused power smashed into the dragon's flesh...and melted. The monster blinked down at Archus and I imagined I could see cruel laughter in its eyes. Archus must have seen that, too, but he held his ground. He was smart enough to change tactics, though.

He shifted his stance and lifted his arms into the wild, sweeping patterns of the more primal weather magic. I'd attended a handful of Leotus's theory lectures on them, but I'd never seen the magic worked. But hanging there, watching Archus fold his motions into the massive clash of wind and water, fire and earth, I could feel the air around me answer. The air sparked with energy, and unseen pressure pushed painfully against my eyes.

Below me as he flowed through the motions his satisfied smile fell into a fierce grimace. His graceful composure became a frantic dance as he fought forces he had merely caressed before.

Though Archus was lost in the magic, the beast was not, and it looked down at him through the eyes of an angry beast, not those of a wizard. So it watched (as I watched) and saw (as I saw) not a terrible wizard casting deadly spells but an enemy arrogantly offering an unprotected heart. I saw the danger and screamed to warn him, but in that instant a bolt of lightning flashed, a pure pillar of heavenly fire slamming down just beyond my reach. My voice was drowned by the twin roar of the thunder and the injured dragon as the bolt struck home.

I blinked furiously, frantic to know what came next. When finally I could see again, I beheld the dragon fallen on its side. A great wound gaped in the shoulder of its left foreleg and bled wet and black all along its ribs. The beast flopped once, then the neck and tail both swayed together and with an enormous strength the animal heaved itself back to its feet.

It fell back on its hind legs and raised up to a terrifying height. The long neck snaked left and right, the beast's eyes fixed on Archus, and I felt sure the thing could simply snap its long neck down and swallow him at a gulp.

But below me Archus kept his eyes fixed on the dragon's head, and perhaps he anticipated the same thing because he moved, shifting left and right, forward and back, almost like a duelist positioning, preparing himself to leap, to dodge the deadly strike.

But at the same time he was already caught again in the dance that would summon another lightning strike. Anger flooded through me—at Archus's arrogance and my own inability to act. I shouted at him, "Watch him, Archus! He has more dangers than his teeth!"

I saw a flicker of irritation cross Archus's face, but he paid me no more attention than that. I struggled against my bonds, but they had no give. "Wind and rain, Archus, let me go! I can help you!" Or I could run. Either way, I needed to be free.

But this time he didn't even frown. He focused all his attention on the storm above, and threw his arms high above his head. A second bolt flashed, searing across my vision, but I heard what I could not see as the dragon's spike-tipped tail lashed forward and drove clear through Archus's body. By the dragon's scream I knew that this bolt too struck true. But the soft, wet sound of the apprentice's body falling against the stone told me the fight was over. And then my bonds were gone, and I was falling.

I twisted in the air and hit the ground hard on my right shoulder. I pulled myself into a roll as I landed, tumbled several paces, and threw myself up off the ground. Still blind from the lightning strike I lurched into a sprint across the rocky ledge.

Fear clawed at my spine, at the back of my mind, and it settled cold and empty into my muscles. I tripped, stumbled three steps and barely kept my feet. My breath burned hot in the back of my throat, short and sharp, and I could feel death all around me. Distraction turned my ankle and sent me sprawling on the stones of the hillside, bloodying my face and my left hand, and I scrambled and slipped three times before I got to my feet.

And then I thought not of Archus, facing down a dragon, but of an old friend and enemy named Cooper. I remembered with a perfect clarity sneering at him and telling him he would die the first time he fought a true enemy. He would panic, and he would die. Some desperate shred of pride deep inside me refused to do the same.

I took one long breath and forced it evenly out. Discipline returned to me slowly. It was not one of the exercises Antinus had taught me, but one I'd learned myself from a battered old fencing text. I drew the fine, expensive sword from its sheath upon my hip and the cold weight of it in my hand did more than all the clever exercises to ground me in reality. In the space of three heartbeats I was on my feet again. By the fourth, I was moving at a sprint.

More of my training served me, then. Still half-blind, as much from fear as from the aftereffects of the lightning, I drew up my memory of the environment around me. I'd seen enough of it, hanging helpless in the air, and I skipped past a spill of loose stones and bounded over a fallen limb even as I heard the dragon suddenly stirring behind me.

Archus's second bolt must have done more damage than the first, and the dragon's own injuries had slowed it more than my frenzied shock had slowed me. It moved behind me now with the rustle of its great wings spreading and settling and the grinding clatter of its tail sweeping slowly across the broad rocky ledge.

I could not escape it in a rush down the hill, not as fast as that thing flew, and I had no hope of climbing higher. Instead I sprinted straight at the cliff face, trusting to a fragile memory and a desperate hope. Off to the left, near the end of the ledge, creeping vines grew up onto the cliff face and pooled against the ground, but in one spot, low against the ground, a shadow stood behind them.

I dove, even as I heard the dragon begin to pace behind me, and I prayed. My right shoulder and hip slammed against the ground, parallel to the cliff, and I twisted as I slid, stabbing my legs toward the cliff face. I braced myself against a jarring impact, but my feet tangled in the climbing

221

vines and tore them free and then stabbed on down into the cliff.

There was a cave, almost a tunnel, little more than a pace tall and half that wide at its mouth. It was a chimney that might have reached deep into the dark heart of the mountain, but it narrowed quickly and I slammed to a stop, hips and shoulders scraping against the rough walls, ten or fifteen feet down into the tunnel.

For a moment I lay on my back in the darkness, staring up at a stone ceiling I could touch without sitting up. I gulped desperate breaths, from fear more than exertion, and I forced myself back through calming exercises until I could reason. My right arm stretched out behind me, above me, dragging the fine sword against the earth. I tried to roll that way, but a stabbing pain in my shoulder and arm told me it was useless.

I clenched my teeth against a nauseating wave of pain, took three slow breaths, then rolled the other way. I pushed myself up with my left hand, then reached out and took the sword up in that one. I pressed forward two short steps, back toward the dim light at the mouth of the cave. I settled into an awkward crouch, inched forward more, still ten feet back, and tried to see what waited for me without.

There was some small sunset light still, and it began to filter through as the sky cleared—the storm energies Archus had harnessed falling back into their natural patterns. But as I crept closer to the cave mouth, something moved across it and total darkness washed over me. Then I heard a snuffling sound, and a cruel red light appeared straight before me.

Firelight danced above and behind a long, forked tongue as slick and black as bitter blood. Around the tongue shone a double-row of teeth, razor sharp and stained with smoke and soot. Then it shifted and the beast withdrew half a pace, firelight still spilling dimly into the tunnel but far enough back that it could cast its gaze down in. The dragon stared at me. I saw myself reflected in its cauldron eye, saw it measuring, weighing, remembering its fight with Archus before.

And then the eye blinked closed. It took a little breath, and a puff of cold air washed up out of the mountain around me, sucked into the dragon's maw, and the flame went out.

Darkness fell.

I could still sense the dragon in the space above me. I could feel its massive presence, hear the clatter sounds of the great body's small motions against the graveled ground. I could not see it, though. I could not guess what it had in mind. It did not simply blast me with its flame, perhaps suspecting I could shield myself as Archus had done. I was too far back for it to reach with claws or teeth, but I thought of the spike-tipped tail that had ended Archus's life. Perhaps it would be awkward, but if the animal could position itself to sling that thing at me, I would have nowhere to go.

I raised the sword before me, steady in my fingers, and I did my best to imitate a dueling stance within the low and narrow cave. I made myself a tiny target, sideways to the dragon's position, and held the blade protecting me from hip to eye. It was remarkable how much of a swordsman's body could be protected with that narrow blade if he knew how to hold it.

But that required knowledge of his enemy's stance as well, and I was blind. I squeezed my eyes tight shut in the darkness, fighting to hold my self-control, and took deep breaths to steady anxious nerves. The darkness pressed in on me, a physical weight, and I wanted to scream my frustration.

I didn't. Instead I bit my lip and reached into my swordsman's calm to grasp at the exercises a wizard had taught me. I forced my mind to relax as my muscles were relaxed, forced my thoughts into discipline as I had trained my body. And halfway through the patterns Antinus had taught me I felt myself fall into a state of quiet self-awareness that I had never quite achieved before. I sensed a bitter weight pressing down on me, immobilizing me, and recognized it as my own fear. I reached out with my will toward that weight, cracked it, and it fell away. The thing that broke and fell was an imaginary thing, no more than a mental construct...but then, so was my real fear.

And as I broke the black weight in my mind, I felt my breath come easier. I felt my arms grow lighter. I reached out again, sensing with my new intuition, and felt the cold, inky darkness that washed around me like water. But when I reached out with my mind I found I could sense through it, feel the stone beyond, feel even the great beast looking down on me. Inside my head, I could *see* it.

And in that moment, for the first time, I understood. In that instant I could truly see. Just as Claighan had said I someday would, in that instant I saw the lines of forces and powers that were at work all around me. I saw the immensity of the mountain above, the durability and weight of each individual stone and the great ageless mountain in one seamless piece.

I could see the cold power of death in my light sword, and the bright, hot flare of blood where I had scraped my hand. I saw dancing threads of air outside the cave, a gentle breeze, and felt even the distant angry magic of the storm Archus had conjured. My body was trapped in that tiny tunnel, in total darkness, but my senses reached for miles. I had always paid attention to my surroundings—more than most—but for the first time in my life I was truly *aware*. I felt like I was seeing the world for the first time. Everything before had been a dream, soft, ephemeral, unreliable. But *this* was real. I had no doubts.

In the midst of all this revelation, though, there was a puzzle. I could see the threads of air dancing around the dragon at the cave's mouth, but I could not see the dragon itself. The dragon was not simply invisible to that second sight, but a terrible well of emptiness. Where the beast's head should have been, drawn in perfect clarity before my second sight, I saw instead a deep abyss into which the light of human power had never shone, a darkness magic could not touch. I understood then what Claighan had seen, what he had known. Perhaps some edges of human workings could injure or irritate this beast, but true magic would melt within that darkness like a snowflake in a blacksmith's blaze.

But I did not need my second sight to see the dragon. Not now. Bathed in understanding, I did what I could never do at Seriphenes's command. I saw the world as it was. The mountain was real. The sky was real. But light and darkness were flimsy, oft-changing things. I could see the darkness that lay around me, but I could see too the memory of the light the dragon's flame had spilled, the traces of sunlight that came and went. I fixed in my mind the image of the cave as it could be. As I wished it to be. I extended my arm before me, the blade held high, and commanded, "Light!"

And it was. A light flared to fill the cave and I saw in perfect clarity. There above me was the dragon, still staring down, watching me with the patience of ages. It hissed in fury at the sudden flare of light, and I remembered what Archus had done before. I felt a great thrill of accomplishment as the beast's head pulled back, open wide in an angry growl—

And then I had a plan. Still in that awkward crouch, still with my sword in the wrong hand, I braced my foot against the cave floor, tightened my grip on the hilt of that perfect weapon. I pressed up, sliding my forward foot along the stone floor an inch at a time, then dragging my right foot after. The dragon came close again, and I saw the fire kindle once more in the back of its maw. I made another little advance, sweating in a sudden heat, and forced myself to hold a fighting calm. I took one slow, measured breath. I forced it out. And with a final prayer, I lunged.

It should have been perfect. I came so close. The dragon never expected any physical threat from me, pinned and puny as I was. I fixed my eyes on the soft, blue palate at the top of its open mouth and shoved my heavy blade forward and up. But my back foot planted for the lunge and then, just as I threw my weight, my boot slipped against a smear of my own blood that I had left upon the stone.

And there was no room in the narrow tunnel for even that much error. My right foot lost its grip and my left foot extended too far. Even as the tip of Othin's blade struck true—I felt the shock as it parted tender flesh—even then I knew it was not the deathblow I had hoped for.

Before I had time for disappointment, my knee buckled and I crashed to the stone floor. I landed hard against the thick, scaled jaw of the beast. My extended arm was in its mouth, and as I came down my own weight ripped my arm open against the beast's double-row of teeth. My flesh tore open from shoulder to wrist. Blood gushed into the beast's open mouth, and I screamed in pain and terror.

In a moment of strange clarity, I watched a single, immense drop of the dragon's black blood pool on the pommel of my sword, and then it fell against my open wound.

In that instant my world exploded in fire, overwhelming every pain I'd ever known. Scrambling, frantic, I pushed away with my good arm, trying to get free, but already I felt the sulfurous poison of its blood coursing through my veins. I don't know when I stopped screaming, or if I stopped screaming, because the fires raging in my soul drowned out any earthly noise. I know I managed to shove myself some distance from the beast, but surely it wasn't far enough to put me beyond the reach of its wrath. In the instants before my world went black I wondered why it hadn't killed me yet. Or if it had.

When I woke an eerie silver moonlight hung in the low fog all around me. At first I thought I hadn't moved, for I was stretched out on a rock floor strewn with gravel, but after a moment I realized the soft shape beside me was the cooling form of Archus. That recognition should have brought some response, but my body was too weak and my mind too numb. I reached again for the calm I had found in two different disciplines, but both eluded me. There was nothing to push against, nothing to push away. I was adrift.

Far above me, I saw the perfect circle of the full moon riding high. I stared at it and struggled to remember. I thought of my injuries, my left arm torn to ribbons. I turned my head, and my awareness washed slowly around as though I were drunk or dreaming. I saw a scar seared into the flesh the length of my arm, a single jagged, sinuous shape from shoulder to wrist.

I remembered the sword that I had left in the dragon's mouth and felt a pang of regret. It had been a terribly fine blade. The thought skittered away, though.

I shook my head. I took a slow breath and pushed it away, but it did little to clear my head. I tried to sit up, but my body did not respond. I was too weak.

I rolled my head and looked around. Not at Archus on my left, but at the other forms that shared this plot with me. Corpses. Victims. All blackened now by the dragon's flame.

I shivered at the thought and wondered how I had come to be there.

I brought you here.

The words exploded in my mind, and I screamed. I screamed until my throat protested, until I could not wheeze another breath. And even in the grips of my terror I felt a moment's strange curiosity. Behind that, as my breath ran out, I felt a deep, rolling laugh inside my head. And I felt the emotion of it, too, a giddy amusement. After a moment it subsided, and the dreadful fear flooded back into its place.

And in the silence, the same voice boomed within my mind. *Who are you? What have you done?* I felt the shape of the question but it was not a matter of discussion. It came like a demand, and I could no more withhold an answer than resist a tidal wave.

I answered without thinking. "*I am Daven, son of Carrick, of Chantire and of Terrailles. I have fought a dragon and died.*" There was only silence, long and pensive, before the voice echoed through my mind again.

You have not died yet, human. First I would know what you have done to me....

I felt the thunder of its wings before the dragon slammed to earth above me. It planted two feet with talons like sickle-blades on either side of me. Its neck arced high, and its head stabbed down at me, teeth flashing. But it did not strike. It stopped far enough away to fix its massive eyes upon me, and it spoke again into my mind.

What is this treachery? How did you get into my head?

I felt the full force of the monster's hatred. It thrummed through my veins, cold and bitter, and I trembled beneath its gaze. I shook my head. "*I don't know,*" I said. "*I only wanted to live!*"

The monster's laugh echoed in my mind again, and I saw fire dance in the back of its throat. *You will not live,* it said. *And yet...I cannot kill you.* There was nothing of mercy behind the words. There was fury, outrage, and it flared up in me as though it were my own. *Tell me what you've done!*

Again I could not resist the command, but I could not answer it either. I shook beneath the beast like a leaf in a furious gale, and after some time it relented. It pulled its head back, and after a moment withdrew a pace. I lay there panting until I could catch my breath, and then I sat up.

My gaze touched Archus then skittered away. I felt the presence of the other corpses again, and fear boiled deep in my stomach. I closed my eyes. *"Why did you bring me here?"*

The monster laughed inside my thoughts. *I brought you here to die.* For a moment silence settled again, and I felt the weight of the creature's patient, ageless pondering. *But you have done something to corrupt my mind, wizard. Something I have never seen, nor has any whose mind I have touched. And I wish to know what it is you did before I kill you.*

It should have been too much for me, but somewhere within me I found a new source of strength. I felt the beast's curiosity, too, and it stirred something within my mind in answer. I should have passed out from the pain or gone blank from the shock, but instead I bent my mind to the question. I pushed myself unsteadily to my feet and looked up into the giant face of the dragon. Cautiously, but with surprisingly little fear, I reached out and touched the tip of one of those sharp teeth. I felt the enormous power of the beast crouched before me, and I shook my head in quiet admiration.

"I did not come here to kill you," I said.

It laughed again. *You could not touch me.*

"And yet I did," I said, musing. "I never meant to. I did not wish to challenge you at all. I only want to leave."

229

Then you are smarter than those you came with, the dragon said, and against my wishes my head turned and my eyes fixed on the dead form of Archus. A hole as large as my fist pierced him just below the sternum. The earth was sticky with his blood. His face was smooth and still.

"*I hated him.*" The words formed in my mind, distant, almost curious. They held no heat now. "*He was a monster.*" I remembered his plan, and I nodded slowly. "*He used me as bait to draw you to him.*"

He needn't have spent the effort. I would have come hunting after his power from a hundred evenings' flight.

I had no answer for that. I shook myself, though, and pushed the gruesome sight of him away. As I did, I regained enough control to turn my head. It was not enough. I took a long step away, and then another. I walked all the way to the end of the ledge before the dragons' thoughts stopped me in my place.

I will not let you live.

"*I only want to go,*" I said. "*If you would kill me, why haven't you done so already?*" The beast didn't answer me. After a moment's silence I turned in place and stared up at the dragon. It reared over me as it had towered over Archus here. And, gradually, I became aware of the resentment and outrage burning against me. It was foreign, unnatural, and with an effort of will I forced it away. I stepped through the exercises Antinus had taught me and they gave me control enough to push the anger from my mind.

Even as I did the dragon roared. It blasted a burst of brilliant red fire high into the night sky and then moved. The spike-tipped tail lashed forward like a whipcrack. It flew like lightning. It drove at me just as it had at Archus.

The force that froze me in place then was not the one that had turned my head to look on Archus. It was not the alien authority that had stopped me short of running. It was fear, deep and terrible, and entirely my own. I froze while the tail lashed at my heart.

But it did not reach me. It slowed, and behind the barrier I'd built in my mind I could feel the dragon's perfect fury as its tail fell limp at my feet. The beast roared again and lunged forward. Talons as long as my arm raked at me and I jumped back. But the tail snaked around again, and though it hadn't been able to stab me it had no trouble wrapping around behind my legs and tripping me.

My shoulders hit the ground hard enough to drive the breath from my lungs and the dragon was upon me in an instant. Those talons slashed forward, straight at my head. But they missed. They scored deep into the stony earth on either side of my throat, but they did not touch my flesh.

The beast roared. It bellowed a rage as deep as the mountain's heart, and seared the sky with an arc of fire that burned into my vision and filled my nose with the stink of soot.

And then it collapsed on the ground before me. I could feel its emotions in a corner of my mind, confusion and frustration and pure, deep hatred.

For a long time I lay motionless, but the beast did not stir. I realized it was panting, catching its breath, and I felt some touch of hope. The monster had worn itself out. It hadn't been able to harm me. I felt a new pang of anger hot on the heels of that thought and shook my head.

If it couldn't hurt me, then I could leave. I climbed to my feet and saw its eyes narrow. It snorted, a hot *huff* of smoky air, but it did not move. I took a long step back, and a growl began in the monster's throat.

I am not done with you.

I shook my head and took another long, slow step away. *"I have no quarrel with you."*

Oh, but you do, the dragon said, and it rolled slowly to its feet. I glanced back, then eased one leg down over the ledge's edge. I found a foothold on the steeper slope below, braced a hand against the trunk of a tree, and lowered my weight down to the hillside.

You will not escape, human.

I watched it. The beast did not want me to go. I could feel the certainty of that in my own head. It wanted desperately to kill me. But something stayed its hand. Hope danced to life, deep inside my heart, and I felt an answering rage from the dragon. I bottled it away and turned my back and started down the forest slope.

I heard the dragon bellow again behind me. It was a force of nature, a timeless power that had apparently survived an assault by half a hundred wizards of various degrees of training—including two full Masters among them—and had absorbed the full fury of a fiercely-powerful apprentice and stretched him dead upon the ground. Even with my mental defenses in place, I felt a healthy fear of the beast I had left behind me.

But it could not kill me. I swallowed once, reached deep for courage, and pressed my way down the steep hillside. I had to struggle to keep my balance, mostly falling from the support of one tree to another. And then a thought crossed my mind. The dragon could not rip or tear me, but could it harm me indirectly? It had thrown me to the earth hard enough to steal my breath. What was to stop it tumbling boulders down upon me from above? As I half-fell down the mountainside, I couldn't help wondering if the dragon could just snatch me up drop me to my death.

I made it another ten paces down the hill before I heard the thunder of its wings. And then talons strong enough to score stone closed around my shoulders with an astonishing care. I felt the barest pressure beneath my collarbone and then my feet lifted away from the earth. With a touch gentler even than the band of air Archus had used to lift me the dragon rose high into the night.

Dizzyingly high. I saw the full expanse of the Sorcerer's Stand laid out in a single inky blot beneath me, the mountain a charcoal blotch in its heart. I imagined I could see the Tower of the Masters on the Academy grounds off to the east, and I really did see the pencil-thin trail of the Brennes curling across the landscape north and east, and where it pooled into a long, low lake I knew the flowered gardens of Gath-upon-Brennes graced its shores.

I should have felt terror from the heights, but it seemed natural. Right. I flashed through the exercises Antinus had taught me and fought a sudden grin at the sight that flooded me. Deep in a sea of elemental air, I swam within a world of whisper-light magic, and though some part of my mind screamed with a fear that the dragon meant to drop me I shook my head. In my mind's eyes I could already imagine a net of empty air, catching me as I fell and lowering me gently down.

I felt the dragon's answering rage, and it swung out in a wide circle that showed me all of the Ardain, from east to west. And in the distance I saw the great sea. Some perverse curiosity rose up in my heart, the same voice that had made me question the dragon's limitations, and I wondered what I would do if it tried to drop me to the sea. I could slow my fall. Perhaps. I *thought* I could.

But that was a simple working. *Seeing* wasn't enough to work the kind of magic the Masters used. I had no clue how to weave a traveling. If the beast dropped me far enough offshore, simple exhaustion would drag me under the waves, magic or no.

I felt the dragon's flash of satisfaction, and its lazy circle turned into a beeline for the coast. My calm shattered. The magic sight fled me. Fear bubbled up in my heart, and even my mental defenses failed. I felt my own fear wash away in the dragon's flush of victory.

"Don't," I cried. "Why? Why are you so determined to kill me?"

You are man, the dragon said. I am serpent. The question needs no more reason than that.

"*I don't want to die!*" There was no nobility in the words, no hint of courage or dignity. I was beyond such things. Terror reigned inside me, but I had barely thought the words before my own fear was subsumed by the dragon's deep, satisfied laughter.

Below us the edge of the earth flashed away, deep blue waters churning far, far away. The dragon soared on, until even at that altitude I could barely see the shore far away. I tried to twist within its grasp, scrabbling desperately for some grip on its talons. If I could hold on, if I could climb up its leg and find a better grip—

Stop that, the dragon grumbled in my mind, and I felt its will bear down upon me. The strength faded from my arms, from my grabbing fingertips. I did as Antinus had taught me, sought my self-control, and gradually regained dominion of my body. I forced my hand up higher, gripping the sharp-edged talon, and my other hand went higher still and found the hard plates like armor that covered much of the dragon's hide. If I could just reach those I could find a grip secure enough the dragon couldn't shake me off.

Stop that! it said again, and I felt a wash of the dragon's impatience and frustration. I felt its will battering at the back of my mind, but my grip on the talon only tightened. If I just remembered my training the beast could not overpower me. If I kept control of my thoughts, I could survive this. I set my jaw and reached higher still.

And then I felt my stomach lunge up into my throat. I was weightless. I felt the air rushing around me. The dragon's grip was gone, and I fell from nearly half a mile above the sea.

I screamed in terror, and in the back of my head I felt an echo of satisfaction from the dragon. I could see it, in my second sight, a deep and perfect emptiness within the night sky. I watched the winds wash against it, around it, and felt below me the ancient, patient, crushing powers of the waters that wear mountains down to sand. I could feel the energy flooding through me, too, the power of my own will, but it was miniscule and fragile against the water and the wind.

Despite the dragon's satisfaction at my scream I could feel a lingering irritation. I had driven it to act sooner than it intended. I found little confidence from that, even as terror clawed at the edges of my vision. I scrabbled desperately to grab at the strands of air around me, but magic didn't work like that. The threads I saw in my second sight were pure power, chaos energy, outside the reach of a wizard's will. I could bend their effects to make a working, but I could not use them directly.

To do a working I had to form a separate reality, and invest it with confidence and will. And focus. But I gained speed as I fell, far too fast toward the earth. My second sight receded, fading with my control, and I flew again through my exercises, and again, until I held some measure of control. And then I began building a reality. I thought of the net I'd imagined earlier. It had seemed so simple a thing. But as I fell faster and faster, the jagged edges of my working rattled apart and it disintegrated. I started over again.

Above me, the dragon swung around and passed back to the east, watching my fall. As I stared at it I saw something new pulsing through that abyss of black nothing. I saw a single weaving, pulsing thread of crimson that danced in a fragile maze throughout the dragon's form. It was mystifying and enticing and, for reasons I could not possibly explain, the sight of it gave me strength.

I needed to survive. I closed my eyes and saw a pillow of air around me, a cocoon soft and slow, a bubble that could absorb the crushing force of my landing and drop me lightly into the waters. The thought snapped into perfect clarity in my mind, and I poured all my will into it. I spoke to give it shape, "Wind, catch me," and I felt a gentle pressure against my back. I slowed, slowed—

And then I struck the water's surface with enough force to shatter bones and crush my body like a flower underfoot. I had taken too long. Far above me I felt the pale pang of deep emotion—satisfaction or regret I could not say—and that thin stream of red danced within the darkness off to the east, and out of sight.

And then the sea swallowed me, and I was gone.

11. The Fisherman's Cabin

I woke to the sound of waves against the shore. Sunlight seared at me, bright and burning red even behind closed eyes. In one great gulp pain enveloped me. No tears came, no cries or even whimpers from a body too broken to complain. Instead I waited in horror as the agony built and built. A shiver dragged a groan from me, and I begged my body to suppress a second one, but it chased down my spine like living fire. I lay there in the sand, pinned down by the burning light of dawn and floundering in pain that lapped against me with the waves.

I turned back to the exercises that had nearly saved me. I reached for self-control, for some manner of distance and calm, but each new burst of stabbing pain shattered my concentration. Where I could not control my mind I struggled to control my body. I tried to move—to lift a hand to shade my face or just to bend a finger—and I cried without tears when my body refused to respond.

Methodically, painfully, I tried to move each part of my body. Starting with my toes, I reversed a swordsman's exercise and tried to tense muscles as I moved up, but I felt no response from any of them. Frustration and pain warred within me, and I longed for black oblivion. It would not come, so I forged on. I struggled with all my strength to twitch a toe, to bend a knee. Perhaps some of my efforts met success, but I felt nothing and dared not open my eyes against the piercing sun. I was too broken to move. My legs didn't work, I knew that for certain. Nor did my arms. And every time I tried to take a deep breath, I felt a sharp pain in my side and chest.

At last I reached the muscles in my neck and head. My jaw dropped open at my command, and then I gave a gasp of surprise that turned into a groan. For several minutes I just lay there, opening and closing my mouth. I felt some thrill of victory that bubbled over into manic delirium, and then a little curling wave jostled my leg, and pain exploded across my mind. I whimpered when I tried to scream and fell into black hopelessness. What good was that small amount of control against the paralysis that held me? What had happened to bring me here? I felt a dizzy wonder that I had survived the crushing depths, but to what end? I was broken and alone. I settled into another methodical investigation then, working through the ways that I might die.

Thirst would get me long before starvation. Exposure might get me faster. Perhaps internal bleeding—or external bleeding, for that matter. I couldn't raise my head enough to check. Or perhaps the dragon would come back to finish the job. It could drop a boulder on me and end things then and there. I closed my eyes and hoped for that. And then another frothy wave exploded pain across my brain.

Consciousness faded away and then returned like some cruel, hateful tide. The sun was higher, then. Hotter. Brighter. I baked in its rays and fought to catch my magic, if only to drag myself up out of the cursed waves. It was no use. My mind skittered like a foal on winter ice, and every working I imagined fractured still half-formed.

I drew a deep breath, and pain lanced in my side. The air escaped me in a rush, and for some time I could only pant and pray. I tried again, cautiously, filling my lungs slowly. It almost worked, but in the end I took too much, and pain flashed again. The sharp stab of it drew a cough that was worse than anything before. And then, thank mercy, I blacked out.

I don't know how long it took, how many tries, but finally I filled my lungs and screamed with all my might. I used up my air and my strength, and for ten minutes or an hour I lay there, panting and trying to fill my lungs once more. When I did, I shouted again, and my voice echoed out across the waters. It shimmered among the frothy waves and drowned beneath the pounding surf and blew away upon the ocean breeze. It took me four tries, and I think a fifth would have killed me, but finally I heard an answering shout that I first guessed was my imagination, and then hallucination.

Then a hand jostled my shoulder, and the pain destroyed my mind.

I woke up in blissful darkness. Agony still clattered against my mind—noisy and constant—but I pushed it away just as I had done the dragon's anger and fought to get my breathing level. I tried to rub at my face, but my arms didn't move. I blinked my eyes open and saw a thin gray light within what felt like a small room. Streaks of orange light stabbed down in front of me, narrow and irregular, and their edges blurred into the mottled darkness.

Fear knotted in my gut at that, but it was just another complaint among the many. I closed my eyes to shut out my damaged sight and focused on the other senses. I heard a dull roar that I thought might bode as badly for my hearing, but after a moment I pushed that new panic away, too, and recognized it as the thunder of the pounding surf. I was in some manner of shelter within a stone's throw of the seashore.

The scent upon the air confirmed it. Dead fish. There was no smell of rot, or open refuse, but even a fastidious fisherman finds himself eventually clothed in the pungent odor of the things. I opened my eyes again, considered the irregular lines of sunlight against the inner darkness, and guessed I was in some poor fisherman's hut, seeing daylight through gaps in a crudely-fashioned wall.

A fisherman. I remembered struggling to scream. I remembered the hand upon my shoulder. He must have brought me back. I took a breath and let it out. My head was up, elevated, but the rest of my body stretched out on some bed or palette. I could smell the stink of sweat, too—of good, hard labor—and faintly the acrid sear of poor firewood convinced to burn anyway.

And then I heard the creak of an ill-made door at my left shoulder, and the orange flicker of firelight intruded on my gloom but did little to clarify it. I squeezed my eyes shut again and choked off a sob.

I felt the fisherman's presence, there at my shoulder, and he waited a heartbeat for me to regain control. Then he spoke with a carefully controlled voice. "Thought you might need something to eat. Got a good broth shouldn't tax you too hard." He cleared his throat and shuffled half a step closer. "Think you can handle that?"

I nodded, and it was a jerky motion. It satisfied him, though. He fell into a crouch, probably sitting on his heels beside my bed on the floor, and then reached a strong, scarred hand under my head and raised me up higher.

Pain stabbed through my stomach and shoulders and a spot on my neck just left of my spine. I sucked in a breath at it, and that brought more echoes from my collarbone, my ribs, and the top of my right hip. A moan escaped me, a sob, and then I passed out again.

It took three tries like that—probably several days—before I was able to eat. And when I did the thin soup was tasteless in my mouth but it burned like fire in my throat, and it set my stomach roiling for hours. I lived in fear that I would retch it up and that the violence of that act would finish me off. When he brought another bowl the following dawn I turned it down.

By noon I regretted my decision. I prayed for him to come back again, whoever he was, and eventually I called out weakly. And then I did as I had done on the beach, gathering my strength and gathering my breath until I could shout. That effort took an entire afternoon, and it earned me nothing. Starving, weeping, I fell back into unconsciousness.

When he came back again it was nighttime, and this time I ate. I ate two bowls, and it soothed my angry stomach, and the fisherman said something to me but exhaustion came on quick and I fell sound asleep.

Then sometime in the night I woke up retching and it very nearly did kill me. The fisherman came to me, turned me on my side, and then set to cleaning it up. I just lay there trembling, gasping for breath, trying to scream. It was a long night.

After that he did not leave. Day and night, he was there for me. He brought food sometimes, but he was careful with how much he let me eat. He gave me water to drink, too. He kept me clean, and I felt him tending to my injuries. He moved slowly whenever he touched me, careful, but his hands were not as gentle as they were strong. More than once he slipped, or gripped too hard, and sent me screaming back into the blackness.

Three times I fell into the dark without quite letting go. Three times consciousness held me too tightly, and though the agony tried to swallow me up completely, I felt something else there in the darkness with me. There inside my head. It was immense and powerful. It bumped like the slow, patient heartbeat of the mountains. It danced like a thread of black fire. It held me up, and I could not fall.

There was a strength within me, something wholly inhuman, and it alone kept me in the world of living men. It knit together broken bones. It stitched shredded muscles back to meat. It prodded me, forever, back toward the light. And after timeless days of blistering agony, it began to heal the light as well. I opened my eyes one weary morning and saw the fisherman kneeling over me.

I saw him. Not just his general shape, but his sunken cheekbones, stringy gray hair tied back in a knot. His weathered skin tanned like leather and the severe slash of his lips pressed into a frown. I couldn't quite follow his eyes, couldn't make out the wrinkles that I knew must mar his hard-worn face, but it felt a miracle to see his face at all.

I smiled. He finished tending a splint around my arm then turned to go—and stopped when he spotted my face. He came closer and tilted his head to one side. "Which one of you's in there this time?"

"Just me," I said. "I can see you."

He pressed a hand to my forehead, warm and strong, and shook his head. "Fever's broke," he said. "First your heart and then your bones and now your sight. Get one more of those and I'll have you hauling nets."

I frowned against his palm, and he pulled the hand away. I sucked in a careful breath, but it was more from habit than need. I couldn't remember the last time I'd felt the angry stab behind my ribs. I let the breath out and took a deeper breath, and this one too came easily. I pressed with an elbow and raised my shoulders an inch higher so I could stare toward his eyes. "What are you talking about?"

I saw him scanning my face for a moment, then he rose and left. I saw the shape of the slatted-door behind him as it swung open, and he passed into the firelight of the little room beyond. He came back with a yellowed glass bottle filled with water and a crust of hard brown bread.

"Time to try some bread," he said. "If you can sit up like that, you'll be needing more strength than broth'll give you. Fillet you a fish first of next week and see how that goes down."

He offered me the bread and I took it, but I did not eat right away. I looked toward his eyes. "You asked me who was in here," I said. "Why? What do you mean about me healing?"

He rocked back on his heels and took a long drink of water. Then he heaved a sigh. "Saw it happen," he said. "Lots of stars that night. The azurefin run by starlight, you know, and I was out making a mighty catch. Saw a shadow across the sky, heard it scream like a horror squall, and then I saw you falling."

I swallowed, and I felt that same old panic and fear bubble up inside. I remembered my helpless fall, remembered the shock of hitting the water. I saw him shaking his head.

"Spent three days looking for you," he said. "Ended up near twenty miles upshore of where you fell. You know that? Should've been dead. Should've been dead a hundred times over."

I nodded. I knew it for the truth. For a while the only noise in the cabin was the crackling pop of the fire in the other room. Then he took another drink and shrugged. "You lived. Times there, I doubted it. Times there, you started to rave. Day I brought you in, your skin burned with a fever like I've never seen. And I've seen sickness. Fever like that can break a man's mind, so it didn't seem so odd...."

He trailed off, and my heart thundered in my chest. "What?" I said.

He shrugged again. "Times, in that fever, you spoke. With a different voice. A hateful voice. Like there was a demon inside you."

I trembled, and it hurt. Not the explosion of pain I'd known before, but discreet blossoms beneath my collarbone and to the right of my stomach. I coughed and groaned, and when my vision cleared I saw him nodding at me.

"Horrible," he said. "Never made a lick of sense. Words that weren't words, you know? First fever lasted seven days, and I figured any morning I'd be hauling you off for the carrion birds."

I closed my eyes. If not for the pain, I probably would have chuckled. Instead, I only nodded. "I felt that way, too."

"Then the fire was gone," he said, and spread his hands in wonder. "Fever was gone. And after that you were still all shattered, but you had a pulse steady as the surf."

"Seven days?" I asked. "And three, you said." He nodded, but cut me off.

"More than that," he said. He chuckled and offered me the water bottle. I took it and drank deep, and he watched me with care. When I finished he nodded again. "Ten days for the first fever," he said. "And then it got bad."

"Then?" I said, and a laugh escaped me. It hurt.

"That's when I started trying to get food in you."

I blinked, startled. "*After* the fever? After ten days?"

He shrugged. "You were never awake. On and off. Took another week just to get you sitting up—"

"I remember," I said. "I hadn't known it took so long."

"Ten days before your first taste of broth, four before your second. And third." His mouth twisted, and I knew the night he was remembering. He shook his head. "Next day we tried again. And then your skin began to burn again."

I shook my head. "I don't remember."

"You wouldn't," he said. "You weren't there. The voice was back. Your brain was all on fire. Twelve days this time—"

"Twelve?"

"Twelve," he said again. "Thirteen when the fever broke, and after that I thought perhaps you were really going to live. Got a real appetite then. Started breathing easier. Stopped coughing blood." He wiped his hands unconsciously, as though washing them clean. "You were mighty broke when I pulled you off that beach," he said. "You know that, right?"

I nodded. He rose and turned away. I twisted, despite the pain beneath my collarbone, and found a little window set into the wall above my bed. He leaned on it, staring out at the sea. "Twelve days of fever when he wouldn't even let me touch you. He raved. He spat at me. He tried to bite me."

I felt a blush rise in my cheeks. "I'm sorry," I said, but he shushed me with a wave of his hand.

"Weren't you," he said. "Times, you spoke to me, too. Not much. But times. And you were always quiet. Like you are now. Little bit afraid. He was different."

I swallowed. I closed my eyes and remembered the great black presence in the darkness. I remembered the furious rage of the beast that I'd felt within my head. I remembered the dragon I had faced. Terrible. Indestructible.

I shivered.

Above me the fisherman nodded. "Brought you broth, but you didn't touch it. Wouldn't let me close enough to feed you. Brought you water, and if I left I'd come back to find it empty. Best I could do for you, and that fever burned hot and long."

"Twelve days," I said.

"Twelve days. And then he was gone again. And you were back. And your ribs...." He sighed. "I've seen a lot of things. You know? I've seen a lot of things. Never seen damage like yours healed by starvation and a fever."

I didn't know enough to tell him what it was. I had suspicions, fears, but even if I dared to give them voice, I didn't know a tenth of what I'd need to make any sense of it. So I held my tongue, and after a time he shrugged again.

"Second fever mended bones," he said. "Shattered legs and broken ribs and an arm I'd've sworn you'd never use again." I grunted as though he'd hit me, and he nodded. "But then it was just a matter of time. Blind and weak and quiet as you were, I figured I could bring you back from death by then. Took four weeks—"

"No!" I shouted, and I saw him twist to look down at me, then back out the window.

"Sure enough," he said. "More than a month of slow and steady from one fever to the next, and then the third one broke my heart."

"Worse?" I guessed.

He shook his head. "Nope. Quieter. Never heard a word from the other one. Could've cooked a fillet on your forehead. Poured the water and the broth into you, listened to your moans, and watched the fever slowly climb. It was worse, but only because it was normal."

"Oh," I said. I nodded.

"Mhm. Figured this one had nothing to do with magic demons. Figured after everything we'd been through, you and me, you were going to die of something stupid."

I chuckled, and I could feel him grin down on me. He sank back down on his heels and nodded toward the bread still in my hands. "Eat," he said. "Eat. Then tell me your name. Been waiting nigh on three months just to ask you that."

"Daven," I said, without starting on the bread yet. It felt rough and real against my fingertips, and I was cherishing it.

"Just Daven?" I shrugged. He frowned. "I expected something grander."

"Everyone does," I said. But then I understood, and I nodded. "I'm a student of the Academy," I said. "I was."

"Ah. Yes." He nodded back at me. "Thanks. Had to be that, huh?"

I shrugged. It was an answer to the things he'd seen. It wasn't really an explanation, it certainly wasn't the truth. But it made sense. People needed sense. Claighan had told me that.

"How long?" I asked, after a while. "Altogether. How long has it been?"

"Eighty days, give or take." I felt his eyes on me, burning, and realized how very little he had asked. How little he had demanded. I felt my cheeks burn again.

"I'm sorry," I said. "Eighty days? You've spent all this time taking care of me?"

"I had the time," he said, and he chuckled. "Not a lot goes on, this corner of the world. Brought a little story with you. That's worth the cost in soup."

"And time?"

He laughed again, a shade darker this time. "Got nothing but time, Daven. Daven." He tasted the sound of it. "Waited weeks just to put a name to you."

"Daven Carrickson," I told him. "Of Chantire. Of Terrailles. And recently a student of the Academy."

He whistled soft and low. "Been all over," he said. "And Joseph." He jabbed a thumb at his chest, then leaned forward and patted my right knee gently. I felt an answering jolt of pain up in my hip, but I concealed the wince. "Get some rest," he said. "Eat that bread. Maybe try you on fish sooner than I thought."

He turned to go, looked back at me, shook his head. "Can't believe you're still alive."

I shrugged one shoulder. "Magic," I said. I made my voice lighter than I felt, and he chuckled back at me.

"Magic. Hah." He pulled the door closed behind him, and the room grew dark again. I tried the bread—one idle bite—and the taste of it woke a hunger in me that I had almost forgotten. I devoured the little bit of crust and longed to call to the fisherman for more. But I restrained myself. Everything in its time.

The light through the slatted walls faded, and after a while the fire from the cabin's other room flickered down to coals, and I lay in deep darkness, thinking. For the first time in months, I could think. I remembered the fisherman's words—first heart, then bones, then sight—but as I lay there I thought probably this fever had given me more than my vision back. I had clarity. I could think.

And I did. I stepped back through the fisherman's story, counting out the days again. Eighty days. Eight weeks on this miserable little bed. Broth could not have kept me alive that long. And no matter what I'd told him, it wasn't magic either.

I thought of the dragon. It came to me in flashes of memory. I saw myself strung up in the air, the immensity of the beast flowing by me on the wing before it struck at Archus. I thought of it reared to its full height, towering over the arrogant apprentice as he called down lightning. I thought of the beast's immense head blocking the mouth of the cave I'd used for refuge. And I thought of the shadow high above me, dwindling with distance, a thin trace of red dancing through its shadow.

Blood. I trembled at the thought but refused to shy away. Blood magic. They'd spoken of it at the Academy. There's power in earth and stone, power in wind and sky, but there's a special magic in living blood. In spilling blood. I'd given some to the dragon, and it had given some to me, however unwillingly.

Something had happened then. I remembered the dragon's confusion as it raged within my mind. *What have you done to me?* it had asked. Nothing of my own intent, but after what I'd seen—after what I'd survived—I suspected there was something in the trading of our powers.

The blackness of it mattered. The emptiness. The magic of man is order. It's power built on reason, understanding, focused will. Dragons, though...dragons are primal creatures. Theirs is the magic of chaos, the underlying powers. It was not the trade of blood that had mattered. Not on a physical level. It was the exchange of *power*, alien power, conflicting powers mingled together.

I hadn't learned a single spell in my time at the Academy, but I had learned boatloads of theory. I nodded slowly to myself. I would not have believed a description of it, but I had experienced it firsthand. No one should have survived what I'd gone through, warrior, wizard, or king. No one. But I had faced a dragon and lived!

And then I blinked, a new memory bubbling up. I had worked a spell, hadn't I? I remembered the cave, the close blackness so like the terrible closet Seriphenes had locked me in. But there in the darkness I had summoned a light. And even as I'd fallen to my death I had managed *some* working of air. It hadn't been strong enough, soon enough, but perhaps it had kept me from dying outright.

I closed my eyes and tried again. There was pain still, an ache as familiar as my own smell, but it was dull and distant now. I stepped through the exercises Antinus had taught me and opened my eyes. And then I licked my lips, suddenly nervous.

Because it was there. Reality laid bare. I could see the fisherman's pathetic little shack, battered and broken upon the shore, a frail speck beneath the maelstrom of energies around us. The ocean churned, deep and bitter and wholly unpredictable. I could feel its power as a threat, a promise of destruction, straining against the leash and pounding its frustration with the collapse of every froth-tipped wave.

I narrowed my focus, drew down my eye, and suddenly I looked down on myself from less than a pace away. I could see the power in me, the weary ebb and flow of my life-blood, but it lay in heavy contrast against a bed of perfect black. Shadow spread out beneath me and wrapped around the edges, and I trembled. The dragon's presence stained me.

I pushed the thought away and looked more closely. I became aware of old bandages and clumsy stitches and in several places splints fashioned of driftwood and twine. There had been a time when that was all that held my shattered bones in place, but I could feel the truth of the fisherman's tale. I could feel bones grown whole again, and in my second sight I could see the flashing shadow that bound the broken edges like mortar.

I stared down at myself for a while, life energy dancing like a kitchen fire, and then I cast out my awareness until I found the fisherman sleeping beneath a threadbare blanket in the outer room. He burned strong, clean, with the strength of his arms and the sturdy power of hard labor. He roared like a bonfire, strong enough to shape his world without a touch of magic, and I felt sadness settle over me when I turned my eyes back to the shadowy, fitful glow of my own survival.

I needed to be stronger. I raised up on an elbow as I'd done before. I tried to heave myself upright, but the strain across my abdomen sent a stabbing pain into my right hip and I fell back. I shook my head and tried again, and once again I fell back panting.

Bodily strength would have to wait. Still, I was pleased with the second sight, and I reached out again as I had done in the cave and found the fragile memory of sunbeams and firelight. I remade my vision of the room, drawing out the light, building it until it shone, and then I spoke a soft word and opened my eyes to find my room as bright as day.

I smiled, but my head throbbed with the effort of it. I found myself straining to hold the image, fighting against the reality I knew was there, and after four hastening heart-beats I let it go, and darkness fell again. Still, I knew that I could do it. I could work magic by my own will. I would have given much to show that skill to Seriphenes.

Seriphenes. The dark wizard's face swam before my vision, and I remembered him as I had seen him last, sweep-ing through a portal to lead dozens of students against the dragon that had tried to kill me. What had become of them? I held precious little fear for the master wizard who had de-fied Claighan's every warning, but what had become of the students? What had become of Themmichus?

I imagined the worst and hoped for the best, and through it all I poured my hate on Seriphenes. On Leotus, who had so happily gone along with the scheme. On Ar-chus, who had dragged me away from all the others and of-fered me up as bait. On the rebel Lareth, who had made that necessary.

I thought of Lareth for the first time since I had left Seriphenes's office, and my mouth twisted in a frown. I owed him more venom than Seriphenes. He was my enemy, true and deep, and I would have given much to face him in vengeance.

But not now. Not like this. I had the second sight, but the extent of my magic was a pathetic little flare of light, and my body was weak as a newborn lamb's. I took up the water bottle the fisherman had left me, drank it to the bottom, then curled onto my side and looked for sleep. There would be work to do at dawn.

12. Chaos Magic

It was another week before I could stand unassisted. The pain persisted, but with some dedicated effort and a far richer diet than I had known in months, I slowly gained my strength. Whenever my body failed me—and in those days it failed me often—I bent my attention to training my mind instead. I worked through my mental exercises again and again, until I could take on the second sight in the space of a breath. I wasted days trying to speed my healing with magical will, trying to imagine myself stronger. But order magic works on expectation, and I felt my weakness far too dearly to believe it gone.

Whenever I faltered, whenever my legs could not quite hold me, I thought back on the spell Archus had used to march me like a puppet across the Academy grounds. He'd woven armor of solid air, and I often thought a trick like that could serve me well. But I didn't know the first thing about that manner of working, and whatever clumsy efforts I made at it ended in failure.

There was another temptation in the magic, though. Even as I tried to understand how to *will* reality so air was hard as steel, I could see the power of that air in my second sight. I could see the energy in a breath of wind like a thread, long and thin and infinitely pliable. It seemed like it would be so easy to reach out and grasp the thread itself, to wrap it around my arm like a string, but I knew that—even more than Archus's clever working—was well beyond my grasp. That was sorcery, the manipulation of pure elemental energy, and Claighan had said even the greatest wizards could not do that.

So I settled for my little tricks—a glowing light, a flaring fire, a breeze to freshen the air in the close little shelter—and mostly focused on strengthening my body. I still could not go far, but soon enough I could feed myself. And then prepare my food. And then the fisherman's too. Soon I was working for Joseph, scaling and gutting, packing and sorting, while he brought in the catch.

There was much work to do. For weeks he had neglected his business, neglected himself in his dedication to my recovery. Now I did everything I could to return the favor. He went out with the rising sun and came back at dusk with a healthy haul. Then while he slept I worked, preparing the catch for him to take out with him the following morning.

So he could start each day with a trip to the nearest market, two leagues south along the coast, and sell fillets direct to the meat market there. And then while he was gone I'd rest. I'd rise. I'd clean the shack or scour the shore for firewood. I'd walk and walk until my legs gave out, then rest and walk back home.

Those first days I barely made a mile, and then eventually two, and it was a great victory to me when I judged I'd gone fully three miles before giving up. A victory. But I remembered days on Jemminor's farm when I had grazed the sheep out across dozens of miles of rolling hills without ever feeling the strain. That thought always killed my joy.

But then one afternoon I found the stone the fisherman had placed. I was five miles from home, the sun well past its peak and drifting out to sea, and I knew I'd have to turn around soon or I wouldn't make it back before Joseph did. Then my right knee buckled, and I barely caught myself short of falling, and I knew that if I went any farther I might not make it back at all. I turned to go—

I spotted the stone among the crashing waves. It was out of place, polished black and smooth, nearly a pace across and just as tall. It was a wonder a man could even lift it.

But clearly someone had. It stood among the surf as a monument, and as I moved closer I felt a deep sense of familiarity. I knew this place. It was where I had washed ashore. I reached back for the memory of Joseph's story, watching me fall and searching north along the coast until he found the spot. I stared up at the sky. I stared out to sea. And slowly I nodded.

The fisherman had brought this here as a monument. Perhaps as a memorial. I watched the mighty waves rolling, crashing in the distance, and I nodded slowly. I blinked my eyes and fell into the second sight, and I forced myself to look upon the deadly crushing power that had swallowed me whole. This was where I should have died. I hadn't.

Weak though I was, fragile though I was, this stone was a testament to my power. To the dragon's power within me. I took a deep breath and let it out. I shook my head. It was from the dragon, yes, but the power was mine. It had served me, not the beast. It had preserved me when the beast wanted me dead.

I sat against the stone and ate my lunch—a carrot, an apple, and dried beef that Joseph had brought back from town—and then when I was done I started back toward the cabin. Just five miles and it would tax me to the bone, but I had *power*. I smiled, I set my jaw, and made my way back home.

Two weeks later I went along with him, down to the little town, and I watched while he negotiated his trades. There was more to it than I'd have guessed—haggling prices, settling terms—but the man worked through it all with an easy familiarity and before noon he had my arms loaded with bundles of goods to take back to the boat.

It was a respectable little fishing boat, single-mast and open-hulled but large enough for three or four if Joseph had had any kind of crew, and outfitted with block and tackle to run a deep dredging net. He never dragged between the town and his cabin—one of the terms of his trade—but there was open water north and west and he never had any difficulty filling his nets.

Now he headed back north, ferrying me home, but there were no perishables among the goods we'd purchased. "Take me out," I said. He looked at me, frowning, and I waved out to the west. "Take me out. I'd like to see a catch."

"Sure you're up to it?" he asked.

"I'm certain of it," I said. "And I'm itching to know what it's like."

"Boring, mostly," he said. "Lots of work. But I could use the help."

So we went, chasing schools and hauling in nets full of flopping fish. I helped him at first, but he'd understated it strongly. Even with the assistance of the pulleys, it took main strength to heave a laden net up, and I soon understood where the fisherman got his strength.

By midafternoon I found a place out of the way toward the stern and curled up to rest. I caught him smiling indulgently down at me, but he never complained. And when I woke an hour later I helped him pull in another little catch before he finally headed home for the night.

I went out with him often, and in that more than anything else I began to rebuild my strength. Two weeks saw me standing beside him, hour after hour, hauling in the nets. Three weeks saw me casting my own over the other side, and soon Joseph was bringing home a greater catch than he had ever managed before.

Then one night when the azurefin were running, we chased along above them by the light of a starry sky. We had almost as much as our boat could carry, but azurefin brought a fine price and Joseph wanted to fill her up. For my part, I'd worked a full day and into the night without the least complaint, and I wanted to see how far I could go. So we agreed and chased the azurefin north along the coast.

And then the rain began to fall, pelting down hot and hard despite the clear sky overhead. We had no other warning as the clouds raced in, but that was enough for Joseph. He dumped the nets and dropped the rigging and had the sails down before I even knew what was happening. He moved mechanically, but I could see the touch of fear in his eyes and a tremble in his hands as darkness fell upon us, and the rain came harder down.

"What's wrong?" I asked, and his lips twisted in a frown.

"Got greedy," he said, without looking up at the storm. He tossed me a length of rope. "Better batten down. Will be bad."

I swallowed against my fear. Waves sloshed the boat now, but they weren't yet much worse than the ones we dealt with every day. Rain came down, but it wasn't a deluge yet. But I knew Joseph. I knew his manners. And I'd never met a more able boatman. If he was afraid....

I followed his example and sank down into the hold, and even as I did the waves grew larger. One splashed across the bow and caught me open-mouthed, and I had to cough and sputter and duck my head before another one washed over me. The rain came harder now, and I saw the flash a breath before a long, low, grinding crack of thunder rolled over the sea. And another behind it. And another.

The boat washed violently to one side and I reached out to steady myself. And as I did, from habit more than reason,

I slipped into my second sight and glanced across the powers that surrounded us.

My blood went cold with fear.

It was the sea as I had seen it before—as I had always seen it—deep and strong and deadly. But it was wild now, stirred with wind and fire, and the power of the storm came not in threads but in sheets. They flashed across the surface, they twisted in the deeps, they flicked and flared and roared in senseless fury. And there among them, like a leaf within a gale, bobbed our tiny little boat, two sparks of life within it easily snuffed out.

A wave tore over us and I saw the sheet of it scream up and slash down. It fell like the blanket of air Lareth had once used to bind me to the floor, and as I saw it coming I almost expected it to crush in the same way. But this was merely water. As it fell it tore across the sturdy bow and broke around the mast. It hit me hard enough to knock me down, but then its force was spent. It spilled into the bottom of the boat and it was done.

But there were more. Thousands more. Millions of the waves churning, boiling up in their frenzy, and with every heartbeat that passed they grew more powerful. Another soared high and crashed almost straight down, and the force of it drove the breath from me and shattered the ship's heavy mast to splinters. And that wave held enough power still to flash away, dragging back out to sea. If Joseph hadn't caught my hand the wave would have dragged me out with it.

And though he pulled me back in, there was no relief in his eyes. There was only dread acceptance. He turned his eyes up into the storm then, and I saw a wave flashing toward us that could shatter the boat as easily as the last had done the mast. And behind it another one greater still. I saw the great sheets of living water thrown up, stretching, folding over us—

Fear flooded through me, and I reached out on pure instinct. I did as I had wanted to do when the dragon dropped me, as I had wanted to do when I could not support my own weight, and I touched the threads themselves with my mind. I didn't bother constructing a visualization, building a reality small enough that I could believe in it but large enough to save our lives. That kind of magic was beyond my grasp.

But the power of the storm was right there. In easy reach. It required no force of will, no fancy tricks of the mind, just the simple physical effort of bending and shaping. I flexed muscles I didn't really have, stretched out my fingers to touch the reality *beneath* reality, and took the fabric of the storm into my hands. I snapped it out around us, as though I were throwing a cloak across my shoulders or spreading a blanket over my bed, and whipped the wave itself out in a dome above our heads.

It roared, wild waters still churning, but it did not fall. It made a shell above us that denied nature and reason, but I held it there by force of will. In my mind's eye I could see through it, and I watched as a larger wave came crashing down, but it spilled against the fabric of my wave and washed into the sea all around us. I felt the wind dance across the waters—threads still, but thick as my arm—and I pulled one down beneath my wave and slammed its end against the stern of our boat.

A jet of wind and water stabbed up out of the sea beneath, and even without a mast the gust hurled us forward. Above us the wave stretched out, curled and crashing and roaring still as though it might fall in the next heartbeat. I grabbed another rope of wind and bent that one, too, and with two of them behind us the little fishing boat flew across the waves like a skipping stone. I carried the wave with us, stretched out and protecting us from above, and we sped toward the shore.

I felt my heart hammering, louder even than the storm in my ears. I felt the ocean's fury slamming against the wave above as though it pounded on my shoulders, and every blow threatened to rip the fabric from my grip. The winds, too, twisted and writhed, and whenever one escaped me our little boat settled to a fitful stop. I found more, though. Another to replace the one that had gotten away, and as another wave crashed down and I felt the water above me slipping from my grasp, I grabbed another thread of wind, and then a fourth, and threw them all into getting us to safety.

With my attention so focused on the elements I had no eye for our position. I threw us east without guidance or care. I had one breath to hear Joseph's frantic scream, to see the terror in his eyes, and then the ship slammed to a sudden, violent stop. Momentum tore me from my place on the stern and heaved me through the air, and the force of the winds I'd summoned flung me further. Joseph tumbled out, too. He held on to the rope secured to the shattered mast just long enough to slow him, so he stretched out long across the sand and tumbled in a low roll while I flew through the air.

The wind never died. It raged against the stern of the boat, even run aground, and flung it up into the air like a catapult's shot. I crashed to earth and stars flashed in my eyes. Darkness rushed at me—all too familiar—but I forced it away as I saw the boat arcing back down to earth. Even if it didn't hit me it would crush Joseph.

So I released the winds within my grasp, and the wave above, and focused all my attention upon the earth. The slow and steady earth. It appeared to my second sight as neither thread nor sheet, but pebbles. Tiny, useless pebbles of energy, but I remembered the huge weight of the mountain built out of these impossibly tiny stones.

I rolled to my feet and threw myself into a long dive. I landed beside Joseph and reached out with the magic of my mind to grab up the energy of the sand. I flung it up in a handful above me and the earth around us exploded up in a great puff. Then the sand fell back down, burying us side-by-side in a shallow grave, and when the boat crashed down above us it scraped on past.

And then the wave drove down behind it. That hurt worse, deadly force delayed but not decreased, and it pounded straight down into the shore along a quarter-mile stretch. I didn't hold the earth above us as I'd done the wave. I didn't have the strength. So the wave splashed down through to soak us again, and then it dragged much of the sand away with it, so Joseph and I both heaved back up out of a shallow pool of mud and sand and sea water, coughing and spluttering. Alive.

It took some time to gather our wits. Then Joseph went to the wreckage of his ship. It was still intact, but nothing close to seaworthy. I watched him from a distance, respecting the privacy of his grief, but after he'd made his assessment he turned back to me without any strong emotion in his eyes. I cocked my head.

"Is she ruined?'

"Ruined," he said, his voice matter-of-fact. "But we're alive." He fixed me with a gaze that demanded acknowledgment, and after a moment I nodded. He nodded back. "And now I understand." He turned back, looking north along the beach, and I knew he was looking in the direction of the stone he'd placed. "Magic."

"No," I said, shaking my head. "I didn't...I just now...." I couldn't put to words what I had done. What I had done was impossible. It was more than magic. It was separate.

The fisherman turned back to me and raised an eyebrow. "Can you get us home?" He made a gesture with his hand, a little arch, and I recognized the shape of a summoned portal. I considered it for a heartbeat, but I had no idea how.

"I don't think so," I said. I reached out with my second sight again, and grabbed at threads of air, but these were not the trunk-thick ropes that had propelled our ship along. That storm was far away, now, and drifting up the coast. The air here was little more than a breeze. I tried wrapping it around Joseph and lifting him into the air, but it only flapped at the folds of his sodden clothes, and he shivered.

I shook my head. "I'm sorry. I don't know how."

He shrugged one shoulder and started down the shore. "Better start walking, then," he said. "Get some boys from town up here tomorrow to see what we can salvage."

I fell into step beside him, numb. I had touched the wind and rain. I had bent elemental power to my will. I remembered the strength of the wave stretched out above me, the battering energy of more waves crushing against it. I remembered tempest winds twisting in my grasp.

I reached out again, testing, and bent a thread of air toward me. I felt only a breath of air over my cheek. A puff against my ear. With the boat I'd used more, though, so I stole a thread of air up off the sea, and another high above. I reached for a breeze that made waves in the grasses higher inland. I gathered them together into a bunch, four little breaths, and combined they were enough to blow a modest wind against us. I remembered the air magic that had been used against me before and wrapped those threads in a cuff tight around my ankle.

But when I strained against it I was able to pull free, as easily as though I were forcing forward against a strong wind. I reached for more threads from the air around me, thinner, spidersilk threads of still air, but these added very little to the strength of my spell, and after the fifth thread the others began to twist free of my control. I reached for a sixth and lost control of two.

And while I tried to catch them back another one twisted free. I grunted, frustrated, head throbbing, and let them all go. Another three paces down I let the second sight fade, too, and settled for the strength left in my legs. It got me home. I fell into my bed, and Joseph into his, and we slept the good sleep of the quiet dead.

It had something to do with power. I figured that. Order magic—Academy magic—took its strength from the will of the worker, but order magic would have been hard pressed to do what I did within the storm. The magic I'd done was different. I gave it shape, gave it direction, but the strength was all its own. I'd done amazing things with the strength of a blustering storm, but I could barely shift a stone with the quiet energy of an environment at rest.

Not a large stone, anyway. Certainly not a boulder. Not a tree. Not something larger like, say, a battered old fishing boat. The thought was strong in my mind the following afternoon as I stood outside a circle of local fishermen examining the wreckage of Joseph's ship. They'd noticed quickly how little I knew of the business at hand, so they paid me little mind as they discussed the options and guessed how much might be salvaged.

Their guesses were grim. I eavesdropped, heart sinking, but Joseph just nodded as though they confirmed what he already knew. Nothing much rattled him. I listened and waited and wondered how I might help. I'd done this, in a way.

I was working on a plan to carve a channel across a hundred paces of beach with the strength of little breakers, when one of the villagers shook his head and said, "Strange days. Dark days everywhere. Dragons in the sky, storms that'll do this, and kingsmen fighting rebels on the plains above Tirah."

That last snapped me out of my thoughts. I pushed through the circle and up to the speaker. He was a little man, and he shrank away from the intensity of my gaze. But I held his eyes. "What about Tirah?"

He shrugged. "The King's Guard's fighting for the baronies out west," he said. "Ain't you heard? The rebels have the heartlands—"

"I know," I said. "I know. But you mentioned Tirah."

Joseph dropped a hand on my shoulder to calm me. "Tirah's old news," he said. "Guard took it three months ago. Didn't realize you'd want to know."

I shrugged one shoulder. "I'd hoped to join the Guard," I said without thinking. "Take up the amnesty."

A look passed around among the fishermen, and I winced. Joseph didn't even bat an eye, and that eased my soul a bit. And none of the others spoke up. There were plenty of ways a man might go afoul of the king's justice, not all of them unfamiliar in territories like this.

Joseph did offer me a look of regret, though. "Amnesty's done," he said. "King put together thirty thousand men. Thirty thousand men on the Ardain proper." He shook his head, astonished, and I felt the same emotion.

"And they still haven't won?"

One of the other fishermen scowled and said, "Brant won't commit his men. They harass and harry, and then they run and hide. The king's men have all the strong-holds—"

"But the rebels have the countryside," another of them said. The same one I'd first accosted. He met my eyes. "It'll be different when the king arrives. He'll put an end to it."

"The king himself?" I said, and I felt the blood drain from my face. I'd forgotten. It had been five months ago, a passing reference, and still I'd felt the flash of significance at the name of the town. But now I remembered Lareth's sun-dark face in the Masters' tower. I remembered him bragging to a helpless student. I remembered him promising to end the rebellion when the king came to Tirah.

"He'll go there?" I said, suddenly frantic. "To Tirah?"

"On his way now," Joseph said. He met my eyes and spoke clearly, as though he sensed how important the in-formation was to me. He couldn't have known why, but he must have heard the frenzy in my voice. "Whole fleet sailed straight down the coast from the Isle. Passed by a week ago. You were gutting fish, but I saw them on the horizon."

The little guy nodded. "I was out there in their path. A galleon full of Green Eagles swept up on me and a full Commander threatened to sink my ship if I didn't tack off to shore. Wrecked my afternoon's take, but it was quite a sight."

I wasn't really listening. I looked down, thinking franti-cally. I asked Joseph, "Where were they going?"

The little guy answered. "Cara," he said. "Way south. Whitefalls is closer, but they're with Brant."

"And well secured," Joseph said. "King probably made Cara yesterday morning."

I swallowed. "How fast could I get there?"

"Take more than a week by sea, with any ship you'd find near here. Over land, most of a month."

"No good," the little guy said. "Not if it's the king you want to see. He would be long gone by then." I cursed, and he gave me a conciliatory smile. "That's how it is. He was anxious to get this over with. He'll be on the road to Tirah already."

Joseph caught my eye. "Cut overland," he said. "Straight to Tirah. Even on foot, could probably beat him there."

I felt my heart pounding. I didn't know this land. I didn't know my way. Tirah crouched at the heart of the Ardain, and I'd seen enough on the dragon's flight to know that put it southeast of me, but it was a journey of a hundred miles easy. Probably twice that, if not more.

I didn't want to go. I liked it here. I liked Joseph. I couldn't see myself ending up a fisherman, but I certainly wasn't yet ready for war. I still needed a few more weeks to recover, a few more months maybe, and this would have been a pleasant place to do it.

And my eyes touched on the ruined boat, on the pricey azurefins rotting under the afternoon sun. I thought of Joseph's livelihood ruined by my magic, and the good I could do him if I were here. But Lareth had a plan to kill the king, a plan only I knew about. And I had a chance to stop it. I had a chance to end this rebellion, perhaps, if I could get there in time. I could save lives. I could save the nation.

I knew what I had to do. I didn't want to go, but I had to. And as I raised my eyes back to Joseph's, I saw understanding in them. He nodded and clapped me on the shoulder. "Seems important."

"It is," I said. "Someone plans to kill the king."

His lips quirked up a smile. "During a rebellion? Big surprise."

I laughed in surprise. And then I laughed in earnest, and he gave me an earnest smile as reward. "Dauk's three leagues due east. End of the road. Farms all around it. Road leads straight to Tirah."

I nodded. My gaze dragged back toward the wreckage of the boat, but I saw him shake his head. "King won't spend long on southern roads. Get a move on. Could be in Dauk by sunset."

"I should," I said. I felt the eyes of all the other fishermen on me. They couldn't have known much about what was going on, but they could tell it was significant. I felt awkward beneath their gaze, but I could hardly go without saying a proper good-bye.

"Thank you, Joseph. I'm so sorry about your boat—"

He shrugged one shoulder and gave that half-smile again. He tipped his head to me in a nod. "Saved my life."

"Only after you saved mine," I said. I hesitated, thinking maybe I should hug him. It had been easier with Sherrim. He saw the uncertainty in my eyes and offered me a hand. I took it solemnly.

"Be safe," he said. "Save the king."

The little fisherman nodded. "Save the country." There was laughter in his eyes. It didn't look like mockery, just astonishment that we were even talking about this. Joseph saw it, and he grinned.

"Kid's a wizard," he told the others. "Sure as rain."

I saw their eyes widen then, all around the circle. I felt a blush rise in my cheeks. I looked at the wrecked boat, glanced back toward the fisherman's cabin, but I didn't have anything to take with me. The dragon had left me with nothing.

I met Joseph's eyes one last time, nodded to him, then turned and headed east toward the distant hills. The little ring of villagers broke to let me by, and I felt them fall closed again behind me. I felt their murmurs rise up, too, and at first I was sure they were talking about me.

But then a little breeze carried snippets of their conversation to my ear, and I realized they were back to making plans to salvage the boat. I was already forgotten. I made it fifteen paces before my will broke and I glanced back.

Joseph stood taller than the rest of them, in the middle of the circle, and he stared past them all, gaze fixed on me. He met my eyes. He offered me a smile. And he waved one short, simple gesture of good-bye. I returned it, tears stinging in my eyes. Then he turned back to the conversation at hand, and I left them all behind.

As I moved up the long beach, the sand slowly gave way to a tough, short grass, but the earth scarcely became more stable. The land was a marsh, soft and wet, and it sucked at every step. I'd never bothered to learn much about the terrain down on the Continent, but I'd seen enough maps while studying at the Academy to have some idea where I was.

There was a space of about twenty miles where the western coastline became swampy lowlands before rising up to the mountains of the southwest coast that stretched all the way to the Fausse. The squelching of mud under my boots and thick smell in the air placed me almost due west of Pollix, some forty miles north of Whitefalls.

I was nearly a hundred and fifty miles from Tirah.

The distance did not daunt me, though it should have. I was still weak, and now alone in a land torn by war, but my thoughts were all on saving the king. I walked for three or four hours while the sun rose high in the sky, stumbling more than walking and covering little more than a couple miles an hour. A thin layer of water and muck concealed the ground from sight, making footing treacherous and tiring. I still felt drained from the excitement the night before, and every other step brought a stab of pain from a bruise on my left hip. Before long I felt warm in spite of the chill in the air.

For several hours I pressed through the marsh, and afternoon was stretching toward evening when I saw a hill rising before me. I felt a flush of relief, bright and hot, at the thought of solid ground. I took another step toward it, and then my blood ran cold.

A shadow flashed across the horizon, right to left, dancing up and down above the broken line of the distant hills. I watched it for half a minute; it dipped lower still, and it was lost to sight. For a long time I stood there, legs aching, heart pounding, staring at the shadows of distant hills. Alone.

That thought stabbed claws of fear into my chest. There was probably not another human being for a dozen miles in any direction. I forced myself to take another step, but my legs felt heavy as stone. I closed my eyes, took a slow breath, and then managed another step. I got moving again. My heart still pounded, my breath came too shallow, and my head ached from the strain with which I stared at the distant hills. But I made half a mile more across the marsh.

And then I saw it again. Far to the south, now, something flashed across my vision. It could have been the shadow of a cloud scudding across the ground, but the angle was wrong. I turned, frozen in fear again, and saw it a moment later. Closer now. A black shadow, swift as lightning, danced in and out among the low foothills.

Then, without warning, it shot straight into the sky. I recognized it instantly. The dragon. Not just a dragon, but the same black beast that had thrown me into the sea. It was all teeth and claws and muscles, and it moved faster than anything that large should be able to.

And the other one moved just as fast. It was larger still, mottled in the color of leaves—dark green along its back

269

and wings, autumn brown along its neck and underbelly. The black dragon arced high in the air and the green flew after it. It screamed its fury and blew a burst of fire that stabbed at the black. The smaller dragon never slowed but whipped its long neck around to breathe a gout of flame of its own in answer.

The green dodged it, light as a butterfly, and closed in. The smaller dragon's tail lashed, vicious, but then the green sank its claws into the other's haunches, and I heard a bellowing roar that seemed to echo, deep inside my head. I could imagine the beast's pain and rage, and I felt my lips curl into a snarl as the black dragon abandoned its flight to turn its own talons on the beast fighting it. They fell from sight, crashing among the hills to the south and east, but still I heard them fighting.

Something inside me pulled me forward. I started moving again, toward the hills, and it quickly became a shambling run that sent water splashing everywhere. After two or three steps I realized I was running straight toward the deadly monsters, and I made myself stop. The hair on my neck stood up, and my fingers itched. I had to fight an instinct to start running again, *toward* the danger.

Muddy water dripped from my nose and eyelashes. I tried to blink it away. I threw a look back over my shoulder, toward the coast, but it was too far. I took another step toward the hills, and then another. It took all my concentration to keep my feet from turning south toward the fray among the hills, but I made myself keep due east as Joseph had sent me. The dragons were busy. I'd pass miles to the north of them. They would have no reason to notice me...and I certainly had no reason to go closer.

My heart raced, but I pressed on. It took me another twenty minutes to reach the first of the hills, but as soon as I was a little way up its slope, I felt solid, dry ground beneath my feet. I sank down to my knees. My body felt heavy as stone. I thought that perhaps I could rest here, regain some strength before pressing on. I climbed until I found a little patch of scrub, hearty bushes growing on the rocky hillside, and I stretched myself out beneath their shadow. I lay on the hard ground and shivered, trying to ignore the pain of fatigue in all my muscles.

Evening stretched toward night, orange and violet staining the clear sky, but I could not sleep. It took me some time to realize why, but when I did, I sat bolt upright.

The dragons had gone silent.

I had heard no sound from them for some time. The noise of their battle had been a terrible thing, but it had at least let me know where they were. Now I scanned the sky overhead, but I saw nothing. I pushed myself to my feet, biting down groans of protest. I crouched low and scurried up to the top of the hill. My legs and back complained, but I felt too exposed to move slowly up that open slope.

At the top of the hill I found a little dip down and then another rise beyond. There were more hills, left and right, all low and rolling but enough of a climb to slow me down. I strained my eyes to north and south, but I saw no sign of the dragons. I fell into my second sight, and it showed me the pulse of the earth beneath me, the dance of the wind and the threat of a little rain come midnight. I saw no dragons, though.

I forced myself to slow and steady breathing. I thought about my choices. I thought about the climb I had ahead. How many months had I spent still on Joseph's sad little sickbed? Too many. And too few days since then had I been working. When I'd toiled on Jemminor's farm this path through the hills might have been an easy stroll, but those days were far in my past.

I eased my crouch down lower, eyes barely raised above the top of the hill, and kept on scanning. My arms shook from holding me up, and my left ankle was just beginning to do the same. I dropped flat on the earth. I stretched an arm up to support my chin, and found myself tucking my head down into the crook of my elbow.

I was too tired. I was too weak to make this trek. Closer to the town now than to Joseph's cabin, but with peaks and valleys still ahead. I hadn't the strength. It was an impossible hope. A moment later a dragon's hunting cry confirmed it.

It was far off to my south, and even as I turned I saw a shadow flick from sight down among the hills. I didn't breathe. For several long seconds I scanned the horizon, but I saw nothing.

A jittery, nauseating energy clawed its way into my weary muscles, then, and I found myself moving without even thinking. Not toward the dragons this time—it was no supernatural urge that drove me—but over the crest of this hill and down the next. Pain lanced through my weary legs and I stumbled going down the hill, too tired to plant my feet properly, but I couldn't slow myself either. Gravity pulled me into a sprint, and I tumbled my way to the bottom of the hill and scrabbled my way up the next.

Shadows flitted over the land. I felt them, to the north and south. And as I made my way east the hills behind me cut off the sun, throwing me into darkness while the sun still stained the sky. I had little hope that darkness would hamper a dragon's hunt, but it made my flight more fearsome. I heard another cry, halfway up the third or fourth hill, and it froze me like a hawk can freeze a rabbit on the ground. I fell into my second sight again, desperately searching the sky, and I saw nothing. Then another cry set me running again, and I made my way to the top of a hill just before the sun set in earnest behind me.

The final red rays spilled down before me, showing a smaller hill yet to scale, and beyond that nothing worthy of the name. Rolling grasslands. Tended fields. In the middle distance I saw the glow of a town like a smudge of brown against the violet night. I felt a flash of hope, shoulders trembling, and threw myself down this slope, too. I ran the sun from the sky. I bloodied my hands and tore my clothes and burned my fear for sustenance.

It was well and truly dark when I finally stumbled into the town. I hadn't a penny to my name, but cold and wet and tired as I was, and shaken by the monsters in the marshland, I felt the need for some company. So I trotted on past dark farmhouses and quiet shapes that reminded me of the green in Sachaerrich. I passed the blacksmith's cold forge and a stable sealed up tight. At the stable, I used stale water from a trough to wash the worst of the blood and mud from my face and arms.

And then I found the inn. It was a small place, one floor with maybe half a dozen rooms to let, but from two blocks away I could see the light spilling out onto the street and hear the rattle of voices in good cheer.

As soon as I stepped through the door that cheer faded, the conversations dwindled, and two dozen gazes swept to me. I saw apprehension in most of their eyes and open hostility in some. A little panic flared up in my chest, but I pushed it aside, remembering the shadows passing without. I forced myself to take another step into the room, hands out at my side and open, empty.

A burly man with a bald head and sharp, pale eyes heaved himself out of a booth on one wall. I saw the motion, but he had two rows of tables to pass, and I had a clear path to the bar. I kept my pace, kept my eyes locked ahead, but I heard the scrape of chairs moving to let him pass off my right shoulder. A handful of men who had been leaning casually against the bar pushed away and moved forward to block my path.

I didn't have much choice but to stop. A moment later the big bald man stepped up, exchanged a grateful look with one of them, and then positioned himself right in front of me. He came too close, towering tall over me, and gave a rumbling growl.

"Who're you then?"

"I'm Daven Carrickson," I said. "From the Academy at Pollix."

He snorted at that, big and dramatic, and rolled his eyes for the rest of the crowd. He raised a meaty hand to finger the tattered collar of my shirt, old rags that Joseph had handed down to me. "A wizard, huh? You don't look much like a gentleman's son to me."

I felt my lip curl. "I'm no gentleman at all," I said.

He chuckled at that, then rolled his gaze around the room again. Some of them joined in his ridicule, offering up throaty chuckles or jeering catcalls. Most of them still looked afraid.

I was a little afraid myself. I could tell what this guy was up to. He saw me as a threat—everyone did—and he was trying to protect his townsfolk. Trying to drive me away before I started begging on the streets. Or robbing. Or worse.

I sighed. I nodded. "The rebels," I said. "The war." Times being what they were, he probably wouldn't let me go with a warning. He'd want to teach me a lesson. I glanced over my shoulder and found it a long way back to the outer door. I met his eyes again. "You've had soldiers passing through here?"

"You're no soldier either," the bully said. "We've had plenty of cutthroats and thieves through here, though, and we know how to deal with them." He glanced over his shoulder to the handful of men still gathered between him and the bar. "Don't we, fellas?"

I had to swallow against a lump of fear. I ducked my head. "I assure you, I'm neither cutthroat nor thief," I said. "Just a weary traveler." I turned my shoulder toward him, trying to break the confrontation, and gestured across the room. "Just grant me an hour by your fire—"

He slammed a palm hard against the front of my shoulder, spinning me back to face him, and the patrons nearest us scraped away. Behind the bully, his fellas took a step closer, ready to help.

I threw a look around the room, hoping to find an innkeeper to come to my aid. The closest I could find was a bartender, and he met my gaze with one as level and hateful as any in the room. No one in the whole common room met my eye with anything other than defiance. I found myself falling onto other habits, scanning the room now as terrain, noting the obstacles I'd have to fight around.

As soon as I caught myself doing that I took a long step back and raised my hands, open, palms out. I had no strength for a fight, and I didn't want to hurt any of these people. I didn't much want to get hurt, either, and that was the more likely outcome. "I'll go," I said. "I'm sorry. I was only looking for some warmth and light. There are dark things out in the night."

"That there are," the bully said, stalking after me even as I withdrew. His fellas fell in behind him. "And we've seen enough of them."

One of his fellas slapped him on the shoulder and pointed at my still-raised arm. "What's that there?" he asked.

The bully peered closer, and I realized he was staring at the pale white scars upon my left wrist, peeking out the end of my tattered sleeve. "You branded?" the bully demanded. "You a renegade from the king's justice?"

That struck too close to home. I stopped suddenly and he stepped too close again. I met his gaze and shoved back my sleeve to reveal more of the wicked scar that snaked all the way to my shoulder. I heard someone gasp in the watching crowd and saw the confusion pass over the bully's eyes.

"That's no brand," I growled at him. "That's the mark of a living dragon. I faced it, and I survived."

A flash of memory took hold of me then—of the black dragon that had nearly destroyed me, and of the dark shapes passing in the night outside—and fear held me in place. Fear gave me courage. There were worse things out there than this bully and his half-drunk friends.

He opened his mouth to sneer more contempt at me, but I shook my head once. "I brought no threat," I said. "I gave no offense." The words came out low, almost shaking with a quiet fury. "All I ever hoped was an hour at your fire."

As I said it I fell into my second sight. The fire flickered and flared on a broad stone hearth. I saw it as a dozen dancing flames, and in my mind's eye I reached a hand across the room and plunged it painlessly into the fire. I knotted that invisible hand in the twisting flames, gripped them tight, then pulled them back to me.

The susurrus of fear that had held the room since my arrival burst into a many-throated scream of true terror. Chairs clattered and tables crashed as the inn's patrons scrambled away from me. To their eyes the fire itself stretched out in a long streamer, flowing like a jet of water from its bed of embers to my outstretched left hand.

I transferred my gaze to the bully, still standing above me. He was frozen in perfect terror, and I felt no pity. I held the hearthfire in a ball between my hands, close to his belly. The living fire struggled to escape, fighting to be free, but I bound it with my will. Every errant flame I bent back into the fire's core, until it blazed like an inferno between us.

"I never hurt you," I said, resuming my rant, "and yet you greeted me with hostility. I—"

I saw him tremble then. I saw tears in the big man's eyes. His fellas had fled him, cowering with everyone else in the room against the cold stone walls. I could taste their fear, thick in the air, and it sapped my strength. It sapped my anger. I lowered my gaze, extended one hand, and sent the fire flowing back into its bed. I saw the bully catch a breath, and it escaped him almost instantly in a shrill little sob. I turned my back on him and left the inn.

13. Of Violence and Blood

Outside, the wind howled. The darkness felt deeper after holding a hearthfire between my hands. It was cold and thick and empty. I squeezed my eyes tight shut for a moment, heard someone in the room behind me burst into tears, and shook my head once. I turned south.

I'd gained a road, at least. And I had places to be. I took a deep breath and let it out. Probably for the best, really. I hadn't time to spare or coin to spend. A stay at the inn had been an idle dream. I set my shoulders, turned my face toward Tirah, and started down the road.

I went perhaps a hundred paces before a tremor seized me. I made it another step and then I shook again, like a doll in the jaws of a furious hound. I fell to my knees and gasped a single sob. Shame burned cold behind my chest. I'd come here hoping to escape that kind of darkness, and instead I had shared it with all these innocent people. I could still see their fear, could smell it in my memory, and it turned my stomach.

And mixed within the shame I felt my own fear. It was the fear that had chased me across the hills, the fear of mighty things unseen. But there was more. I had as much to fear from men as monsters. The bully in the bar had reminded me of sins I'd long forgotten. I *was* a fugitive of the king's justice. I had enemies at court and at the Academy. I had enemies among the king's garrison and in the rebels' highest ranks. The world of man was bent against me. The only peace I'd truly known had been at Joseph's cabin. And I had walked away.

A shiver wracked me and another sob escaped. I missed that rotting cabin. I missed the man who hadn't challenged me, had never sneered. He had shown me only kindness that brought me from the edge of death and brought me into my power.

My power. I ground my teeth. My power that had torn his boat to tinder. My power that had filled these hearts with fear. My power that I could not quite control. Better if I only had the sword.

But even as I thought it, I remembered the king's soldier I'd spitted on my blade. I shook my head and clenched my fists. I was a threat, a danger, a monster as terrible as the beasts that roamed the night.

This town's bully had known it. Archus had known it, and Seriphenes, too. Cooper, mocking me on the hills outside Sachaerrich, and everyone who'd ever heard my father's name and shunned me in the streets. They'd known and sought to chase me out.

Everyone but Joseph. I pushed myself up to sit on my heels and dragged my ragged sleeve across my eyes. He'd given me a home. He'd given me respect. He'd taught me a new trade, and shared his wealth, and perhaps I could have stayed there all my life. Let rebellion wrack the land. Let Claighan's nightmare dragonswarm roll across the earth. They wouldn't touch some fisher's hut forgotten on the shore.

I took a breath. I dried my eyes and thought of my friend Joseph. I thought that I'd go home—

And then I heard a sound upon the road. It was the crunch of stone beneath a boot and less than half a dozen paces behind me. Fear and fury flashed through me, and I flung myself to my feet. I sprang backward, opening distance between me and this intruder. And as I jumped my eyes darted to take in every detail. My hand flew to a sword that wasn't there.

It was no attacker, though, no mob come to chase me from the town. It was one man, barely older than me, with work-worn hands and friendly fat cheeks. His eyes were wide, startling white within the night, and he threw his hands up and flung himself to the ground. He screamed, "Don't hurt me!"

The shame bit deep into my gut again, and my shoulders fell. After another heartbeat I stepped over and helped the young man to his feet. He wore a wedding band upon his hand and met my grip with easy strength.

"I'm sorry to have frightened you," I said. He laughed, nervous, and I winced at that. "I will not hurt you. Just go."

He stood before me. He adjusted his shoulders, then took a breath. "I'd rather not," he said. "I'd rather hear your story."

"You'd never believe it," I said.

"That interesting, is it?" he said. A smile peeked out at the corners of his mouth, then came out for real. "I could hardly complain at that."

I shook my head, then nodded down the road. "I'm needed in Tirah." It made a better excuse than Joseph's cabin. "I should go."

"Not at night," he said. "That's foolishness. Even for a wizard." His face went pale at that and he gulped, but he recovered in a beat. "I have a room. And a warm fire. And my Becky can make you a supper to warm the soul. Stay with me a night and I will carry you halfway to Tirah tomorrow."

"Carry me?" I said. The rest...it sounded too good to even think about. "Why would you—"

"I've business down in Ammerton," he said. "And a team too fine to haul a cart, but you'll be glad of them tomorrow."

I looked more closely at his eyes. I shook my head. "That's no answer." I glanced back at the door of the inn. "Why would you offer me this?"

He paled again, just a touch around the eyes, but I saw it. He didn't look back at the inn. "It wasn't right to treat you that way," he said. "And I could use a dangerous man on my side, if I'm to take the road to Ammerton. And because...." He trailed off. He finally broke eye contact, looked away, and gulped again. "Because I am afraid of darker things than you."

That much I could believe. I remembered the dragons fighting just miles from this town. I couldn't have been the only one to see it. This man was a helpless farmer, forced to take his cart down the long miles of the empty road. I remembered the loneliness, the emptiness of the land all around me. Whether I went back to Joseph's cabin or on down the road to Tirah, I had that desperate solitude to look forward to.

That decided me. I'd impressed him with my show of fire, but I wouldn't be half so handy against an attack as he hoped. But his horses could move me faster, and I'd appreciate his company as much as he hoped for mine.

"Daven," I said, extending my hand, and he grinned again.

"Rann." He said. I nodded my head, once, and he led me back to the stables to fetch his cart.

His farmhouse sat on a plot that would have made Jemminor jealous, with a stable of his own and a house for the farmhands besides. His Becky made a fine meal indeed, and he showed me to a bed more comfortable even than the one I'd had at the Academy. I woke an hour after dawn, still sore and still tired, but better for the rest. The farmer had his cart already packed and waiting, and I watched his wife fret and fluster over him for a dozen minutes before he finally kissed her once, warm and firm, and said his sweet goodbye.

"I'll be back tomorrow," he promised.

And then we took to the road. He asked for my story and ended up telling me his. He was the second son of a minor baron. His older and younger brothers had both gone off to war behind the royal banner. One for love of country, one for fame. Either one, it seemed, would have made a better farmer than young Goodman Rann. The family home was fallen on hard times, and he had to make this journey.

The story passed the time, but it cut at my heart. He didn't tell me how his brothers died, or exactly when his father passed along. He didn't tell me what it was that drove the farmhands from his fields, devoured his livestock, and ruined his crops. He spoke of accidents and fickle fortune, the way a farmer would, but I could see the edge of darkness he dared not address outright.

There were dragons in these hills. I saw no sign of them by daylight, as we rolled swiftly south along the farmers' road to Tirah, but I could see the signs of them in Rann's story. I could feel their effects in the mob's response to my appearance last night. The dragons had brought hard times, chaos, even where they hadn't yet shown their true forms.

I thought again of running off to Joseph's cabin. It was a wish, a dream, but not one I could long indulge. I knew too much. I knew what wrecked the farmer's lands. I knew what screamed in the night. And I knew it was just the beginning. We would need more than brave men or hiding places. We would need an army. We would need organization. We would need order.

A memory of the rebel wizard Lareth flared in my mind, sharp and clear. He knelt beside me, almost giggling, and told me he would kill the king. I had no love for the king, but the nation needed order now. Lareth's reckless stroke would doom the world. I looked over at the farmer on the seat beside me, set my jaw, and turned my eyes toward Tirah.

We passed through Nauperrel and Undermest and a dozen little towns with names known only to their farmers. We passed beneath a clear blue sky, sun riding high, and lunched in an inn where three of the King's Guard bragged of a recent victory over a band of rebels. Or perhaps a band of brigands. It was hard to tell from their description, and I got the sense the Guardsmen didn't much care.

We passed the afternoon in pleasant silence, the morning's gloom long lifted. Birds sang in the air, cattle grazed in unfenced fields, and Rann began to hum a merry tune. The dragon threat was easy to forget.

I carried it in my heart, though. I remembered what I had seen, the dragons' fight at dusk, and even as the goodman whistled, I watched the sun sink down. How much of it was timing? Would the dragons come out as evening approached? The road bent from east to south, and shadows stretched across it as we moved closer to the hills. I felt a shiver chase down my spine. Timing and terrain. There was more here to fear.

But nothing came for us. Evening settled down, and my eyes ached from staring at the land rolling by on our right, but Rann noticed nothing and soon he had us rattling over cobblestoned streets and settling to a stop near an inn as large as any I'd seen outside the City. Stableboys came to fetch the reins, and Rann hopped down to the ground.

I moved automatically, following him, and for the first time really looked around. "Where are we?" I asked.

"Ammerton," he said, as though it were obvious. "You've never been?"

I blinked at him. I looked back up the road, the way we'd come. "But you said—"

He nodded. "We made most of a hundred miles, in time for supper." He jerked his head toward the inn. "Come on. They make a fine pork cutlet here, and Simeon's going to be waiting."

I started to go with him, but I remembered I had no money to my name. The farmer had bought me my lunch, but I could hardly expect the same courtesy at the end of our journey. Still, I had no desire to be out on the road with dark coming on, and his company would find me welcome at the fire. I could find a place in a corner to sleep and strike for Tirah in the morning.

So I followed at his side as he opened the door. The place was huge. And empty. A bartender nodded to us as we came in, and a worn old man hunched over a beer in one corner, but otherwise the common room was deserted. Rann grunted with the same surprise I felt.

I nodded toward the old man. "Is that Simeon?"

"No," Rann said. His voice was distant. "Simeon is Becky's cousin. He's supposed to have seed and stock for me." He stood for a moment, then shook his head and started across the room. "Ol' Gregor," he called. "You seen Simeon? He was supposed to meet me—"

The bartender shook his head, grave, and Rann's pace faltered. He read something in the bartender's expression and his face went pale. "Something wrong?"

"Just got news an hour ago," the bartender spat back. "Something happened out at Drew Gail's farm."

"What?" Rann asked. "What happened?"

"Hard to say," the bartender said, and he dropped his gaze. "Crazy rumors coming in, but whatever it is, it's bad. Folks went out to check on him, Simeon among 'em."

Rann didn't listen to the rest. He turned on his heel and sprinted for the door, clutching at my sleeve as he passed. I knew what he was thinking, and I didn't like it. He bolted to the stable, caught a stableboy by the collar, and screamed at him for his cart.

"Rann, wait," I said. "Wait for word to come back. We don't know what's happened."

"I know," Rann said. "And you do too. These people won't admit it, but I've heard the things that scream in the night." His face went ashen. "Oh, Simeon."

"How far is this farm?" I asked, while stablehands bustled to prepare the cart. "Do you know even where to find it?" I had to ask it again before the farmer heard me.

"A couple miles outside town," he said. He nodded, almost frantic. "Not far." His breath caught, and I saw his lip tremble.

I put a hand on his arm. "Rann," I said, trying to comfort him, and he whirled on me.

I saw rage flash in his eyes, but it was born of fear and it fled a heartbeat later. "I tried to warn him," he said. "The hills aren't safe. Nobody listened, but I noticed it was worse in the hills. And in the woods."

I swallowed. "You don't actually know," I said. "It could be anything."

He shook his head. And then his eyes found mine, and I saw compassion settle in them. He sighed. "I'm sorry," he said. "I have to go, Daven. I have to go check on him. He's family. But this is no business of yours. Go on."

I shook my head. "No, I'll come with you."

He reached into a purse on his belt and counted out a handful of coins. He offered them to me. "I know you can't afford a room. Get yourself something to eat."

I pushed his hand away. "I can't take that," I said.

"You did as much as I needed," he said. "You made my trip a brighter one." His eyes flashed at that, and he dropped his gaze. He swallowed.

I looked back at the inn one last time then shook my head. "I should at least see it through to the end," I said. The cart rattled up and I nodded to it. "This is what you wanted me for anyway, isn't it?"

His eyes widened in surprise, then moistened with gratitude, and I felt a stab of shame. I couldn't offer him the help he wanted from me. I couldn't do anything to stop a dragon. But he needed company more than anything else. He needed hope. I hauled myself up onto the seat and then stared down at him. "Come on," I said. "Let's see what all the fuss is about."

Darkness fell as we rattled out of town, and a chill wind sprang up. Rann paid it no mind, but I had to huddle in on myself for warmth. Out on the king's road again, the farmer kicked his horses into a trot, and the little cart flew along. The moon was not yet risen but the stars shone bright from a clear sky and gave enough light to see.

Rann barely needed it, though. He seemed to know the way by heart. He urged his horses on, faster and faster despite a hard day's work, and when he turned them off the main road onto a rutted little path back to a farm in the hills, he barely slowed at all. We were half a mile from the road before I saw the firelight.

It was a furious, mad flickering, and with it came a rustle of noise. I had trouble distinguishing much over the thudding of horses' hooves and the clatter of the jouncing cart, but there was certainly a clamor in the night ahead. Rann took us around a curve, up over a hill, and a rundown farm-house came into sight below us. The farmer slowed the cart and jumped from the seat before we had even stopped. I leaped after him.

Beyond the farmhouse stood a little clearing, a fenced yard perhaps a hundred paces across. The small pond at one end of the yard would have made good watering for a modest flock, though there were no farm animals in sight. But near the pool, in the mud at the edge of the water, was a dragon. Inky black, larger than a house, and wounded.

It lay sprawled, one hind leg stretched out awkwardly behind it. Its sides heaved, and I saw great gashes gouged through the armored hide. Black blood stained the earth, and more slicked its long, sharp teeth.

And then I recognized the sound. It wasn't the scream of fighting monsters, but the shouts of an angry crowd. They gathered on the field, in a half-circle around the stricken dragon, wielding crude clubs or cheap swords or, more often, sharp-edged farm tools. They carried torches, too, flickering firelight that threw hideous shadows among them. They were the townsfolk of Ammerton. Perhaps even Simeon was among them, and Goodman Rann sprinted down to join them.

But I did not move. Something like cold water washed down my soul, and I lost the focus in my eyes. I could hear the angry rumblings of the crowd, feel their living fury, but I felt something else, too. I felt pain, deep and deadly. I felt despair and impotent rage. The dragon huffed and grunted, and I saw the closest humans press away from it, but instead of a gout of flame the dragon only managed a little growl and a puff of light. The farmers took confidence from that, and crowded closer yet.

They hoped to kill it. And something of that other presence in my mind told me they could kill it. It was too weak, too wounded. Instead of elation, I felt sadness. I felt a flash of frantic desperation. I took a step forward, into the silver starlight, and looked down on the mob below me.

And then something took hold of me. An eerie sense of hope flared in my chest, and without meaning to I fell into my second sight. I looked down on the army of men, pressing close and deadly, and I saw the slashing steel of their weapons like living death. I reached for it, as I had reached for wind and rain, but no effort of my will could touch the worked-metal. I saw it straining, yearning toward the empty blackness of the dragon—and the pulsing thread of red that danced within.

But there were other powers here. There was earth all around them, and water behind the dragon, and even the biting wind that had risen while we drove. I ignored them all. Something in me bent my mind on the fire that danced above a hundred waving torches. I felt my lips pull back in a silent growl. I stretched out a hand, grasped the living flame from the torch of the foremost farmer, and hurled it like a stone to the ground at his feet.

It exploded in a burst of sparks, and the grass caught fire. The farmer screamed in terror, and I heard a roar of victory from the dragon. Then without thinking I did it again, with a flame in the heart of the group, and I heard their panic as they tried to escape the wild fire. Then I grabbed ten flames at once and hurled them to the ground. I grabbed a dozen more and snuffed them out. And then the rest, so darkness fell between one heartbeat and the next, apart from the vicious fire spreading out around their feet.

And then they broke and fled. I saw Rann among them, and he supported another man who hobbled at his side. They came toward me, and a flush of shame and confusion that were entirely my own washed over me. Then of my own volition I turned and fled, darting into the shadows beneath a nearby grove of trees. I hid there as the stampede of terrified townsfolk flooded past. I hid there as Rann helped his injured cousin into the cart. He called for me, three times, but then Simeon groaned and the dragon roared again below and Rann broke and sent the cart careening back down to the road.

I watched it go until I could hear its rattling wheels no more, and then some compulsion turned me back toward the dragon and pressed me three paces forward out of the shadows of the trees. I looked down on the dragon, and it looked up at me. For a long moment we stood like that, lit only by the flicker of spreading fires in Drew Gail's pasture. I reached out with a thought and crushed the fires out.

Before I could do more I felt that other presence in the back of my mind again. Not just the subtle compulsion that had directed my hand before, not the siren call that had pulled me toward the warring dragons in the night. This was a whole presence, one I remembered from the night long ago when the dragon had dropped me into the sea. I felt its pain. I felt its fading anger, and its growing curiosity. I felt its gratitude, too, and the quiet thrumming thrill of survival.

And I felt its desire, compelling me to come forward and present myself before it. I stopped my feet, swayed for a moment, and then that pressure redoubled. I could feel it swell inside my head, stronger and stronger, but I fought it. The dragon's will pressed hard, driving against my spirit, but my mind had grown strong and my will stronger.

I stood upon the hill above the dragon and forced back that second awareness until it was only a seed in the back of my head. I could not push it any further; I could not push it out of my mind, but I could contain it. For several minutes I stood under the starry sky, sweating in spite of the cold, until I felt the aggressive force relent.

I raised my eyes then, met the beast's gaze, and it only stared at me. Without the overwhelming presence of that other awareness, I felt a flush of animal terror beneath its gaze. I trembled so hard I could not contain it, but I didn't break eye contact. I did as I'd done before, fighting my own emotions as I'd done the dragon's, until I owned control of my mind once more.

Then I took a long step down the hill, toward the beast. It huffed a breath, shifted its head, and waited. Deep inside my mind, I felt a touch of surprise from the beast and just a hint of admiration.

You have grown much, little human. I could still hear the voice in my head, but now I had some idea how. I could feel the thoughts reverberating from that kernel of his awareness, feel them coming out of his mind and echoing into my soul. *I would not have guessed. But here and now you have my gratitude. You saved me, Daven. I owe you lifedebt.*

I took a slow breath, forcing the monster's emotions apart from my own, and stoked the little flame of my fury. It had controlled me. I concentrated on that place in the back of my head, the link between the dragon's mind and mine. "*Hello again, dragon. I have done you a kindness tonight that you did not deserve.*"

Do not call me dragon. Dragons are many but I am one. Call me Vechernyvetr, Daven. Know my name as I know yours. We are bonded now, closer than I would have guessed possible.

"*Vechernyvetr, then.*" Even in my mind the name felt powerful and strange. I frowned. "*I should have let you die.*"

Why is that? The thoughts were accompanied by surprise, offense, where I had expected sarcasm. I almost shouted at him aloud, but I was not sure he would have understood my language. Instead, I spoke in my mind.

"Why? You tried to kill me! You dropped me in an ocean to die!"

But you are not dead. You are quite well. Strong. The day I met you, you could not have done what you did today.

I tried to hold on to my anger, but it slipped like water through my fingers. There was truth in the creature's words. I took a step closer, holding myself as tall as I could. *"You are a threat. You are a monster. I would be happier if you were dead."*

The dragon answered me with a rolling laugh. I know that feeling well. But it is as I said. There is a bond neither of us can easily break. And it has proven useful tonight.

"To you, perhaps." I felt irritation curl my lips. "It cost me a friend, an easy night's sleep. A meal or two—"

These are petty things, the dragon said. It rolled its great eyes, and shifted in the mud. You lost one night's sleep and gained the gratitude of a force of nature.

I felt an eyebrow arch. "And what is that worth?" I asked. "The gratitude of a monster. A dragon helpless and already halfway dead, no less."

You judge too quickly what you do not understand. I will be well enough to pay my debt. I am tired and weak, but far from helpless. Dragons heal quickly. By midnight I shall be well, and then I can settle our score.

I frowned at that and moved closer to the monster. Somewhere far in the back of my mind, near the place where I had tucked the dragon's thoughts, an animal part of me wailed in fear. But mostly I was not afraid. Mostly I was curious. I stepped up to the injured leg, the one stretched out awkwardly at the dragon's side. I raised a hand that didn't quite touch the long, jagged gash that split the dragon's hide and muscle down to bone.

The moon came out then, slipping free from a light band of airy clouds and peeking over the trees. A beam of silver light traced across the earth and fell upon the dragon's hide.

From that far corner of my mind I felt a flash of relief so sharp and sudden it broke through all my defenses and washed over me as though it were my own.

When I fought it back, surprise and confusion held its place. *"Moonlight?"* I thought. *"There is no magic in moonlight."*

Arrogant little humans, it said. There is so much more magic than your own. The moon is a mighty power, ever-changing mistress of the chaos night. She is our queen. There is no injury to my kind that cannot be healed between sunset and dawn. I will be well by midnight.

Beneath my hand, the dragon's wound began to heal. I watched ruined flesh stitch itself together again, watched armored hide remade beneath the silver light of a waning moon. *"Incredible."*

The dragon huffed, an irritated sound that sent a blast of hot air washing all around me. *You are a boring little pet*, the dragon said. *But it is as I said. I owe you lifedebt. What boon will you ask of me?*

I thought about that for a long time, and I could feel Vechernyvetr wondering at my silence. Finally, I shrugged. *"It will be midnight before you can offer it, so I will wait until midnight to decide. I must think long and hard on this."* I sensed the dragon's compliance, and then the beast settled down to doze while it healed. I felt its weariness within me, and a little echo of my own, but hunger quickly overwhelmed it. Lunch seemed a long way away, and I couldn't guess when my next meal might come.

I made my way to the pool at the end of the little yard, taking on my second sight as I did so. There were little whispers of life within the water. The farmer's pond was deeper than I'd expected and well-stocked as I had hoped. Short bursts of light blinked through the slow, ancient energies of the water itself as fish darted after prey, away from predator. I reached out carefully with my mind, binding the water into a shell around one of the larger fish, then brought it rushing like a bubble to the surface. With a little smile of satisfaction, I reached out and plucked the fish from the water.

I found the memory of fire among the quiet embers still hot in the farmer's field, but it took more effort than I'd expected to coax them back to flame. I'd nearly succeeded when I felt the dragon shift behind me. I had one heartbeat's warning before it coughed, and belched a tiny stream of fire that washed like water across the ground before it. Hotter than a forgefire, the dragon's flame lit the trampled grass, and I grabbed a thread of it and bound it with my will before the fuel itself crumbled to ash. I heard the dragon's satisfied chuckle deep in my mind, and then it was asleep again.

I cared little about its amusement. I had everything I needed. I cleaned the fish on the pitted edge of a sword abandoned in the townsfolk's flight. One fish and an open fire made a small and simple meal, but after my hunger it was a feast. When I had eaten my fill the moon was already shining high, but Vechernyvetr still slept.

I eyed him for a moment, wondering what favor I could ask of a dragon. My mind returned again and again to the threat upon the king. Whatever else I wanted, nothing compared to that danger. I'd spent two days now chasing blindly after a solution to a problem much too large for me, and here before me was an answer.

I found a place to rest my back against the dragon's warm hide and stared up at the stars while I considered options. I found no definite plan before a yawn cracked my jaw, and soon after that I shook myself from a light doze and tried to focus. The rhythm of the dragon's breathing defeated me. I fell asleep in earnest and only woke hours later when the dragon shifted in place. It hesitated for a heartbeat, just long enough for me to catch myself, then threw itself off the ground with a mighty power. It lunged into the air, huge wings hammering wind down upon me, and thrummed up high into the night.

"You are well then," I thought, aiming it at the knot of emotion thrilling in the back of my mind. The beast answered me with joy and with a flood of power that left me almost drunk. I pushed it back.

I watched the dragon dance among the stars, watched it stretch stiff muscles, and I reached out with my own senses toward the spot in my mind. I imagined I could feel its motion, feel that rush of air and movement that even now I could remember.

The dragon soared for a moment longer, then frustration bubbled through, anger, and it banked long and slow and settled once again before me. It stalked slowly closer, cauldron eyes fixed on me, and huffed another forge-hot breath.

I must go, the dragon thought. I have other burdens than yours to settle. So decide now or accept the delay. What would you have of me?

"I would have an end to war," I thought. "The duke Brant has brought rebellion against the king, and the wizard Lareth fights for him—"

A growl escaped the dragon, a low and terrible sound, and I felt a flare of impatience from it. *I have no interest in the politics of man.*

"This is more than politics," I thought. "The nation is on the brink of chaos. Lareth plans to kill the king—"

I do not have time for stories, the dragon said. If you have a task to ask of me, then ask it.

I clenched my fists. "I want you to win the war."

That sounds like more than one night's work, the dragon answered. It sounds a greater threat than the one you saved me from.

I shook my head. "You needn't kill them all," I thought. "Attack them in a gathering and crush their numbers."

Your rebels do not gather, Vechernyvetr said. My kind can feel a gathering of arms, and only from the sea has that kind come. These are the soldiers of your king, I believe.

I sighed and nodded. "Then not even a gathering. Just Lareth. Can you kill Lareth for me?"

Can you tell me where he is? the dragon asked. I didn't even answer, the frustration that flashed through me was response enough. The dragon lowered its head. *Could you kill a single bee within a swarm, if I named him for you? No. I cannot kill your wizard.*

I scrubbed my hands across my face. The dragon was scarcely any help at all. I caught my breath and shook my head. *"Fine,"* I said at last, knowing how much I squandered a dragon's lifedebt. *"I ask you to carry me to Tirah. It will save me two days' travel—"*

The dragon's answer came as angry laughter in my mind. The monster threw itself into the air again, battering me with the downdraft of its wings. *Do I look like a beast of burden to your eyes? You silly little man. I am a beast of violence and blood. Ask that of me and it is yours, but I am not a pony you can ride.*

With that, it rose high into the sky. I strained after it, shouting in my mind. *"You owe a debt, and this is all I need! I have no use for violence and blood!"*

The dragon was a shadow against the star-specked sky, a motion fading north. Its answer came from far away, but clear within my mind. *You will,* it said with confidence. *You humans always do. As much as we and more. The time will come, and I will heed your call.*

I heard it, or imagined it say *Farewell,* as final as I'd ever heard. I watched until I could see nothing of its shadow in the sky, then I fell to my knees. And then I sighed.

14. The Wizard's Plan

I left the farm at a sprint, clutching the rusted, pitted sword at my side and straining to see by the moonlight. The heavy weapon slowed me, and the rutted road tripped me again and again, and finally I abandoned the blade and limped on out to the king's way. I walked for a mile while I caught my breath. My mind raced, trying to sort everything that had happened.

The dragon had compelled me. I knew that. No matter that it had offered me a boon reward, I had not by my own will done anything to save it. I certainly wouldn't have turned the villagers' fire against them.

But even as I thought it, some treacherous corner of my spirit reminded me I'd done just that the night before when I was surrounded by hostile locals, weak and tired and afraid. They had threatened me, and I'd used their own fire to drive them back.

I hadn't hurt anyone. Not either time. I couldn't imagine the dragon showing such restraint. But why would I have saved it?

I remembered the trace of red that danced within the dragon's darkness. It was my blood. I knew that now. The mark of my power within the beast. A part of me. Could it have been as simple as that? I'd felt just as threatened here as the night before? I'd chased them away to preserve that piece of me?

I remembered the blinding agony of the dragon's acid blood against my wound. I remembered the dragon raging that I had done something to stop it killing me. I wondered if I might look the same to another wizard's second sight—all flare of light and life, but with one thin strand of black as dark as nothingness.

It made sense. *Something* had kept my broken body breathing. *Something* had given me inhuman strength to survive. For that matter, *something* had given me the gift of chaos magic—a kind of sorcery most wizards didn't dare attempt.

I could feel it in me, then: the thread of ancient, terrible strength, and the core of power that drove me. I tapped into it, beneath the light of the rising moon, and while Vechernyvetr soared north to his acts of violence and blood, I ran toward Tirah to stop one.

I made perhaps a dozen miles, flitting like a ghost through villages long since gone to sleep. I stopped to drink from a township's well, I snatched a pear from a roadside orchard, but mostly I just ran.

I passed another sleepy town with four hours still till dawn, and then fences fell away until rolling plains stretched wide in all directions. I slowed beneath the stars in the heart of the wide open plains and felt the immensity of it. And then I yawned, until I feared I would crack my jaw, and I missed a step and barely caught myself short of falling.

Dragon blood or not, I needed to get some sleep. I left the road, hoping to find a spot with fresh water to rest an hour or two. I'd seen the glint of moonlight on an oxbowed river once or twice along the way, off to the west beneath the shadows of the hills. So I bent my path in that direction, hoping the river had followed me this far.

I found it, not a mile from the road. Low and wide and slow, the river snaked across the verdant plain and made a great peninsula before me where one tree grew. An ancient oak spread its mighty branches over a little spit of land.

Where embers glowed beneath a cooking pot.

I stopped in my tracks, weariness and dragon's strength alike forgotten in a sudden fit of fear. I fell to my hands and knees, crouching in the too-short grass, and strained my eyes to see.

A dozen men sat close around the dying fire's coals. They held tin cups or bowls, and I smelled the faint aroma of a stew. My stomach rumbled, but they were too far away to hear it. I saw swords and knives on their belts, and a crossbow leaned against the trunk of the proud oak. There were sturdy boots and light chain shirts, but not a scrap of uniform among them.

Rebel soldiers. Or brigands. Either way, these men were trouble. And as I watched one of them snatched the cook-pot and dunked it in the river. He brought it back and dumped water on the coals, barking orders as he did. I heard groans and complaints, but the men around the fire began to rise, to gather their things together.

That was the sign that it was time for me to go. I had no desire to meet these men alone beneath the moon. I turned to slip away, skulking low as a hunting fox, and I was almost lost to sight when I heard a word that stopped me dead.

"Tirah."

I strained to hear above the sudden pounding of my heart. The man who spoke assisted me when he raised his voice in sharp objection. "There's no way! We'll never beat the king there. It's more than forty miles—"

"We don't have to," another voice growled back. "The wizard has made arrangements. We only need make it to Nathan's farm." I scampered back, peering past a little bush, and saw the man who'd doused the fire. "Still a long night's walk, but do you really want to sit this one out?"

He didn't get an answer right away, and I crept closer trying to get a better look at the expressions of the men in the circle. "Cowards," the leader growled. "Every man of you! Don't you understand what this represents? The king and, what, a couple dozen Green Eagles? We'll have three hundred men. We'll step out of empty air and win the war in the space of an hour."

I saw them shuffle, saw them exchange glances that never quite met the leader's eyes. The one who'd objected earlier spoke up again. "It's a little frightening, though, isn't it? Trusting the wizard?"

The leader drew himself up tall. He stared down his nose at the men around him, then shook his head in disappointment. He turned on his heel and snatched up his crossbow. "Stay, the lot of you," he said. "There's glory to be had. There's victory. And you'd do well to consider how the wizard treats men who let him down. He'll remember, mark my words. He'll remember who was there. And who wasn't."

With that he left, stomping south along the river's edge. The others stared after him for a heartbeat, then exchanged a quick, quiet conversation. Then they, too, hurried off after the leader.

I watched them go. My mouth was dry, my arms were weak. Twelve deadly men, and I was unarmed. I thought of the miserable old sword I'd left by the path at Drew Gail's farm, and of the magnificent blade I'd lost before when I first tangled with the dragon.

Of course, I wasn't entirely powerless. I raised a hand and felt the breeze playing between my fingers. I stretched my senses out to the patient, rolling depths of the river and felt the weight of it. Oh, I was far from helpless.

It didn't matter, though. If I'd been barely a day out of my sickbed and half-blind, I still would have followed them. This was it. This was the rebel wizard's plan. I'd expected it in Tirah, but this made so much more sense. He had an ambush planned on the Cara Road.

I slipped after them, lagging far behind, but never far enough to lose sight of them. All he'd need was a portal to bring them through, just as the Masters had sent us to hunt the dragon in a forest half a day's ride away. Claighan said such things were dangerous, but Lareth had shown no hesitation to work travelings. If he could bring three hundred men into the heart of the king's contingent—if he could drop them right on top of the king himself—the wizard could do just as he'd threatened.

I tracked them through the night, across a ford and into rolling hills, then up to higher ground beneath the shadows of true mountains. By dawn the ground we crossed was steep and treacherous, more rock than earth, but the soldiers that I followed made more noise than I could have hoped for and hid my presence as much as anything I could have done. They were jittery, anxious and excited for the day ahead.

And as they moved they joined another party of ten, then later fifty men who rose up from the earth like morning dew. I fell farther and farther back, wary, but no one ever looked my way. Their eyes were fixed on their destination. The sun was not yet risen, but it tinted the sky when the army I followed angled back down out of the hills, toward the plains, and I could see beyond them the neat lines of tended fields.

A ripple of excitement passed among them, and they moved faster. Despite my best efforts I fell behind. Just before dawn I lost them, though I knew the general direction they'd been headed. As the sun rose on the far horizon I crept up a little, long-forgotten footpath to the top of a gully and almost stumbled into their midst. They had stopped running at last, and as I came to the top of the hill I could see why.

They stood in an unfenced yard around a whitewashed farmhouse alone on the verge of a sprawling pasture. A ball of hazy green flame the size of my fist hung in the air, dancing with an eerie flicker, and more than a hundred men gathered around it. They kept their distance, leaving a circle nearly ten paces across at the center of their crowd, but every man among them stood attentive and stared at the flame.

From my place outside the gathering I could only barely hear the voice, but I had no doubt it came from the flame. "...timing is crucial," it was saying, and thin as it was I still knew it for Lareth's. I felt a knot of fury in my stomach. "Be ready."

I slipped into my second sight, considering my options. They carried no torches or I'd have dispersed them as I'd done the townsfolk of Ammerton. But here I saw no fire anywhere among them. Even the green flame that carried Lareth's voice seemed to be an entirely artificial construct. I could see the light of the energy that drove it, but it had no substance, no thread for me to bend to my will. The wind had died down low again, too. The power bound into their weapons and armor called to me, but even when I tried I could no more touch the metal than I could the green flame of Lareth's will.

Still, I could do something with the earth. While I was considering my options, though, I heard Lareth's voice hiss, "Now!" In an instant the ball of flame unfolded, attenuated, and flashed out into a rectangular window taller than a man and ten paces wide. A portal.

And the soldiers washed into it. I saw fear on some faces, saw shifting feet in the furthest rows, but still they moved. From both sides they poured into the traveling like sand rushing into the gap of an hour glass, and a hundred men disappeared from Nathan's farm before I could so much as slow them.

A cold, sickening fear flashed through me. I'd just watched them go to kill the king! I heaved myself up over the edge of the gully even as the last of the rebels moved through the portal. I sprinted as hard as I could across the trampled grass. I caught a glimpse through the gateway of a steep rocky slope, spotted with scrubby trees, and far below was the wide path of the Cara Road.

My feet pounded, as did my heart. My breath seared in my throat. My vision blurred as I turned all my focus to desperate haste, and I flashed through the portal a heartbeat before I felt the whispering pulse of the wizard's will stretching out to close it.

I made it through, though. I made it through, and burst out at a full sprint above a steep fall. I heard the little sounds of surprise among the soldiers around me. I sensed them, vague shadows among the trees, spread out all along the slope, as thick as the trees themselves. I might have heard the rasp of a sword, or even a softly barked order.

I could scarce respond to it. I was falling. My first step through the gate stretched too far before it hit the earth, and it hit loose soil that gave beneath it. My second step found no purchase at all, and then I was falling forward. I reached out my arms to catch myself, still in my second sight, and instead of hitting the earth I seized the elements with my mind and bent them to my need.

I caught the air, weak and still but strong enough to slow my fall. I shaped the earth beneath me, slamming my will down the slope ahead of me, changing a rough and rocky slope into a path as smooth as the flat of a blade. I snapped it in my mind, like a housewife snapping a bedsheet, and trees and boulders danced aside to clear my way. Even wrapped in air I nearly faltered when my foot struck the path I'd made, but my next step hit true and then I was running down the mountainside as easily as a paved street.

Far below I saw figures on the king's road. These wore uniforms—the deep green of the king's personal bodyguard, and the soldiers' red and blue. There were more than I'd hoped, but not enough. Not enough by far. They moved easily, unafraid, swords sheathed and eyes fixed lazy on the distant horizon instead of the hills around them. Of course. The advance scouts had already checked these hills for an ambush. They'd come and gone before Lareth opened the way.

Terror nearly overwhelmed me then. I felt it batter at the control that had let me remake the mountainside. I tried to push it away, but I saw an arm reach out at me as I passed. It missed, dirty fingers closing inches from the end of my sleeve. I heard another cry behind me, still muted but sharper now, and knew I was in trouble.

My second sight failed me then. My strength went with it, and if not for my momentum I probably would have fallen where I stood. Instead I sprinted on down the hillside, helpless to do anything else. I forced the deadly men around me from my mind, and focused all my attention on the cavalcade below. I threw myself toward them with great leaping strides.

As soon as I thought they might hear I bellowed, "Look to the hills!" I heard complaints from the rebels around me but I fought to ignore them. "Look to the hills!" I screamed. "Ambush! Ambush by the rebel's men!"

I'm not sure if the soldiers on the road below me heard any of the words, but they responded with merciful haste. Pikes and swords flashed into hands and the loose spread of soldiers fell into a tighter formation. The Green Eagles were faster, falling back against the carriage that must have carried the king and drawing crossbows while their eyes searched the hill. And even as they responded, I heard an order pass along their lines and every man among them spurred his horse faster. They flashed through the pass with surprising speed.

Still hoping to take some advantage of their surprise, the rebels came boiling down out of the hills to fall upon the king's men. I saw the woods ripple like an anthill opposite me. The same must have been happening all around me, too. Arrows flew in both directions, and the first charge of the rebels even got close enough to swing their swords, but superior arms and training threw them back and the king's mounted party slipped away.

And as they left, they took my only hope with them. Still sprinting down the hill, I watched them go, leaving nothing but furious rebels around me in all directions. I heard their frustrated wails, heard the whistle of arrows bent in my direction—mostly from above—and heard the orders raging openly now to take me down.

I scrambled for my second sight, but I could find no shred of calm. I tried to see my surroundings, to guess where I might hide, where I might run, but everywhere I looked I saw murderous faces bent on me. A dagger flew past my shoulder and buried itself in a tree as I flashed by. A sword flicked out into my path and caught my leg. It didn't bite deep, but it scored a painful track along my hip.

Down below me rebels crowded onto my path, waiting, but no force of will could have stopped my rush down the hillside then. Pain burst fire-bright behind my eyes as a thrown stone hit my shoulder from behind, and then another larger than a fist hit me in the small of the back and sent me tumbling head-first down the hill.

I slid to a stop at the feet of the group who had crowded into the path, and I saw among them the leader who had doused the fire back at the camp beside the river. His face twisted in a furious sneer. His leg went back. His boot flashed forward. The darkness fell.

I woke in pain bound in a wooden chair in the middle of a tent. Coarse, strong cords bit into my wrists behind my back. I could see nothing in the tent but this one chair. And the wizard Lareth.

He crouched before me, resting on the balls of his feet, staring up into my eyes. He grinned when I focused on him and showed me all his teeth. "Oh, it's you," he said, delighted. "I thought it was you. I thought it must be you. I had to see the eyes to know for sure, though."

I tried to answer, but my jaw wouldn't work. Pain stabbed through my head, and I winced against it. A groan escaped me, and Lareth chuckled.

"They were not kind to you," he said. "Just...not at all. And can you blame them? Really? After what you did?" He shook his head, admonishing.

I gained control enough to grunt, "I saved the king."

"You did at that," he said, with a grudging nod. "For now at least. It's far too bad. I had another plan for if this failed, but it's a tricky one. And harder for the way you spoiled the first. You gave the trick away, I think. They saw your magic, and mistook it for mine, I fear."

I tried to shrug, but the bindings were too tight. I glared down at him. "What do you want with me?"

"As it happens," the wizard said, "probably more than you'd suspect. I want your help."

"I'd rather die."

"You likely will," he said, without missing a beat. "But you're too good a chance to let slip by."

I closed my eyes, remembering the pain this one had inflicted when last he'd had me in his hands. "How?" I said. "What could you want from me?"

"Your power," he said. "Simple as that. I remember you, you know. I remember a time when all I had to do to steal your strength was stop you drawing your pretty little sword." I swallowed, remembering too.

He cocked his head to the side and looked at me down his nose. "And then you went off to die. It worked, too. You died. Everyone says you did."

"Everyone is wrong."

He shook his head. "Archus died. Leotus died. A dozen students died." A fist of sudden grief clenched at my heart, but he rattled it off as though the lives were nothing. "And yet somehow you came through much stronger than before."

"Who died?" I said. He blinked at me, as though confused, and I had to clear my throat to ask again. "Who died? You said a dozen students. Was...was Themmichus among them?"

He frowned at me. "The Eliade? You know an Eliade." He laughed, short and sharp, and shook his head. "No. I think I would have heard. Your Eliade's alive."

I'd never known his family name. In all the time we'd spent together, he hadn't offered it and I'd never thought to ask. Eliade rang familiar, though. I frowned, trying to find the memory, but it washed away in a moment of relief and then a flood of weary fear.

The emotions must have shown on my face, because his grin wavered, then twitched back into place at the last. "Ah, there," he said. "And we return to the business at hand. Where did you gain your power?"

I shook my head. "I have no power." I fought to gain my second sight even as I said it, but the calm eluded me. For the first time in months I stepped consciously into the exercises I'd learned at the Academy, but they rattled beneath my fear and pain. My focus fell apart, and all it left behind was Lareth's cruel smile.

"I know your name," he said. "I know how much you cannot do. But I was also there. I saw, upon the hills. I saw you shape the earth. I know a half a dozen Masters who could not explain the thing I saw—because they are too arrogant to doubt the things they know—but I know what I saw. You...are a sorcerer."

I shook my head. "I will not help you. I'm loyal to the king."

"You're foolish then," he said, with pity in his voice. I looked up and found him shaking his head. "In earnest, boy. Why would you serve the king? It's he, not I, who stole your chance at fame. It's he, not I, who set you on that road. It's he, not I, who crippled Master Claighan and set bounties on your head."

"But he is king," I said. "This is his land. It's not about me. Your rebellion costs more lives—"

"It isn't mine," the wizard said. "It's mine to end. I want what you want, Daven. I came to speak with Brant, to end his defiance, and saw that words would not do it. And, worse, I saw the king's army wouldn't do it either. This war would have stretched out for years. It's *been* brewing for years. The only end is ending that king's life."

I sneered at him. "Clever words—"

He raised a hand and cut me off. "Now listen, boy. I know you're practically a shepherd still, but hear me out. Just think. The war is real, for good or bad. Rebellion's here. You have a choice between two sides, but in the end it's all just politics. I cannot fathom what you'd find to love in that fat king's defense. But here, to me, it matters not at all. I've made your choice much simpler by far."

I took a slow breath and met his eyes. "What is my choice?"

"Join me," Lareth said. "Or die."

"Should I forget the things you've done?" I said, incredulous, but he nodded as though it were the most obvious thing in the world.

"Of course you should," he said. "Deal with the world as it is, not as you would have it be. The things I've done are done. But here and now you have a chance—"

"You wouldn't..." I said, and trailed off. I shook my head. "You couldn't trust me."

His lips pulled back to show his teeth. "I could in time," he said. "Not here and now. But give it time, and you will find a bit of everything your heart desires."

I shook my head. "You do not know my heart."

"I know every man's heart," he said. "You long for power. You long for admiration and respect. You long for liberty. Perhaps you long for friends." Every line struck me like a blow to the gut, but I fought to keep it from my face. He grinned anyway and spread his hands wide. "We have that here. For you, there's that and more."

"You're murderers," I said.

"We're soldiers," he replied. "That's what you wanted, no? To join the Royal Guard? Forget the Guard. Their pay is low and they promote by blood. But we...." He chuckled again, and waved a hand at me. "But we promote by power."

I swallowed against a sudden lump in my throat. I'd tried. I'd dreamed. I'd longed to join the Guard for all the reasons that he said. I saw these men as murderers, cruel and cold, but then I'd seen the same from a Green Eagle on the hills above Sachaerrich. I'd seen the same from a garrison of Guards in Gath-upon-Brennes, where they had put a bolt through Claighan's back.

The Guards had done that. Not Lareth. The king had called us traitors, when I had done nothing at all. I took another long, slow breath, and searched the wizard's eyes. He couldn't really be offering me this. I felt my lip curl, felt the cruelty of his deceit, and shook my head.

"You don't mean it," I said. "This is just another torture."

He sighed, and though he still smiled I saw sadness in his eyes. He shook his head. "I'm not prepared to cut you free and offer you a sword," he said. "I'm not so mad as that. But I believe you've got the strength we need, and if you only see you'll join our cause."

I held his eyes for a long time, searching. My heart pounded, my shoulders ached. I shook my head. "What would I do?"

"You'd kill the king," he said. He held my gaze for a heartbeat then nodded, as serious as I had ever seen him. "In one move you'd right the wrong you've done, you'd earn your place among our ranks." And I would burn to ash my hopes for any other life. I'd bind myself to the rebels in a way I could not break. He didn't say it, but I could see it in his eyes. He nodded.

I asked him, "How?"

"With fire," he said, and his smile came back. "You may not know, but he's enshrouded in more magic than this world has ever seen. One man, defended from the sling and stone, defended from the wizard or the wolf. We might have caught him in our trap, but I could not have burned him down. I needed time and clever care to break the spells. But you...."

He shook his head, and then at last I understood his smile. It wasn't madness—or not entirely madness. It was genuine joy. Hope. I believed him, then. Believed his promise, his offer.

"But not pure fire," I said. "They didn't protect him from that?"

"But not from living flame. Not sorcery," he said. "I'll send you through to him. A traveling. I'll send you to his court, in Tirah's heart, and you can beg an audience. Then bury him in fire." I shivered in horror at the thought. He shivered in anticipation.

"I cannot kill—"

"You can, my boy," he said, and placed a gentle hand on my shoulder. He held my eyes. "It's bleak, I know, but one man's death can buy an end to war. One sacrifice in flame could save us all."

Some of the fanatical gleam faded from his eyes, and he seemed to focus more clearly on me. He swallowed and dropped his gaze. He rose. "You'd save us *all*," he said again and nodded toward me. "This is your chance. The king will reach Tirah by even bell. I'll give you until then to make your choice."

I closed my eyes. I felt considerably steadier now. I nodded, as though in acquiescence, but behind my eyes I stepped once more into the wizards' calming techniques. I'd see how well Lareth could defend himself from the magic that could kill the king. I reached toward my second sight—

And pain lanced through my head. I screamed. I thrashed so hard I toppled the chair onto its side, while the burning cold of ice seared the backs of my eyes and blinding fire flared within my mind. Somehow I heard the wizard's sigh through all the pain and heard him cluck his tongue.

"The king is not protected from your power," he said. "But I am no such fool." I dimly felt the flash of light as the tent flap lifted. "Till even bell," he said, and he was gone.

Someone came and cut me from the chair. The agony faded back, slow as a falling tide, but I had no strength to resist the hands that took me from the ground and carried me away. I felt the heat of noonday sun, and heard the rustle of a busy camp. My porters moved with a quick efficiency, carried me a couple dozen paces at once, and then heaved me like a heavy sack of grain into the darkness of another tent.

I spilled across the floor, rolling until I bumped up against something soft and yielding. Something warm that jerked and cried out in surprise. Something that smelled like sweat and fear...and a summer sunset.

I shifted my shoulders despite the pain until I slipped back off her and rested flat on my back. I twisted at the waist to get my legs stretched out straight and then took several slow breaths while I searched the myriad aches and pains for anything that might represent a serious injury. The worst of it was still the pain in my head, though, and that was fading.

I opened my eyes and found myself staring up into a fall of dark hair, and eyes the gray of slate. With just a touch of blue. She frowned down at me, equal parts confusion and concern, and I heard myself laugh. It was barely more than a cough, but I shook my head and stared up at her.

"I know you," she said. "I... I met you at the palace."

I laughed again, though this one didn't come out much better. "You're the Eliade," I said at last. "I know your brother."

She shook her head. "It's impossible. It can't be you."

I smiled, lips pressed tight, and used a shoulder to lift myself up off the ground. It was awkward with my hands tied in the small of my back, but I got halfway up, and then she overcame her shock enough to help me the rest of the way.

She held my gaze for a long time after that, then she shook her head again. "You're... you're really him, aren't you? The shepherd from the palace. And Themmy's little hero. And a soldier. And a wizard." The words came fast, breathless, and I remembered Themm telling me long ago that he'd written home about me. I saw confusion pinch the girl's brows. "But he said that you were dead."

I felt my gaze drawn back toward the wizard's tent. "Not yet," I said. I frowned as well and turned back to her. "What are you doing here? Are you one of them?"

She pulled back and sat up very straight. Her chin came up, proud, as I had seen Themmichus's do. "I am fighting them," she snapped. I looked at her hands, unbound, and checked her ankles for some shackles. She had none. When I met her eyes again they flashed with fierce contempt.

"They underestimate me," she said. "Do not make the same mistake."

"I never would," I said. "But what are you doing here?"

"These are my lands," she said, full of righteous fury still. I frowned at her, and she waved toward the back of the tent. "We are at Teelevon. The seat of my father's lands. He is the only loyal servant left in all the south Ardain, so Lareth made his camp around our town. He holds us under siege—"

"Your town is just out there?" I asked, hope flaring, but she spotted it and shook her head.

"We're on the brink of ruin," she said. "Our fighting men are gone, our weapons confiscated, our food stores plundered."

I felt my shoulders sink. She sighed. "I know," she said. "*That's* why I am here. We had no other hope. I slipped away in the night and tried to pass their lines to find some help."

"That was brave," I said.

I saw the twitch of muscles as she set her jaw. Her eyes flicked to the tent's opening, then back to mine. "I'm not done," she said in a little whisper. She moved closer to me. "You saw I have no bonds. I'll give it until sundown and then run. If you think you can keep up—"

"No," I said. "I know this Lareth. He's a careful man and a monster when pushed. Do not assume he's underestimated you just because your hands are free."

She scowled down at me. "Then what should I do? Just hide? Just wait? Just see what Lareth's men might want from me?" Her voice quavered at the end of that, and I felt a stab of sympathetic pain. I closed my eyes.

"I see," I said. I nodded. "But we must be smart. Even if you have to run...we should at least coordinate our efforts. He'll come for me at even bell. I'll make you some distraction—"

"Why?" she said. "What does he want from you?"

I met her eyes for a heartbeat, but I could not hold the gaze. I dropped my eyes and sighed. "To...to kill me, I suppose. To have my answer."

I felt her eyes on me, measuring. A long time passed in silence. At last she asked, "What has he asked of you?"

I sighed. "He wants me to kill the king," I said. "He's offered me a place among his men, if I will just...." She gasped in horror and I nodded. "He would send me there tonight."

"To the king?" she said. "To Cara?"

"Tirah," I said. "The king relocated today."

She gripped my shoulder with an almost painful intensity. That drew my eyes at last, and I found her staring down at me with a fire. "You must go," she said.

"I cannot kill the king."

A frown bent her lips, and then she shook her head. "You are a hero," she said. "To be here at all. And you will take the rebel's offer."

I blinked at her. I shook my head. "I won't," I said.

She stopped me with a finger on my lips. "You will," she said. "You will go to Tirah. And you will warn the king. You will tell him the wizard lays siege outside my town. He has been waiting for an opportunity like this, to find them all gathered in one place. He'll come to wipe them out—"

"And save us both," I said. She nodded, serious. Hope flared in my chest and then died in the same heartbeat. I shook my head. "I think you underestimate the wizard. He must expect some attempt at betrayal."

"Then you must convince him," she said. "But I think he is not as smart as you suspect. Madness sometimes looks like genius."

I considered her for a long time. Her eyes burned with hope and angry passion. Perspiration touched her sun-dark skin. I remembered the pretty, confident girl who had flirted with me in the palace, but here before me was a warrior. "You have an uncommon courage," I told her. "How can you be so sure that I have the same? That I will be your hero?"

"I know it from Themm's letters. And from the fire in your eyes from the moment I met you. And from the quiet little rage that trembles in your voice even now." She smiled, and I saw a touch of tears in her eyes. "I'd almost lost all hope until I saw your face."

I swallowed and shook my head, but she held my gaze. I took a deep breath. "I will do everything I can to save you, Lady Eliade."

"Isabelle," she said. "Always just Isabelle."

"Isabelle," I said. I swallowed again and thought back on our pleasant encounter in the halls of the palace. I licked my lips and forced a laugh. "Did you... did you find your prince?"

Her eyes were hot on mine. After a long moment she gave me a little smile. "Half a dozen," she said. She moved a little closer. "But not a one to my liking. Too proud, too soft, too quiet. I think I could make good use of a shepherd though." Her eyes glittered.

I felt a heat burn in my cheeks and dropped my eyes. "I only hope to serve you," I said. She came closer still and I felt her warmth. I met her eyes and said quietly, "We are not safe here."

"I know," she said. Her voice came very soft. "And I am so afraid. But what is there to gain from letting that show?"

I nodded at that. "I'm thinking about the night," I said. "About our plan. I think it would be best if you didn't run."

She arched an eyebrow at me. "You don't imagine *I'm* so proud and soft and quiet, do you? I can be a hero, too."

I shook my head and tried not to think how soft she might be. "No," I said. "I know your courage and it gives me fear. We have a plan. But if you run...these are not all careful men. Even if Lareth doesn't have some trick in place, if you run and they chase you...they will not be kind in capturing you."

She held my gaze for some time before she said, in that same quiet voice, "They were not kind before."

I felt the blood drain from my face. I looked away, and she placed a comforting hand on my shoulder. "I am strong enough to do what must be done, Daven."

I nodded. "And that has changed," I said. I met her eyes. "*That* is what I'm telling you. You don't have to run. I will bring back the king with his army. Let them rescue you." She opened her mouth to argue, but I leaned closer and held her eyes. "Please, Isabelle. I intend to bring deadly men to do battle in this camp. Promise me you won't step out into that."

"But what if you fail?" she asked.

"I will not fail. For you, I will not fail."

She chewed her lower lip again, eyes on something far away. At last she said, "If they discover you've betrayed them, I could lose my chance."

"And if you run before I can bring you help," I said, "you could lose your life. Trust in me. Stay here."

She took a deep breath and held it. And then she nodded, once. "I will trust you," she said at last. And then more quietly still, "Everything rests on you."

I swallowed again, and met her eyes, and tried to match her courage.

15. In Tirah

We had little more time after that. She told me what little she knew of Tirah and of the king, and she assured me Themm was safe and well. She shared a bottle of stale water with me and half a loaf of bread. She was trying her hand at the thick knots that bound my wrists behind my back when a heavy footstep outside the tent stopped her. She drew away.

The ones who came for me were two big guards, and from the looks in their eyes they knew about the role I'd played at their little ambush. They were none too gentle as they dragged me from the tent, but they let me keep my feet. I walked between them across the camp, learning everything I could of it.

There were campfires everywhere. Dusk still hung in the air, but I could see the glow of campfires holding back the night in all directions. There must have been hundreds of tents. There could have been thousands. Straining my gaze into the distance, I could see a faint curve as the smaller clusters of tents bent toward the north, encircling the distant town.

My escorts led me to Lareth's tent. It was huge—easily three or four times the size of the dusty brown tents the soldiers used. This one was nearly a pavilion and stained a deep black that gave it a powerful presence at the heart of the camp. A guard outside the tent ducked in first, spoke briefly, then came back out and waved me on ahead. My escort stayed behind. I cast one last look around, trying to memorize every aspect of the camp's layout, and then ducked on in with my wrists still bound behind me.

I expected some kind of luxury. Instead I recognized the same tent I'd been prisoner in before. The chair had been righted and beyond it—in a corner I hadn't been able to see before—a simple bedroll lay in disarray. An open bottle of wine stood beside it, and a pile of leather-bound books. The wizard held another in his hand.

Now, too, there was a cold green flame hanging in the air off to one side. I felt my eyes drawn to it, and I saw Lareth turn to face it, too. He nodded slowly. "Impressive, is it not?" he said. "Or perhaps you do not know. So take my word, it's an impressive thing. A thing of my own making, even more."

He shook his head. "But you cannot see even a fraction of the thing." He stepped closer and waved a careless hand. As he did, a pressure I hadn't known was there eased in my head. "Go on," he said. "Look with the wizard's eye, and see what I have wrought."

I hesitated, the memory of pain still far too clear. He smiled at that and shook his head. "I mean to send you north to kill my foe," he said. He waved again, a slicing gesture, and I felt the bonds on my wrists fall away. I massaged life back into my hands. He nodded. "You'd do me little good without your power. Now try."

I hesitated a heartbeat longer, but if he only wanted to hurt me he had plenty of other ways to do that. I closed my eyes and stepped through the exercises Antinus had taught me so long ago. They drew my focus from the pain and fear. They helped me press those things down, to push them back, until I was nothing but my concentrated will. I breathed once, in and out, and opened my eyes to the world of energies and powers.

318

The tent held none. I realized for the first time there was no flame in here, no light but the cold green glow of Lareth's artificial fire. The air was still, the earth was out of reach. The only energy I could see in the entire tent was Lareth's—the strength of life that made him glow like a star, and the tiny reflection of that flame in his mystic fire.

Out of curiosity I reached out to that fire with my senses, but I could not grip it. My will passed right through. I could see the shape of it, though, could sense the purpose behind the working. It pulsed with the energy of a traveling, all bound up and hovering on the brink of realization.

I dropped my second sight and found Lareth watching my eyes. Too late he put on a careless grin, but I had seen the calculation, the measurement. I waved to the flame. "It's just a way to save a working?"

"It's...something on those lines," the wizard said. "It binds my will in place and time, unfolding without thought when I intend."

"And this one is for me?"

He showed his teeth. "This one's for you," he said. "This is your traveling toward Tirah. It opens when the sun is set."

I nodded slowly, mostly for his pride. "Quite impressive," I said. "I've never seen its like."

He snorted and shook his head. "Come," he said. He stepped across and took my arm, his thin fingers hard around my biceps. "We have some moments left before it shall unfold." He steered me toward the tent's entrance. As we stepped out into the falling night I saw again the myriad glowing campfires, and for a heartbeat I considered reaching for them.

Lareth stopped me with a slight pressure on my arm before he stretched an arm toward the tent where Isabelle was waiting. I saw another cold green flame above its peak. I felt a pit of ice in my stomach, and from the corner of my eye I saw Lareth slowly nod. He said nothing.

"And what is that one?" I asked.

"A simple thing," he said. "A ball of fire. Not...." He chuckled, amused. "Not the cold green sort, I should say. But hot. White hot. And larger than a house."

"And what...." I had to lick dry lips. "What trigger unfolds that one?"

"You," he said, and at last he played no games. He turned to me, cold and serious. "You, and her. If she should run—"

"She will not run," I said.

He grinned again. "She won't," he said. "And so already you have earned your keep. You did an admirable job of that. I think she quite believes that you will handle everything."

I swallowed. His eyes danced with a deadly light, and he nodded slowly.

"It was a ruse, of course," he said. "Betray me to the king? You're far too sharp to go through with that plan." His eyes flashed and his voice turned cold. "Do as you're told. Do only as you're told. And come back once it's done—before the dawn—and you can *have* the girl. I'll make her yours, to do with as you will."

I had to fight for a breath. I couldn't tear my eyes from the cold green flame. "Before the dawn?" I asked.

"By dawn," he said again. "The king is dead by dawn, or Isabelle instead."

I spun on him. "I can't guarantee that," I said. "I don't know Tirah. I don't know the king's disposition. I don't have any access to him—"

"Oh, but you are quite the clever lad," he said. "You'll find a way. I've every faith in you. Come now, your flame unfolds."

I fell into my second sight and reached for the working that hovered over Isabelle's tent, but I could no more touch it than I could the one in the tent. I could grab the campfires, though. I could burn this whole encampment to the ground. I could open the earth and swallow Lareth's tent. But Isabelle would die. I might die, too, but then and there that didn't bother me too much. That had been almost inevitable since the moment I dove through Lareth's portal at Nathan's farm.

But Isabelle... she trusted me. She needed me. To save her home. To save her. I felt a frantic desperation clawing at the back of my breastbone. I forced my sight away, and turned my back upon Isabelle's soft little prison. In Lareth's tent, the portal waited. He raised an eyebrow at me, impatient.

I knew what Isabelle would want me to do. I had no doubt. She had already risked her life to save her lands and she hadn't hesitated to ask me to do the same. This was larger than either of us. Her choice was made. She would want me to bring the king's forces to end the rebel threat no matter what the cost. I took a step toward the portal and felt cold sweat between my shoulder blades.

Perhaps I could still find a way. Perhaps I could still save us all. But before the dawn? I frowned at that. The deadline made it harder. I'd thought I might have a week—a day, at least, to bring the cavalry from Tirah—but one night? I shivered and took another step.

Off to the side, the wizard laughed. "You've drama fit to fill the king's theater, child. Just go and get it done. I'll shower you with coin. I'll name you first lieutenant of the sword. I'll teach you everything the Masters won't. Just kill the king and end this war for all."

I stopped one pace from the portal and met his eyes. "I want the girl," I said. "I want Isabelle unharmed. For that— for that alone—I'll do this deed."

"It's yours," he said, impatience almost making it a growl. "Just go!"

I closed my eyes and stepped through to Tirah.

The largest of the Ardain's duchies, Tirah is only rivaled by the capitol itself. And like the proud city, its lords have long felt due a greater role. Lareth had called this war inevitable, and in a way it was. As long as I had known anything of the nation's politics, I'd known of the festering rebellion in Ardain. Even when I was a boy my father had spoken of it as an old and tired thing.

There was wealth on the continent. There was pride, and culture, and tradition. A thousand years and more these lands had owed their fealty to the FirstKing and his heirs. And yet, for just as long, they'd toyed with breaking free.

I found the clear reminder of that the moment I stepped out of Lareth's gate. I stood within a hall of quarried stone, and an eerie recognition settled down on me. I hurried ahead, to a wider crossing corridor, and looked left out into a courtyard bordered by a gold-wrought gate.

It wasn't the capitol palace. It stood upon a square as flat and low as everything else in central Ardain, but the layout was the same. The structure was the same. They'd made a copy of the royal palace here in old Tirah. I turned to the right, instead, to the great arching double doors that would have opened upon the king's throne room. Here, it could be just the same.

Lareth had done it. He had brought me to the very door of the king. A dozen guards stood at attention outside those closed doors, every eye fixed on me as I stepped into the corridor. Two of them wore the uniforms of the Green Eagles as well, and they stood apart. I had to pass between them to approach the guards at the door. Those guards raised pikes to block my way before I'd gotten halfway there, but I shook my head.

"No," I shouted. "I'm no threat to the king. I bring dire news. The wizard Lareth plans to kill him here! I must get word to him."

I saw a look of concern pass among some of them, but it did nothing to gain me passage. If anything it raised their suspicion. Two of the guards stepped out into the hall and leveled their pikes at my heart. I slammed to a stop, hands raised and empty.

"I'm not a threat," I said. "I am no threat at all. Do not admit me. I don't care. But take a message to the king. It's vital that he hear—"

A hand clamped hard upon my shoulder—hard enough to make me wince—and turned me from the guards to face a Green Eagle with fresh scars on his cheek and neck and hand. From the look of them, they might have been received at the morning's ambush.

I paled. "Please, sir," I said. "We must move quick—"

"We will," he said. His voice was low and harsh, like a spill of gravel. "But you will not. Come with me. Ellone, inform the Knight Captain. I will take this one to the barracks hall."

He never relaxed that grip upon my shoulder. He turned and left, and if I had resisted at all it would have snapped my collarbone. I went along, some flare of hope bright and hot within my chest. We went four paces and Ellone had barely moved from his position on the wall when suddenly the doors flew open behind us.

The Green Eagle who held my shoulder slowed just long enough to glance back, and I turned back, too. And there was the king. Ten paces away. He looked no different than he had the night he chased me from the City. Storm clouds raged in his eyes, and he stomped into the hall all full of fury. I tried to turn to him, to call out warning, to beg his aid, to end this war—

I'd barely moved at all when my escort sensed the motion and, without warning or even apparent effort, flung me to the floor. I landed hard and bounced. I rolled onto my back and tried to rise, but before I knew what was happening I felt the Green Eagle's sword against my throat, just below my jaw. "Hold fast," he said, and I froze.

The king whisked by without a glance in my direction. He grunted as he passed, "Well done, well done," and the soldier over me nodded his quiet thanks. Then Ellone, the other Eagle, resumed his place against the wall. I saw the king slipping away down the hall.

"Wait!" I screamed. "Your Highness, no! I have grave news!" I cut off short when the cold steel of the Eagle's blade pressed harder at my throat. The king flew on, altogether unconcerned.

I felt a flash of fury then. Torches lined the hall. Fire. Fire everywhere. I remembered what the wizard had said about the king's safeguards and wondered how many threads of flame I would need to catch the man's attention. I wondered how many it would take to burn him down to ash.

I knew it would take just one cold steel blade to end my life. It would take less than an inch, the work of the flick of a wrist. I swallowed delicately and held my tongue. I gained nothing by rousing their suspicion. Better to wait and convince them later. I held my place while the bodyguard on the king's heel stormed after him.

One among them paid me more attention than the king had. A Green Eagle in the full uniform, with extra bars of rank on his shoulders. He stopped to share a word with Ellone, and then another bit of praise to the soldier who had so handily silenced my outburst. And then he cast a glance down at me—

And I recognized him. He had advanced in rank but I knew the long, scarred face and the eyes so full of hate. He knew me, too. His eyebrows came down sharp and in a blur his sword, too, was at my throat. "Get him clear!" he bellowed to the guards who followed the king. "Now! Now! Ellone, to the king! We have a traitor here!" I heard the hustle of movement down the hall as the king's escort hurried him away.

I tried to shake my head, but I could barely move without opening my throat. My eyes strained wide. I showed my open hands and croaked up at him, "I mean no harm. I have come to warn you."

"You have come to die," Othin said. He pressed the blade harder, and I thought perhaps he meant to kill me then and there. He stopped just short of that and growled. "Where's my sword?"

I almost laughed as the answer came to mind. His sword was in a dragon's cave somewhere, or perhaps on the bottom of the ocean. He didn't truly care about the sword, though. He knew me. That was the point. He meant the question for a reminder of the dishonor I had done him.

"It is long gone," I said. "Everything between us is well and truly gone," I said more strongly. "Othin, please. Hear me. The king's life is at risk, as is his friend's. The baron Eliade—"

He kicked me, hard, just below the ribs. It shut me up. He grunted. "Get this one to the cells. I must secure the king, but I will be along for him soon enough. He may know some magic. If he does anything—anything at all— then run him through."

With that he left. I lay upon my back, staring up at the Green Eagle who had thrown me there. I met his gaze, trying to keep the bitter anger from my eyes. "The rebel wizard Lareth can open portals to the king," I said. "He was behind the assault on the Cara Road this morning."

I saw the soldier's eyes go wide at that, and I nodded carefully against the cool steel of his blade. "He has a force of several hundred gathered in one place, ripe for attack. They must be the bulk of the enemy's force, and Lareth himself is the gravest threat by far."

The Green Eagle narrowed his eyes, considering me, and I showed him my empty hands again. "I know their dispositions," I said. "Take me to the cells. Lock me up. I do not care. But bring me the king, or even the Knight-Captain, and I will tell him everything he needs to end this rebellion here and now."

His eyes narrowed as he considered me. Then he withdrew his blade and jerked his head. "On your feet." I scrambled up and he gestured with the naked blade. I started walking.

He turned me down a side hall, opposite the way the king had gone. We were soon alone, and for several slow paces I considered my options. I fell into my second sight and saw the flicking fires, saw the ponderous weight of the worked stone. I could have burned the guard alive or buried him in stone. But he was not my enemy. I could have trapped his feet and run, but what would I have gained? My only hope was meeting with the king, or sending word to him, and my only chance at that lay in patient obedience.

So I went quietly. The cells lay in a wide wing of the palace and looked nothing like I'd imagined. I had expected cramped little pens in a cold, musty dungeon. The room he threw me in was every bit as large at the one I'd had at the

Academy and, after a cursory glance, it proved better appointed than that one, too.

Its inner wall was not of solid bars, but the worked stone gave way to a barred window from waist-high to crown which would have allowed a guard easy oversight of anything a prisoner might get up to. The outer wall offered a window, too, likewise covered in iron bars. I could see the stars pinpoint bright against the violet night without.

My escort left me there. I pleaded with him one last time to carry my word to the king, but he gave no response at all. He saw me in my room, summoned a guard to lock my door, and then he left. I tried the guard, too, but he paid me less attention even than the Eagle had.

But Othin had promised to come for me. It was little comfort. I'd met the man once, he'd tried to kill me, and I'd left him looking like a fool. I shivered at the memory, at the hate that had burned in his statue eyes, and it hadn't faded a shade in the year that had passed since then.

This was bigger than either of us, though. The man was Knight-Captain to a king deep in hostile territory now. That had to take precedence over any old insults. I took a deep breath and clung to that thought. He would listen. He would have to. I spent ten minutes planning what I would say, but no one came for me. I noticed the guard on duty pass by my window four times on slow patrol. I clenched my fists and reviewed everything I'd planned. My guard passed by again.

Half an hour passed. An hour. I cried out to my guard, but he ignored me. I tried to catch his sleeve as he passed, but he knocked my hand away with a violence that bruised my shoulder against the bars of my window.

I watched the moon rise outside my prison walls. I thought of Isabelle, of the wizard's light green flame prepared to turn the girl to ash. I thought of Lareth, happy and free, waiting for word of my success or failure. I pressed the heels of my hands against my eyes and ground my teeth in fury.

I could still do it. The king *was* an arrogant old fool, surrounded by terrible men. He'd branded me a traitor when I was nothing of the sort. I watched my guard patrol once more past my window and thought how easy it would be to pull the roof down on his head. I extended mystic senses to the stone blocks of my wall and felt the shape of earth within, the tiny beads pressed tight and hard, and saw how easy it would be to scatter them like sand and open a way I could step right through.

Midnight came and went, and still I sat alone and waited. I cursed the Eagle's name. A woman's life hung in the balance. The *king's* life did as well. If this strike failed, the wizard could send an army next. They'd have a harder time of it than I would have. They would certainly kill more people than I needed to. But they could win. If the king ignored my warning the wizard's men could take him unprepared.

I ground my teeth and stared out at the moon. The man was going to die anyway. I pounded a fist against the stone wall, which only bruised my fist. That was the worst part of it, though. Arrogant as he was, the king was going to die. The wizard would win, with or without my help. If I waited here Isabelle would die as well. And me. I closed my eyes and nodded. They thought me still a murderer. They had no plan to listen to my plea.

I forced a slow and calming breath, but it didn't work. Fury burned deep in my heart. I wanted to do violence. Lareth deserved to die, but the king just barely less. And Othin with him. I turned my hateful gaze back to my door and felt my lips pull back from my teeth. These men could not hold me. I tried to fight it down, to reach for sanity, but rage washed over me like ocean waves, and I could barely even catch a breath.

And then I understood. I felt it, coming not from me but from that spark within my mind. I closed my eyes and drew a breath, and felt the exhilaration and fury of a predator on the prowl. It buzzed in my veins, it put strength in my arms, but it was not my own. I walled it off, forced it back. I reclaimed my mind and felt the bloodlust fade.

Then I reached thoughts toward the spot and asked it, "*Vechernyvetr. Is that you?*"

My own pet wizard, the dragon answered, its voice deep and distant in my head. Oh, you will enjoy this night. Blood will flow.

"Are you close?" I asked. "I need your help. Right now. Tonight. I call your debt."

Oh, but death is in the air. The words came rich with ecstasy, and I heard a thin, piercing cry far out in the night. Another answered it, and a moment later another. I felt a little pulse of anticipation from the dragon. *A gathering of arms like I have never seen, and at its heart a working of man and magic brighter than the sun.*

The king. I shivered. "*You're drawn to power,*" I said.

To human power, yes. To scatter and destroy. I'll burn his army to the ground—

"But wait!" I cried. "There is another, worse. The wizard Lareth. The one I told you of. He has a thousand men—"

I see their stain, the dragon said, uninterested. *They are a spot beside the sea, a star against the sun.* I could feel the thoughts growing stronger as the dragon flew closer. It screamed again, piercing the night, and I imagined I could see it moving against the stars in the middle distance. *I taste their fear*, it said. *A city full of men to set aflame.*

My heart began to beat faster. "*I'm here,*" I thought. "*Would you destroy me too?*"

You're wrapped in stone and steel, the dragon said. I see you. I see your pain and fear. I'll show you better things. I'll show you what it's like to kill and burn.

Violence and blood. I remembered the promise the dragon had made beside the farmer's pond. *"Free me,"* I thought, making it a command. *"Tear me from my cage and pay my price. I need your violence and blood."*

You would take me from this fight? it asked, disbelief and betrayal behind the words. First let me kill the king! I see him, high above the earth, wrapped in stone that I could tear like leaves, and wrapped in spells that I could shed like water. He will be fun to slay.

Even held at bay, the dragon's bloodlust bubbled in a corner of my soul. I could feel the same pleasure the beast anticipated, the surge of power and pride at crushing out a life that blazed as brightly as the sun. A predator spirit within me wanted to crush the man who had imprisoned me here.

Another colder part of me considered the possibility as well. Let him do what he meant to do. It was a force of nature, not my hand, that would kill the king. It would be enough for Lareth, though. It would be enough to save Isabelle, and no blood on my hands. I only had to wait, which was the only option the king or his Knight-Captain had given me.

Just wait and Lareth would give me my reward. The injustices done me would be settled. I felt the dragon closer still, felt its hunger bright and hot within my mind. Moments yet, and it would be over. Then I could go and claim my prize.

My prize. I thought of Isabelle. Lareth couldn't give me her. No man could offer her. She'd called me her hero, for this. For now. I thought of Themmichus, her brother, who had shown me kindness when no one else would. I thought of Claighan who had brought me into all of this to save the kingdom from pressing darkness. I thought of Joseph, who had brought me back from death and sent me off to save the king. I thought of the chaos that would fall all across the land if the king were to die this night.

I took a deep breath, closed my eyes, and stretched my will toward the beast as though it were a breeze I meant to bend. *"Come for me,"* I said. *"Leave off the hunt. There's more important work to do."*

I pressed against it like a child trying to topple an ancient oak. I could not have forced the dragon with all my might, and yet it budged.

Oh, very well, it said. I sensed a petulance that felt quite out of place in a force of nature, but acquiescence, too. *But you must give me blood.*

"Oh, there is blood," I thought. My stomach turned at what lay ahead, but I set my jaw and turned toward the south. *"There's blood enough to spill."*

Then come to me, the dragon said. *Come, and we shall fly.* With the words I heard the thunder of its wings. It roared outside my cell, and without the strength of dragons in my veins I would have fallen to the earth and cowered. The bellow split the air and rang against the steel bars of my cage. It rumbled in my chest and made me weak.

And others answered. More even than the two I'd heard before. Half a dozen bellows broke the night. *"How many are here?"* I asked. *"Is this the dragonswarm?"*

Vechernyvetr answered me with a chuckle that rumbled in my chest like its bellow had. This is not the waking, child. This is half a flight, a tiny hunt. The waking comes, but this is just a taste.

I heard the screams of men. I heard stone shatter and the roar of dragons in full flight. *"They'll kill us all!"* I cried.

They wouldn't mind, it answered. So come quickly. If we must leave, then let us leave.

"But the city!" I cried. "We can't just leave them to die."

There's soldiers here and wizards enough to give my brothers chase, it said. They can do far more than you.

"I can't just leave—"

Where armies gather, men will die, the dragon said. *That much is beyond your control. You decide for you. And for me, tonight.* I felt its resentment at that, but it snorted just outside my window and I felt the heat of it through the window. *Are you coming, or can I go and kill the king?*

I nodded. I took my second sight, and with a thought I tore the outer wall of my cell to sand. I stepped out through the gap and into a dark courtyard lit only by the flicker light of wildfire in buildings nearby. I shook my head. *"We cannot let them do this."*

We cannot stop them, the dragon said. We can only choose another life to end.

The dreadful words fell like stones into my soul. I shivered once, and set my jaw. I turned my eyes to the south again and nodded. *"Lareth,"* I said. *"That man deserves to die."*

16. Beneath the Silver Moon

I rushed to the dragon's side and reached a hand toward the plates beneath its shoulder, but it batted me away with a casual gesture. I fell three paces away and the monster rolled a baleful eye at me. *I am not*, it said in quiet contempt, *a horse*.

I climbed back to my feet, scowling across at the beast, then a thunder of flame and fury flashed by overhead. It was a ruby-red dragon, barely half the size of Vechernyvetr, but it was still terrifying. I flinched closer to the shade of the stone wall. I heard a shouted order in the direction it had flown and saw a volley of crossbow bolts slash up toward the dragon on the wing. I nodded toward it.

"They will fire on us, too," I thought. "It could mean my life if I'm hanging in your clutches again this time."

For a while the dragon said nothing. Then it rolled its massive eye, dropped one shoulder low to the ground, and snorted at me. I rushed to find a place at the base of the dragon's neck, hooking my ankles around spines on its collarbone and gripping tight to the armored hide. Before I'd fully caught my grip, the dragon sprang without warning. As we rose into the air, I saw the formation of the king's guard that had fired on the red. They spotted us, too, and a dozen crossbows snapped up in our direction.

"*Vech!*" I screamed, but the dragon was already moving. It banked away, tail slashing out behind us, and flapped its great wings twice to fling us high, high into the air. I heard the order barked again, but even the bolts of the Guard's heavy crossbows couldn't drag us from the sky. If any found the dragon's armored hide, the animal gave no indication. It certainly did not slow.

Which way? the dragon asked, but for a moment I said nothing. I lost my breath, staring down upon the city of Tirah from high above. Half a dozen dragons swarmed above it, flashing in and out like hummingbirds, hovering in place to rain down fire.

The city itself seemed mostly untouched. Houses, shops, and squares stretched out for miles around the replica palace, and though there was plenty of panic I didn't see a single fire among them. The dragons focused most of their attention on the palace, where soldiers rushed like ants. And farther out, outside the city's walls, the king's army washed out to the horizon in all directions. It was a camp like Lareth's, but cast across the earth as far as the eye could see. Ten thousand men. Or more.

Vechernyvetr's brothers fell among them like living chaos. I felt cold.

The dragon's voice intruded on my mind again. Which way, little man? If you don't tell me soon I'm going back to kill the king.

"They'll kill him anyway, won't they?" I asked.

Perhaps, it said, but it didn't sound convinced. They're younger wyrms and have no plan to work together. They'll have their fun, they'll spill some blood, but they will not do as I could have done. I could hear the beast's regret at the missed opportunity.

"South," I thought, then tried to form an image in my head. "Toward the wizard's camp. You said you'd seen their stain—"

Of course, the dragon said. It banked again, rolling on the wind, and I felt the dragon's thrill wash through to me. I embraced it, looking out over the sleeping world, and strained my eyes as the dragon bent its path south.

Are they prepared for me? it asked. Will they expect a dragon?

I laughed at that. "Never," I thought. "This land has barely seen a dragon in three thousand years."

The dragon's answer came slow and thoughtful. *It has not been quite so long as that.*

"Even so, they wouldn't expect this. Not a planned assault. I was in their camp four hours ago, and they were half asleep."

These are warriors?

"Bandits, really, organized by a local lord. The worst among them is the wizard—"

I fear no wizard, the dragon said.

I laughed. It had a hint of darkness to it and just a touch of madness. *"I look forward to seeing what you can do with this one. But first...."* I thought about what I'd seen in Tirah, the ordered camp beset by raging dragons, the city all in panicked disarray. *"But first, let's take his power. Scatter all his men. They're rabble and it must have been quite a feat to gather them."* I nodded to myself, seeing a real solution. *"If we can put them in flight, it will take months to build that threat again. Time enough for the king to end it."*

The dragon weighed the plan for a moment. Then I saw its giant head dip in a little nod. *You ask a fair favor of me, Daven. I will serve you in this.*

Far below me, the earth spread out like a map. I strained my eyes to see, but even by the light of moon and stars I caught only the barest impression of the land. After some time the dragon dropped lower, and I saw that it was following the twisting path of a river. I knew it—the same wide, slow river that I'd forded while following the rebels. Here, though, it cut a deep, straight path through harder rocky earth. It slashed south beside a hard-packed road and led toward the distant glow of a town.

335

And campfires like a starry constellation. I swallowed and felt the anticipation building in the dragon's heart. I shut my eyes and caught my breath then stared ahead at tents arrayed in scattered clusters entirely unlike the neatly ordered rows outside Tirah.

My stomach surged up into my throat when the dragon suddenly dove. A burst of my own terror broke through the dragon's hungry euphoria and tore out of me in a scream. The dragon answered me with a scream of its own, that soul-deep bellow that had shaken me in the palace of Tirah. But now I felt it closer, wilder, burning in my blood with the dragon's hunger and its rage.

Then we were above the rebels' camp. We swept in from the northwest, far from Lareth's black tent, and I saw below me the tattered little tents of the footsoldiers. I saw the soldiers' faces, too, twisted with shock as they startled from their sleep. The dragon raked a claw at the earth, scattering a smaller camp, and I saw the weapons they had bent against the king, the cookpots full of food stolen from the nearby town. I saw men thrown dozens of paces across the earth, broken and bloodied. I saw their fear, and it tasted sweet in my lungs.

"Burn them down," I thought, and the dragon dropped its jaw. Fire fell like rain across the earth, washing out over the tents and sending rebels running for the hills. Not one among them defied us. Not one stood his ground or tarried even long enough to grab a weapon. They ran like wild hares before a fire.

I thrilled at it until the dragon dipped closer to the ground and snapped a running soldier up in its mighty jaws. The man screamed once before the dragon swallowed it in a gulp. My stomach rose up again, in twisting nausea this time, and I shook my head to shake away the memory. *"Just scatter them,"* I thought. *"Just chase them all away. We need not kill every one among them."*

Violence and blood, the dragon thought, sharp with reprimand. *That is the price of power.* It flew on, though, and swooped down on another stretch of camp that it scattered with another gout of flame. It swept its tail along behind us, snaking back and forth along the ground and scattering tents and men like so much dust.

While the dragon raged around the wide circle, I searched ahead. I scanned the horizon for any sign of the wizard's tent, and as we drew closer I fell into my second sight instead. The beacon light of the green flame hung bright and clear over Isabelle's tent. Orienting off that I found the wizard's tent, too, broad and black a hundred paces on. I pointed uselessly, and tried to guess how I could drag the beast's attention to it.

I needn't have bothered. Chaos held the camp now, soldiers washing ahead of us in terrified waves like cockroaches, but as we drifted toward the wizard's tent he came out calm and ready. The rebels passed him in a panic, but the wizard merely turned his head in our direction and raised a hand.

I brought my arms up to shield my eyes a heartbeat before fire flared. A searing bolt of white-hot flame lanced up to strike the dragon on its breastbone, less than a pace below my hands, and I gasped against the heat of it. But I felt no echo of pain from the dragon. Instead it screamed a roar of rage that should have driven Lareth to the earth.

The wizard merely turned and raised his other arm. I felt Vechernyvetr gulping air to burn, but the wizard before us twisted his hand, stabbing it upward, and I saw a cloud of abandoned blades flash up into the air. Swords and knives hurled toward the dragon like stones from a sling. Even as that wall of steel flew up the wizard turned and threw another blast of flame that melted to nothing in the depths of the dragon's black power.

But a sharp-edged sword barely missed my ankle before it buried itself hilt-deep in the dragon's shoulder. The beast convulsed, and hammers of pain slammed against the back of my mind as a dozen other bits of sharp steel stabbed through its hide. The stricken dragon bucked in mid-air and flung me from my perch.

I had a moment's warning before I hit the ground. I landed hard, rolled, and tried to throw myself back to my feet. Instead I stumbled and sprawled. I raised my head and shielded my eyes against the light from a gout of dragon's flame. I wrenched up to my feet, stumbled, but stayed up-right. I took one step toward the wizard, hoping to hit him while he was distracted, but the dragon was already gone, flown past. I could feel astonishment and agony through the bond in the back of my head. Lareth had done more to hurt the dragon than either of us had thought possible.

I felt a fury peel back my teeth as I rushed toward the wizard. I fell into my second sight as I ran and gathered liv-ing flame like riverstones. A dozen paces away I let fly a ball of blistering flame, aiming for his head, and threw another right behind. I gathered dragonfire too in angry ropy waves and flung it at the wizard.

But as I watched, the flame fell back. It washed away. The wizard turned to me and all the fire I threw unraveled like my tattered hems and fell to shreds. I screamed in rage and snatched a skinning knife abandoned at a fireside. Still in stride, I brought my arm back and threw for his heart.

The knife flew straight and true, but Lareth shook his head. He wore that same smile. He flicked a hand as though he were swatting a pesky insect, and the knife skittered past him. Then he swung at me, from five paces away, and a burst of will that looked like wind met me like a battering ram and sent me sprawling.

The air went out of me. Pain flashed when I tried to catch my breath, and white-slashed darkness pressed in on my vision. I put a hand down to climb to my feet, but I couldn't find the strength. I fell on my back with a groan.

"*Vech...Vechernyvetr, where've you gone?*" I cried. I could feel the dragon, not far off, but it was hurt. Hurt worse than it'd been when I found it by the farmer's pond.

I did not know.... it said and trailed off. I coughed a painful sob and tried again, and this time found at least my knees. I struggled up in time to see Lareth step up over me. He smiled, but there was murder in his eyes.

"You constantly surpass my every guess," the wizard said. "I've never even heard of aught like this. And still you fail." He shook his head and sighed. "And now you'll die."

"I've scattered your men," I said, and it came out a hiss. "I've broken you."

He laughed, deep and low. "You've barely scratched my skin," he said. "There's men enough who'll want what I can give. There's time enough to find another force. There's nothing really changed, except for you. You might have been a handy one, but I'll be safer with you dead."

I growled and reached for the threads of the campfire at my hand, but he frowned, he whispered, and that same agony exploded in my head. He nodded slowly, eyes stretched wide. "I am the end of war," he said. "Why can't you see? You will before you die. Not kings, not sorcery or steel can lay me low. Not dragons on the wing. Not living fire." He grinned, and there was madness in his eyes. "You should have killed the king or never have come back."

His eyes narrowed then, and he leaned closer. "Why did you come?" he said. "You have no love for death, I know that much. You'd barely come to wreak your wrath for the touch of pain I shared with you." And then his eyes snapped up, above me, to the tent. To Isabelle. "Aha!" he said, and I felt a stab of fury and terror.

"I came for you!" I shouted, hoping to draw his attention away from the girl.

He ignored me. "I can unfold the knot at will, you know," he said. "Another trick I could have taught to you. I'll burn the girl to ash for what you've done." He raised a hand toward the tent.

I threw myself at him. I lunged from near the ground and hit his knees with my left shoulder. He tripped and fell away, but as he went he cried. It wasn't a sound of fear or anger but of command. Even as he hit the ground his will lashed out at me like cruel whips. I ignored them, swinging fists in my fury, but he caught my arms in shackles made of air and crushed them to my sides.

I growled and without thinking reached out with my second sight again. It worked, somehow. The working he'd used to bind my arms must have robbed him of the will to bind my mind. I grabbed the fire's flame and threw it at his face. He screamed. He stumbled back. He wrenched the bonds that held my hands and swung one at my face, a phantom punch that sent me sprawling, but a heartbeat later he had to let them go to fight away the flames.

I pressed the essence of fire harder, hotter, while I struggled to my feet. I burned the sparkle from his eye and the smile from his mouth. The air reeked of burning flesh and rattled with his scream. He waved a slashing hand, and my mind exploded once again.

I fell to my knees beneath the pain, and the flame dissolved. It left behind a face half seared to black, pitted and cracked, smoldering red still in places and ashy white at the edges. His unburned nostril flared and his good eye flashed with rage. He stepped forward and swung a boot that took me in the face and sent me sprawling.

He stood over me, panting, and put his full weight behind a heel he drove against my chest. I couldn't catch my breath, could barely think, and he loomed above me like bitter death. He pointed a hand down at me, and I saw that it shook. "I'll break you, child. In body and in soul. I'll break you till you beg me for your death. I'll make you pay for everything you've done!"

I tried to snarl an answer, but he shook his head and waved a casual backhand that cracked a vicious blow of will against my jaw. Pain flashed behind my eyes, brighter than the stars above. I clung desperately to consciousness, blinking away the lights, and saw a shadow cross the starry sky.

I grinned. He struck me once again, but I laughed. *"Kill him!"* I ordered in my mind. *"Kill him now. Kill him, please!"*

The dragon struck, fast as a cobra strikes. It fell to earth hard enough to shake the ground beneath my shoulder. It landed behind the wizard, wings still spread, and fangs as long as my arm flashed at the wizard's head. Somehow the wizard dodged them. He felt the dragon's presence, and he leaped away. He spun in the air, his arms lashing out, and once again a storm of hammered steel lashed through the air.

I screamed, "No!" I twisted up but I could not reach my feet. I leaned upon my knees and screamed again at the staccato bursts of pain as blade after blade drove deep into the dragon's armored hide. The mental defenses I had built collapsed. They washed away beneath the thunder of that pain, and the dragon's awareness flooded into me.

I felt its agony so sharp and hot it drew a sob from me. I felt its rage clenching my hands into fists. I felt its quiet, patient hunger, too. I opened my eyes and saw the world that the dragon saw. Blood flowing, life failing, I saw the tiny, fragile man before me. I snorted a hot huff of breath that exploded from my nose and drank a deep draught of air.

I had no fangs of my own, no fire within. I felt the dragon's strength beneath my weakness, its fury beneath my fear. I felt a power blind to deadly pain. Across from me, the dragon heaved itself onto its feet despite its injuries. I touched that same strength and rose up to my feet behind the wizard.

Time turned slowly. The wizard raised a hand, a gesture that seemed casual as it dragged through the air, but I would not let him slay the dragon. I reached down to my side where a sword should have been and snarled that there was nothing there. And then I grinned, fierce and terrible, and my power was upon me.

I reached out with my will and called it up. I felt the wizard's spell again, the explosion of pain within my mind for daring to touch elemental power. But there was a dragon in my head. I shared the pain with my fearsome ally, and man and beast we shrugged the pain away. There was killing still to do, and for that I needed fangs.

I stretched my empty hand toward the earth and poured my will into it. In beads as fine as crystal salt the earth reached up, pouring against gravity to form a shape beneath my hand. It made a simple hilt that molded to my hand. It stretched into a crosspiece and then stabbed out before me in a long, slender blade.

I took the campfire in my other hand and poured it over the blade. I bent the moving air to shape a cutting edge, to strip the point until it could pierce steel. Within a breath I made my sword, forged hot from living nature. Then I took it in my hand and called the wizard's name.

"Lareth!" I shouted, and he turned before he could make the killing blow. At first he only glanced and saw me there. His good eye opened wide in horror. He spun and there was power in his hands, glowing bright and hot, but I was not afraid. I brought my sword up in anger and in pain. I brought it down in violence and blood. It pierced the wizard through and pinned him to the ground. I roared. The dragon roared. The sounds were one.

And then the agony was gone. The surge of pain within my mind dissolved. The bright green flame above Isabelle's tent winked out. The wizard at my feet coughed blood and tried to smile. His hand fell limp. Panting for breath, I held his gaze and watched the life ebb out of him.

Just before it went, a heartbeat before he died, he breathed one word of power and disappeared.

I blinked. Blood slicked the ground and stained my earth-wrought sword. Fire roared behind me, all around me. I could smell the acrid smoke, the scent of death and destruction that lay upon the plain. I turned slowly and looked upon the dragon.

"He's gone," I thought, stunned.

He's broken and he's dead, the dragon said. *His power's burned, and he cannot heal the way a dragon does.* With that thought came another wash of pain that drove me to my knees, and I had to gasp for breath before I could wall away the dragon's awareness again. I shook my head and ground my teeth until it passed.

Vechernyvetr shifted awkwardly before me, trying to settle its weight on injured legs. I saw the moonlight playing over the beast's hide, stitching it together again, but there was much that needed fixing. I stepped closer, compassion welling in me. The dragon snorted and rolled its cauldron eyes.

Spend no pity on me, little man. You're hurt worse than I, but we will both survive. The dragon chuckled, deep and low. You fight with fury. You could almost be my brother. You have my admiration.

I shuddered at the memory, but I knew it for a compliment. I bowed my head to the dragon. *"I could have done none of it without you."*

I know, the dragon said. *My debt is paid.* It shifted again, testing injured legs, then turned its head to look down on me. *My debt is paid,* it said again. *We are not friends. You know this, yes?*

I nodded. "I know," I said. "And yet you have my thanks."

That means nothing at all, the beast replied. Its long neck snaked up high, head whipping left and right to look out over the plains, and then one eye tracked down to me again. *Men will come, as they came before. I should not tarry here. My debt is paid.*

I swallowed and nodded. "Of course. I understand," I said. "Your debt is paid. Now go and live."

And you as well, the dragon said, and it leaped to grapple with the sky. Wings as wide as a village green flapped twice, three times, and the beast was gone.

I had to find my strength before I could go to Isabelle. I did my best to quell the fires that raged through the camp, and bound up one single flame like a torch above my hand. Then I turned toward the prison tent, my heart racing, and bent a gust of wind to lift its flaps. I stepped inside.

Like a rose in the desert she was there, sitting on her heels in the quiet darkness. Her eyes were wide, and I saw tears of fear upon her cheeks, but she had never budged. She'd waited. She had trusted me to bring her rescue.

She blossomed when she saw me. Light and hope and joy flared on her face, and she threw herself to her feet with more energy than I could have imagined. She flung herself upon me, arms around my neck and kisses on my face, and it was everything I could do to keep from falling. The sword dropped from my hand. My light blinked out, and the sword splashed like water and ended as a pile of dirt beside my feet. My attention was all elsewhere.

She paused in all the kisses to peek past me. She seemed very small then, fingers knotted in the threadbare fabric of my shirt and body pressed close against mine. She stretched up on her toes to see more clearly, and I heard a little squeak escape her lips. I raised a hand to brush at her hair and whispered softly, "It is done."

"You've killed them all!" she said with wonder in her voice.

I shook my head. "I've set them all in flight," I said. "I think I killed the wizard, though. And put a fear in all the rest they will not soon forget."

She nodded, blinking, and I saw tears in her eyes. "You did it," she said. "You really did it. My shepherd boy. My beggar from Chantire."

I laughed at that. "You do remember well."

The tears escaped her eyes and she reached up in frustration to wipe them away. "I didn't know.... I heard it all. I had to wait. I had to wait, and never knew, and then with all the screams—"

"It's done," I said, with a quiet ease I did not truly feel. I raised a hand to brush the tears from her cheek. She didn't need to know everything that had happened. She knew enough.

She leaned her forehead against my chest and I heard a little sniff. Without looking up she asked, "Where are the rest?"

"The rest?" I said.

"The soldiers. The king, his wizards, all his men. Where is the army? Are they out giving chase?"

I laughed again. I could not contain it. "The king? He would not come. He wouldn't even hear my plea."

"Then how...." She stopped, and her eyes were very wide again as she raised her gaze to mine. "You did it by yourself."

I swallowed. I didn't tell her that a dragon helped. She raised a hand to my face, awe in her eyes, and did not quite touch my skin. "You saved my home. You saved my life. You... alone."

I ducked my head to break her gaze. I sighed. "I could not let him win," I said.

She laughed, a sharp and startled sound like a pheasant breaking cover. "Of course," she said. "You couldn't let him win. So you alone bested an army to rescue me and mine." She shook her head slowly. "There is magic in you, Daven. It was there before the wizard ever found you."

"You don't understand," I said, but she stopped me with a finger on my lips. And then a kiss. It was softer, more hesitant than the flurry of little kisses she'd given me before. She pressed close against me, and she was warm. She held the kiss for a handful of heartbeats, then pulled away and had to catch her breath. I had no hope of catching mine.

"You are a hero," she said. I opened my mouth but she stopped my objection again. "You are my hero."

I had to swallow before I could speak. When I did I dipped my eyes in a little nod. "Lareth's force is broken," I said. "But we should go. This is no place to linger."

Her eyes flashed, and she chuckled low. "Will you escort me home?"

"I will," I said and offered her my hand. I stepped before her from the tent, straining my ears for any sound of struggle. In the distance fires still raged, but as we walked that way I reached out with my will and snuffed the dragon's flame. I left campfires here and there to light our way, but mostly I smothered those as well. A dozen paces down I drew another sword out of the earth, in case of need.

But there was none. A hundred paces brought us to a band of townsfolk come to investigate the disturbance. They cried out in joy when they saw Isabelle and rushed up to us. One and all they stopped a pace away, eyes flashing with gratitude and concern.

Isabelle accepted their warm sentiments for a moment, then waved them to silence to offer a hurried explanation of what had happened. Heads shook in quiet awe, and when she gave me credit for the devastation all around me I saw a tremor of fear pass among them. They did not quite meet my eyes. But when Isabelle sent them on ahead, to carry word back to the town of what had happened, they bowed low and rushed away.

She caught one of them just before he left, and said with quiet authority, "Find my father first. Tell him everything I've told you. And tell him too that the hero's name is Daven. Themmichus's Daven."

Then she let him go. I watched it all, anxious to bring Isabelle after them to the safety of her father's house, but she showed no hurry. She strolled instead, as though we were walking in a city garden, and held my empty hand between two of hers. My heart pounded as we went, and it was not entirely for fear of rebels coming back.

When we arrived at Teelevon I found a little town without walls or gates, little larger than Sachaerrich on the green. It was not yet dawn, but everyone in town seemed to be there, gathered in two crowds with a broad path down the center of the green. At the end of that path was a house that could have put Jemminor's to shame—a mansion on the green, fronted by a wide patio atop a dozen marble steps. And on the porch stood a man I'd seen once two lifetimes ago, a glimpse through a distant door.

Isabelle's father, the Baron Eliade. He was a friend of the king and a Lord of the Ardain. He waited with attendants at his side, and down upon the green a hurrah went up as we approached. Isabelle never stirred. She squeezed my hand more tightly and watched me instead of the crowd as we approached her father's house.

He did not frown at me as we approached. He did not narrow his eyes or ask suspicious questions. He held my eyes with a tearful smile. "She said she'd bring us help," he said, and I heard the husk of tears in his voice. "In a note." He swallowed and shook his head. "I thought her lost."

"Oh, Papa," she said, chiding, and the old man burst into tears. Big and strong and full of joy, he threw himself at me, and I flung my sword aside or he'd have been hurt. He wrapped me in his arms and heaved me from my feet in a great bear hug, and behind me a cheer went up to shame the one that had gone before. The whole town cried out.

I drifted in it all like a man at sea. I could find no solid ground, no touchstone to reality, except Isabelle's hand. She never took it from my arm, and her long, cool fingers held my focus. I heard her laugh again, "Oh, Papa, please!" and Baron Eliade released me and stepped back.

"Teelevon," he cried to all the crowd. "My girl is back! Our Isabelle is safe. The siege is done. We're saved, by this man's hand!" He spun me, then, to face the crowd, and for a moment I lost Isabelle's touch. She found my other arm, and gripped it with both hands, and turned her smile on the crowd below.

The baron still proclaimed, "His name is Daven! Wizard. And a friend of our family. Forever." He dropped a heavy hand on my shoulder, warm and strong, and in a lower voice he mumbled, "Thank you, boy. I cannot say enough. You have a home here as long as you might want one."

Isabelle tore her gaze from the crowd at that and fixed it on my eyes. I felt a sudden nervousness in her grip on my arms, a fear that was entirely out of place in her expression. She lowered her voice and said, "Will you please stay? You're welcome here. Will you please stay?"

I looked at her and laughed. It was absurd. Her eyes shone bright beneath the silver moon. They glinted, and I saw the hint of tears. She had taken my laughter for rejection. I bent my head closer to her, blocking out the noise of the crowd. I stared into her eyes. "I shall do whatever you desire," I said to her. "I am your shepherd after all."

Her eyes danced at that. She caught her breath, and then she smiled. She reached up to touch my face. "You'll be my prince. But that is talk for tomorrow." She leaned against me again and took another breath. "For now, you are our hero, and this can be your home. Is that enough for you?"

I could not have answered her, but she did not seem to need one. She leaned against me, and waved out to the crowd, and I could feel her breathing.

This could be my home. It was enough. I had honor, and hope, and a place to lay my head. I stretched an arm around the girl and she did not object. I had a family here and friends. I had everything I wanted.

In the back of my mind there burned a weary pain, reminder of other things. I had Vechernyvetr's guesses but I knew not what had become of the attack on the king's garrison at Tirah. I did know there were dragons in the world and more waking. Vechernyvetr had confirmed it.

There were still rebels, too, and the wizard had escaped. I'd given him injuries far worse than the ones that had lain Claighan low, but I could not trust him to die easily. I had an enemy in him.

I had powerful adversaries at court as well. And I would have more, if they survived the dragons' attack, for the way

I'd left my prison cell. The king still thought me a murderer and a traitor. And his Knight-Captain, Othin...twice now I'd slipped the officer's custody and stained his pride. I had enemies enough to make a strong man tremble.

But that was a matter for tomorrow. For now, I had survived. For now, I was a hero. For now, I had a home.

That was enough, for now.

About the Author

Aaron Pogue is a husband and a father of two who lives in Oklahoma City, OK. He started writing the high fantasy world of the FirstKing at the age of ten and has written novels, short stories, and videogame storylines set there. He's also explored mainstream thrillers, urban fantasy, and several kinds of science fiction, including the popular science fiction crime series Ghost Targets which focuses on an elite FBI task force in a world of total universal surveillance.

Aaron is also a Technical Writer with the Federal Aviation Administration. He has a degree in Writing and has been working as a Technical Writer since 2002. He's been a writing professor at the university level, and is currently pursuing a Master of Professional Writing degree at the University of Oklahoma. He also runs a writing advice blog at UnstressedSyllables.com and is a founding artist at ConsortiumOKC.com.

CPSIA information can be obtained at www.ICGtesting.com
Printed in the USA
LVOW101438210312

274154LV00003B/19/P